The Galaxy's Finest: Specter

Raziel Andrade

Copyright © 2024 Elijah Andrade

All rights reserved. No portion of this book may be reproduced in any form without prior permission from the copyright owner of this book.

The characters and events portrayed in this book are fictitious. Any similarity to real persons, living or dead, is coincidental and not intended by the author.

No part of this book may be reproduced, or stored in a retrieval system, or transmitted in any form or by any means, electronic, mechanical, photocopying, recording, or otherwise, without express written permission of the publisher.

ISBN-13: 979-8998551703

Cover design by: Anze Ban V.
The Writers Guild of America, West Registration Number: 2282114
Printed in the United States of America.

To my family, friends and everyone else who supported me along this journey. Thank you. Special thanks to the brave men and women in the armed forces, you all are truly the galaxy's finest. Thank you for your service.
May this story be a reminder that even in the darkest of times, a single beam of light can still be seen for miles.

"The year is 2442, the planet once known as Earth has become a planet of boundless water with very few cities, mostly forts, bases, scrap metal collection centers and camps. Humanity figured out a way to leave Earth and travel to other Galaxies with sustainable air, food and water supply. The people of Earth rejoiced as they began their new lives in new galaxies. People enjoyed the peace of a new life away from the problems of their dying Earth. They were happy and free to travel to whichever planet or galaxy they desired. Vespis is the Core planet of the Waylif system, it is where every and all governing issues were held. Unfortunately, the peace would not last long. Months after humanity's arrival to their galaxies, a dark force rose out of the Cheloria System, they were known as The Chelorian Confederacy. They were hellbent on control of all the galaxies in the universe. They allied themselves with systems with the same ambitions as them. The Confederacy, fearing the humans had the same idea of total dominion over all, repeatedly attacked and demanded that the humans leave immediately and surrender their home planet. War was the last thing on everyone's minds, it all could have been avoided, but the Confederacy left them with no choice. With an alliance with other star systems, war was declared on the Chelorian Confederacy. Thus starting a conflict lasting for over two decades and showed no sign of an end in sight. The alliance came to be known as The United Starlight Coalition. It would take more than a miracle to end the bloodshed of these great galaxies. It would take a team of extraordinarily brave men and women. It would take the galaxy's finest."

PROLOGUE
The year: 2468

Is it hard to believe that this all started long before the first gun shot? Before the first bomb was dropped? Before the first missile strike? That's what I believe anyways. We didn't want this. We have wives, husbands, kids, pets, families, not to mention dear friends and the sanctity of our homes. All the people we left to fight in a war. It's a nightmare we did not start, a fight we did not want. I could've run away. As soon as I got the grim message telling me I had been drafted, I could've run right through a wall like one of those cartoon characters from when I was a kid. I miss those days. How could I have run away, though? I was taught by my mother and father to avoid the fight, but be prepared for it if it comes. I could've avoided the fight, but some things you just can't run from, though, especially if running could get you locked up or killed. Hell, right now, I think I'd prefer either of those options. At least it'll get me out of here. We've taken the light away from so many men and women who have come to fight. Not just men and women, children too. Most of the younger soldiers that come onto base are so naive and know nothing of war, it's understandable at that age. I was the same way when I joined. They'll break soon enough. They all break eventually, whether it's the realization of their own mortality or the harsh environment. It becomes real. It's a harsh, rude awakening. You're never ready for it, but when it hits you, you stay ready from then on.

My name is Corporal Clark David Parson, originally from Eugene, Oregon on Earth. The one piece of advice

I always give to the soft, pampered children who come through our doors is that of my parents, "Avoid the fight, but be prepared for it if it comes." My father, Thomas Parson, a college Professor, named me after Superman's alter ego, Clark Kent. He believed I was destined for greatness and always told me that one day I'll be a hero, like the Man of Steel himself. The sad, bitter truth is, I'm no hero, not even close. He and I loved our comic books. Every day after school, if I wasn't riding my Telore Speeder, we would talk about our favorite heroes for hours on end. I don't get to ride my Telore as much as I used to, but my parents say they still have it in storage. My mom, Caroline Parson, had no idea what the hell we were talking about when we spoke about heroes, but she would watch us and smile in bewilderment. Dad frequently told her he married his Wonder Woman. I wish I had someone like that. I had a twin brother, Kent, but he unfortunately died when we were kids. My parents always tell me he is always by my side. I don't talk about him much or what happened, though. To most common citizens, I am a hero, a brave soldier, fighting for their freedom and safety, risking life and limb for the galaxy. That's what we all want to believe. Most days I feel like the villain, or more appropriately, like a blind, braindead henchman for the evil masterminds behind this bloodshed.

    It's not all bad. I thank whatever unseen force in the universe that no one in my patrol squad has been taken away from us, yet. I'm not much of a prayer, if at all, but I hope and beg that we all come out of this alive and well. We just want to go home. Some of us joined the fight to escape their family, hoping to find a better one here. They've all come to see that they had it easier back home, no matter how their home and family life treated them. It is hell in every sense of the word. Death surrounds us, bodies everywhere and here we stand, engulfed by fire and evil. I can't close my ash stained eyes without seeing an innocent child who was just playing on the street gunned down or a mother being taken away from her family by force.

I'm stationed on a planet named Nesteru in the Dommis system, a galaxy that's part of the Chelorian Confederacy. Nesteru has fallen under control of the Chelorion Confederacy, the people beaten and slaughtered for not believing in the war and what it stands for. Nesteru is a beautiful, but dying planet. It is the closest in its Galaxy to their Sun, the heat is difficult and damn near impossible to deal with. We are positioned in the city of Tefion, to be exact. One of the few surviving cities of Nesteru. All of us went in thinking the people were violent animals that would be a constant issue, imagine how shocked we were when most of the people greeted us, offered us food and water and treated us as equals.

Even when you're not out there fighting, there's more pain and suffrage waiting for you elsewhere. Something as simple as patrolling the city during heatwaves, sun beating down upon our faces, carrying around forty-three pounds of equipment, moments away from collapsing due to exhaustion. Despite us being the enemy to these people, despite what little currency, food and supplies they had, they all were so quick to jump to our aid. For instance, there is one older lady, Anisah, I always see her on my patrols, she didn't speak much English at first, but we'd always greet each other every time I went out. When I had a few moments to spare, she would teach me some common Nesterun phrases over cups of her homemade tea. Fitting that her name means "friendly" in her culture. In return, I'd teach her some common English phrases. She was extremely smart, picking up on the phrases very quickly. Not only smart, but witty, which leads me to believe she knew English all along and was just messing with me. No matter, though. My mother taught me that time spent smiling is time well spent. In this time of our lives, smiles, genuine smiles, were hard to come by.

These amazing people have lost almost everything. Their homes, their businesses and unfortunately, their lives.

To make matters worse, the people who did that to them are just walking around their city, carrying rifles and explosives. A part of me is terrified when my group and I go to patrol the area, we just think one day we are going to be attacked. While most of the people are kind and took us in, seeing us as ordinary people, there are others who don't see us the same way. To them, we are the enemy. One individual came up to us and yelled that we were "evil spirits" sent to "destroy their home". To be fair, that isn't entirely false. If the roles were reversed, I know I would feel the same way. It's not like we like it any better, most of us hate what we are doing.

    There are other members of this army who take sadistic joy out seeing these people in pain. One in particular, another Earthling from Dallas, Texas, Specialist Blaine Johnathan, what a piece of work he is, finds joy in enemies suffering. It sounds childish, but he has always been my competition, ever since Basic Training at Fort Benning, down in Georgia back on Earth all those years ago, back when Earth was filled with life. I was just a kid back then, scared and alone, away from my family and friends. We were all kids, but Carlston, he was a big guy, short blonde hair, broad shoulders with a seemingly permanent scowl on his face. I'm not sure what it was exactly that made him target me all these years, I never spoke to him unless I had to, I kept any rude or unnecessary comments to myself. I tried to be a ghost to him. My whole life I tried to avoid violence and confrontation, unless it was necessary. Blaine did the exact opposite. I never tried outshining him, he probably thought I was trying to be better than him, which if we're being honest, is not that hard.

    Growing up, I never really had many friends. Any chance I got, I stepped away from the crowds of my schools and went directly to the campus library. My time spent at home was filled with reading books, filling my head up with as much knowledge as possible. I had a fascination with mythology, I loved reading about other cultures around the world before it all went downhill. They're all fascinating, but one stuck with me in particular, Norse mythology from the Scandinavian region of Earth. I was enamored with what they used to believe in. All their powerful gods and figures going on larger than life adventures and journeys, getting in battles against giants and monsters completely captivated me.

Back in the days of Vikings, they believed that if you die in battle, with a weapon in hand, you will be carried to a land known to all Vikings. Once you are dead on the battlefield, a group of female warriors known as Valkyries will carry your soul to the Hall of the Slain, Valhalla, a paradise where you can eat and drink as much as you want without a care in the world and fight alongside the Gods of their land. To them, that was their heaven. Each culture has their idea of an afterlife but for me, Valhalla just stayed with me. To die in battle has always been an honored and respected act, even to this day. That's a big reason I choose to stay in the fight. So that one day, if my time comes in "glorious" battle, I will be sent to the Hall of the Slain with my brothers and sisters.

Going back to SPC. Blaine Carlston, perhaps he was threatened by me, not physically but more so intellectually. What he had in body strength, he lacked brain power. I wouldn't say he is stupid, I can't stand him, but that man has bailed me and my squad out multiple times whenever we worked together. Whether it's just him taking everyone out one bullet at a time or him cleverly navigating his way through enemy lines undetected, it's actually pretty remarkable, especially for his size. For that, I respect him. To a certain degree. I have respect for all men and women who risk their lives daily, even if they're people like Blaine. I guess I hate him not just because he acts like an inhuman monster most of the time, but because I know if he really tried, he could run a squad of his own one day. He has the potential to be one of the smartest of us, but chooses to act like an idiot. A real shame.

It seems he and I will always be at odds, but sooner or later it will be time for us to put the childishness behind us. I already try to ignore the heat between us, yet Blaine can't go a day without acting like a schoolyard bully whenever I see him. We have a job to do. We both want out of this mess, I'm over it, personally, but Blaine must grow up. Maybe, we just have to fight, but that will have to be put to the side. I have no doubt Blaine can beat me in hand-to-hand combat, but to just get one shot at him, one shot to get him to shut up would be something I'd remember for life. Maybe a shot to the face will make him respect me. I've never cared if anyone respected me or not, but the Coalition is supposed to be a team, everyone equal. Blaine has the idea he's better than everyone. One day, he will have to prove it. All of us will have a day where we all must prove ourselves and be the people we were born to be.

A BIG PLAN WITH LITTLE HOPE

I look around and I see everyone's faces. Beaten down, stained with ash and little hope in their eyes. A truly saddening sight to behold, it never gets any easier to see. It's a miracle that the Coalition has lasted this long. The systems in the Coalition are strong allies, but we lack supplies, troops and hope. The Chelorian Confederacy cleverly allied themselves with systems whose main export is weaponry and military supplies. Xenem, in the Dommis System, is allied with the Confederacy and unfortunately for us, Xenem makes the finest weapons in all the galaxies. The Coalition allied themselves with systems of superior intellect, so what we lack in weaponry, we make up for in intelligence, but that doesn't help the fact that we still needed weapons.

Since the beginning of this war, the planet Foli, in the Skylock System, has been the supplier of military goods for the Coalition. Folins are clever and creative, naturally they volunteered to make the weapons and supplies for us. They've been great allies to us. What they create is no Xenem weaponry, but they are damn close. As amazing as Foli is, they're only one planet. The rate that they're producing supplies is just too slow. My superiors have asked the process to be sped up, but everyone on Foli is either already working day and night or out here with the rest of us fighting. It's amazing we've lasted this long.

As it is, we just took a big hit the other day. My base, Fort Kjialfa, was attacked by Confederate forces from Nesteru.

Hundreds dead and many more injured. I got out with only a few scratches. I just can't seem to die. That attack hit us hard. I was asked to fill out a damage report on the situation, while submitting the report, I overhear some people talking. I'm not one to eavesdrop, but these people sounded serious. I peek into the room they were in and it was a group of high ranking soldiers from the Coalition army, my higher ups. I decide to sneak into the room, but I cann't recognize all the figures. The room is dimly lit and I am hiding, trying to lay low, but I still recognize the one speaking. It was Lieutenant Jovell Serro, from Tilo, in the Waylif System. It was easy to recognize him with his all white eyes, booming voice and long, white hair. With everyone talking over each other, I'm not able to hear much, but a few things I hear standout.

Amongst the chaos, I hea LT. Serro say only two things,
"We have no choice."
"It is time."

Baffled, I have to stay and listen more to find out what the hell is going on. The room quiets down as Serro walks to the center of the room,

"Ladies and Gentlemen, we have no choice. We are faced with a threat who is better equipped and more advanced than us. That being said, we have had this plan for a while to create a special squad, a group of soldiers, the best of the best, who will infiltrate the Chelorian Confederacy systems and take out their leaders, factories, bases, they will take out everything. It will not be easy, but with the right leader and the right people, we can end this war, once and for all."

A group of soldiers? Best of the best? Ending the war? Sounds too good to be true. The room remains silent, I can feel the tension and shock throughout the room, even I am in shock. After a few moments, someone steps forward,

"You are a mad man." the man says sternly while leaving the room.

Everyone else in the room follows him out, luckily no one saw me hiding. As more people leave, I hear Serro pleading,

"Please, everyone just listen to me. I have been cleared to create this team. I just need all of your help!"

All of them gone, all but one. A man, sitting alone in the back of the room, lit up only by his burning cigar. LT. Serro sits down and lowers his head in defeat without saying a word. After a long sigh and a dry chuckle, he lifts his head up,

"Well, Miner," he continued, "I should have figured you would be the only one mad enough to listen. So, what do you say?"

The figure in the back stands up and approaches Serro,

"Just one question," the figure turns to my direction and continued, "CPL. Parson, what do you think of this fine idea?"

A part of me questioned whether I should remain hidden, but instead, realizing I have already been caught, I slowly stand up and approach them both trying my best to keep my head up, ready for any punishment that undoubtedly will come my way. I look to the right and Serro looked bewildered and infuriated simultaneously, I look to my left and through the cigar smoke, I see it's Staff Sergeant Richard Miner, a legendary war hero from Earth, No one actually knows where exactly on Earth he is from, he keeps information about himself as hidden as possible. He is part of my division, most of us just refer to him as "Sarge". He doesn't seem to mind. I've spoken to him maybe a few times, both times were to get orders from him, but nothing else. He looks impressed and has a slight grin. LT. Serro charges towards me, his yellow eyes burning with rage. I instantly think to myself "This is it for me."

Without giving me a chance to speak,

"What are you doing here, Corporal?" he shouts in my face.

I open my mouth to speak, but he holds his hand up,

"Is it customary on your planet to sneak into meetings among your superiors where you are most unwelcomed?"

"No, sir, I apologize." I respond as quickly as I can.

"I care not for your apologies, what were you doing

sneaking around, hiding like an insect? Are you spying for the Confederacy?"

I quickly shake my head

"No, Sir, never! I was submitting a report and I overheard all the yelling and decided to see what was going on. I can't explain how sorry I am, sir!"

Serro clearly wants to say more to me, but he looks back at Miner, remembering what they were talking about,

"Will you lead, SSG. Miner?" he asks.

Sarge took his cigar out of his mouth and blew a cloud of smoke and nodded. Serro looked back at me with anger and pushed me aside, leaving the room.

"Boy, those Tiloans sure do have a temper, don't they?" Sarge says.

I was stunned silent taking what just happened all in.

"May I be excused, sir?"

That is the only thing I am able to say. Miner doesn't respond. He looks off in the distance for a brief moment in contemplation, rubbing his stubble on his face and looks back at me. He takes his cigar out of his mouth again and smiles,

"So, are you in, kid?" he asks.

"In, sir? I don't understand."

"Come on, kid, don't act stupid. I saw you peeking right from the start. Pretty impressive how you avoided detection from everyone else, I could use a man like you for this job. You heard the situation and what needs to be done. So, I will ask again, but only once." he walks closer to me, "Are you in?"

I had no idea what to say. To be in a squad with someone so legendary leading the charge is an honor. I just wanted more information before doing anything I'd regret. I've already had my share of regrettable actions here as it is. I start babbling uncontrollably, but Sarge just sticks his hand up, which seems to have magically shut me up.

"Quit your babbling! Yes or no?"

I take a deep breath,

"It would be an honor, sir, thank you."

Putting the half smoked cigar back in his mouth, he laughs,

"I'll talk to Serro and clear your name."

As he walks away, he tells me he will get the info he needs then assemble a squad and to keep quiet and tell no one about this plan. Who knows if I would've been his first pick for the squad or any pick for that matter had I not been snooping at the right place at the right time? My thoughts are running wild. I have a mixture of emotions, happy, surprised and scared, just to name a few. On the one hand, I feel honored to even be considered for such an important role, to be a part of a team that could end this nightmare is something only one could dream of. On the other hand, where are we going to find people crazy enough to do this sort of thing? If it was easy, it would've been done a long time ago.

My face is pale. I turn to walk away, but I'm still in shock. Not only because of the squad, but because of what happened with LT. Serro. I've been yelled at before by drill instructors, enemies and many other people but never have I been yelled at for breaking a rule or doing something as idiotic as spying on a meeting I had no business being at. Now, I'm wrapped up in this mess. Hopefully, Miner can clear my name. I'd hate to be on the bad side of a highly respected Lieutenant, especially one as esteemed as Jovell Serro, what he has done for this army is remarkable.

Days go by awaiting to be asked to meet with Miner to go over the rest of the squad and what the plan is exactly, but nothing happens. Maybe it was just all a dream. A very bad, ludacris dream. Miner told me not to tell anyone of this operation, but it was hard not telling anyone. I had to tell someone, but I didn't want to disappoint him. I'm guessing he spoke to LT. Serro and decided against me being a part of the squad, Serro was furious, he could have convinced Miner to drop me. Thinking about it more, my anxiety begins to build, that thought weighs heavy in my heart.

About a week goes by, I come back from patrolling Tefion

and I'm greeted by a Private in my bunker who I have never seen before,

"Sir, my name is PVT. Charlie Kemper. SSG. Miner has requested you meet him."

Well, it's about damn time. Charlie takes me to an abandoned city away from camp. It's not much, I remember this place, though. It was the city of Dezip, destroyed during a major battle a few years back, which wiped out everyone and everything. We tried liberating the city but instead, we helped bring it to ruins. PVT. Kemper looks like he had no place in this fight, he is from Earth, Montana to be specific. He looked to be about 18 years old, buzzed brown hair and hazel eyes filled with hope.

"What are we doing here?" I ask.

He doesn't't say anything, he points to the left and there was Miner sitting down in a crumbled down building that once was a Bar.

"You requested me, sir?" I ask as I approach him.

Sarge nods,

"This was my favorite part of this hellhole planet. It really was something. Why is it that everything good never lasts?"

Sarge lowers his head. I can't come up with an answer or any words for that matter, but I do agree with him. He remains silent after that, he takes a swig of his flask filled with a drink called Fulka from Vespin, it tastes similar to what Sarge calls "Good Ol' Whiskey" back on Earth. There were a few moments of nothing but silence, the only thing you could hear was the cold wind blowing past us. It was clear this place meant a lot to Sarge, despite it being part of the Confederacy or technically under its control.

Sarge lifts his head back up and offers his flask to me. I'm not much of a drinker, but I don't want to be rude, especially right now. I take a swig and hand the flask back to Sarge.

"I'm sorry, sir, but there's nothing we can do now." I say somberly.

Sarge stands up while groaning,

"That's where you're wrong, Son. We can and *will* do something."

The sudden mood change took me by surprise. Sarge puts his hand on my shoulder,

"We are ending this, kid. Us and the rest of the squad."

He brings out a crumpled up piece of paper and slams it down on a nearly broken down table that was barely standing. He walks off to look at the city of ruins. Confused, I approach the piece of paper. It's a list. It's the squad.

A group of 10 people, Sarge and myself included. My heart drops as soon as I see who else is on the squad. I thought my vision was impaired, but no. Sarge is having 7 Privates be a part of the squad. Not only did he recruit 7 rookies for this squad, but he also added Blaine Carlston. I'm baffled by the people on the list, but I just don't understand what exactly Sarge has planned. I snatch up the piece of paper and march towards Sarge, never would I ever charge up to anyone like this usually, but I am overcome with rage.

"With all due respect, sir, but what the hell is this?" I ask.

Miner says nothing. I was fully expecting to get backhanded or reprimanded, but nothing happens. Sarge takes a sip off his flask and smiles.

"You think I'm crazy, too, right?" he asks while laughing.

Ignoring what he said, I shake my head,

"Sir, you can't be serious. All these Privates, not to mention SPC. Blaine Carlston, he is a sadistic ass!"

I'm fuming and Sarge can tell.

"Do you trust me, kid?" Sarge asks.

A part of me wants to say no and tell him he's insane, but I know better,

"I trust you, sir, but this list is just down right a bad idea. You know what we are trying to do here requires years of experience, I'm not even sure if I could do this, either, sir."

Sarge looks down again, saying nothing. I think even he knows this list and this plan is just too crazy to achieve. I saw

14

no sign of Sarge redoing the list, a list that I would love despite it not even being up to me.

I feel I have no choice. I drop the list to the floor,

"Sir, I'm sorry. I'm fine with risking my life for our people but this is suicide, especially with a team like this. I'm afraid I can't do this."

It kills me letting Sarge down, especially after everything. I walk away and head back to PVT. Kemper. I ask him to bring me back to base. He looks at Miner for confirmation and Miner gives a single nod. I guess he realizes our meeting is over too, seeing as he isn't trying to stop me in any way.

For a while, barely any words were said between PVT. Kemper and myself on the way back to base. I can tell he's disappointed by the outcome of the meeting,

"I knew it was good to be true. I guess I was just holding onto hope thinking I'd be able to go home and see my girls." he says with his voice breaking.

"Girls? A bit young, aren't you?" I ask,

He shrugs his shoulders as he weeps for his family back home. I want to hear about them, it's a good way to fill the silence.

"No matter, tell me about them."

Kemper smiles thinking about his girls.

"I have a girlfriend, soon to be wife, Kara, she just gave birth to a baby girl, Laura. Haven't met her officially yet, but I see photos of her all the time when I speak to Kara." he continued with tears falling down face. "She's the most beautiful thing I've ever seen."

He wipes his tears as he finishes speaking while showing me a photo of his girls. Kara is beautiful and Laura is an adorable baby. I wish I had what he has.

"You're a lucky man. I hope you will go home to them soon." I respond.

You'd think he was trying to guilt trip into joining that mess of a squad, but I know when someone is being genuine.

I want to go home too, but there's just no way anything will happen with this squad that was created. At least, I have a better chance at survival not being a part of that squad. Still, though, if Miner does find people for his squad, I do hope it works out. As great as he is, the list was just too concerning. Blaine alone would kill us all before the enemy did. I do feel guilty though. I know I'm letting people down, not just PVT. Kemper and Miner. The thing is, I have no issues with rookies. My issue is that this mission requires a team of seasoned soldiers who knows what they are up against. I feel the recruits just won't take anything seriously, too much is at stake. Has Miner actually cracked? The man is past his prime and has seen enough carnage and chaos to make the best of us go insane. He truly is a great man from what I've heard, but maybe a legend is just what he is, someone who once was great, but has become something empty, a shell of a former war hero.

Returning back to base, I hear news of an attack on Felv, a city on Vespis. The attack was by Xenem, a planet in the Dommis System and an ally of the Confederacy. Rather bold of them to attack such a big planet in Coalition territory, but from what I've heard, their attack was a success. Taking prisoners as well as hundreds of lives. This just gets better and better. After hearing the news and trying to process what I just went through with Sarge, I go into my Quarters and see that a letter was placed on my bed addressed to me from Felv. It's from my parents. It is a bit of a shock, seeing as how I don't typically receive letters from my parents that often, or from anyone in general. The letter was written on paper in a sealed envelope. My parents have always been old fashioned, preferring paper over technology. I sit down and open the envelope and find a crumpled up piece of paper covered in dirt and what appears to be blood. It's not like my parents to put together something so messy. Worried and confused, I read the note.

"Clark,

By the time you get this, we will be long gone. Xenem is attacking our city and their soldiers are closing in on our home. We

are not able to really understand what the soldiers are saying to us or others but it looks like they are taking prisoners with them, to where? We have no idea. We're fine, besides some cuts and bruises, but we don't know what plans they have for us. It's safe to assume that we will be taken back to Xenem to be kept prisoners or worse. Clark, if you are reading this, be strong and don't be afraid, you're our Man of Steel. We will be okay. We are sure the Coalition is working on a plan to get us all back. We have hope and so should you. We hope we will see you soon. We love you. Be safe.
Love, Mom and Dad"

    I shoot up out of my bed and pace back and forth. I'm freaking out. Those Xenem bastards are ruthless. The USC has bigger things on their minds than a group of civilians taken captive. I hate it, but it's the truth. They're only hope is me. After a moment, it hit me what I have to do. I need that squad that the Miner was creating. Putting my faith in a group as ridiculous as the one Miner was creating isn't easy. Any other circumstance, I still would not join the squad, but if this group of kids are to supposedly go to Confederate planets and take them out one by one somehow, then this would be my chance to help my parents and end all this.

    Looking out the window, I see PVT. Kemper sitting down on a cargo box looking at the photo of his family he had shown me. I march up to him and demand he takes me back to Miner. Without any hesitations and with a smile on his face, he takes me back to the crumbled down Bar in Dezip. I see Sarge sitting in the same place and in the same position I left him in. He raises his head and sees me approaching,

    "Did you forget something?" he asks.

    Pretty obvious he knew I'd be back sooner or later. I show Sarge the letter from my parents. After reading, Sarge puts down the letter slowly and rubs his eyes.

    "Are we really surprised that those lunatics did something like this?" he continued, "That being said, I am sorry, son."

    I myself am still processing everything, a millions

thoughts and emotions are running through my head. I simply can't think straight. I suppose I'm mainly just wondering why this happened or how. From what I remember, Vespis has one of the best planetary defenses in all the Galaxies. I imagine they all put up a fight, but in the end, it doesn't matter. Knowing my parents, they did not put up a fight or gave any resistance, which is smart. My whole life, they've always been there for me and I've tried my best to always be there for them, but I failed. It's my time to fix that. I'm all over the place trying to think of what to say exactly to Sarge. Nothing comes out. Finally, I come up with words to say to Sarge.

"If this squad of yours is to do what it was meant for, then I'm in, but only if we get my parents back when we hit Xenem, sir."

It feels odd giving demands to someone like SSG. Miner, but at this point, I don't care and it's clear that he does not care, either. After brief moment of silence, he gets up and looks at me for a few seconds, maybe to see if I'm being serious or if I'm just as crazy as he is, which I probably am. This plan is still crazy and borderline moronic, so, what the hell am I even doing? Perhaps I just have a death wish. After his glance into what seems like into my soul, he grabbed his beaten up helmet and smiled,

"Well, kid, let's get those sons of bitches. We got a deal."

THE TEAM

A few months have gone by now. It feels like years, though. We're told we're the galaxy's last hope. The few who know about us call us the "Galaxy's Finest", at least that's who they say we are or who we are supposed to be, but we have not earned that title, yet. Our official title is Specter, a squadron led by SSG. Richard "Sarge" Miner, also known as, "Specter 1". If you picture what a seasoned soldier looks like, that's Sarge. He has long, scraggly gray hair, a five o'clock shadow and constantly smells of cigars. Sarge has been a part of every major conflict involving our people for the past five or so decades. According to Sarge, our name comes from the fact we are supposed to be specters, ghosts, unseen and unheard. Ironically, we make more noise than any other group or squadron. A squadron who isn't supposed to exist having a name seems odd, but we're told we're different from a typical black ops unit, but we sure sound like one, either way, I go with it. We're all honored to serve with him, or under him, I should say. He would have a higher ranking, but he is not the most liked person among the USC. It's petty and childish, but that is really the only reason he has not moved up further.

    I still can't believe he actually wanted me to join this squad. He told me he wanted me after seeing how I was able to sneak into a secret military meeting undetected, also after hearing a few Drill Sergeants and other soldiers give me praise for my hard work and initiative during my time with them, he was impressed. I have never cared for any praise given to me during this whole mess, but at least I got the attention of Sarge, I was given the codename "Specter 2". After me, we have SPC.

Blaine Carlston, "Specter 3", we needed a brute and Sarge saw the good in Blaine, somehow, and requested him, too.

I still have a complete lack of respect for those kids who are entitled, cocky, naive and know nothing of war. So, naturally, I have one of those kids. Private Bradley Whithers Dillon, from Manhattan, New York on Earth. He was given the codename "Specter 4". He is the spitting image of what a rich kid looks like, a smug smile, gelled back blonde hair, green eyes and not a single scratch on him. It shows he's careful, at least. I still ponder why he decided to enlist, a pampered elitist, trust fund prima donna leaving his cushy home back in New York to fight? Any time someone asks him why, he gives the same frustrating response, "Wouldn't you like to know?"

I've grown a liking to the next kid, Private Carden Munrick Reddina, "Specter 5", from the planet Foli in the Skylock system coming from the city of Patsan, an ally of the Coalition. From what Sarge told me, the moment he got on base, he didn't try to impress anyone by flexing his knowledge or muscles. When there's off time, you can find him in his bunker reading or drawing pictures of ideas for new inventions. He's the only rookie in my squad who has ever come up to Sarge and I for advice. Most recruits are too afraid to ask questions, thinking that we would say something along the lines of "You should've learned that during training." Yet, Carden had no issue with asking questions. I personally believe that there is absolutely nothing wrong with asking questions, Sarge feels the same way. Back when I was a Private, he taught me a good soldier always asks questions. Folins and other planets in the Skylock System look similar to humans, the way to tell them apart is the teeth and eyes. All black eyes and their teeth, sharp as hell, but no reports of them ever biting or eating anyone or anything meat based. As far as we know.

Going down the list, we have two brothers from Earth, specifically from Liverpool in the U.K. Private Martin Baxter Lane and PVT. Mitchell Brandon Lane, "Specter 6" and "Specter 7". Twins. How great for us. Both of them have bright, curly red hair and brown eyes, essentially impossible to tell them apart. Few months now with them and we can't get many words out of either of them, but they do their job well and they like to keep busy, that's all that matters. Not much else info I could give about them, not yet at least. They're quite a mystery to us all. The last three of our group are women. Naturally, Blaine wasn't crazy about the idea of women serving with him, especially since one of them was born Male, but identifies as a Female. He has the mind-set that women are fragile and weak and would slow us down, but they are quite the opposite. All three could definitely kick Blaine's teeth in, but he would never admit that.

Private Kierra Pauness Shuua, "Specter 8", from the planet Matu in the Cammora System, specifically the city of Lakena. Perhaps one of the smartest members among us, there is no problem that isn't solvable to her. Gives Carden a run for his money. It was an adjustment having someone from Matu a part of our ranks. We didn't see many of them really anywhere. Their people always kept to themselves and kept out of any issue that arose around the galaxies as much as they could. I guess the threat of being conquered by an evil Empire was enough to get them moving with the crowd. Despite how reclusive Matu is, their people are kind and wise, yet often quiet. Nonetheless, they are a great asset to the USC. Blaine never makes eye contact with her when he reluctantly speaks with her because of the way she looks. Everyone in the Cammora System shares the same appearance, red and white hair and eyes, but Kierra was born with blue and red eyes. She doesn't speak much about it. She doesn't speak that much in general, sounds like me.

Next soldier, a human, from Earth, specifically Nashville, Tennessee. Private Rachel Warner Denza, "Specter 9". Born Richard Warner Denza, to a single father who abandoned her when she told him that she was Transgender. It broke her heart, she was just a kid, but she sees now that she is better off without him. She has long wavy brown hair and hazel colored eyes which she claims is one of her favorite features about herself. She always tells us how the USC gave her the family she never had, but Blaine's hatred and misunderstanding is a constant reminder of her dead-beat father. We just wish Blaine would shut his mouth and do his job. Never has there been a time when Rachel didn't step up for her squad, no issues with going first into enemy territory, firing the first shot, throwing the first punch or helping one of us when any of us fall. A true heart of gold. Sarge sees a wall of medals in her future, and if we're being honest, most of us do too. The only issue, she is quick to anger, especially when it comes to her gender identity being questioned or used as the subject of a joke. She will fight anyone who gives her crap over it. Maybe she wants to prove something, I'm not sure, but we're working on controlling it. As Sarge would say, "Save it for the battlefield."

 Last, but not least, Private Somma Terra Juna, "Specter 10", from the capital city Felv on Vespis, core planet of the Waylif System. If you need to know anything about any planet or any system, Somma is the right person for the job. She spent her life studying all that surrounds her and her people. She knows every location, every hideout and any and all danger that lurks around the galaxies and not to mention, a hell of a tracker. She is technically the oldest of the ten at 1,023 years old in terms of Earth years, but you wouldn't even believe it. To people on Vespis, she is on the younger side. On Earth, she would pass for a 23 year old woman. Admittedly, she is absolutely beautiful. Like everyone on Vespis, her eyes are a mixture of silver and white and sparkle like diamonds as does her skin. She has long silver hair that goes down to her lower back. It shimmers and flashes when she moves around, almost as if she has shooting stars in her hair. It's really something to see. The only real struggle with her is we have to cover her up extra on stealth operations, but she doesn't seem to mind. She is actually amazing when it comes to stealth and secrecy. It's impossible to hear her footsteps and she covers herself so well that it's pretty difficult to see her. She has to use black gloves and an extra layer of cloth to wrap her hands and a face mask to cover her neck and face, as well as wearing a black hood to cover her hair, it's an entire process. To be honest, I am a bit jealous of the way the whole ensemble looks. If she gets too stressed, her skin tends to get brighter and can even get to a point of a blinding light if she gets to a high level of stress. On Vespis, everyone's shining skin and hair is showing, making it impossible not to stare. To put it into perspective, due to everyone's shining skin, from space, Vespis shines so bright that it is considered the "Sun" of the Waylif System, it even gives off heat, yet we are somehow able to visit the surface without sustaining any burns or harm of any kind. In my time with PVT. Juna, I've found out that Vespin blood looks like liquid silver mixed with red, it's an interesting sight to see. It is said that their blood carries some sort of powerful healing properties that can heal even the worst wounds. There have even been some stories of people who are not from Vespis sustaining fatal wounds that were healed soon after Vespin blood that was donated was injected into their system. If it enters the victim's bloodstream within a day or so, it's fully healed, it still leaves a scar, though. I don't quite understand it, then again, these are just stories. Who knows if it's true? I don't think many people understand Vespis, but nonetheless, it's a truly fascinating planet.

    She still carries child-like wonder when we travel from different planets, but as smart as Juna is, she isn't one for war. It's not that she's scared or a coward, she just hates the idea of it and never wanted to join the fight. That immediately tells you how bright she is, no pun intended. She only joined to make her father, General Pyren Juna, proud. In Waylif, GEN. Juna is a legend. He pushed her to join due to her extensive knowledge of the galaxies and of course, to keep his family legacy of serving in war. Their whole family legacy was in service of Vespis and he wanted his offspring to carry their legacy. From what I know, she is his only child and she doesn't want to fail him. She keeps her family life personal and I know better than to try to question it further. She worries too much about the responsibility she has as the only child of a legend and as a member of a well known and respected military family. I know she makes GEN. Juna proud, though. Lucky for us, Somma speaks English, as does everyone else in Specter. It would make this job ten times harder if none of us could understand each other.

The Coalition's uniforms are different from ours, theirs is black with blue accents, but our uniforms are black with white accents and our Specter number on the right side of our chest and the United Starlight Coalition logo on the left. The USC logo is a white star with other similar colored stars surrounding it. As far as the uniforms go, it's a small difference, but we are supposed to be separate from the regular military for the Coalition. At first, I was confused as to why Sarge wanted mostly rookies on his squad. Apparently, he fought pretty hard for them to be with him. Had I been a worse person, I still wouldn't have joined the squad after that letter from my parents. After all, I originally used to think rookies wouldn't help us much during firefights or day to day operations. I know that's what Blaine thinks. Which is why I'm surprised he was fine with joining. Either way, after all these years with Sarge, I've learned he always has a good reason for everything, so I trust him. He always looks out for his own.

As I mentioned before, I'm quite the expert on Norse mythology and its tales. There have been a few nights where the squad and I are resting around a roaring fire on base or while setting up camp on the road and during those times, I would tell them classic Nordic tales. Tales that would inspire them like the stories have inspired me. After a long day, it's my job to boost morale and so I tell them stories of the God of Thunder, Thor, defeating monsters, giants and other evil forces. Using that as a metaphor for us. We are facing monsters and giants and evil forces of our own and my hope is that we will all rise up and defeat these monsters and giants just like

Thor and all the other gods did.

    We've been through a lot in our short time together. I guess the harsh, hard-hitting reality of war has hit everyone by now, but they never mentioned it. PVT. Juna was the only person who spoke about it with me. I still remember that day, seems so long ago. Sarge put Blaine and myself in charge of helping the rookies get better acquainted with our new temporary base camp at the time, which ended up being Fort Kjialfa. Nothing about Kjialfa was hidden or a secret, I questioned why we were even sent there. I figured as long as it was temporary, we'd be okay. Sarge wanted Blaine and I to go there to help the others with any sort of training they still may need as it has proper supplies and a decent shooting range and other training facilities. "Babysitting" Blaine called it, he never had the same connection to the Sarge that I had with him. After a while, I understood his methods and his requests, but Blaine never cared to get to know Sarge better to understand how he works. To Blaine, the great SSG. Richard Miner was just another old man telling him what to do. Blaine has a hard time giving respect, but demands it from everyone else. Face to face, Blaine wouldn't dare question authority or show a lack of respect to Sarge. It sure is easier talking shit about someone when they're not present.

    Technically speaking, as Specialist, Blaine had the authority to help the rookies by himself, but Sarge wanted me to help. Seeing as the only thing Blaine and I could agree on was what type of training was the best, we brought the rookies to the shooting range. Despite their requests to pick whichever gun they wanted to fire, we had them practice with their respective mandated weapons. A Hentfay rifle and a Baunafiss handgun, the finest guns Foli has to offer. Even though the rookies in Specter have been in battle and has fought bravely, they needed work on their aim, among other things. First thing is first, though. We trained on base, Blaine and I gave them their guns, explosives and a few other toys to get more familiar with. I feel as though when Blaine and I put our differences aside and actually work together to a common goal, we seem to think alike and one thing we noticed was the rookies all had the same issue when dealing with firearms. It's something we both have noticed during firefights in the past, they all would close their eyes when they fired their weapons. Nearly got them killed many times. They're lucky to be alive. I approached everyone,

"You know, you aim better with your eyes open."

PVT. Dillon rolled his eyes at me, which, with him, is a daily occurrence and it still is. Any other higher ranking soldier would beat his entitled ass, but Blaine and I let it slide. For some unknown reason. It's probably why he always does it, because he knows he will get away with it. He can think what he wants, but in reality, it is just because we know one day he will realize we are right and he will then listen to us. PVT. Juna overheard us giving Dillon advice and quietly interjected. Blaine approached her,

"You have something to say, Private?" he shouted.

She lacked eye contact and kept a quiet demeanor. I could tell she was scared and nervous. I tried to move Blaine away from her, but he shoved me away, continuing to yell at her.

"Don't tell me your people are deaf, too! You want to say something?"

He clearly wasn't here to make friends, but by then, I knew how the squad worked and operated. I remember I grabbed Blaine by his collar and threw him towards Bradley. I look back at PVT. Juna who looks defeated. I bring her to the side,

"What's the problem here?" I ask.

She looked up at me with her sparkling Vespin eyes, only the sparkle wasn't as bright,

"I am scared, sir." she said quietly, "We are all scared. Not just scared of these loud guns and cannons. We are scared we will not see tomorrow, or our families and homes. I cannot speak for anyone else, but I close our eyes because each time

I fire a gun or throw an explosive, the loudness is deafening and the only other thing I hear is shouting and screaming everywhere. When I open our eyes again, there are bodies on the floor, blood on the walls, and burning buildings with ashes in the air. I cannot breathe. How do you handle that?"

I recall thinking "She finally gets it." I had hoped it would have been someone else who got the rude awakening. Even though she is technically years older than us, we saw her as the youngest among us and we still do. She knew Blaine wouldn't care, I guess that's why she wouldn't say all that in front of everyone. At this time, she and I had gotten a bit closer to each other, close enough to where I'd say that's why she confided in me. Any time a soldier gets hit with reality, I tend to just shrug it off, but I guess it's different with her. It hurts seeing what this war is doing to everyone. It has taken a toll on all of us.

These kids were thrown into action almost immediately after meeting us all. Having to fight for your life as soon as you come on base would scare anyone. I'm proud of them and how far they've come. Despite some flaws, they were doing great for rookies under their circumstances. I thought if PVT. Juna and everyone else could keep a cool head, they would survive this nightmare. We all would. I knew I had to say something to her. I couldn't just let her emotions and feelings go unnoticed, but what could I have said?

After a brief moment of reflection over what I just heard, I grabbed her rifle and put it away, averting eye contact while trying to think. I came back to her with some water and offered it to her. She was shaky, but grabbed the cantine and took a sip to calm herself. I looked back at her,

"Look, I'm scared, too. Even SPC. Carlston is afraid, even if he won't admit it. We fight so we don't have to be afraid anymore. I'm not going to stand here and lie to you saying it's going to get better or there's a light at the end of this dark tunnel of death and decay. We are at war, you are a soldier and it is your job to fight and get the job done, so you can go home, so we can all go home. Protect your home so you have a home to go to at the end of this. Just stay calm, listen to your orders from your superiors and you and everyone here will be fine. We got your back. You're dismissed."

Her face was hard to read, but she seemed to understand. With a slight nod, again avoiding eye contact, she picked up her rifle and went back to the group.

It seems so long ago, but I hope she is doing better. I haven't checked on her recently, but I always mean to. After all this time, we're still in Fort Kjialfa. We have been waiting a while for Sarge to give us any sort of assignment or take us to the new camp. Blaine and I send everyone to train with their weapons again, we don't know what else we could do while we all wait. After about an hour of training, Sarge finally shows up in a Transport craft to hopefully take us to the new camp. We constantly have to move to new locations so no one finds us, it's pretty frustrating, but at this point, we are used to it. This is actually the longest we have stayed in one spot. As we enter the craft we see Sarge in the driver's seat holding a hologram pad. Sarge never used those pads. Just like my parents, he preferred paper. He looked frustrated, hitting the pad and shaking it,

"Damn thing can't do anything!" Sarge yells.

Glad to see he's in a good mood. Blaine and I look at each other and naturally, Blaine signals for me to talk to him.

"Get everyone the ship. Don't kill them while I'm gone" I say while walking towards Miner at the front of the ship,

"Hello, sir, is everything alright?"

Sarge took a swig of his flask,

"Whatever happened to pen and paper? Am I the only one who still uses it?"

I had no idea how to answer that, but I'm on his side in the matter. My parents and I prefer pen and paper too.

"Technology is hard, sir." I respond, unable to think of anything else to say.

In hindsight, that doesn't sound good, but either way, Sarge ignores what I said, trying to fix his pad as everyone gets situated onboard,

"Alright, you muts, listen up!" Sarge yells at us all while taking off.

Up until now, our impact on the war as a secret squadron has yet to be anything of impact, few cities and minor planets liberated here and there, but not much else. Which is why we're hoping Sarge has something big in mind.

"First, Reddina, get your ass over here and fix this damn pad!" Sarge demanded.

PVT. Reddina runs over and within about three seconds his pad was fixed, although if we're being honest, his pad wasn't even broken, it was just not turned on. With one issue resolved, we're still waiting for what Sarge has to say.

"Ms. Juna, please teach the class about the wonderful planet of the day, Xenem." Sarge requested.

PVT. Juna smiles and quickly brings out her pad with her notes on it, her face lights up, more than usual. She was always happy teaching people about her expertise. Blaine sighs and rolls his eyes,

"Something wrong with your eyes, Carlston?" I ask.

"Nothing's wrong."

All bark, no bite, classic Blaine. Miner asking PVT. Juna to tell us about Xenem made it seem like we are going after my parents and also liberating the planet, only one could hope.

"Of course, sir!" she exclaimed. "Xenem is the fifth planet farthest from their sun in the Dommis System and they are the main supplier of weapons and equipment for the Chelorian Confederacy. The planet itself has barely any life forms on it, barely anything at all, really, besides factories and camps. Their Chancellor, Valkis Tyro, is a brutal and harsh man who tortures and forces his people and prisoners to work non-stop for him and the Confederacy. Their soldiers have no issues killing men, women and children. They would never dare question Valkis. Truly, a horrible place."

Well, I'm glad to hear my parents are there. Anyone with a brain in the USC knows about Xenem. I've heard many horror stories about what goes on there. Xenem is a green, gray and red planet. It's believed the green and gray are produced by the factories and polluted toxic waste flowing into their waters and up in the air. The red from all the blood of travelers who were unfortunate enough to visit. It's a place that no sane person would ever set foot in intentionally, luckily, we're clearly not sane.

"That's too bad, but what does that have to do with us?" Blaine asks.

"Well, SPC. Carlston, we have a job to do, if that's alright with you." Sarge continued, "We've done good work so far, but it's barely anything compared to the hell we are about to bring down."

We all look at each other with concern in our eyes. We're not sure what the plan is exactly, but from what Sarge was saying, this sounds like we are starting to get the real work going. The mix of emotions we were all feeling was noticeable. The rookies were frightened, naturally, even I was a bit shaken. None of us ever did something like this. All the years in service and neither Blaine nor myself came close to doing something like this. We all know what we signed up for, though. Sarge continued,

"Our plan? Take out their supply factories and free their prisoners." he then looks at me,

"All of them." he says with a nod of his head.

While that's all well and good, we still have no idea how we will do something like that. 10 of us against an entire planet with a brutal dictator calling the shots? Sarge better have an amazing plan. We simply can't walk in and wreck their entire planet. It's harder when the Chancellor and his soldiers are one of the most ruthless creatures in all the galaxies. We have to be smart about this. Luckily, Sarge picked up the smartest kids he could find who were ironically stupid enough to join this squad.

PVT. Shuua raises her hand up,

"SSG. Miner, a planet like Xenem is going to have quite a lot of ground and air defense systems, how do you suppose we get in?"

Aerial and ground defenses didn't even occur to me until she mentioned it. It's a valid point, how the hell do we get in and more importantly, get out? This would be the first major move we've made so far. I trust Sarge, but even he has to realize how difficult this is going to be, even if we are the "Galaxy's Finest". We're all ears waiting for Sarge to tell us what he has planned exactly.

"Good question Ms. Shuua!" Sarge continued while jumping to hyperspace, "If we can get our hands on a Xenem ship, we can sneak our way in. How we get the ship, I leave up to your superiors. You all better hurry, we don't have long. Dismissed."

Fantastic, now we have to get a ship? I suppose that's not the hardest part, but it'll take some doing. Blaine and I look at each other and shake our heads. Even someone like him can tell this is going to be a hell of a lot to pull off. Jumping out of hyperspace, we reach our new location within seconds. Our new camp is on Tarena, the deserted planet that started this war. We've only been here one other time. We destroyed a military fort not too far from where we're at. We're just outside of the small, war torn city of Lornas. No one really lives here anymore, from what I understand, Xenem uses it for storage and supplies. Many planets and cities under their control are used for the same reason. As we enter Tarena's atmosphere, Blane nudges my shoulder,

"So, what's the plan?" he asks while scratching his head.

As if I formulated a plan within the past thirty seconds. Granted, I don't see any plan really being the smartest, but I need more time, everyone knows Blaine won't think of anything, anything brilliant at least. I'm not even the smartest person on this squad if we're being honest, it's Blaine and myself's seniority that makes it seem like we can be tacticians. If anything, I'd ask either PVT. Shuua, Reddina or Juna. Sure, they're kids, but they're bright. Smarter than I'll ever be. Regardless, we will come up with something. All these years at war and under command of some of the best leaders in all the galaxies, we'd be foolish if we didn't learn anything from all these years. One of the Lane twins, Martin, I think, walks up to us,

"Excuse me, CPL. Parson, SPC. Carlston?"

"So, he does talk! What is it, kid?" Blaine responds.

"My brother and I have heard from others that every so often, ships pass by over our new campsite, going where? We have no idea, but from what we have heard, they look like a Xenem ships. They could be wrong, but if not, perhaps that is how we get our ship, assuming we can take it down somehow. We'll keep a look out for the ships."

I nod my head once without saying a word and Martin nods back as he walks away. It's not a bad idea, but as far as I know, there's no way to take down a ship quietly. Luckily for us, not doing anything quietly is essentially Blaine's specialty. He somehow always has explosives with him, even explosives we don't carry on base. Still, I'd like to figure out a way to quietly bring one their ships down, perhaps some sort of EMP. Either way, we finally land at our new camp, Miner sends everyone to set up camp. Before everyone runs off, I gather the whole squad,

"Listen up, PVT. Lane has informed us of possible Xenem ships that pass us by from time to time, if we can take out one their ships quietly with some sort of EMP, that would be our best chance at getting one down, PVT. Reddina and Shuua, please work with each other on developing the EMP, dismissed."

PVT. Reddina and Shuua look at each other then bolt towards an empty spot to set up their work stations, I ask the rest of the squad to dig up whatever they can about Xenem, we have to fully prepare for whatever is to come.

"Are you sure you don't want a big explosion? It'd look pretty great in the night sky." Blaine asks, as if he will have anything to do with the development of the EMP.

I won't even give him an answer, hoping in time he will

see the stupidity of what he just asked, I won't hold my breath, though. It's been a few days since we landed and set up camp, everyone is hard at work. The Lane twins are at their watch posts documenting the frequency of the amount of time the ships pass over us. PVT. Reddina and Shuua are both hard at work creating the EMP. PVT. Denza, Juna and Dillon are finding out everything they can about the ships and Xenem defenses. The moment she stepped foot on our new camp, without being asked, PVT. Juna had the idea to wrap herself, covering her hands and face. It's smart of her, though her skin hasn't been too bright for a while, her hair and skin still shimmer. We can't risk someone seeing her from afar. Every day so far, she has only taken her wraps off in private to change them out. I don't doubt it's uncomfortable, I personally appreciate what she's doing.

    Blaine and myself are watching over everyone, trying to help whenever and wherever we can while Sarge went back to USC Headquarters, on Vespis, to try to gather intel on Xenem, along with helping the survivors of the attack. Most of the United Starlight Coalition doesn't even know of our squad's existence and we would like to keep it that way. That being said, it's going to be hard to pull this off while keeping our squad a secret from everyone else. A Xenem ship randomly going down will almost certainly raise suspicion from each side of this war. I head over to PVT. Reddina and Shuua to ask if there is a way to ensure that the attack is as quiet as possible. I know that a ship going down isn't exactly the quietest thing in the Galaxy, but if anyone can figure out how, it'd be Reddina and Shuua. After all, Sarge recruited them for their brains.

    Both of them look very focused, not letting anything distract them, but their stations are a mess. Years ago, before this war started and I was back home with my parents, I'd help my parents cook and they both had a saying, "A clean and organized kitchen is a functioning kitchen." To others, it may seem like one of the millions of lessons parents try to teach us, but they're right about this. I carried that lesson throughout my life. I approach PVT. Reddina and Shuua, I see both of them moving everything around their stations trying to find specific tools they need. Looking at what PVT. Reddina is working on, I can tell he needs a Vertiz Screwdriver. In the rummage, I see the screwdriver he needs. I pick it up and tap his shoulder, he turns around and sees me holding the tool.

"Thank you, sir. Where was it?" he asks,

"A clean and organized station is a functioning station."

I look at both PVT. Reddina and Shuua while handing him the screwdriver, hoping the lesson got through to them, both responding with a nod.

"Yes, sir." they say at the same time.

As I walk away, I hear objects moving around, I turn around and see them both organizing everything. It's a simple, but effective lesson, I'm glad they listened. I decide to head over to the twins who are still documenting the frequency of the amount of time the ships pass. Not sure how much help I can really be, but I'm just walking around checking on everyone. The twins see me coming and both quickly stand up with the hands behind their backs called to attention.

"So, what have you both been seeing so far?" I ask,

PVT. Lane, Mitchell steps forward,

"Sir, we haven't seen any ships pass by for some time. It's rather odd, from what we've heard, a few days ago there would be Xenem ships passing us almost every hour, but there hasn't been much going on as of late."

That certainly is odd. It seems unlikely anyone in the USC would lie about something like this.

"Just keep looking out and report any more strange occurrences to me or SPC. Carlston." I respond as I walk away.

Lastly, I go to check up on the rest of the squad who are still researching all things Xenem. Blaine is there with them, but I can tell he's lost. Again, he never was the brainy type. PVT. Juna has taken the lead as far as research goes seeing as she knows the most about Xenem, but even she doesn't know everything.

"SPC. Carlston, can you please leave us and patrol the base, I'll stay with the group." I say to him.

Blaine rolls his eyes while picking up his gun and heads out. Our base camp is small and isn't even known about by anyone besides the squad, so we have to be careful of our surroundings.

"So, has anyone found anything new about Xenem?" I ask,

"Sir, we found out the Xenem used to be allies with Vespis." PVT. Denza says, while handing me her pad, "Apparently, they were on extremely good terms. That is until Chancellor Valkis Tyro rose to power years ago and has completely cut ties with Vespis."

It's shocking to say the least. I grab the pad to take a closer look, it's a photo of the President of Vespis, Pontell Bovi, and former Chancellor of Xenem Lerot Holek together in front of a beautiful mountain range on Xenem.

"Where was this photo taken?" I ask.

"That is what Xenem used to look like," PVT. Shuua continued, "before Tyro took control. He completely demolished all the natural beauty from their world just for his factories and death camps."

The pad shows a photo of Tyro, he doesn't look too friendly. Pale, wrinkled skin, piercing green eyes, crooked nose with a scar over his mouth. It's amazing what one person can do in a matter of years. I give the pad back to her , PVT. Juna grabs the pad from her and looks at the photos,

"Xenem used to be so beautiful!" she says with that classic sparkle in her eyes.

"Thank you for saying so, child." we hear from behind.

We didn't recognize the voice, we quickly turn around and draw our sidearms and see Blaine with his hands up. Two Xenem soldiers with their guns pointed at his back approach us followed by someone else. A Captain.

THE INTRUDER

"Now, now, everyone, there is no need for all the theatrics. We have simply come to talk." the Xenem Captain says calmly.

No question that these guys are from Xenem, but the left side of the Captain's face was burned, the skin wrinkled and his left eye pale white as opposed to his right green eye. Those from Xenem have toxic green eyes, his damaged eye was the first thing I noticed. Putting his appearance aside, my sights are still on him. I look at all three of them,

"Hard to believe that you just want to talk when you have our friend held at gunpoint, where I come from, we don't talk that way." I respond.

The Xenem Captain gives a dry chuckle, amused by my answer, he orders his men to lower their weapons and he holsters his gun.

"Now, how about we talk?" the Captain asks in a sarcastic tone.

I look at the rest of Specter, they've never been in this position before, to be honest neither have I. I signal my squad to lower their weapons. Some follow my orders immediately while a couple others, such as PVT. Denza and Dillon were reluctant to do so. After a few moments, everyone put their weapons down. I look back at the Captain,

"Have a seat."

The Captain takes a seat at a nearby table. He pulls out an oddly shaped bottle and takes a sip of it. He offers some of his drink to me,

"What the hell do you want?" I ask, ignoring his offer while looking dead into his piercing green and white eyes.

"My name is CPT. Auldin Leezol, I have been watching you for a while, I have been watching all of you."

I look around to everyone else with concern and confusion. CPT. Leezol leans in,

"So, CPL. Clark David Parson, from Eugene, Oregon, born May 25th, 2443," he continued, "Yes, you are most definitely Mr. Parson. Pale face, long black hair, tired brown eyes, tattoos all over your arms, hands and fingers, ouch, by the way! Now, do you really think this weak group of kids, yourself included, will 'save' the galaxy', not to mention your dear parents?"

I'm stunned. So many thoughts run through my head, I've never been in a situation like this. Leezol chuckles,

"Do not worry, we have not done anything to your parents, yet."

My mind is racing, how did he know about us? About me? Did someone tell him? Were we not careful enough? More importantly, is this the end? I remain silent, whether it's strategic reasons or just my state of shock, I'm not sure. CPT. Leezol clearly isn't an idiot and picks up on my shock and confusion.

"I apologize, I imagine this is all very confusing and dare I say, scary, for all of you. If it makes any of you feel any better, you were not easy to find. I suppose the name Specter is quite fitting. We have only known of the existence of your squad for about a month now, so I congratulate you all on that, plus the amount you have done within months is quite impressive." Leezol says.

He turns to his soldiers who still are holding Blaine by his shoulders,

"Not bad for a group of mostly kids, right, men?"

The soldiers say nothing, keeping a close eye on everyone. With fury in his eyes, he shoots up out of his seat and throws Blaine out of the way, he violently grabs both of his soldiers by the throat,

"I asked you both a question! You answer me when I talk to you! Understood?" he yells while gripping their throats tighter.

The soldiers gasping for air, nodding their heads, after a few more seconds, Leezol lets them go and sits back down and turns his attention back to me as if nothing just happened. The soldiers quickly pick Blaine back up and continue holding him back. Leezol is truly terrifying figure. I feel we could have made a move while he was distracted by his soldiers, but I think we're all stunned and frozen in fear. After I gather my bearings, I lean in,

"What do you want?"

Leezol sighs and pulls out a knife from his belt, it's beautiful. The handle is made from a rare type of wood only found on Xenem called Colia and even then, I've heard it is exceedingly rare to find. It has amazingly detailed carvings of Xenem letters and symbols. The blade, serrated and razor sharp to the touch with a sentence engraved on the blade in their native language. I tilt my head in wonderment looking at the knife, Leezol catches me staring,

"It is remarkable, is it not?" he asks with a sinister smile before stabbing the knife into the table, inches in front of my hands that were placed on the table.

That breaks the trance I was under, I once again make eye contact with Leezol as he chuckles.

"I will tell you what we want. Answers."

"Answers for what?" I ask.

Leezol extends his hand toward one of his soldiers, the soldier gives him a hologram pad, Leezol pulls up a picture and hands me the pad. I grab the pad and see who's in the picture, it's Sarge.

"You know this man, do you not?" Leezol asks while grabbing the pad from me.

He stands up and walks around the camp going to every member of the squad showing them the photo.

"You all know this 'great' man, I know you do, the question is, who is gonna open their mouths and tell me all about him? His strengths, and more importantly, his weaknesses, among other things."

He walks past PVT. Juna, who is noticeably shaking. Leezol turns to her and smiles,

"Oh my! A Vespin! Oh, how beautiful you are, child. I can tell, even with your face covered up like this. My, my, those eyes, they never cease to amaze me. Did you know those sparkling diamonds you call eyes are said to hold the brightest hidden stars in all the galaxies?" he says as he turns to everyone, "At least, that is what we were taught on Xenem."

She is shaking more than before as she looks at me, but in a split second, Leezol quickly brings out his knife and violently grabs her face, bringing the blade inches from her left eye,

"Those eyes will be an excellent trophy! Or perhaps a new set for myself? Unless, you tell me about Miner! I know you know him, you all know him! What is it going to be, child? Where is that old, broken antique? Where? Answer me, now!"

Everyone tries to get to her, but the soldiers bring out their guns and aim for us. I try to charge at Leezol, but one of the soldiers rush to me and hit me with their gun. I fall to the ground, but the soldier grabs me by the shirt to hold me back. The blade slowly gets closer to her eye as PVT. Juna tries resisting, pulling away with all her might while screaming in frustration and fear, but Leezol is too strong. We are all yelling and begging for him to stop. The blade, inches from her eye, about to make contact, when all of a sudden, we hear a gunshot, the knife is shot out of Leezol's hands. Stunned and furious, Leezol drags PVT. Juna in front of him as a shield, when seconds later, we hear another two shots and both of his soldiers go down.

Perplexed, Leezol demands that whoever the attacker is reveals themselves immediately.

"Not bad for an 'old, broken antique', right, Leezol?" Sarge asks sarcastically while emerging from the bushes nearby holding an old, beat-up sniper rifle with a cigar in his mouth as he approaches Leezol.

"Here I am, Captain, you mind letting my team go now?"

Leezol laughs while holding onto PVT. Juna tighter, putting his knife to her throat.

"Oh, I do not think so, Miner. How about you drop your weapon instead, and perhaps you can still save your Vespin pet here. After all, it has been a while since we have had a little chat, old friend." he responds.

All of us are still frozen even though there are no guns aimed at us, we're taking in what's happening, especially hearing that Sarge and Leezol used to be friends. Sarge takes his cigar out of his mouth and laughs,

"Friends? Is that what we were? Back on Earth, friends don't betray each other and try to kill one another! You were my brother!" he yells while aiming his gun at Leezol.

We've never seen Sarge like this before, it was heartbreaking. Leezol snarls,

"You are still as foolish as you were the day this war started! You became the enemy when you picked your side, Chancellor Tyro wanted you, he wanted you and Ben, remember little Ben? What did you do, though? Run to the Waylif System, you coward! Oh, but that is not the end of our tale, is it Miner?"

We have no idea what he means, or who Ben is, but one thing is clear, Sarge is shaken. Seems uncertain if any of us, even Sarge, will make it out of this. Sarge looks at PVT. Juna, he can tell that under all the wraps, she is filled with stress and fear, her shine begins to pierce through her wraps more and more. She is becoming a ball of pure light. He motions at her to wait for his signal. Sarge looks back at Leezol,

"That's all in the past now. Sorry, Captain, but coming here wasn't a *BRIGHT* idea. Juna, now!"

PVT. Juna elbows Leezol in the stomach with all her might and quickly unwraps her face, blinding him and everyone in front of her for a few moments, including myself. That's when PVT. Shuua comes up behind Leezol and puts him in a sleeper hold until he's unconscious. PVT. Juna collapsed to the ground along with Leezol. Everyone rushes over to them. PVT. Denza and Dillon go to cuff Leezol and take him inside one of our tents for interrogation when he wakes up. The rest of us quickly cover up PVT. Juna with what little vision we had at the moment. After we cover her up and the chaos settles, everything goes silent. The only sounds that we hear are our heavy breathing and of course, the heartbreaking sound of PVT. Juna crying. At least the worst is behind us.

About an hour has gone by and Leezol hasn't woken up yet, despite our best efforts. We decide to wait until he wakes up on his own, so while we wait, Sarge takes some of the squad to help him find the ship that Leezol and his men arrived in and had the rest of us stay back to keep watch. I walk around camp and it's quiet, with no one speaking, the only sound we hear is the blowing of the cold wind. I look around and everyone has their heads down, I see PVT. Juna sitting down with a blanket around her that PVT. Shuaa brought her. She has a cup of water in her hands and PVT. Denza has her arm around her, but she isn't really drinking. No one should ever go through what she went through today. As I finish walking around the camp, I step on something hard, curious and lift my foot up to see. It's Leezol's knife that was shot out of his hand. I pick it up and take a closer look at it. Within seconds, PVT. Juna shows up seemingly out of nowhere and snatches the knife from me, pacing back and forth with it with anger.

"PVT. Juna, please give me back the knife." I request in my most calming voice possible.

She shakes her head frantically,

"No, you bury this, you bury this knife right now, get it out of here." she demands while her voice breaks.

I understand her reaction, but I'm sure Sarge is going to want to see it. I approach her and reach for the knife, but backs away and points the knife at me. There's only so much we can let her get away with, all things considered, but if she is trying to threaten me, that's another story.

"Where is he?" she asks with her hands shaking.

Given the state she is in and the weapon she is holding, I can only imagine what she wants to do to CPT. Leezol while he's down. I demand that she puts down the knife immediately and to sit back down, but she ignores my demand and stares at the knife while her hands tremble with anger and fear. PVT. Shuua slowly walks up to her with her hands up,

"Please put the knife down. You have been through a lot, but you need to remain calm." she says in a soft, comforting tone.

We hear footsteps approaching, it's Sarge and the rest of the search party. They all stop and look at Somma holding Leezol's knife and blankly staring at it. Blaine chuckles,

"You'd think that Juna would've gotten her fill of seeing the knife up close." he says.

Next thing we know, out of nowhere, the seemingly hypnotic trance PVT. Juna was under broke, she turns her attention to Blaine. She marches over to him and punches him square in the jaw, knocking him to the dirt, as I stated, these girls could easily kick his teeth in. She tries to punch Blaine again while he's down but PVT. Denza and Shuua pull her back and take her to her tent.

"Carlston, get your ass off the dirt." Miner demands while rubbing his eyes,

Blaine quickly gets up and stomps away while Miner walks past me.

"What the hell was all that, Sarge?" I ask.

Normally I wouldn't talk to him like that, but we were held captive by a guy who supposedly knew Sarge. There's a lot about Sarge that's still unknown, he's a bit on a question mark, so I'm not that surprised I never knew about Leezol. The question is, why would Sarge not tell us about him? Sarge didn't answer my question, he walked away and looked off in the distance. Blaine and I look at each other, we both go to see what's going on with Sarge. We find him at a cliffside near our Camp, his arms crossed and his head shaking.

"I'd say there's a lot you need to explain, Sarge." Blaine

states.

The sarge, again, shakes his head, but he is muttering something. We lean our heads in to hear what he is saying, but we can't make it out. A few moments later it becomes clear what Sarge has been muttering.

"It's not possible."

Blaine and I look at each other again with confusion.

"What's not possible, sir?" I ask, Sarge quickly turns to me and grabs me by my collar, "Leezol, it's not possible, he is supposed to be dead!"

We're left with more questions than answers. We slowly take him back to camp and sit down with him.

"Tell us everything, sir" I say as calmly as possible even though I have a million thoughts and questions going through my head. Sarge sighs and remains silent for a few seconds, he chuckles,

"How much time you boys got?"

We remained silent, waiting for him to finally tell us everything.

"Well, back when everything was normal," Sarge continued, "no planets hated each other and the Galaxies were filled with peace and beauty, me and a buddy of mine, Ben Gawti from a planet called Kana, we enrolled in the army and we didn't fit in, I know, what a surprise. The recruits were horrible and hated the fact that me, in particular, was from Earth. At the time, people from Earth were still relatively new to everyone in the different Galaxies, so many of the recruits thought they were better than me, except one, Auldin Leezol and Ben Gawti."

The thought of Sarge and Leezol not only being recruits together, but friends is a huge shock. Sarge stands back up and turns to us,

"He was our brother and we were his. We had different ideologies, but it never affected anything until this damn war started and his whack-job ideas aligned more with the Confederacy's views, so when the time came, he joined them, and Ben and I stayed with the Coalition. Doing so caused him to hate me ever since. Why he was looking for me now after all this time? Well, I'm as lost as you both."

Blaine and I had no idea what to say, when PVT. Reddina walked up to Sarge,

"Pardon me for overhearing, sir, but did you both have to join the fight? If your ideologies affected your friendship when the war hit, then why did you both want to serve?"

A fair question. Sarge rubbed his eyes, it was clear talking about this bothered him, but we needed to know more.

"It was bound to happen, we both came from families who have fought in previous wars, so the pressure to join the fight became unbearable. You think PVT. Juna was the only one pressured by her family to join?" Sarge responded.

His answer caused PVT. Reddina to tilt his head, he had one last question.

"Would it not have been possible for you both to put your differences aside and fight side by side? Maybe that could have avoided that horrible injury on Leezol's face if you were with him, sir."

Sarge remained silent and glared at Carden.

"That's all for tonight, everyone get some rest. We have much to do." Sarge said as he walked away.

After getting some sleep, we all wake up around the same time. What happened the night before still haunted us. Everyone is silent as we all meet at the center of the camp, PVT. Juna is the last one to come out of her tent. After a few minutes, we see her slowly walk out with her eyes to the ground, she walks up to Sarge and pulls him aside. Before Sarge goes with her, he gives us our orders. We're all packing our gear up to leave camp since Sarge feels we've been compromised and if Xenem knows we are here, then it's safe to assume more will be after us. Luckily, the search party found the Xenem ship we can use for our operation, assuming that plan is still in action. We begin loading our gear onto the ship, but I see Sarge and PVT. Juna talking in the distance. She still has her eyes to the ground and Sarge looks frustrated and concerned, more than usual. All I hear from Sarge is "You're dismissed." PVT. Juna walks away, looking even more defeated than usual. Ten minutes go by when I see her carrying her gear, she's silent and focused on getting her gear ready, when she usually is giddy, especially when going to a new planet. Finally, I go up to her and ask if she's okay, she sighs and shakes her head.

"What happened with SSG. Miner?" I ask,

"I thanked him for saving me, then I tried to submit myself for court-martialing."

"You are being too hard on yourself."

PVT. Juna brushes off what I said, she just shakes her head. She puts down her gear and looks me in the eyes, holding back her tears,

"Sir, not only did I disobey multiple orders from you, but I also struck SPC. Carlston and attempted to do it again. You are both my superiors, I have immense respect for you, but I let my emotions get the better of me. I feel like I am not ready to be part of this squad and serve with everyone. I do not know what I am doing here."

I have no idea what to say, it now makes sense why she and Sarge took a while talking, but I can tell that Sarge didn't let her submit herself for court-martialing. I pick up some of her gear off the ground and carry it onto the ship. As I put her gear on the ship, I turn back to her after a moment to think of what to say. I take her to the side of the ship and sit he down on a nearby rock and kneel down next to her,

"Listen, there's no denying that what you went through is horrible, no one should ever be in that situation. As a Superior of yours, I take responsibility for letting the situation get to that point and for that I truly am sorry. Leezol was simply stronger than you, stronger than all of us, but your brothers and sisters had your back, you're alive. As far as what happened with SPC. Carlston and myself, don't worry about it. Get the rest of your stuff on the ship. Remember, we need you."

She's stronger than she thinks, she'll be okay. Blaine

walks up to me and looks at PVT. Juna and looks back at me,

"I let her hit me, to make her feel better."

I ignore him and head back to the camp to gather more of my gear when PVT. Denza walks up to me and lets me know that Leezol is awake. About time. I tell her to get Sarge, he should be there to question him. I stand by the tent Leezol is in to wait for Sarge, but the entire squad is walking with him. I look surprised, as everyone enters the tent PVT. Dillon smiles and looks at me,

"There's no way we're missing this." he says.

Glad to see life or death situations haven't changed him. We all enter the tent to see Leezol sitting in a chair tied up, but he's laughing.

"Which one of you put me in that hold? Could not have been you, Vespin, we were having fun, as I recall." Leezol says while cackling.

We can feel the hate running through PVT. Juna at that moment, but she stays calm and ignores him.

"We'll be asking the question!" Blaine says, but Sarge has him back off as he steps forward while looking at Leezol, keeping eye contact the whole time,

"Everyone, leave us, besides Carlston and Parson. It's time you answer our questions, Captain." Sarge says calmly while clenching his fists.

After trying to get answers out of the prick for about thirty minutes, we've got nothing, but we're not giving up on what we want to know. Much to Blaine's chagrin, we haven't resulted to torture, yet. Leezol treats this like a game, he either ignores what we ask or just laughs at us while insulting us.

"Oh, Miner, oddly, I have missed you!" Leezol continues, " You know, boys, back in his day, your SSG. was quite the shot, I suppose that's how he got the drop on me and my men."

Again, evading the question. Sarge walks up to him and places his hand on his shoulder,

"Come on now, Auldin, help your brother out here. How did you know about us?" he asks.

Leezol scoffs and shakes Sarge's hand off him,

"Brother? Really, Miner? After everything that has happened? I tire of you all. Bring in that Vespin girl, we seemed to really be getting to know each other." he says while laughing.

It's a chilling laugh we've heard too many times now. Why we haven't resulted to harsher means of getting our answers is beyond Blaine and I, but at this point, this is a waste of time.

We hear someone enter the tent, I go to check who it is, but before I can check, PVT. Juna bursts through holding Leezol's knife and approaches him. Blaine and I try to grab her, but she shrugs us off. Sarge didn't try to stop her at all, if anything, he moved out of her way.

"Here I am, you sick monster!" she yells while putting the knife to Leezol's throat.

"There she is! Oh, and my blade! You found it, thank you, my dear!"

PVT. Juna is fuming, but she looks at the knife then back at Leezol and smiles,

"Not that long ago where you had this very knife up to my face, funny how things work out!" she yells while grabbing Leezol's face bringing the knife closer and closer to his green eye, "How do you like it? You monster!" she yells as I try to interfere, but Sarge stops me.

I think he wants to see what happens. She gets closer to his one good eye and now Leezol is the one trying to get away. Something in PVT. Juna snapped, she is not backing down. The timing of it makes sense, the horrors of war got to her already, but now she is diving deeper into what makes it a nightmare, the anger and hate. She already felt fear in the past, but it seems like an animal has been unleashed now. We don't dare get in her way at this point. For the first time ever, we can see fear in Leezol's eyes, it appears he didn't think what comes around goes around. A part of me is happy for PVT. Juna, this probably feels great for her. Then again, this whole ordeal is going to traumatize her, but if it fuels her and gets us answers, then we can't get in the way, not yet, at least.

I can't say I have ever done something like this, though I wish I had. A part of me wants to look away, Blaine is leaning in to get a better view and Sarge is standing back with his arms crossed. I don't think any of us knew PVT. Juna had this in her. This side of her is something completely unrecognizable. It feels odd saying so, but I'm a little afraid of her. If I got in her way, would she show me the same treatment? I hate Leezol just as much as anyone here, but I want to interject and stop her. Sarge's face, per usual, is impossible to read. I don't know if he approves of what's happening or not. He is letting all this happen in front of him, I guess that's how we know he is okay with these methods that could only be described as barbaric. I personally prefer to show mercy, if given the choice, PVT. Juna thought the same way, but with how Leezol threatened her life, it seems to be a situation of what goes around comes around. As the blade is brought even closer from his eye, Blaine cheers for the knife to go closer, Sarge and I remain silent. I can't imagine how all this sounds from the outside. I know everyone wanted to see what was going to happen. It must sound like a horror movie, it definitely looks like one. The knife, now inches away from Leezol's eye, but he hasn't said anything. He just yells in frustration and resistance, just like how PVT. Juna was doing when the roles were reversed. I begin to wonder if he will even talk at all, it seems obvious he's willing to lose his good eye over the intel we want. When hope starts to feel lost, we hear Leezol yell in frustration,

"Alright, damn you, I will talk!"

FARTHER AND FATHER

If a blade to the face was all it took to make Leezol talk, then we probably should've just started with that. Either way, PVT. Juna did what none of us could, I just hope Sarge doesn't get too angry at her. She slowly pulls the knife away from Leezol,

"This is truly a nice knife, I think I will keep it." she says with a grin on her face while twirling the knife and walking away.

We are all shocked at what we just saw. PVT. Juna, for the first time, walks away from Leezol with a smile on her face, even with her face wrapped again, we can tell from her eyes, she is proud and smiling.

"Look who is stronger now." she says while passing me.

We've never seen that side of her before, it seems being so close to death made something inside her snap. I have always had general respect for her, just like I do with most people, but after all this, she has truly earned my respect. At last, it's time we get our answers. Sarge chuckles as Somma leaves the tent, he turns his attention to Leezol, breathing heavily and looking at the ground, Sarge walks up to him,

"Well, old friend, unless you would like that 'Vespin girl' to come back, I suggest you tell us what we want to know."

Leezol growls at Sarge, but even he knows there's no way out. It seems like he's finally going to talk.

"For the final time. How did you find out about us?" Sarge asks.

"About a month ago, Xenem was having a meeting with the allies of the Confederacy," Leezol continued, "everyone was talking about the recent attacks they have taken over the past months. We knew no ally in the Coalition would ever be so aggressive or bold. Eye witnesses and survivors of the attacks informed us that there was no army involved in these attacks, but 10 people. We thought those witnesses were mad, but security footage and data were scrambled so we had no choice but to trust them. We heightened our defenses, but did that stop your pack of children? No!" Leezol shakes his head and looks at Blaine and I, "You boys sure got a talented group of people, we thought we would never find you all. That is until when you attacked a Fort I was visiting on Tarena, not far from here. I barely made it out, but during that attack, who did I see leading the charge? My old friend, the great Richard Miner, so I brought it upon myself to be the one to track you all down."

Sarge is stunned silent, but he is still unsure how Leezol found us. Leezol laughs, "Oh, I thought you were dead after all these years. I wished you were dead. I could not believe my eyes when I saw you. With an old photo of you, I had everyone under Confederacy control to look for you and if they saw you, they were to tell me immediately. Lucky for me, a scout spotted you as you were leaving Vespis and followed you back to your little camp here. So, we sent spies to see what you were up to, but sadly, I sent morons who had no idea what they were doing. They could not figure out what you were doing . None of that matters now, though, because here we are, face to face once again, old friend."

How could we be so stupid? "The Galaxy's Finest" got caught within months, not a great look. PVT. Dillon walks in the tent and looks around, he notices we're all visibly defeated and confused from what we just found out from Leezol. He gives a nervous chuckle,

"I'm sure this is a great time for this, but GEN. Pyren Juna is here to see us."

Out of everyone who knew about our group and whereabouts, I should have known GEN. Juna would know. We leave Leezol tied up and leave the tent to see GEN. Juna with his arms behind his back looking off in the distance. He looks the same every time I see him. A massive scar on his face, going from his mouth, up his cheek, going across his right eye. He wears the same eyepatch over his wounded eye with the Vespin seal and of course, his left eye with the typical Vespin sparkle, but somehow it doesn't feel as magical as other Vespins. Almost like there is permanent anger and frustration behind it. Once Sarge sees GEN. Juna, he walks up to him laughing and puts his hand on Juna's shoulder,

"Damn, Juna, have we got a story for you-" Juna shrugs Miner off his shoulder and interrupts him,

"What happened here, SSG. Miner? This is a mess! There are bodies and guns on the ground, care to explain? Perhaps I should not have cleared this squad with LT. Serro and the others. Most people told us this squad would not work and it was a bad idea, maybe they were right!" GEN. Juna says with what seems like hundreds of thoughts running through his mind.

For the first time, Sarge looks scared and is at a loss for words. I decide to step in,

"If I may, sir? GEN. Juna, my name is CPL. Clark Parson. Myself and SPC. Blaine Carlston have been assisting SSG. Miner with this squad for these past months. What happened here was an unfortunate breach of security that we both take full responsibility for."

Juna looks at me and scoffs,

"Earthlings, I should have figured."

I don't let his insult bother me too much, I remain silent. Even Blaine, for once, holds his tongue, but rolls his eyes, unfortunately GEN. Juna catches him. He marches towards Blaine,

"Am I wrong, Earthling?" he asks mockingly.

Blaine opens his mouth to answer, but GEN. Juna sticks his finger up, shutting Blaine up and continues,

"Honestly, what security did you have here? I see multiple points of possible breaching standing here right now! Despite your ranks, I can tell you both lack any basic tactical thinking!"

It's getting harder to not talk back. I tried holding my tongue, but it's near impossible now. Just as I was about to speak up, Somma steps forward,

"Father, that is enough!"

GEN. Juna turns around and sees her,

"Oh, no, Somma, my child, please do not tell me you are still with this old fool and this mess of a squad! Think of your family!" he says with pain and frustration in his voice.

She looks down in shame, probably because she knows he's right, this really is a mess. To all of our surprise, Somma looks back up at her father and walks towards him.

"This 'mess', father, has been more of a family to me than you have ever been for a long time now!" Miner tries stopping her since he's still a General of the army, but Somma ignores him and continues, "I am valued here. My skills are put to good use. You pressured me to join this army and now that I am actually in a place where I am happy, you call it a mess?"

At this point, Sarge is letting them go at it. GEN. Juna is fuming, he turns to Miner,

"You would be wise to teach your squad how to speak to their superiors-" Somma grabs him and turns him back to her, interrupting him,

"My 'superior'? You are my father! Maybe treat me like your daughter instead of just another soldier you control!"

GEN. Juna says nothing and walks away. He left Somma without saying a word to make her feel better in any way. This is only my second time meeting him, he may be a legend on the battlefield, but he sure as hell isn't what a father is supposed to be. As GEN. Juna leaves camp, I look at Somma tearing up and it breaks my heart. I step forward in anger,

"Sir, she could've died last night! Did you know that?" I ask knowing damn well my ass is on the line here.

Everyone is glaring at me shaking their heads signaling me to stop, but this isn't okay, nothing about this is okay. I don't care who he is. He turns back to me,

"Well, I can see why. Most Earthlings lack defense and strategy. At least Miner used to carry those qualities before he went insane, now he has nothing, you all have nothing!"

His words cut Sarge deep. It cuts all of us. PVT. Lane, I want to say it's Mitchell, out of all people, steps forward, too,

"SSG. Miner may be 'insane', but he's been like a father to all of us, especially PVT. Juna." he says with a passion in his voice I have never heard. His brother follows him,

"We all come from nothing, sir, Miner has given us more than we could ever have imagined."

It's always so strange to hear either of the Lane twins speak, I often forget they're British. Sarge smiles proudly. GEN. Juna looks around and sees all of us are against him.

"I could ruin all of you with counts of insubordination! Somma, you are coming with me. Just because these fools are going down the wrong path, does not mean you have to too." he says.

Somma shakes her head, she is staying with us "fools". He marches towards her to grab her, but PVT. Denza, Dillon, Shuua and Reddina all step in front of her blocking GEN. Juna. He laughs,

"My dear Somma, when this ship goes down, and it will go down, do not come crying to me and asking me for help. You may have nearly died, but you are dead to me. I do not have a daughter anymore."

We all watch as GEN. Juna leaves our camp. Somma has tears in her crystal eyes and goes to her tent, understandably upset and hurt. The rest of the squad leaves her alone, they can tell she needs time to herself. Sarge, Blaine and myself go to each other.

"Okay, that guy needs a smack or maybe a hit to the face with the butt of a gun, either way, I will volunteer to do it." Blaine says.

Sarge scoffs,

"Yes, well, GEN. Juna has always been that way. I never liked him and obviously, he never liked me very much, either."

I look at GEN. Juna heading for his ship and turn to Sarge and Blaine,

"Did you guys find it odd how he never asked or talked about how Somma almost died or ask if she's okay?"

Sarge shakes his head in disapproval and looks back at him.

"What did you expect?" Blaine responds.

This is a rare moment where I actually agree with Blaine. We hear Leezol laugh from the tent he's tied up in,

"Oh, good old Pyren Juna, I rather liked him to be honest."

I think we completely forgot about Leezol with all this other crap going down. It feels odd, he's her father, why wouldn't he even ask? Sarge grinds his teeth,

"You're right, Parson. He never talked about it. Screw it, let's make him talk about it. Shall we?"

Sarge marches towards Juna, after a moment of hesitation and looking at each other, Blaine and I follow him. To be honest, I never planned on this happening when I mentioned Juna's disregard to his daughters near death experience, but I guess Sarge had enough with all of his shit.

"Hey, Pyren!" Sarge yells out as he marches towards him entering his ship.

Pyren turns to us quickly in anger to see who disrespected him,

"Is there something I can do for you, *Richard*?" he asks sarcastically, mocking Sarge.

I am not sure what is going on inside Sarge's head, more than usual, all I know is he's gonna get us all in trouble going on like this. It seems like Leezol showing up in Miner's life again really rattled him, he is all over the place.

"Be careful, Miner. Again, you know I can end your career and this 'squad'" GEN. Juna says, but, Sarge scoffs,

"Now, I'm no father and I'm not the girl's father, but I have damn sure been more of a father to her than you probably ever have!"

GEN. Juna points his finger at Sarge, opening his mouth and preparing to speak, but Miner swats his finger away and continues before he can interrupt,

"Jesus, Pyren! She is your child! I'm not sure how you treat your young on Vespis, but your kid is hurting and instead of being her father, you are being her General."

GEN. Juna rubs his eyes in annoyance, but perhaps he is just mad because he knows that Sarge is right. There is debris around us from a battle many years ago, Pyren sees a piece of a downed aircraft and takes a seat on it, sighing,

"Gentlemen, look around." GEN. Juna continued, "We are surrounded by this desert wasteland, filled with pieces of metal, wood and even burnt, decayed bodies. We all know that war gets to us all sooner and later, my Somma told me a while ago it hit her what war really is, poor girl. I treated her like a soldier because I was trying to prepare her for all of this. No man, woman or child should go through this disaster, but here we are and now my daughter almost died. I figured if I treated her like a soldier more, she would get used to being a soldier. I did not foresee her having to kill many people at all and see so much death and ruin. It was rather foolish of me to think otherwise."

It's odd seeing GEN. Juna open up like this. He has always been such a crass, rude individual. Now we see, GEN. Juna isn't exactly a bad father. He's not great, but he tried to be a good father in his own unique way. It seems over the years he lost his way and got lost in all this mess. As most of us do. I decide to step forward, I clear my throat,

"If I may, sir, your daughter is a great soldier, despite all that has happened. So, at this point, I think she needs a father more than a General."

GEN. Juna nods his head and pulls out his pad, he opens a file named "Diamond" and it is filled with images of Somma and her family before the war. She looked so happy. Her whole family did, including GEN. Juna. I'm not sure what happened to the rest of the Juna family, though.

"There is not a day where I don't look at these images and hope my "Diamond" is okay. An attack like what happened last night cannot happen again. Understood?" GEN. Juna says.

Everyone, including Sarge, nods their heads. We finally have some understanding, I just wish he told Somma this himself. I'm sure all this would have meant more coming from him rather than us. GEN. Juna boards his ship and leaves, as we head back, we see Somma out of her tent watching the ship leave. It's unclear whether GEN. Juna wanted us to tell Somma what he said, but I think it'd be best if we told her. She deserves it. As we enter the camp, we go up to Somma and Sarge puts his hand on her shoulder,

"Sit down, kid." he says calmly.

Sarge walks Somma to a nearby table and sits her down, he asks that they be left alone while he tells Somma what GEN. Juna said. We all sit down at the center of camp waiting for Sarge and Somma to finish. It takes us about an hour or so for him to tell her everything and try to talk her through how she is feeling. Somma looks naturally shocked, who wouldn't be? As legendary as he is, GEN. Pyren Juna clearly wasn't a good father despite his best efforts. We saw it all right before our eyes. We're all from different planets and galaxies, but we all know a bad parent when we see one. After a brief moment of silence, we hear Somma chuckle from a distance,

"Diamond" she continues while wiping her tears, "He has not called me that since I was a child."

The sentiment means a lot more to her than we originally thought it would. Blaine, Sarge and myself all saw the file name and heard GEN. Juna call her "Diamond", but I think we dismissed it. In truth, it seems we were just as shocked as Somma hearing him speak so fondly of his daughter that the nickname went over our heads. Good thing we remembered it, though. It really did lift Somma's spirit.

All this family drama had us all forgetting our guest of honor, Mr. Auldin Leezol. The rest of the squad stays with Somma while Sarge, Blaine and I head back to him. As enter the tent that Leezol was kept in, we hear his sinister chuckle, once we come face to face with him again, he looks at us with a smirk,

"Wow, was that the real torture? Having me wait hours tied up? Or was it all that family nonsense? Either way, I told you what you wanted, let me go!" Leezol yells.

Perhaps keeping him here waiting all this time causing him to break more was a happy accident. Miner walks up to Leezol,

"Oh, I just got my friend back! Why leave so soon? I thought you missed me, buddy!"

Leezol laughs and shakes his head,

"Oh, yes, I did miss you, my old friend. I could not wait to see you again and watch your life disappear from your eyes by my hand, let me loose, cowards!" Leezol demands while shaking trying to get his restraints off.

The man that Sarge knew seems to be truly gone. The question is, does Sarge realize it, too? It's a possibility that Leezol was a good person in the past, before all of this, but I've seen what this war has done and whoever Leezol was when he and Sarge were friends, is now gone. As wise as Sarge is, I just don't think his eyes are truly open in terms of who his friend once was, versus how he is now. The question is, if the time comes where we need to take out Leezol, will Sarge be the one to do it? After what he's done to me and the rest of the squad, any of us would be glad to pull the trigger, assuming Sarge wouldn't stop us. Despite his laid back attitude and joking demeanor, Blaine and I can see that Sarge should not be here. We fear his emotions will make things worse. He's an amazing leader and soldier, but Sarge is cracking. We can tell.

I am not a betting man, but I'd wager getting inside Sarge's head, making him snap, is exactly what Leezol wants. Why not? He knows Sarge, perhaps better than anyone. All these years knowing him, he must know his likes, dislikes, his dreams, but even worse, his nightmares. When Leezol first showed up at our camp, he asked for Sarge's weaknesses. I think he already knew the answers, but perhaps, was hoping to gain more information to help him with his hunt. We still have no idea what exactly he's capable of, seemingly, only Sarge knows, but a part of me is too scared to find out more. As valuable of a prisoner he is, the longer he is here, the worse it'll get for all of us. He has made the squad's lives hell and he has only been here less than a day.

It's a safe bet to assume the people of Xenem know something is wrong and have sent backup. With everything that has happened, I'm not sure if we can take any more bloodshed, at least for today. The point is, we need to leave.After more back and forth between Sarge and Leezol, I finally am able to drag Sarge out of the tent to speak about a plan going forward. Leaving Leezol with Blaine alone in the tent probably isn't the smartest move, but I need to get Sarge out of there.

"What the hell are you doing?" Sarge asks.

I understand where the confusion and anger is coming from considering I grabbed his arm and pulled him out of the tent without saying anything. To be honest, I wasn't really thinking, but like I said, I needed to get him out of there. I don't know anyone who has dragged their superiors, let alone a legend, like I have and lived to tell the tale. Sarge shoves me away, but I step in front of him, blocking his path. His normal pale blue dead eyes, now were seemingly on fire. I swear, Sarge seemed ready to go back in the tent and fire off a few rounds into Leezol's head, but sadly, we still need him alive. Sarge always knew how to keep cool, but with Leezol, it is different. I am genuinely unsure of what is going to happen.

"Sir, this is what he wants. He needs us to get angry and most of all, distracted. You know of all people how sick and clever he is, so please do not do anything that'll put us in an even worse position." I plead to Sarge, but he doesn't say anything.

He looks back at the tent that has Leezol is in, then looks back at me, seemingly calmed down. He sighed,

"I'll go help the other runts pack up." he says before grunting and storming off.

I come back to the holding tent and see blood all over the floor and walls of the tent and to no surprise, Blaine wailing on Leezol. I think we all knew eventually Blaine wouldn't last long one on one with someone like him, we know how good he is at getting under people's skin. I run up to Blaine and stop him from inflicting any more pain on him, but it seems I may be too late. Leezol is slouched over and not moving.

Initially, I was pretty happy seeing this sick bastard unconscious, it was finally quiet, but we still need him, Blaine might've screwed us.

"What did you do?" I ask Blaine, nearly unleashing all my stress and anger from this whole ordeal onto him.

Blaine remains silent, standing over Leezol's unconscious body on the chair while breathing heavily, as if he doesn't even know what he has done. After a moment of nothing but heavy breathing from Blaine, he looks at me and back at the lifeless body,

"What happened?" he asks quietly, looking more bewildered than I have ever seen him.

I say nothing, waiting for him to realize what happened. Blaine sees Leezol's limp body and, like a child, pokes him to see if there is any movement. I look him dead in his eyes,

"I was wondering the same thing. What happened?" I ask sternly.

Blaine rubs his eyes trying to remember what occurred, and finally, he looks ready to talk. Blaine takes a seat and lets out a shaky exhale, he looks back at me,

"About a minute after you and Sarge left, it was silent between Leezol and myself, then the he starts running his mouth-"

"So, you try to kill him?" I ask, interrupting him, but Blaine just shakes his head and continues,

"Then, he mentioned my family, throwing out seemingly empty threats towards them that I just brushed off my shoulder. It sounded like the typical attacks you hear from guys like him, but it was more than that. Parson, he knew everything about them, their names, their jobs, their addresses, everything!" Blaine says before stopping to take a breath.

It's not surprising to be honest, we all know how clever and vile this guy is. He probably knows everything about all of us. He already proved he knows basically everything about me..

"Then what happened?" I calmly ask Blaine.

He wipes the sweat from his forehead,

"Despite him revealing all the info he knew, I kept my cool, but after a while, his threats got worse and more personal. He described ways he'd torture them all, it was horrible. I finally had enough and threw a punch at him in an attempt to finally shut him up, but he just laughed, so I hit him again, and again yet all I heard was laughter, sick, twisted laughter. It came to a point where I kept going, not even realizing that he could drop dead at any moment, as nice as that would've been, but I just really wanted him to shut his damn mouth."

I guess with trying to get Sarge to walk away outside of the tent, we didn't hear all the chaos inside. We all know how twisted Leezol is, so what Blaine says definitely sounds like the truth, but Leezol is a valuable prisoner to us, we need him alive.

As sympathetic and understanding I am of Blaine and his actions, I remain silent.

"Right, well, let's get him up." I tell Blaine.

He hesitates, but after a moment, he too realizes we still need him. He nods his head and walks towards me and Leezol's body. As Blaine and I work on waking Leezol up, we hear someone enter the tent,

"Alright, what's the holdup?"

It's Sarge. He enters the tent, holding a cup of coffee, one of his favorite beverages from Earth that didn't contain any alcohol, unless he, of course, added some himself. He stops walking as soon as he sees the body next to Blaine, whose fists are covered in green Xenem blood. Sarge chuckles,

"Thanks for starting the fun without me!" he exclaims.

His reaction comes as a bit of a shock to me, I would've thought he would be pissed, but then again, it's Sarge. He approaches the body with a little smile on his face, completely unphased by what Blaine has done.

"I must say Carlston, you did a hell of a job. Remind me to call you next time I get in a scrap at the bar!" he jokes while laughing.

While Blaine would usually laugh at a joke like that, he said nothing. I break the silence by stepping in front of Miner,

"Sir, what are we going to do? Don't we still need Leezol?"

The calm and joking demeanor of Sarge fades as he nods his head. He takes a sip of his coffee then throws it on Leezol's face, we finally get some movement. After everything that happened the past night, every one of us in the squad, myself included, would've been thrilled with Leezol being dead. As weird as it is to say, I'm a bit glad Sarge got him up. Leezol's eyes begin to open slowly, he looks to the left and sees Blaine,

"Good work, Mr. Carlston. I'm almost impressed." he says before spitting blood at our feet.

The regret of keeping him alive starts to set in. Sarge sighs,

"Carlston, get out." he demands,

Blaine listens and quickly leaves. Sarge walks behind our recently revived prisoner and puts both of his hands on his shoulders. Leezol flinches, but Sarge chuckles and grips his shoulders tighter.

"You know, old friend, I could kill you right now, with a little effort and your neck goes in all sorts of directions it shouldn't. I also could have let you die after Mr. Carlston's effective beating that I wish I saw. Do you want to know why you still draw breath?"

"Because you and your pets are weak!"

Sarge laughs before quickly moving his hands into the

neck snapping position and starts to gently twist,

"This is it, Auldin! Are you gonna be a pal and help us out some more or is your time up here?"

Sarge starts to twist farther and farther, Leezol's face is clearly in pain, his eyes darting back and forth looking for a way out, but Sarge isn't playing anymore. A similar situation to his previous experience with Somma.

"Last chance, buddy!" Sarge yells as Leezol struggles and tries to resist.

I make eye contact with Leezol and he looks at me like he is waiting for me to do something to stop Sarge, but I'm done playing too, besides, this is Sarge's choice whether he lives or dies. I shake my head while looking at him, letting him know this is it for him. Leezol is strapped to the chair tightly, yet he still tries to break free in any way possible, but eventually, he realizes there's no escape out of this. After moments away from a broken neck and having dealt with immense pain and fear among other things all night, Leezol lets out a scream of pain and one more push of resistance with no success, the screams getting louder, it's hard to watch.

"Dammit, I can help you all get to Xenem! Miner! I will get you to Xenem!" Leezol yells.

It is twice now that being inches from death or major bodily harm has gotten what we wanted from Leezol. I still can't say I personally approve of the methods used both times, but at long last, we get somewhere. I can only hope that somewhere is not an early grave for me or anyone in Specter.

PLAN B

The room goes silent, Sarge and Leezol are both breathing heavily. Sarge has a proud smile on his face, compared to Leezol's face filled with exhaustion and fury.

"Oh, what was that, buddy?" Sarge playfully asks as he slightly loosens his grip,

Leezol's face fills with fury, more so than usual.

"I am a smart man, I know when I am beaten, as ashamed as I am to admit it." Leezol says.

The wonderful folks of Xenem are pretty notorious for their bluffs and poker faces, we don't know if he's not lying or not.

"Parson, let him go." Sarge demands.

I hesitate, but Sarge darts his eyes to me and I know if I do not do what he asks, as dangerous as the order or task is, I'm in trouble. I nod my head and deactivate Leezol's restraints, despite my best judgment. We put cuffs on him before we get him up and moving. We can never be too safe, especially with Leezol.

"Don't try anything stupid." Sarge says to Leezol,

Leezol scoffs,

"That is funny coming from you."

Sarge takes hold of his shoulder as we exit the tent,

"Gather 'round, runts! Our friend here has some news for us!" Sarge yells.

We are all at our guard, hands to our holsters and eyes on Leezol. Sarge laughs at how on edge we are, but he knows we have every right to be concerned, if we could, we would all kill him right now, we had all night to do it, why not now? The only reason we are all letting him still draw breath is because we have a plan and no psychotic Xenem soldier is going to derail it, more than he already has. Our plan might finally be moving into motion.

PVT. Dillon takes his gun out of his holster as he walks up to Leezol and aims the gun at his head,

"Give me one reason why I shouldn't pull the trigger and end this?"

Most of these kids are too quick to anger, to be honest we all seem to be that way. Sarge tells him to stand down, PVT. Dillon looks back at Leezol and barely contains his anger, but not before Leezol laughs,

"Yes, pretty boy, you need me, now, listen to your owner, you filth!"

PVT. Dillon scoffs and looks at Sarge who nods, he smiles and nods back, as if they were on the same page and had the same thought, within an instant, PVT. Dillon pistol whips Leezol. Blaine laughs,

"Can we take turns?" he asks while cackling,

I am actually wondering the same thing. Leezol spits blood out of his mouth and laughs, but all that mockery won't change what he is about to tell us all. The rest of the squad eagerly awaits what Leezol was brought out to say. I was in the room to witness and hear what he said before his much deserved demise at the hands of the legendary Richard Miner, but a part of me doesn't believe what I heard, so I wait with everyone else. Sarge making the decision to trust Leezol is questionable. We all noticed a while back that Sarge makes questionable decisions, but over time we all began to trust his judgment, as odd as they may seem at times. Sarge laughs at PVT. Dillon striking Leezol, but quickly gets back to business, he clears his throat and looks back at us,

"Our good friend has decided to help us on our little quest, ain't that right, buddy?" he asks Leezol while patting his shoulder.

To no surprise, Leezol is reluctant to talk, but we do get

a nod out of him, which is good enough for us. Sarge shoves Leezol to the ground,

"Now talk, the floor is yours CPT. Leezol, quite literally!" he jokes,

Leezol says nothing and slowly gets up and looks at all of us one by one with disdain. He groans before speaking,

"I admire your interest in Xenem, but your foolish plan to take one of our ships and flyright in would never have worked! Did you even consider the fact that we check the passengers in all ships going in and out? Your little journey would have ended right there. Oh, what a sight that would be."

Leezol is most likely telling the truth, all the people in the squad whose job it was research Xenem and their defenses clearly didn't go that far into their research, I guess our camp being invaded is pretty distracting. They seemed to have focused on the history of Xenem rather than their present. I should have been more vigilant and tried to steer them in the right direction. After hearing what Leezol told us, we all look at each other with worry and panic in our eyes, it seemed like we had such a fool proof plan.

"So, what do we do?" PVT. Denza asks,

We're all wondering the same thing, we need answers. Leezol, whose hands are still cuffed, chuckles while slowly approaching her, their eyes lock onto each other, trying to show their dominance and lack of fear, but eventually, Leezol is the first to break eye contact,

"Something about being beaten half to death and nearly killed by you fools has put me in a helping mood! I will get you into Xenem, I will take you as far as the surface. After that, you run free to try to accomplish your pathetic mission. Just know, after you are in, my hunt for you all will not be over. Given the chance, I will take each and every one of you out one by one."

I would expect nothing less, we know he is not an ally, but a means to an end. A very messy, blood filled end.

"You're a diamond, pal!" Sarge says to Leezol before barking his orders at us to get packed and ready.

Most of our stuff has already been packed on the Xenem ship Leezol arrived in, the squad worked fast during our interrogation with the then imprisoned Leezol. I take out my pad to release the cuffs on Leezol, but before I hit the release button, a hand blocks me from doing so, it's Somma.

"PVT. Juna?" I ask.

She looks up at me without saying a word, but I can see in her eyes that she needs to say one last piece to Leezol. Hoping I can trust her, I nod my head and Somma approaches Leezol,

"You do not trust us and we do not trust you, nor do we like you. You think you will hunt us after this? No! We will hunt you, *I* will hunt you, and make sure you see the fall of your bloodstained home and then, only then, I will kill you myself." she says before walking away.

Leezol looks as shocked as me, but remains to keep his worry-free attitude. I undo his cuffs, he sarcastically claps his hands in her direction as she walks away,

"Well then, let the games begin, Vespin!"

After being stunned with what Somma, out of all people, said, I quickly get on the ship with him and everyone else. Things are about to get real interesting. The idea of being on a ship with Leezol doesn't really excite any of us, but we are pretty much out of options and need a decent plan.

How exactly do you plan on getting us all through with no issues?" PVT. Denza asks Leezol as we take off, heading for Xenem.

Leezol, once again, scoffs,

"Use your imagination."

A clearly unsatisfying answer to a question we are all wondering.

"Just answer the damn question!" Sarge exclaims, but unphased Leezol remains.

He is always toying with us, we're just lucky he has no choice but to answer us. Leezol sighs as he realizes the fun is over, he looks off into the vast empty blackness of Space then looks back at us,

"Chancellor Tyro has a blockade surrounding Xenem, it would be a fool's errand to try to pass through with pure luck, even your brainless mut Carlston would not dare try it. So, when the time comes, you all hide away and I shall take control of the ship. The blockade sees me driving a Xenem shuttle and should not be suspicious."

I hate to admit it, but it's a pretty solid plan, hell, it seems to be the only plan. We were all well aware that Leezol could easily screw over as soon as he reached the blockade, as much of a disaster that would be, we felt confident that he valued his life more than getting rid of us. Each of us stood ready to take him out within an instant, so any wrong move, he's dead and he knows that. After everything he put us through, killing him seemed like such an amazing idea, I'm sure Somma has been thinking of every way to kill him. She's young, stressed and on edge, hopefully she can keep her cool and not jeopardize our team. Blaine is the squad's trigger-happy fool, we don't need another one. After half an hour of pure silence while traveling to Xenem, we finally arrive.

"Alright, we are here, everyone get down, hide!" Leezol demands.

We are not fans of him barking orders at us, but we look at Sarge and he nods, so we listen. PVT. Reddina quickly runs up to me and hands me an odd looking device,

"Put it in your ear," he says to all of us, "PVT. Shuua and I developed earpieces a while ago to help us all understand other languages, an instant translator, if you will. We have not programmed all languages yet. We still need to add Vespin, Taren and many others. We were able to put in translations for Xenem and a few other languages for this operation. I figure this is as good of a time as any for a test run, seeing as we do not know what we are about to get into." he quickly hands everyone else an earpiece before finding a hiding spot.

I do wish they were able to insert all languages. I understand we were thrown into this last minute, though.

Luckily, when humans reached the other galaxies, many planets, including Vespis, Tilo, Matu, mainly allies from the USC, they all learned English and other languages from Earth soon after. So, I guess it's not too upsetting that PVT. Reddina and Shuua didn't have time to put every language in for translation, I just hope the languages they did put in are able to be translated with no issue. Aboard the shuttle, there were many compartments for us to hide in, Blaine had trouble finding a space big enough to fit him. We were running out of time and Blaine needed help getting into a space, so after one good push from me, he was in. The plan almost jeopardized because of inadequate storage space for our meathead fiend to fit in tells us that we are really not ready for this, but Sarge still has faith in us and the plan, so we have to follow and hope for the best, while also hoping that Blaine isn't crushed, as fun of a thought that is. We feel the shuttle slow down, I peek out of my compartment and see an entire army in front of the shuttle blocking Xenem, fear begins to take over me, "This could be it" I say in my head.

We hear a static come through the speakers of the shuttle,

"*Identify yourself!*" the voice on the speaker demands.

Leezol looks behind him to see if we're all hidden then looks back at the blockade. He pushes the communication button,

"This CPT. Auldin Leezol."

So far, this translator is working like a charm. No one responds to Leezol identifying himself, Xenem is one of the strangest and hardest languages to learn and understand, it's impressive how well the translator is working so far. Leezol tilts his head,

"Odd," he says, "a patrol ship is approaching us. This does not look good."

Sarge pokes his head out of his hiding spot,

"What's going on?" he asks,

Leezol shakes his head in disbelief and quickly pushes

the communication button and starts questioning the two patrol ships approaching, but he gets no responses.

"What did you do?" Sarge yells,

"Nothing! I-I-" Leezol started stuttering, unsure of what is happening or why.

Sarge looks around and punches the wall next to him,

"Damn! Fine, let them come and board us if that is their plan. Just act natural, Leezol. The rest of you, including myself, will stay hidden. All of you shut up!"

I'm not sure what the plan is at this point, I guess we're just winging it and hoping we don't get shot, per usual. Outside of the shuttle, we hear locking mechanisms and air hissing, we are about to be boarded.

Trying to get the tiniest peek, I see the shuttle door open and two Xenem soldiers march into our shuttle as Leezol stomps his way over to them. I'm praying the translator won't fail us here. Leezol growls as he looks at soldiers,

"What is the meaning of this?" he asks.

The two soldiers look around before standing at attention,

"Greetings, honorable CPT. Leezol, you were gone a long time, we were sent as a precaution to see if it was really you."

"Of course it is me you fools! Now get off and let *us* through!"

The soldiers bow their heads and begin to leave, until one soldier stops then turns around,

"'Us'? Sir?"

I shake my head in frustration, but continue to listen.

"Me! I meant me, now go, that is an order!"

The soldier slowly approaches Leezol,

"Forgive me, but who is on this ship with you?"

Leezol forces out a laugh and grabs the soldier by his uniform,

"You are disobeying orders, leave, now!" Leezol demands.

The soldier nods and walks away, but stops and turns

around,

"We were told you left with PVT. Seket and Halor, sir, where are they?"

Leezol nods his head,

"Yes, unfortunately we ran into an ambush and they were lost in battle, any more questions, *sir*?" Leezol asks mockingly.

"You did not send any word of this attack or casualties, sir, that is not like you."

Leezol stares down the soldier with the same look he has been giving me and the squad all night. The soldier finally decided to back off and leave. As he walks back to his ship, he hears movement in a trunk. As he walks towards the exit, he quickly flips open a trunk and sees PVT. Dillon staring blankly at him.

"Who are you?' the soldier asks while aiming his gun at him.

PVT. Dillon says nothing, he is at a complete loss for words. The soldier puts his finger on the trigger ready to fire, when out of nowhere Leezol grabs the soldier by his collar and demands he drops the weapon. The soldier slowly moves his weapon from PVT. Dillon and shoves Leezol off of him, aiming his gun at him. Baffled and furious, the soldier growls,

"I have no idea what is happening or who else is on this shuttle, but I am taking you all to Chancellor Tyro, now!"

Leezol sighs,

"Oh, you fool, you should have listened."

Leezol quickly smacks the gun away from him and grabs the soldier's sidearm and shoots him in the chest. The shot alerts the other soldier who runs back in to see what happened, after seeing his partner on the ground, he bolts back to his own ship to fly away to undoubtedly alert everyone else to open fire. Leezol runs back to the pilot seat and accelerates forward to stop him. Leezol, given up on care or secrecy, opens fire on the escaping ship, but misses as the ship turns back to us and opens fire back, but also misses. In a matter of seconds we got ourselves a dogfight.

"Leezol, you have lost your damn mind!" Blaine yells while stumbling out of his hiding spot.

Leezol is twisting and turning our shuttle so fast, we can't even properly get out of our hiding spots without stumbling around. All of this noise alerts the other Xenem ships who now pursue us. Sarge manages to power his way to the seat next to Leezol and glares at him,

"What's the plan here?" he asks while being thrown around like the rest of us,

Leezol shrugs,

"The plan? Not to die I would say!" he exclaims while forcing the ship into a dive to avoid getting hit, but still, our ship takes some damage.

"Damn! He is good, I cannot get away from him!" Leezol yells while trying any maneuver he can to outsmart his foe.

One of the Lane brothers. Martin, pulls me towards him,

"If I'm not mistaken, there's a turret gun in the back, it could be useful."

I nod and tell him to hold onto something as I run to the back the best I can.

"Hey, Leezol, is this turret gun in working order?" I ask

Leezol doesn't respond, so I'll have to start shooting and find out. On the gun, I see a screen with a bunch of buttons, all with what I assume are Xenem words that I do not understand. Like a child, I start hitting random buttons, but nothing is firing, until, of course, the center button is hit and a shot gets fired towards one of the pursuing ships.

"What are you doing back there?" Leezol asks,

"Trying to save us!" I respond while opening fire.

I must admit, being a tailgunner in a dogfight is pretty fun, if you ignore the possibilities of your ship going down, it reminds of games I played as a kid.

The fun doesn't last long, I miss multiple shots, these Xenem pilots have always been very skilled, everything I try, they evade. With pure luck, I am able to take one pursuing ship out just barely, but is it not enough to "save us" as I claimed I would. PVT. Denza wobbles her way to me,

"Maybe we can send an EMP out there to immobilize most of them, it's worth a shot."

A solid idea, PVT. Reddina and Shuua didn't get to finish their special EMP, we have to use a standard one and hope for the best. I for one had no idea we even had any EMP's left after Blaine used them to "see if they really worked." I never got over that.

"If you can find a way to send one out, do it. Take PVT. Juna with you to help, I think she's about ready to pounce on our pilot right about now." I say to PVT. Denza.

She grabs Somma by the arm, they both go to the back of the ship to an opening hatch while holding a couple of EMP's, they look back at me through the window, I nod, signaling them to move forward with the plan. The door opens and a blast shield is raised for their protection, but they are still able to send out our little gifts to our pursuers. I see a couple of EMP's pass by and head towards the Xenem ships. Within an instant, a blue flash explodes in front of me and the ships that were chasing us completely stop and start floating around aimlessly. About time one of our plans worked. Unfortunately, it does not get all the ships. Even with Leezol's admittedly skilled pilotry, we have yet to escape. A wave of black ships come out of nowhere and get in shots with incredible accuracy and precision unlike the previous ships. Their attacks completely destroy the tailgun. After clearing the smoke in my face, I turn back to the rest of the people on the ship,

"Tailgun is out! There are new ships chasing us, who are they?"

Leezol takes a look and his eyes widen with pure terror and shock, his lips trembling,

"Oh no, it is the Black Guard."

"Who are the Black Guard?" PVT. Shuua asks,

"Elite hand selected warriors from Xenem, formidable in combat, survival, flying, anything." Leezol says while trying to stay on the defensive because he knows he cannot outgun them.

Somma pulls out her pad from her satchel. My guess is she found more information about Xenem and their military than I thought. She goes through some pages and lands on one,

"He is not wrong, this is bad." she says while handing me the tablet that was put on a page that she wrote about the Black Guard from her studies.

With all the flipping, turning, diving and dodging, I can hardly read, let alone stand still, but I begin to read the best I can:

"The Black Guard:
Ruthless, calculated and driven, among other extraordinary traits that fill me with fear. I would be terrified if I was ever to run into them. The Black Guard are hand selected by members of the Xenem military to receive highly extensive and brutal training ranging from hand-to-hand combat, aerial combat, firearm efficiency and all around problem solving skills, everything, really. I have heard of them before from Father, but I always thought he made them up to scare me into training harder. From what he told me, we would need a miracle to get out of any situation with them alive with just cuts and bruises. STAY CLEAR!"

In the page, are photos Juna found from people's past interactions with them, bodies on the floor with gunshot wounds so precise and direct to the head, you'd think a machine did all of it, the rest of the photos show the all around death and destruction The Black Guard brings upon their victims. I must say, it is impressive, but then again, we are being chased by them, so my admiration quickly turns back to fear. We thought being chased and shot at by regular Xenem ships was tough, but these guys make me miss them.

More and more of The Black Guard show up, again, seemingly coming out of nowhere, firing at us from each and every direction. I had hoped if I was to die, I'd die fighting, not being tossed and flung around a now broken down Xenem ship. Leezol pushes the communication button, trying to engage contact with The Black Guard,

"Stop your firing! I am CPT. Auldin Leezol, what you are doing is treason!" he exclaims.

The ships stop firing and Leezol finally stops our ship. It's weird being able to stand still for more than a second.

"What's going on?" Sarge asks,

"I am not sure, I have never been on the other side of these chases before."

All of sudden we hear the sound of something charging up, the sound starts to surround us, it's is coming from The Black Guard, a dark and gravely laugh comes through our speaker,

"It is you who has committed treason. You fired on your brothers. You did this to yourself!" the voice exclaims.

At that moment, immensely powerful, charged up shots come from all of the ships around us, completely immobilizing us, causing the already irreparable ship to spin out. Alarms are going off around us, fires start to consume the ship and panic among us starts to ensue.

"Leezol, do something, you damn fool!" Sarge demands while falling over like the rest of us.

In the distance, Leezol sees a nearby planet, trying to keep a cool head, he grips the steering mechanism and thrust them towards the planet. Leezol leans forwards using all his strength, the ship starts to stabilize bit by bit and soon enough, we start heading towards the planet, I guess better a crash landing than endlessly spinning out in space facing impending doom, but either way, this ship is seconds away from exploding.

"You really think this is better? Crashing in the middle of nowhere on an already broken tin can?" Blaine asks,

Leezol glares at him, but doesn't respond, focusing on the best possible way to get out of this alive. We begin to enter the atmosphere of this unknown planet, our ship, on fire and spinning through the sky, begins to reach closer and closer to the ground. Everyone holds on to anything they can, ready for a crash landing.

"Hang on!" Sarge yells as we brace for impact.

"I'm going to kill you, Leezol!" Blaine yells as we finally hit the ground.

Everyone is on the floor of the ship and, luckily, is not hurt from what I can see. I quickly get up and look around,

"Is everyone okay?" I ask while helping everyone up.

Everyone nods their heads, probably too shocked to speak, but at least they're okay, okay as they can be. Leezol rubs his eyes,

"I have no idea where we are, my screen will not turn on, we are going into this blind, no data or anything, what a mess."

It never gets any easier to say this, but he's right, we are lost. Sarge looks outside the window at the desert wasteland,

"Well, I guess we have to leave this flaming trash can and see what we can find out, everyone, breathing masks on, Leezol, open the hatch."

I see a medicine box and open it to grab any supplies we may need. I see 10 breathing masks, as much as this kills me, I grab the mask and toss it to Leezol who seems like he does not have one on him. Leezol looks back at me with a shocked and confused expression for a moment, but nods at me in appreciation afterwards. I hand everyone else masks, I give Somma hers, she looks at me with worry in her eyes,

"What about you? You will not have a mask."

"Don't worry about me."

"Thank you, sir, but I have one of my own that I keep with me. Please wear yours." she says while grabbing a mask out of her bag.

I smile as she hands the mask back to me. The hatch opens up and this place is nothing but sand.

"Nope, absolutely not!" Blaine yells while shaking his head,

During Blaine's outburst, Sarge smacks him across his

head,

"Let's go, move it Carlston! All of you, move!" he yells.

We all put our masks on and slowly make our way out of the ship to take a look around, it's as we thought, a complete wasteland. The sky is ocean blue, but there is a smoke trail coming from our landing. The sand glows random colors in different spots, I am not sure what that means, but it seems harmless.

"What now?" PVT. Reddina asks,

Sarge looks around trying to see if he can see anything,

"I guess we'll start walking and see what we can find." he says with little to no confidence in his voice, an uncommon occurrence with a man like him.

The lack of confidence in Sarge's voice makes us all worried, but we have no choice, we have to follow along. There is a heavy wind that blows sand towards us, making this trip even worse. I'm not sure how long we will last out here in these conditions. We all stay silent and keep our heads down, even with breathing masks, the sand and wind are strong and a true force we have never felt before. After walking for about an hour or so, Leezol squints his eyes, looking off in the distance,

"Look!" he exclaims.

He points to a small village in the distance about a mile away. We approach the village and the villagers walk towards us with concerned looks on their faces. We try to show we mean no harm, but nothing changes. Sarge steps forward with his hands up and approaches the villagers,

"Hello, we mean no harm, we just need sanctuary, a place to rest for a day or two, if that is okay. May I ask where we are?"

I have never heard him speak so softly or with such kindness. A villager, a poor looking man with gray skin and blue eyes who's missing his left leg, being held up make a wooden crutch, wearing torn up clothes and looks to be what people on Earth would refer to as his "Golden Years", steps forward and bows to us,

"Hello, travelers, my name is Geb Tawin, please forgive us, we are not used to people stumbling our way, but you are safe. You do not need those breathing masks here, either. Tanli offers life's luxuries to all! I can offer you a place to rest, you can stay at an outpost near the Quarry for now. I am unsure how long you all are planning on staying, but when you are ready, follow me. My friends, welcome to Tanli Village!"

TANLI VILLAGE

It is a small and quaint village, one I have never heard of. The villagers seem friendly enough, keeping their distance from us, though. Makes me wonder why Mr. Tawin was the only one friendly enough to approach us. We take off our breathing masks and begin to follow Mr. Tawin to the outpost he mentioned. We stay pretty quiet, politely nodding and smiling at villages as we pass them by, except for Leezol, keeping his classic scowl.

"I am sure you will all love it here, the people are kind and we have many Quarries filled with Noli. I am a Noli Extractor myself! A Noli Quarry is not too far from the outpost, it is just a little further." Mr. Tawin says while leading us.

"So, Mr. Tawin," Sarge continued, "you said you're an extractor of something called Noli and you mentioned Quarries, what's that all about?"

His face lights up, obviously pleased to answer the question,

"Oh, yes! Noli is a valuable and precious stone we use to power our village, very powerful and beautiful, but we must be careful, the ones that are used for power and energy are highly flammable if not handled properly with care and attention."

Sarge nods his head, then taps his shoulder,

"One's used for power? Are there other kinds of this Noli stuff?"

"There are pieces of Noli that have no use to us because they do not hold enough power, we usually use them for jewelry and such due them lacking enough power to be flammable or really any sort of use or threat. You can tell the difference between a powerful piece and a scrap, but both are beautiful, you will see. I will show you when we get there, my friends! We are almost there."

Mr. Tawin has a soft, kind voice, it is clear the war hasn't affected him and his people, not that much at least from what we can tell right now. It felt odd only having Sarge speak, it probably didn't sit right with Mr. Tawin either, so I finally decided to ask something too,

"Excuse me, sir, would you mind me asking what planet we are on?"

He chuckles,

"Young man, do you not know your planets?" he joked, "Oh, I jest, I am sorry, my friend, you are on Kana, home of the glowing sands and, you guessed it, Noli!" he exclaimed, lifting his arms in the air in celebration.

Truly amazing seeing someone this happy, especially at this time. Sarge's face lights up,

"We're on Kana? I've only ever met one other person from Kana, but I've never actually visited!"

"I have heard of Kana in my studies, I was always curious about it, but I never thought I would get to see it!" Somma exclaimed.

I can tell the joy and wonderment that was lost in Somma for a while now is starting to come back as we pass by more glowing sand. I have to be honest, I'm amazed, too. Mr. Tawin laughs,

"Well, you all are certainly welcomed here!"

He has so much kindness, I do wonder, though, is he and his people unaware of what is going on around the galaxies right now? Should I mention it?

"Excuse me, Mr. Tawin, SSG. Miner, may I speak to you for a moment?" I ask Sarge who's at the front of our group with Mr. Tawin,

"Pardon me, Mr. Tawin, SPC. Carlston, take point with Mr. Tawin here and-"

"Apologies for interrupting you, sir, but," Mr. Tawin

continues after politely interrupting us, "Please, everyone, call me Geb! No need to be so formal with me."

"Noted, *Geb*, thank you!" Sarge says before heading back towards me,

"So, what do you think, kid?" he asks while patting me on the back.

"It certainly is a nice place, sir, but I wanted to ask, should we ask him if he is aware of everything going on? Sure, this village doesn't seem in the best condition, but the people seem happy and unaffected."

"I see what you're saying," Sarge responds, "I'd wait till we get to the outpost before asking any more questions, leave it to me, for now, enjoy the sights, kid!"

We finally reach the outpost. It is a small structure, but it has stools, cots and other places to rest. Luckily, there is also water. Blaine sees a nearby cot and with all his grace, collapses onto it. Sarge and I help everyone sit down, Sarge even lets Leezol take a seat before him. It's the least he could do considering Leezol technically saved our lives. Sarge pulls up a chair and offers it to Geb, but he kindly rejects, shaking his head and offering it to Sarge instead. Just like with the masks, there isn't enough for everyone. I decide to lean on a post with my shoulder with arms crossed, leaning my head against it. While everyone takes a few moments to relax and get settled, I close my eyes. After a brief moment, I feel someone tap my arm. I open my eyes and see Somma in front of me, smiling and handing me the stool she was sitting on. I smile and shake my head,

"I'm okay, you can have it."

Somma looks down in defeat and frowns, putting her stool back down before sitting.

"Thank you." I quietly say while gently placing my hand on her shoulder.

Somma looks up at me from her stool and smiles, bowing her head. With all of us finally situated, Geb steps forward,

"May I offer anyone anything?"

"Waters, please." Sarge requests.

Geb nods his head and brings each of us a cup of water, he takes a seat on the ground and looks at each of us.

"We have never seen anyone like you all here before. Where do you all come from? If you do not mind me asking."

"We DO mind!" Leezol snaps.

Leezol's crass and rude behavior will probably get us in trouble here, he seems to have no place in what looks like a peaceful village. He doesn't speak for us, so I choose to speak up,

"Apologies for our- associate. My name is CPL. Clark Parson, from Earth." I say while extending my hand to Geb to shake his hand.

Geb looks confused, seemingly unaware of what a handshake is. He slowly grabs my hand and once I shake his hand, he smiles with curiosity and wonderment,

"Fascinating! Yes, I have heard of Earth. When we all heard stories of people from a planet called Earth reaching our galaxies, we were all amazed, I never thought we would get any of you here, how exciting! Is anyone else here from Earth?" he asked.

Answering his question, Sarge, Blaine, PVT. Denza, Dillon and the Lane twins all raise their hands. Geb smiles at them in amazement.

"I recognize the rest of you, Tanli and all of Vonra was once the center of all trade, the entire planet deals in trade with other planets, not as much as we used to, but we still try to get around when we can." Geb continued as he looks at PVT. Reddina, "I see here we have a young man from Foli, I would know those eyes from anywhere and those teeth, very sharp!" he jokes as he turns to Somma, "Oh, my, how beautiful you are! Diamond eyes, sparkling pale skin and hair, you must be a Vespin! How wonderful, Vespis, Sun of Waylif! You know, Vespis is the reason why my people have a home here!"

Somma smiles and bows her head in appreciation. Geb

turns to PVT. Shuua,

"Now, let me see, you, young lady, are a mystery,. The hair of the wise Matu, but your eyes, one is blue?" he asks,

She nods while lacking eye contact, she was never comfortable with her eyes. Geb notices her mood change when he mentioned the eyes,

"On my planet, blue is the color of the rarest sands here. Let me tell you, it is very beautiful, but does not appear too often. Blue is a very lucky color! You hardly ever see that color for sand here in a lifetime. You have rare, wondrous blue in one eye and the wisdom of Matu in the other, fascinating! Your eyes are one of a kind, my dear, be proud!"

PVT. Shuua smiles and bows her head to him,

"Thank you, Geb, on Matu, others do not see it that way. It was hard living where everyone was 'wise' and made you feel like an outcast, it makes you think they are right. I do not talk about it much."

We've never heard her open up like this before. Geb grabs her hand,

"Wise does not mean intelligent, a simple man can offer wisdom, but it may not be sound if he lacks intelligence."

That very well may have been what she has needed to hear for a long time. Geb looks at PVT. Denza,

"You there, not to sound rude, but you look rather odd, I cannot quite figure it out-" he says before I interrupt after seeing Rachel sigh in frustration,

I decide to answer for her to avoid her possibly raising her voice at him,

"She is transgender, Geb."

"Oh, I apologize, I do not know what that is."

"It's a concept from Earth, when someone isn't comfortable with the gender they were at birth, they identify as whichever gender they feel comfortable with and tend to dress and look like the gender they identify with."

Geb looks at her,

"Well, are you happy this way?"

"I guess." PVT. Denza responds,

"No, yes or no, are you happy this way?"

"I am."

"Then I am happy for you!" Geb exclaims,

His support fills her with shock and happiness. She was never used that response when it came to her gender. After PVT. Denza thanks him, we hear a groan come from Leezol. He stands up and approaches Geb,

"So, Geb, tell me where I am from." he says while leaning closer to Geb, trying to intimidate him.

"You are of Xenem."

"Oh, come now, you are teaching us all these fascinating little facts about Earth, Vespis, Foli, what about Xenem? Talk to me about Xenem, Geb."

Sarge interjects, shoving Leezol,

"Back off! Apologies, Geb, we-"

Geb lifts his hand up stopping him from continuing,

"It is no issue. Well, when I was a boy, Xenem was a beautiful planet. I was lucky enough to visit during former Chancellor Holek's reign. I saw him speak while I was there. He was so wise, so smart, so-"

"Weak!" Leezol interrupts, "Holek was a weak, spineless child! He-"

Blaine gets up and punches Leezol in the face before he could continue. Geb shakes his head,

"Thank you, but no need for that. Please, continue."

Geb has more patience than all of us combined. Leezol slowly gets up,

"What is this? What are you trying to prove?" he asks Geb,

"Do I need to prove anything to want to have a conversation? For all his great and kind deeds, yes, Holek was not the best leader, he was taken advantage of by many people, including his own staff, he rolled over to most opposition, too, so to an extent, I agree, he was weak, sometimes, but overall, he was a *LEADER*. My time spent in Xenem, I constantly spotted him working with the public, building gates and structures and he never asked for money in return for his work or did not threaten his people or force them to bow, he worked with the people because he knew he was there in a position of power because of the people, back when their people could vote for their leader. He was a great man, in my opinion."

Sarge smiles, I could tell he likes Geb, we all do.

"Come on, Leezol," Sarge says, "Doesn't he remind you of Ben, he was always smarter than you! Geb seems to have you outmatched."

Leezol doesn't say anything back, he stays silent and walks back to his resting spot. Geb sighs and stands up. He looks off towards the Quarry, he suddenly turns around, slowly walking towards us,

"Breaking down rocks for a living teaches you that once things are broken down, you get to truly see what is valuable, precious, beautiful, and what is just dirt." he turns to Leezol, "Leezol, sir, if I break you down, what will I find, value or dirt?"

The mood has completely shifted, we all go quiet, except for Leezol, who begins to growl,

"Is that a threat?" he asks.

The sudden mood change is unlike anything we have seen from Geb. Granted, we have not known him long, but challenging Leezol is bold. Trying to change the subject, I interject,

"So, Geb, you were going to show us this Noli stone, right?"

After a brief moment of tense silence, Geb turns to me,

"Yes! Come, you all must see!" he says while grabbing his tools and waving his hand for us to follow him.

We all get up and starting walking towards the Quarry, Geb turns to us,

"Now, you all must be very careful here, I lost my leg here because I was not careful." he says while carefully approaching our destination.

We reach the Quarry, it's a lot bigger than I was

expecting, we're almost blinded by the shine of all the Noli stones,

"The shine is almost blinding. Friends of yours, PVT. Juna?" Sarge jokes.

For the first time in a long time, things seem normal. No one chasing us or trying to kill us, it's nice. As we approach a hill leading down into the Quarry, Geb stops at the top,

"Okay, friends, the hill is steeper than it looks, be very careful. Does anyone need any help?"

"Yeah, you may need to hold Parson's hand!" Blaine says mockingly, laughing so hard he accidentally falls down the hill. Geb watches him tumble down,

"Yes, that right there, do not do that." he says while pointing at a falling Blaine.

We can't help but laugh, even Leezol gave us his famous cackle watching the big oaf fall. We carefully make our way down the hill where we find Blaine wiping the dirt and debris off of him and muttering angrily,

"Stupid... Dirty... Ridiculous... "

"Maybe you're the one who needed to hold someone's hand." I say while helping him with the debris.

Geb gathers us around,

"It just occurred to me, I do not know all your names! How rude of me not to ask! I have the sense you are all soldiers, brave warriors! I would like to know your names, though." he asks.

We all look at each other and nod, Sarge steps forward,

"I'll do the introductions, yes, we are soldiers, Geb. I am SSG. Richard Miner, this is CPL. Clark Parson, this genius who fell down the hill by laughing is SPC. Blaine Carlston, then we have PVT. Bradley Dillon, Martin and Mitchell Lane, Carden Reddina, Kierra Shuua, Rachel Denza, then last, but not least, Somma Juna. Oh, yes and this is CPT. Auldin Leezol."

We all bow our heads in respect, except Leezol who glares at Geb. We tend to not give our names and rank to anyone, but we figured that information would be safe with

Geb, Sarge can tell when we can trust someone or not.

"A pleasure to meet you all, shall I address you by your ranks?" Geb asks.

We all tell him that's not necessary, considering everything he has done for us but, naturally Leezol speaks up,

"You call me CPT. Leezol." he demands.

Geb nods his head, understanding the demand while Sarge rolls his eyes. Geb approaches the wall he has been working on for what looks like years.

"Would anyone like to know how to get Noli?" he asks.

We all nod our heads. Geb approaches the rocks and smacks it a few times with hard strikes with his hammer until pieces of rock and debris crumble down, revealing a greenish-gray looking stone, it looks a lot like the stone Labradorite from Earth. The stone Geb found has a bright white flash, it looks unreal. Geb grabs it carefully, after wiping the debris off, he walks towards us,

"My people believe this stone was a gift from the Kana god of beauty, Noli. As you can tell, the stone was named after her. She found the world in need of more beauty and sent us the glowing sands and soon after, she sent us pieces of her heart which we believe are the Noli stones." he explains while giving us a closer look.

He puts the stone in his bag carefully then approaches the wall again,

"Let me see if I can find you all a safe piece that you can keep. Oh! I see some." Geb exclaims before striking the wall again, causing rocks and dirt to crumble down.

His strikes reveal a piece of Noli with a rainbow shine to it, Geb finds quite a few pieces and grabs them all,

"Now, the rainbow still has significance and connection to the great Noli, while the white flash has the power to help us survive, it is believed that soon after the sending pieces of her heart to us containing only white flashes, Noli created a different type of stone, but still used pieces of her heart. She created a rainbow and trapped it inside other pieces of her stones. She sent them to us as a symbol of thanks for using her gifts to survive instead of selfish gain." he continued, "If you all would like, I could carve these stones into a shape or design of your choosing, perhaps turn it into a beautiful necklace? I could carve something that means a lot to this team?"

"That would be great, we will think of something and let you know, thank you, Geb." Sarge responds.

The sky begins to go dark and we head back to the outpost, Geb starts a fire for us to gather around and rest, we all sit down. We see Geb bring out plates from his bag,

"Luckily, I have enough food for all of you, then tomorrow, I will take you all into the village and help you get some supplies."

"Thank you, Geb, but curious, do you live at this outpost?" PVT. Reddina asks,

"Oh, yes, well, you see, Carden, life has not been too kind to me or really anyone in Tanli for a while now. All of us here were originally from a city named Vonra, it was nothing fancy, but it was home, until CPT. Leezol's friends arrived and started taking over, taking the city and pushing everyone out who would not blindly fall to their rule. That is how most of us ended up here." he continued, "We were lucky enough to find this abandoned outpost for shelter. We have been here ever since."

"I had nothing to do with that invasion, Geb, I was not even there when it happened." Leezol interjected.

Geb shrugs his shoulders at Leezol's statement, as if to say "It's all in the past now." Even then, it's not like Geb to not have some sort of response, I guess when it comes to what happened, he does not have much to say about it, anymore, at least.

"Food is ready!" Geb exclaims, snapping back into his old self.

He brings each of us a plate with a piece of meat on it. I'm not sure what it is exactly, but my parents taught me that when food is free, just shut up and eat it. Only after, you say thank you. We thank Geb for the food and he sits down with us, but doesn't have any food for himself. Leezol sighs, he rips half of his meal in half and hands it to Geb,

"I am sorry about what happened to your home." Leezol says somberly.

All of our eyes widened at the same time, each of looked completely baffled, but knew better not to question what we just saw. Geb smiles,

"Thank you, CPT. Leezol," Geb continued while handing the half back to Leezol,"but that is not necessary, I am not hungry. You all need to eat, big strong soldiers need their food!" he says while getting up to grab water for us all.

Geb is proving to be a most generous host. Once he hands us the waters, he slowly sits back down,

"Well, what fun is a fireplace if no one tells any stories? " he continues, "Does anyone have any tales?"

Somma points at me with excitement,

"CPL. Parson knows many stories, stories about these amazing gods and giants from another universe!"

Geb chuckles and looks at me,

"Well, Clark, tell us about these gods and giants! If you would?"

A part of me was filled with fear, hating to be put on the spot like this. After everything we've all been through, I figure they need a distraction, so I might as well put on a show. I smile and look around at everyone with playful intensity in my eyes,

"Well, heroes, legends, warriors, friends, shall I regale you with another tale from The World Tree?" I ask while standing up and doing my best hero pose.

Everyone cheers and laughs, Leezol's laugh is more so him laughing at me and what he assumes is my embarrassment. I think for a moment trying to think of a story to tell, when I finally remember one of my favorite figures from Norse mythology,

"This is the tale of Huginn and Muninn, Ravens of the Chief god Odin. Even a god cannot see everything and still run the universe, so Odin has his two Ravens assist him. The Ravens tell Odin everything they see and hear. He sends Huginn and Muninn out at dawn to Earth, otherwise known as Midgard, the birds fly all over the world before returning at the end of the day, regaling Odin of everything they saw and heard from their travels, so if you ever see a pair of Ravens flying around, it is most likely the great Huginn and Muninn. If you see Ravens flying near you, it's believed that the gods are with you, so we must always fight bravely in hopes that the Huginn and Muninn and the gods will see us and offer their protection and strength."

As I finish, I bow dramatically like a court jester, just to give my story a bit more fun and dramatic energy. Everyone begins to clap and cheer, Geb laughs and claps, but leans in,

"A wonderful tale! I do not know what a 'Raven' is, though." he says while tilting his head in curiosity.

His confusion is understandable, I can't expect other planets to have the same knowledge and animals as mine. I remember I had to teach members Specter who weren't from Earth what different animals and objects were too.

"Ravens are birds from Earth, depending on where you were, people either regarded them as evil and bad luck or wise and magical. The story comes from a region on my planet known as Scandinavia, where Ravens were seen as sacred creatures who held wisdom and major connections to the gods. I try to preach Scandinavian stories and lore to the squad due to them having lessons of strength, wisdom and courage." I explain to Geb.

Geb looks down in contemplation,

"Fascinating," he continues, "What do they look like?"

"Well, they're a black bird, long beaks, black eyes, medium in size, I guess." I respond.

Geb nods, again in contemplation, like he is planning something. As it gets later in the night and the fire dies down, we start getting ready to sleep. I volunteer to take the first watch while everyone else sleeps, despite Geb assuring us that no one will bother us, we still want to be safe. It's a peaceful night. Sounds of the desert winds blowing past are the only sounds I hear. It's calming. An hour into the watch, I hear quiet footsteps behind me, I quickly draw my knife and turn around. I'm relieved to see it's Somma, with a confused expression on her face, undoubtedly wondering why I pulled my knife out. Her face and hair, both fully unwrapped, it's not too often when I get to see her long, straight silver colored shimmering hair down. I must admit, she looks beautiful.

"Oh, PVT. Juna, sorry about that, why aren't you sleeping?" I ask while putting my knife away.

"I could not sleep. I really do not think we need watches, sir."

"After what happened, I'd rather be safe than sorry, if you or someone had died when Leezol and his men ambushed us, I wouldn't be able to-" I stop myself before continuing, "All of this has just become one big mess, it's hard to trust we will be safe anywhere." I say while looking off into the sea of sand that surrounds the outpost.

Somma looks down in reflection of what happened to her on that night.

"I cannot believe the man who almost killed me is sharing sleeping quarters with me, with all of us. A part of me is scared to sleep because I think he will try to kill me." she says while looking at Leezol asleep on a cot.

"You know we'd never never let that happen, *I'd* never let that happen, I have your back, just as you have mine, you'll be safe, I'll make sure of it." I say trying to reassure her safety. Somma smiles and moves her shimmering hair out of her face. I look at Leezol, too, a chill runs down my spine,

"If anyone is in real danger here, it's me." I say under my breath.

"What do you mean?"

"Other than Sarge, who else leads this squad? He put that on me from the very start and we have made many enemies over time, people I'm sure who would love to see me dead." I continue while looking down, "It's hard trying to keep everyone safe, even with SPC. Carlston and Sarge taking charge at times, all these people chasing us- chasing me, wanting me dead, I feel alone. Alone and to be honest, completely in the dark. I don't know what to do."

It felt weird telling someone this. I probably should have kept all that to myself, but there is something about Somma that makes it easier for me to open up. My whole life, I never expressed how I felt, not even to my parents. I dealt with issues internally, alone. I could have asked for help if I needed it. I had supportive, loving parents, but hiding pain and dealing with it on your own kept everyone worry-free. If I don't tell anyone anything, they won't stress or worry. I'd hate to put that on anyone. Despite all that, Somma has always been very easy to talk to. After a moment of silence, Somma approaches me,

"Even in the darkest of times, a single beam of light can still be seen for miles." she says softly as she starts unwrapping her hand, revealing her shimmering hand.

She slowly reaches for my hand and holds it. The shimmer of her hand causes my hand to glow. To be honest, I have no idea what to say. For a while now, Somma and I seem to be closer to each other than anyone else in Specter. The only thing I am able to come up with is appreciation,

"Thank you, that means a lot to me." I say with a genuine smile on my face,

It's been so long since I had a real smile. While continuing to hold my hand, Somma looks up at me,

"You are a hero to us, you may not see it, but you have done so much for me and the rest of us, everything you have taught us, getting us out of trouble and making sure we are safe. My father may not see it or care, but me and everyone else here is blessed to have you lead us, everything feels safer when you are around. That is how I feel, at least."

Little shocks me at this point, but that makes me fall silent, only letting out a soft chuckle,

"Wow." I whisper with the same smile on my face.

"You can talk to me about anything, I do not want you to feel alone. You may think I do not notice, but I can tell when something bothers you or hurts you. I wish I could help more."

"You're too smart for me to hide anything, I never stood a chance." I joke, "Don't worry about me, I'll be okay, you should get some sleep."

Somma chuckles and walks away before stopping and turning back around, she quickly walks back to me and stands on her toes, kissing me softly on the cheek.

"Goodnight, sir." she says with a shy smile before heading back to the outpost.

I touch my cheek in shock, unsure if what just happened was real or some illusion brought on by the dessert. A few moments pass when I hear a loud, obnoxious yawn behind me as heavy footsteps approach, Blaine pushes me to the side,

"Alright, scram, I'll take watch, I guess."

I say nothing in return due to shock. I head to the post I was leaning on earlier, I sit down, leaning against it to finally get some sleep. What a day. The next morning comes, my eyes are closed when I hear humming, I slowly open my eyes and see Geb packing up his satchel,

"Good morning, Geb." I say while getting up.

Geb quickly turns around and smiles,

"A very good morning, indeed, Clark! May I offer you anything to eat?"

"No, thank you, but if you can prepare something for everyone else, we'd appreciate it."

Geb nods his head and begins bringing plates out,. Half an hour later, everyone else is awake and eating. I sit down away from the group, I pull out my pad and pull up a photo of me and my parents from when I was young playing at a park near where we used to live.

"We'll get them back, son." Sarge says, standing right behind me.

"You're quiet, old man!" I respond playfully as I put my pad away.

"This old dog still has some surprises." he continued, "So, obviously, the plan was a disaster, we need to think of a way out of here and back to Xenem, fast. I don't know about Leezol, though," Sarge looks over at Leezol, "Xenem surely knows about what happened, there is no way they'll let him cross through the blockade now, so what do we do with him?"

Personally, I don't care what we do with him. Releasing him poses not much of a threat, besides the possibility of him killing us. As for Xenem, he's no longer welcomed back to his home and I don't think he would even go back after what happened. Killing him is a fun idea, too. Then there's letting him stay with us, after all, he is a solid pilot, as much as it pains me to admit it.

"I'll let you decide what to do with him, sir, after all, he's your friend? Nemesis?" I ask.

"Something like that."

Sarge heads towards the rest of the squad to see if they're ready to get moving. We're all carrying our weapons and equipment, we hear Geb chuckle,

"You will not be needing all that, Tanli is a peaceful village, no one will bother us. We are running simple errands. You can leave your clothes and gear at the outpost. I went into the village this morning and bought you all clothes, it should fit you all well enough."

We're all given baggy gray shirts and pants, they're not the most comfortable or well-fitting, but it beats carrying our equipment and wearing our uniforms. We slowly put our gear down and dress down to the casual clothes Geb kindly bought us. It's our first time seeing each other dress down like this, even Somma is fully unwrapped. Of course, Leezol didn't care for the casual clothes, opting to keep his uniform on. I'm not sure if the concept of casual clothing is even something that crosses people's minds on Xenem. Either way, he's been with us since his attack and doesn't have other clothes besides his tactical gear. Geb tells him we can try to find him something else to wear in the village, Leezol isn't so keen on that idea, but reluctantly agrees to do it. We all follow Geb to Tanli, it's about a 10 minute walk,

"Okay, my friends," he continued, "I know you all are probably not used to civilian life, but that is okay. Just treat everyone with kindness and respect and they will do the same to you."

"When we got here, we were respectful, but everyone just stood there and watched us in need until you came along." PVT. Denza responds.

"You see, Rachel, Tanli is not used to visitors, especially visitors who look and sound different from us. They did not mean any offense by it, they were shocked and they will be shocked again, but like I said, be kind and they will be kind. Oh, each of you, take these!"

Geb hands each of us some pieces of metal that look like coins, he tells us we can use it for our supplies. We reach Tanli and Sarge gathers us up.

"Okay, we are here for supplies, got it? Parson, the Lane twins, Juna and Dillon. You five search for supplies. The rest of you, with me and Geb, we'll ask around about a way out of here and see what we can find out. Dismissed!"

Our groups go our separate ways, none of us, besides Geb, knows the language here, so this is going to be hard for all of us. Hopefully with the translators in our ears, we can understand what they're saying to us, but how we will be able to have a conversation or ask questions is going to be an issue. Sarge has Geb with him so they will be fine as far as communication with others goes, but as for me and my group, I guess we will have to see. My group heads towards small buildings and posts that look like they sell certain items. We pass by a shop that sells clothes and everyone, but me, stops,

"Is there a problem?" I ask,

"No problem here, sir, but aren't you curious what Tanli has to offer?" PVT. Dillon asks as he motions into the store.

The Lane twins and Somma smile and nod in agreement.

"Fine, but only for a little." I reluctantly say as we head

into the store.

The shopkeep turns around and sees us, she tilts her head in curiosity,

"Oh, yes, the new travelers. Welcome. Do you speak Vonran?" she asks,

We shake our heads.

"You understand me, though, yes?"

We nod our heads,

"Interesting. Well, take a look around then."

It's nice to see one of the languages PVT. Reddina and Shuua were able to add is Vonran, that makes things easier. I stay at the front of the store while the others walk around. It's a nice place with unique looking pieces of clothing. PVT. Dillon walks up to me with a large, crazy looking hat with many different colors on it.

"For you, sir!" he jokes.

I hear the shopkeep snicker behind me, Somma and the Lane twins join us at the front laughing,

"Put it on!"

"Do it!"

"You will look amazing!"

They all cheer, I roll my eyes and break a small smile. I snatch the hat from PVT. Dillon and put it on. I immediately feel ridiculous, but everyone is getting a good laugh out of it, including the shopkeeper.

"How do I look?" I ask sarcastically.

Everyone is laughing too hard to answer, but they give thumbs up. Somma approaches me and fixes the hat to make it look straight,

"Very handsome!" she says while finishing fixing the hat.

She rubs my shoulder before heading back to everyone else who is still laughing. I figured what happened with Somma and I last night was a dream, but perhaps it was real, which, to be honest, I'm not complaining about. With everything that has happened, it's hard to even think about consider relationships, at least, hard for me. Then there's the question of should it even happen? We live dangerous lives, constantly being shot at, chased or hunted. I do think Somma is truly beautiful and a great person, I've always been able to open up to her, but at any moment, either me or her could get killed or hurt, do we really want to have to deal with that? It's bad enough having anyone in the squad be in danger, but someone I have an actual relationship with? Another story. Plus, I'd need to be unbiased towards all members if any issue was to arise between members of the squad. Maybe, at a safer time and place I could entertain the idea of me and Somma being more than friends or teammates on some suicide squad, whether she agrees is a mystery to me.

After we put the hat back, we walk out of the store. We look at the other shops when suddenly we hear cries,

"Thief! Someone stop him!"

The cry came from a nearby shop with a man running away from it.

"Stay here." I tell the group before chasing after the thief.

After a while of running, I manage to catch up to the thief, but he's very fast and agile. Hurtling and jumping over boxes and large items in his way, he's definitely making me work for it. After chasing him for a few more minutes, I'm finally able to lunge at him for a tackle. Once he is on the ground, I start hearing laughter around us, five men come out of hiding and slowly walk towards me and the thief on the floor.

"You have our friend there, stranger." the man on the left says with a shifty grin on his face while continuing to approach me.

I snatch the bag of stolen items away from the thief and quickly stand up, the thief gets up and joins his friends who are getting closer to me. I'm clearly outmatched, especially since Geb told us to leave our gear behind. I can tell I am in for a beating. I look around and put my hands up while holding the bag,

"I am not sure if you can understand me, but just walk away, I'll give these back to their rightful owner, I won't say a word to anyone."

The gang looks at each other in confusion, until one shrugs his shoulders and hits me across the face with a rusted pipe.

I hit the floor and before I knew it, I was getting beaten by everyone around me, using fists and blunt objects. Is this it for me? Is this how I die? I am unable to get up or fight back, I am constantly being beaten down more and more. The only things I see are white and red flashes with glimpses of my blood on the floor, I slowly feel my life draining away from me, until the beating suddenly stops. I hear the men start yelling in pain, with the little vision I have, I see their bodies hit the floor, a few seconds pass when I hear a voice,

"Scum."

It's Sarge. He picks me up off the ground, I could tell I was a bloody mess,

"Damn, son, you sure can take a beating!" he says while putting my arm around him so he can help me stay up as we head back to town.

There were a few moments where I went in and out of consciousness during the walk back, but I was able to stay awake for a little once we reached the shops. My mind was fuzzy and I couldn't make out what people were saying, the only things I was able to make out were,

"Oh, my god!"

"What happened?"

"Can you hear me?"

"Get him some bandages, now!"

I was able to barely see the shopkeeper who had his items stolen. He is standing outside his shop looking at me, I wake myself and let go of Sarge. I slowly limp my way to the shopkeeper and hand him the bag in my shaking, bloodied hand. He looks at the bag in shock and bows his head in deep appreciation. That's the last thing I see before I collapse and go unconscious. What a wonderful way to start off my time in Tanli.

A GENTLE MOMENT OF PEACE

Everything is hazy, I can barely open my eyes, all I hear is everyone shouting in panic and confusion,

"Put him on the cot, quickly!"

"Who did this?"

"Shut it, get him some water, quick!"

I feel terrible and probably look worse. Do I regret going after the thief? Right now, a little. Doing the right thing is hard most times, as rewarding as it can be. I couldn't just stand there and let that thief get away with his friends. I'm able to open my eyes a little to see Geb pacing back and forth,

"Oh, Clark, I am so sorry. I did not think this would happen. Why did this happen? I'm sorry, my friend." he says frantically,

I weakly wave my hand at him, trying to let him know not to worry about it, it's not like I can really talk at the moment. I close my eyes again and hear PVT. Reddina approach us,

"Here is the water, sir."

"Thank you, stay with CPL. Parson, is that clear, PVT. Reddina?" Sarge asks,

"Yes, sir."

He sits down next to the cot I'm laying on, he approaches to help me drink the water, but I lift my hand up and grab the water from him and take a few sips before handing the cup back to him.

"Damn!" Leezol exclaims, "How did I let this happen?

How did I let a group of some street vermin beat you down before I could?"

"Leave us!" PVT. Reddina yells at Leezol.

To be honest, Leezol's jokes and attitude is welcomed compared to what I just went through. I feel PVT. Reddina wipe the blood and dirt from my head, he sighs and starts to say something, but stops before finally saying what he wanted to say,

"I am sorry, sir. I- I am sorry."

He has nothing to be sorry for, but I am unable to tell him that. I don't want him thinking it's his fault that this happened, he wasn't even there with my group. Had he been there, I still would have wanted him to stay back. Despite being unsure if this is even a good idea, I fall asleep. Somewhere within my rest, I started seeing flashes of what happened. The hits, the blows, the blood and the sounds of the men cackling, everything. I was reliving it. The scenes kept replaying in my head, it came to a point where I started yelling and shot up in my cot. I looked around, it was night, everyone was asleep. I feel a hand gently touch my shoulder,

"Hello, hero."

I look back and it's Somma, she gives me a smile that seems to make me feel better. She helps me lay back down. I chuckle,

"Hero? Yes, I'm sure this is exactly what a hero looks like."

"I think so, a hero who takes the blows just to help someone, that is a hero to me and I am sure to many others, too." she responds with a smile while putting a cold rag on my head.

Her smile starts to fade, I can tell something is bothering her,

"Is everything okay?" I ask,

"I was not there, we were not there. We did nothing, I just stood back and did nothing. I know you told us to stay put, but I should have followed and helped, but instead, this happened."

"Please don't worry about that."

"Thankfully, SSG. Miner was there to stop it, we could have lost you."

I chuckle again,

"Don't worry, you guys can't get rid of me that easily."

"How lucky for us." she continued with a bright smile, "Lucky for me."

She looks at me and our eyes meet, it's baffling how bright Vespin eyes are. Somma smiles and gets closer to me, softly placing her hand on my chest. Despite what I thought earlier, I decide to give in. I gently grab her and pull her in, and just like that, Somma and I share a kiss.

I know I had concerns over this, but in all honesty, this was unavoidable. I don't want to die wondering what could have been, but instead look back on what did happen, and this, I will forever look back on and remember. After we move away from each other, Somma's eyes sparkle more than usual, she says nothing and smiles, she holds my hand,

"You must rest now." she says softly before gently kissing my forehead.

I close my eyes, once again thinking this was a dream or more accurately, a hallucination from blunt force trauma. Either way, I hope this is real. I spend the next few days resting, going in and out of consciousness. After days of healing and feeling pretty useless, I wake up one morning to the feeling of someone poking the wounds on my face,

"Blaine, I know it's you, why are you poking me?" I ask with my eyes closed.

"Just wanted to see if it still hurts, how do you feel?"

"A little better, thanks." I continue, " What did you and everyone else find out about this place? Anything about a way out of here?"

"Sarge will tell you all about that, you need help up?"

I'm not used to Blaine being this kind or helpful, I shake my head and slowly get up. It takes me a couple moments, but I finally stand up and limp towards Geb,

"Good morning, Geb." I say, he quickly turns around,

"It is the Hero of Tanli, hail, hero!" he exclaims while dancing around like a jester,

I smile and shake my head,

"You're calling me a hero, too?"

"Everyone is! Everyone in Tanli has been talking about you and what those horrible fiends did to you, just awful!" he responds while patting me on the back.

"Awful" is a pretty good representation of what happened. I hear Sarge call me over to him. I limp my way over to Sarge,

"How do you feel, kid?" he asks,

"Still sore, but I'm okay, did anyone find out anything interesting about this place or how to get out of here?"

"Yes indeed, I got plans in the works. I'm working with Leezol on the plan, believe it or not! I gave everyone some time to themselves, it's been a rough few days, especially for you! So, rest, be with the squad, I'll gather you all when it's time. Be careful, kid."

I'm not sure what to do exactly, having the day off doesn't happen often with us, I better take this chance while I can. From my bag, I grab my old coat that looks almost as beaten as I do, I put it on with my black tank top and usual Specter pants and boots. Having time off, I have the freedom to let my hair down. One of the perks of having long hair is that it goes in my face, hiding how terrible I look. If I had it my way, I'd always have my hair down. I decide to head back to Tanli. It feels strange, though, everyone is bowing their heads to me, treating me like I'm the hero everyone says I am. Calling me "The Hero of Tanli" feels weird. It doesn't feel right, I don't think I deserve all this praise. In the distance, I see a shining, shimmering light. Looking closer, I see it's Somma walking around the village. I decide to surprise her since she's probably unaware I am up and walking- well, limping.

Somma enters the clothes shop we all went to before the whole thief incident. I move the hair out of my face and grab the colorful hat PVT. Dillon had me try on. I put it on and walk up behind her,

"Excuse me, miss? Do you think this hat suits a gentleman like myself?"

Somma quickly turns around and her face lights up, she laughs and launches at me with a hug, she squeezes me so tight I almost faint. She lets go, she looks so shocked to see me,

"I had no idea you are able to move now! How do you feel?" she asks, speaking at a million miles per hour.

"Still a bit sore, but I'm okay. How are you?"

"Better now! I was so worried about you, we all were, I still cannot believe what happened."

"Me too, but don't worry about that, okay?" I tell her trying to put the whole ordeal behind us.

Somma nods her head and smiles at me with relief in her diamond eyes. The shopkeeper approaches us,

"Pardon me, but I just wanted to say what a wonderful thing you did for Sarsey, he truly appreciates what you have done. You are a very brave man, a shame those men are still walking free, though. Hopefully they do not bother you again." she says.

Knowing she doesn't speak English, I bow my head in appreciation, which we've all had to do a lot here. Somma and I walk out of the store, she holds my hand,

"Now people will think twice before attacking you." she jokes,

I do, in fact, feel safer with her. I squeeze her hand tight, fearing I may hurt her, but I'm not used to holding anyone's hand. We head towards the shop who had the thief,

"I am sure he wants to thank you!" Somma exclaims.

We head inside the store. It's my first time in the store, they seem to sell an assortment of items. Jewelry, accessories, toys and so on. The shopkeeper walks up to the counter and sees me,

"It is you! It is really you! By the gods, you are alive and well!" Sarsey runs around the counter and starts shaking my hand and continued, "Sarsey Wilnew, at your service! I was told you do not speak Vonran, not a problem, just pick out any item you like and it is yours!"

A very kind offer, Somma and I take a look around the store for a little when I see a brown leather necklace with a silver arrow pendant on it. It has a piece of brown leather wrapped around the arrow, too. A single silver feather pendant hangs next to the arrow, making it even more interesting. It's a really nice looking piece. I pick it up to take a closer look. I think it would be great if every member of the squad had one. After all, where I come from, arrows and feathers represent direction, purpose, intention, freedom, honor and spirit, among other things.

I bring the necklace to Sarsey. I'm not sure how to ask if there's a way I can get ten of the necklaces, let alone know how to speak Vonran in general. I put the necklace down in front of Sarsey and hold up ten fingers, hoping he would understand what I am asking. He tilts his head in confusion, I point at the necklace then hold up ten fingers again, Sarsey's eyes widen,

"Oh! Would you like ten of these?" he asks,

I smile and nod my head while pulling out some of the coins Geb gave us, expecting to have to pay for the rest of the necklaces,

"Put that away, my friend! The ten are yours. It is the least I can do!" he exclaims.

I can't help but feel bad, it's a small shop in a crumbled down old village and Sarsey is giving me ten items for free. Sarsey returns with 9 more necklaces in a pouch and hands it to me, I bow my head in appreciation and put down some coins on the counter and slide them to him, he shakes his head with a smile, but I hold my hand up and push them closer to him. He reluctantly take the coins,

"May the gods smile upon you!" he says as Somma and I walk out of the store after bidding him farewell.

I grab one of the necklaces out of the pouch,

"May I?" I ask Somma, wanting to put the necklace on

her.

She smiles and turns around, moving her hair out of the way. Her hair gave off a near blinding flash, I should have expected that, though. I put the necklace on her,

"Now, here we have a beautiful warrior."

Somma giggles while looking at the arrow and feather pendant,

"I love it!" she continues, "I'm sure the others will love it, too, thank you, Clark-" she stops herself and tilts her head, "or CPL. Parson?"

"It's alright. Clark is okay."

"If you want, you can call me by my name, I think we are past 'PVT. Juna'!" she responds while rubbing my shoulder.

I address everyone by their ranks, Somma is now the only exception. In my head, I have been calling her by her first name for a while, but out loud, I addressed her by her rank, too. Things are clearly different now, I don't know how it's going to go if the others hear us slip up and call each other by our first names while I still address them by their ranks. All of this seems so surreal. I can't remember the last time I even had a girlfriend, assuming that's what Somma and I are. It's strange, no one is shooting at us or hunting us down, we all have free time to do whatever we want. It all seems so normal. I still haven't forgotten the goal, though. I know we still have to get out of here and head to Xenem to, freeing my parents and all the others who have been falsely imprisoned there. For now, I figure I should enjoy this while I can.

Somma and I hold hands while we walk around Tanli, her face and hair are uncovered, shimmering in the sun of Kana, causing the villagers to stop and stare in amazement.

"They are all staring at me, should I wrap myself up?" she asks in a defeated and embarrassed tone,

"No, they've just never seen someone like you before, you wouldn't believe how long it took me to not get shocked every time I saw you when all this started. Besides, I like seeing you."

I really don't think the stares had any malicious intent behind them, how often does anyone see someone with shiny, shimmering skin and silver hair? We eventually reach a cliffside overlooking the colored sands, a truly beautiful view,

"Where is your necklace?" Somma asks,

I grab the necklace out of the pouch,

"Would you like to bestow it upon me?" I ask playfully.

Somma smiles and nods, I need to kneel down a bit so she can reach around my neck to put the necklace on. Somma is the shortest member of the squad, we would always use her to get into small or tight spaces, I'd say she is a little over 5 feet tall, just barely. Compared to me, almost being 6 feet tall, we make a hell of a duo.

Once I kneel down, I move my hair out of the way and she puts the necklace on me, the next thing I know, she wraps her arms around my neck in a hug from behind,

"I hope this arrow protects you and keeps you safe, like I will." she says.

She is the only one I've ever opened up to about how I've felt about all this chaos over time. She has also been by my side for months now, she has seen what I've been through. When she says something like that, it truly hits me. She's always been a sweet girl, not just to me, but to everyone. She never deserved anything that has happened to her recently, if anything, I needed to vow to protect her. I kissed her hands which were still around me,

"Thank you." I whisper.

It was the only thing I was able to say without getting too choked up, not only because of her kind words, but because it made me think of what happened to her with Leezol, I still think how I should've done more. I've never been that great with words and expressing my emotions. I still feel the need to let Somma know how I've felt about that whole situation. I turn around and hold her hands and bring her down to my level on the ground, looking at her, her smile and eyes, I forget what I was going to say. Within seconds, I remembered what I was going to say. I looked in her in the eyes again, trying not to be entranced for the second time,

"Somma, my safety should be no concern to you, I failed you-" I stop and look off in the distance towards the cliff so she wouldn't see me tearing up, I look back at her and see a concerned face,

"What do you mean?" she asks,

"That night, with Leezol and all of us I-" Somma stops me,

"No, Clark that was not your fault, do not worry-"

I interrupt, holding her hands tighter,

"No, I need to say it, please." I continued, "That night we all messed up, I messed up. I was so concerned with the planning, how we get into Xenem, how we got out, making sure we did everything safely. I didn't even see the threat that was right in front of us, even with Blaine watching out, we still got caught in that mess. Every night since then, I see it in my head, I can't sleep without seeing that knife get closer to you, I should've done something, I don't know, disarm the other soldiers, try to run to you again, hoping I don't get shot. I never thanked Sarge for saving you, for saving us. It's clear I couldn't save you and I'm sorry you had to go through all that, I'm sorry I couldn't save you. I'll always be sorry."

Somma looks down with tears running down her face still holding my hands. She quickly wipes her tears and rubs her thumb along my left hand tattoo of Huginn and Muninn, the ravens from my story.

"Do not be sorry, it is okay. I do have one question for you, though. These are the birds you told us about the other night?" she asks.

I nod my head.

"From what you said, they are wise and brave, traveling around the world learning and seeing all sorts of things, good and bad, yet still find the strength, bravery and energy to return home and go out again the next day, they remind me of you."

I can tell she is trying to steer the conversation in a lighter direction, for the sake of not ruining our time with any more stories of sadness and regret, I let it slide. I smile and kiss her cheek. Even though I knew what she was doing by steering the conversation somewhere else, it was still clever. She has always been very bright. People like PVT. Reddina and Shuua are so smart that they overshadow how smart Somma is. She's quiet, so she never speaks up to prove it, but Sarge and I always knew.

"I hope you know, I will keep you safe, always." I say,

Somma wraps me in a big hug, again almost squeezing the life out of me,

"I know you will."

We sit down on the cliff overlooking the sands, I pull Somma in close to me, I notice the sands changing color, sometimes red, sometimes blue or purple, every color.

"The people here call this the Heleia Fields, named after the lady who discovered it. I learned about it while you were healing, it is incredible!" she exclaims,

"It really is. Why does the sand change color?"

"I do not know, even the locals do not know. They just believe it comes from their gods, a gift, I suppose."

The wind starts to pick up and I feel Somma get closer to me for warmth, I take off my coat to give it to her.

"Thank you, but I do not want you to be cold, too." she says, trying to put the coat back onto me.

"Don't worry about me, I'll be fine, I don't want you to be cold."

I put my coat over her, it looks massive on her,

"How do I look?" she playfully asks,

"Beautiful."

It feels strange openly telling her she is beautiful and treating her as someone more than a soldier and teammate. For so long, most of the time when I would speak to her was to give her orders. Somma smiles and kisses me on the lips. I wonder if this place is really magical because there's definitely a special feeling here, everything just seems happier. My coat is pretty old and worn out, it's a dark gray military coat with holes in it from the numerous time I have been shot at, burn marks from fires and explosions and tears from dragging this coat through hell over the years, but it keeps me warm and serves its purpose, I'm not trying to win any fashion contests here with this coat. I can't remember where I got it, it's been with me since I joined the war. I would always wear it when Specter was starting out, before we were given our official uniforms. There were quite a few operations we did with me wearing the coat, it probably didn't look as bad before Specter, but now, it's a mess. It was never a clean coat, but I didn't do it any favors by wearing it when this all started out. Somma looks at the coat and starts looking at the gunshot holes, burn marks and all the other damaged parts of it, she points out one burn mark in particular,

"Where did you get these from?" she asks,

"It was on Pikez, Blaine blew up some explosives with me too close to the blast and I got blown away with the coat catching fire. What a mess that was. I think you were with others trying to find transport off of the planet."

"What about this?" she asks while pointing at a gunshot hole close to where my heart is,

I look at the hole, I remember exactly how I got it, but I don't like to think about it, nor do I think Somma would want to hear about it.

"I don't think you want to hear about that one." I respond while looking down in shame.

Somma looks up at me, placing her hand on the scare where my heart is, the same place where the gunshot was placed on the coat,

"Please tell me."

"It was after the first operation we did. It was on Nesteru as a newly formed squad, as you probably remember, it was a disaster, little to no planning involved, my first time trying to lead everyone while dealing with the stress of my parents being taken. No one listened or understood what I was saying over all the noise and chaos. All the men tried to be heroes multiple times, Blaine kept trying to take the reins as leader, we didn't even complete the job, we had to retreat."

"I remember."

"I've never been in that situation before, when we returned, Sarge was furious at me. He told me he made a mistake picking me for the job or making me a leader under him. For a long time before then, I had been dealing with issues on my own internally and after that disaster and Sarge's rampage, I had no one to turn to for help, I tried to figure it out on my own, but this, it was getting too much and I knew that it was only beginning. I didn't want to deal with it anymore. I figured we would never reach Xenem and help my parents. I went back to my quarters, and-" I stop and slowly inhale and exhale before continuing, "I tried to take my own life, hoping a shot to the heart would do the trick."

Somma says nothing in shock, she slowly pulls the collar of my shirt down, revealing the scar of the gunshot wound on my heart, it barely missed. Somma lightly gasps and covers her mouth with tears filling her eyes, her skin begins to shine brighter from stress, she kisses the scar and places her hand on it,

"Never again. Never try that again, please" she begs,

"Don't worry about me, it's okay."

"No, it is not okay, I will worry about you, I will always worry about you. We cannot lose you, we need you."

For the longest time, I convinced myself no one needed me, for anything other than to lead a suicide squad or die in battle for them, with everything that happened with my parents being taken, all the screw ups with the squad and everything in general, I only saw black, but it is like Somma told me, "Even in the darkest of times, a single beam of light can still be seen for miles." Reliving the past caused me to go silent, I heard what Somma said and I do appreciate it, but I don't respond. Without me realizing, I start shaking and breathing heavily, I feel my heart racing and can't seem to speak even if I wanted to. I start gasping for air and that is when I realize, I'm having a panic attack.

It's been a long time since I had one. The past keeps replaying in my head, even the whole thief situation is plaguing my mind, causing me to gasp for air uncontrollably, I can't stop. In all the inner turmoil, I suddenly hear a calming and beautiful voice,

"Look at me." Somma says,

She gently grabs my face and moves it in front of her, her thumb rubbing my cheek seems to have calmed me down a little, but not nearly enough to end what I was dealing with. She says nothing as she smiles as if she knew it would calm me down seeing her smile and looking into her eyes. She pulls my head to her head, putting her forehead against mine. She closes her eyes, it seems like she was absorbing my pain and panic.

"I am here, be calm, I am with you." she says softly.

My breathing finally begins to slow down, she gently lays me down on the sand and lays next to me, putting her arm around my body, holding me tight. Maybe it's not the Heleia Fields that are magical, perhaps it's Somma or some Vespin magic she carries. As I calm down, I feel myself about to pass out, the last thing I hear is Somma sniffling.

I wake up in the middle of the night and feel Somma holding onto me while she sleeps. I try not to move so I don't wake her. I place my arm around her. I have some time to think to myself. The main question going through my mind is, "What is she going to think of me after what we talked about?" Most people are not that great when it comes to stuff like this, Somma has shown she is not like other people, she is better, but I still worry.

Somma and I spent the week together exploring Tanli getting even closer, usually coming back to the Heleia Fields to sleep. Most nights, Somma has nightmares and I can never really sleep anyways, so I'm always there to comfort her. The week comes to a close when Somma and I decide to sleep, once again at the Heleia Fields. As the night goes on, I lay awake, but sadly, Somma is having another rough night. She starts moving around, her head starts shaking, like she is fighting some evil force,

"Clark, no! Please do not go. Come back to me!" she says while asleep, I pull her closer to me,

"I will always come back. Always." I softly say before kissing her head trying to help her go back to sleeping peacefully.

I see her smile, she stops moving around frantically and finally, is back to sleeping peacefully. I can't help but feel like if I never told her about what I did in the past, it would be one less thing to worry her or cause her fear. I finally fall asleep after a few hours, the rest of the night we sleep peacefully in each other's arms.

I feel the sun beat down upon my face and feel Somma rubbing my hair, which admittedly feels relaxing. I slowly open my eyes and see her sitting up, smiling at me,

"Why can't I always wake up and see you?" I ask playfully,

Somma giggles and helps me up,

"How did you sleep?" she asks,

"I slept okay, what about you? It sounded like you had a rough night."

"Oh, yes, it is just another nightmare, I try not to make noise, I am sure it bothers everyone who tries to sleep, I am sorry if I disturbed you."

"Don't apologize, if you don't mind, though," I continued, "I heard you mention my name in your nightmare, what happened?"

Somma slowly stops rubbing my hair, she looks down and sighs,

"It felt so real, more real than usual."

"If you don't want to talk about it, I understand." I respond while holding her hand,

"I guess we all went on some operation. Something

horrible ended up happening where one of us had to stay behind and face certain death. You immediately volunteered to stay behind for us. There was fire and destruction everywhere, I tried to stop you. I begged you to stay, not to go. Even in dreams you are still a hero. I knew you staying would end up killing you, but I still begged you to come back to me. At that point, the dream seemed to stop and all I heard was your voice, 'I'll always come back. Always.' then all the flames faded away, everything faded away. That was when I was finally able to sleep." she says with tears running down her face and her skin starting to shine brighter.

This is what I was worried about. I knew if Somma and I had a relationship, the fear of losing each other would be devastating for both of us. We're happy together, but the fear of losing her weighs heavy. Somma looks into the Heleia Fields,

"I know we are soldiers before anything else, but I wish things were different. The dream made me realize I could lose you at any point, whether it's someone killing you or you sacrificing yourself for us. I know I cannot ask you not to do that, but-" she stops and starts weeping,"but I cannot lose you. Not now, not ever. This war has taken so much from me, but I will not let it take you from me. Maybe I'm being selfish, but I have feared losing you for so long."

I have so much I want to say, but I end up hugging her tightly. I can't promise her I won't do what needs to be done for the squad and the USC, Somma knows that. I can promise I'll do whatever it takes so I won't need to do anything that would take me away, though.

I feel Somma crying as I hold her, knowing I need to comfort her. She is such a kind person, it really is a shame she deals with all this loss and dark thoughts.

"Listen to me," I say while holding her, "sadly, we both know I can't abandon my job, same with you, we're part of a squad with a job to do, but Somma, I promise you I will do whatever it takes so you or I or anyone doesn't have to sacrifice themselves and die, remember, I have your back just as you have my back. I will keep you safe, no matter what."

Somma sniffles and chuckles, after a few moments she giggles,

"I love-"

Our communicators make a static sound interrupting her and we hear Sarge's voice.

"Alright, runts, head back to the outpost, we got some news."

Somma and I look at each other and smile,

"Well, you heard him, 'runt', let's go!" I say playfully,

Somma laughs and starts walking next to me and holds my hand,

"I did not know what a runt was when I first met him, the first time he called us that, I had to research what they were, runts are cute! I thought he was complimenting us."

"No, Sarge doesn't do compliments. Although you are cute, that's for sure." I respond.

Somma playfully hits my arm and laughs. We reach Tanli Village, after walking through it, we pass by the location where I nearly got beaten to death by those thugs, my dried blood is still on the ground. I stop walking and walk towards the blood, Somma looks down in shame and holds my hand tighter.

"I am sorry, Clark."

I let go of her hand and walk towards the blood, I kneel down and gently touch it. Flashes of the beating, the yelling and the sight of my blood pouring out replay in my head. I'm frozen in place, filled with a mixture of fear, anger, anxiety and frustration with those thoughts coming back to me. I feel Somma gently place her hand on my shoulder, she knew I was frozen in panic,

"It'll be okay." she said.

"Everyone is calling me a hero, when all I did was take a beating for a bag of items, no one was brought to justice, the people who stole from Sarsey, the people who beat me to near death, they still run free. Yet, somehow, I'm a hero."

"You stopped people from stealing without hurting anyone, those men will face judgment soon enough, but you stopped them. You did not shoot them, stab them or use your hands, I know you, Clark, even without weapons, you could have fought them all off, but you are better than that. A hero is kind, strong, courageous and brave. You are a hero, and not just to me."

She always knows what to say, never ceases to amaze me. Somma gently pulls on my arm to get me away from the dried blood and continue heading back to the outpost. I slowly stand up and back away, Somma grabs my hand and pulls me further away which seems to break me away from the trance.

On our way through Tanli, we see PVT. Shuua exiting the small structure in the village that Tanli had made their library. I'm not surprised to see her come out of there. She spots Somma and I and waves at us, we wave back, but she looks lower and sees us holding hands, she doesn't say anything, she smiles and heads back to the outpost, we follow behind her. Before we join the other at the outpost, Somma stops and kisses me on the lips and hugs me,

"I could not have spent the week with anyone better. Thank you." she says while holding me tight.

She lets go and we approach everyone else, Sarge walks up to Somma holding his communicator,

"If you could manage to keep your hands off each other, PVT. Juna, your father wishes to speak with you, join us after you're done."

"My father?" Somma asks while tilting her head,

She slowly grabs the communicator and walks away. I should have figured Sarge would somehow be one the first to find out about Somma and I, if PVT. Shuua never saw us, he definitely would have been the first to figure it out. Not that we were hiding anything, but still, he is too smart for us to hide anything. Sarge pats me on the back,

"Funny, isn't it? At first, you wanted nothing to do with this squad, now, you and Ms. Juna are a couple of lovebirds. I don't mind kid, I'm happy for you, just don't let it affect you or the squad."

Sarge's approval means a lot to me, he has always been like a second father to me, to all of us, really. I expected him to get pissed off and force us to end whatever it is we have going on with each other, as horrible as that would be. I approach the rest of the squad, they're all sitting down waiting to hear what Sarge has to say. Ten minutes pass by and Somma is still speaking with GEN. Juna, their conversation doesn't exactly sound pleasant, I can't understand what they're saying in Vespin, but Somma is walking back and forth and shaking her head. The only phrases I'm able to understand are,

"Why?"

"How could you?"

"You cannot do this!"

"This is not right."

After a few more moments, I see her head go down and finally, I hear her say something I don't understand in a defeated tone, she slowly walks to us,

"Hey, are you okay?" I ask while rubbing her back.

Somma nods her head without looking at me. Obviously, I can tell something is wrong, but I knew I would get nowhere if I kept asking. Sarge walks past Somma and grabs the communicator from her hand, she doesn't seem to realize he took it because her hand is still out as if she was still holding it. Sarge looks off into the desert and looks back with a proud smile on his face. It's a devilish grin, but one that fills us with hope rather than fear. I can only expect something truly great seeing Sarge with this much confidence. After pacing around for a few moments with the same grin, muttering to himself, he laughs,

"Ladies and gentlemen, we have our way out of here!"

IN NEED OF SMOKE

It's bittersweet, on one hand, I'm glad we get to leave and finish the job, or at least try to. On the other hand, as strange as it seems, I really will miss Tanli, not because most people here see me as a hero, that's actually one of the things I'm glad to get away from, but in general, the people here are friendly and courteous, Geb is a perfect example of that, and it's beautiful here, too. I'm a little sad to go, maybe when all of this blows over, I'll return.

"That was GEN. Pyren Juna that Ms. Juna was speaking to, he found us a way out of here!" Sarge exclaims.

We all look at each other the same disgusted way. We remember what happened the last time we had an experience with GEN. Juna. Seeing how off Somma has been acting ever since she spoke with him makes me even more skeptical. Blaine raises his hand,

"All due respect and all, but can we really trust this guy? He never supported this squad and has never once treated us with any respect. Why is he all of a sudden trying to help us?"

This is one of the rare moments where we are all wondering the same thing as Blaine.

"Carlston, you forget your place!" Sarge exclaims, "I've known him a long time, yes he can be difficult, but so can I and you can be, too. Besides, he's a General, he puts his own first before any petty squabbles he has. Now, if it is alright with you, may I tell you all the plan?"

Blaine decides to shut up and let Sarge speak.

"Do you all remember when our good friend, Geb, told us he used to live in the city of Vonra before Xenem invaded? Well, as it turns out, we received intel from GEN. Juna that there is a Central Command with an airstrip that has hundreds of ships that are just sitting there. Now, within Vonra, there are Xenem soldiers stationed there, so expect a fight. The fine people of Tanli agreed to help us with this assault if we can get their city back and loosen Xenem control over them, if not completely."

None of us respond, we've all grown tired of messing with Xenem, we're already on their radar as it is, including Leezol. Sarge scoffs,

"What's wrong with you all?" he continued, "Look, I know our run with Xenem has been one-sided, but we need to create some smoke, cause some problems for them so they get distracted and won't notice us slip into their hellhole planet. This is not up for discussion, get your gear ready, we leave in a few hours. Dismissed!"

Everyone slowly gets up to get ready, I gently grab Somma's arm and pull her to the side,

"What's going on? What did your father want?"

Somma grabs my hand and kisses it,

"Do not worry, I will tell you later. I have to get ready." she says while slowly letting go of my hand.

She spoke with less enthusiasm in her voice than usual, so contrary to what she said, I will worry, but like Sarge told me, I shouldn't let anything affect me or the squad and what needs to be done. It's hard for me to not go after her, but I need to get ready, too. Everyone is getting their gear ready for the assault, PVT. Reddina is packing medical equipment, Blaine is packing his explosives, everyone is packing their essentials. I finish packing and start to put on my war paint, it's nothing too crazy or creative, they're just black lines across my cheeks with black paint around my eyes inspired by the Vikings. I look over at Somma and she is slowly wrapping herself up. Being experienced with wrapping herself, she typically finishes up within minutes, but she's taking longer than usual, she is still distracted from what her father said.

The two times I have seen her talk with him ended with

her being upset and hurt, it makes me wish he would stay out of her life, but he told Sarge, Blaine and I that he truly does have loving intentions behind what he does and how he treats her. Still, I wish he wouldn't hurt her so much. Somma stops wrapping herself and sits down and looks off in the distance. I walk up to her and grab her black wraps and sit down in front of her,

"May I help?"

Somma gives a small smile and nods her head. I start wrapping her hands up enough so there is no shine or shimmer showing from her skin, she wears gloves, too, but at times, even that is not enough. After her hands, I begin to put the face mask over her. Before I begin, I stop and put the face mask down, I sigh and kiss her on the lips, hoping that would make her feel better in any way.

"You know I'm always here for you, you can tell me anything." I say, placing my hand on her thigh.

Somma places her hand on mine,

"I am scared. All this is not going to end well."

Somma grabs my hand tight, like she is holding on for dear life,

"We will be okay, we're almost out of this mess. I know we will all make it out together." I respond.

Somma gives a small smile and nods. I finish helping her put the face mask on, only revealing her eyes. She slowly puts her hood on, even completely covered, she looks beautiful. I feel pretty defeated that the attempts I made to make her feel better, even a little, failed. I take the liberty of packing up her things without saying anything, knowing anything I could say that might help would ultimately take me nowhere. It was a silent few minutes, but I eventually finish. I place her bag next to her and walk away without saying a word. As I walk, I feel Somma grab my hand and pull me back, I turn around and see her looking at me with tears in her eyes. I slowly go down to my knee and look at her confused, tilting my head.

"Stay by my side?" she asks.

"Always."

I kiss her hand before walking away as the transport craft arrives. Everyone starts putting their bags and equipment on it, we're using a Ranna, a small transport craft. It's a filthy, almost broken down craft, but it runs and it'll get us to Vonra, according to Sarge. The people of Tanli found it to help us get to Vonra. I grab Somma's bag and put it on the Ranna for her while she finishes getting ready. I head back to my cot to grab my things. Blaine grabs me by the shoulders and shakes me around,

"So, you and Juna, what's going on there?" he asks,

"Not that it's any of your business, but I'm not sure. Do Vespins even know what a girlfriend and boyfriend is? Do they have different phrases and meanings for them? I never asked her, but she and I seem to really like each other, so I don't want to hear anything from you."

"Hey, man, I don't care. Hopefully she doesn't do some Vespis magic on you or something!"

I shove him away as he laughs, I grab my gear and put it on the transport. Geb decides to stay behind and spread the word on what we're trying to do to gather support and lift morale among his people. Before I get on the craft, I help Somma get on and she sits in the back, I get everyone's attention,

"Excuse me, everyone? Before we go, I want to give you all something." I pull out the pouch filled with the arrow necklaces, "The shopkeeper who I helped with the thief was kind enough to give us these necklaces as thanks, they have arrow and feather pendants on them. I felt it would be a nice piece for us to wear as a squad, considering on Earth, and maybe on your home planets, too, arrows and feathers represent direction, purpose, intention, freedom, honor and spirit, among other things. As you may have noticed, PVT. Juna and I already have ours on."

"That's not the only thing we've noticed." Blaine jokes, clearly referring to my relationship with Somma.

I smack his head as I walk past him. Luckily, no one seems to have paid attention to what he said. I hand everyone a necklace. Everyone smiles before thanking me and putting it on.

"Where is mine?" Leezol asks mockingly,

I roll my eyes at him and get seated on the transport. I sit in the back next to Somma,

"You were right, they loved it!" I say to her while holding her hand,

She smiles and lays her head on my shoulder. Things seem a bit better, but something is still off with her. I'm sure she will tell me what's going on in time, sometime after the assualt, hopefully. It's a slow five hour long drive to Vonra, especially in this beat down craft. If everything goes well, this is the last time that most, if not all, of us will be seeing the colored sands. There are still as encapsulating as the first time I saw it.

"I wish we could stay here." Somma says to me quietly.

"I do, too, but once this ends and we have time, we'll come back here."

"This is a bad idea." she says with her skin starting to shine through the wraps.

Her stress is getting too high already and it is concerning me,

"What do you mean? What's going on?"

Somma doesn't respond, she squeezes my hand tighter as she keeps looking at the sand.

"Listen up, runts!" Sarge continues, "Here's what's gonna happen, when we get to Vonra, expect resistance, not too much, though. From what Leezol told me, Xenem uses Vonra for storage for their power cells, ships and equipment with a small number of soldiers guarding them. It sure seems like they can spare a ship, but they probably don't feel the same way, so Leezol will try to get us a ship himself. Assuming the troops in Vonra aren't aware of what went down with Leezol and The Black Guard, they should let him right in and he will tell them he is taking us back to Xenem for questioning. Once they figure out what is really going on, and they will, you better expect trouble, so we're in for a fight. Remember, we need smoke, chaos to leave them blind. Any questions?"

We say nothing, the plan seems pretty clear. Sarge pats Leezol on the back. He stands up, letting Sarge drive while he speaks,

"When we are close, Miner will let me drive this filthy bucket to meet the soldiers, do not worry, I will not expose any of you or the plan, as fun as that would be. At this point, I hate Xenem more than I hate all of you. All those years of service to them and they try to kill me? Fools! Xenem can burn for all I care, so if I can help achieve that, then I can tolerate being with you all for a little longer. When we get there, just shut your mouths and let me do the talking."

He really does have every reason to go against Xenem, I know that this is a temporary alliance, but having someone who knows the ins and outs of Xenem and their military is really helpful and maybe after all this, he will not want to kill us like he used to. All this is taking way too long, I have to remain hopeful my parents are still alive. There hasn't been a single day that I have forgotten about them. Their capture is the main reason I agreed to join the squad.

After a few hours, we get close to Vonra. Sarge stops the craft and let's Leezol take over, before he starts driving, he approaches us,

"All of you, I'm putting cuffs on you. We want to make it seem like you are prisoners, give me your hands."

The squad reluctantly puts their hands forward and lets Leezol cuff them, he approaches Somma, he smiles at her,

"Oh, Ms. Juna," he says in a mocking tone while cuffing her, "We have not spoken much since we first met, a pity. Perhaps we-"

"Leave her alone, keep it moving." I interrupt.

"How sweet, defending your lady, yes, I know about it, too. What a gentleman you have, Ms. Juna." Leezol says while cuffing me.

Somma stares at Leezol with fury in her eyes, I'm sure she hates being cuffed by him, we all hate it. Leezol starts driving the craft towards Vonra, the cuffs make it hard for me to hold Somma's hand, so I play my hand on her thigh, I just want her to know I'm there for her, even in cuffs. She seems to be isolating herself lately, but she has me and the rest of the squad. She places her hand on my hand, a few minutes later, she grabs the face mask on her face and pulls it down. She looks at Vonra ahead of us and looks at me,

"Clark?"

I look at her in confusion. Her skin is still shining bright.

"Why is your mask down?" I ask.

Somma leans in and kisses me on the lips passionately.

"I do not know what exactly is going to happen with me or you or everyone else as we move forward with the plan. I know this might be too soon, but-" she stops and takes a breath, "Clark, I want you to know, well, I *NEED* you to know, I love you." she says with a smile on her face, but tears fill her eyes.

The timing and setting seems strange for sure, telling me she loves me while being cuffed, cuffed by an enemy we have a strange alliance with, and heading towards a Xenem controlled city in a rusted, nearly broken down ship. Even then, it still filled me with surprise and joy to hear her say that. I would've thought I'd need time to say it back to her, but I didn't. Somehow, I just knew I loved her, too.

"I love you, too. Don't worry about the plan, it'll be fine, we're the 'Galaxy's Finest'!" I exclaim.

I kiss her lips and put her face mask back on. I rub her cheek with my thumb the best I can while being cuffed. I look into her eyes before we reach Vonra as it instills me with confidence, but also fear, fear of what may happen if I lose her. I promised to keep her safe and stay by her side, and I plan on doing just that. I'll do anything I can to not just keep her safe, but everyone, even Leezol, as annoying as that is.

"Everyone, shut up!" Leezol demands before approaching Vonra's blockade.

A Xenem guard steps in front of the craft with his hand up to stop us. Leezol slowly brings us to a stop,

"I am CPT. Auldin Leezol, I am bringing these criminals to Xenem for questioning and I need a ship. May I enter?" Leezol asks.

The guard doesn't respond, he slowly walks around the craft and looks at each of us on board. He walks back to Leezol,

"I know these people, these are those 'Galaxy's Finest', yes?"

"Yes, you would not believe how difficult it was to track them down, but most vermin are hard to find."

"Well, very impressive, sir." the guard says as he waves at his men to open the gate.

The gate slowly opens showing a deserted city, it's a horrendous sight. Crumpled down, burnt buildings and structures, dead bodies on the streets, some were burnt, some were shot or worse. Sarge shakes his head,

"Geb was lucky to make it out alive, this is some kind of hell."

The rest of us are at a loss for words, including Leezol, we were in a total wasteland out of a nightmare. Leezol sighs,

"With the explosives Carlston packed, we can set up bombs all over the Central Command base, that is also where the ships will be located. We set the bombs off, cutting the base's communications with Xenem, eliminating their stored equipment and resources and some soldiers, too, but there are hundreds of others stationed around here, so like Miner said, this will not exactly be a simple job. I hope your children know how to fight, Miner."

I close my eyes and take a few deep breaths, in my head I hear Somma's voice, *"You are a hero to us, you may not see it, but you have done so much for me and the rest of us, everything you have taught us, getting us out of trouble and having our backs. My father may not see it or care, but me and everyone else here is blessed to have you lead us, everything feels safer."*

I open my eyes and stand up,

"Alright, listen up! I hope you all remember what SPC. Carlston and I have taught you over our time together. When you shoot, keep your eyes open, stay focused, breathe and do not panic. Always remember, these are not your fellow soldiers in a practice field firing blanks or fake ammo, this is real. These soldiers will kill you if you give them the chance and will not think twice about it, we expect you to treat them with the same generosity. Have each other's backs, help where you can, communicate, stick together and no matter what, fight until the end. We've been in gunfights before, but this will be different, but I know we can make it out of this alive. SSG. Miner selected you all for this squad for a reason, show him why! We're Specter, the 'Galaxy's Finest', we can do this. Remember your training and good luck to you all, are we clear?"

"Yes, sir!" the squad says as a whole.

I sit back down and Somma puts her hand on my thigh, "Our hero."

I can't help but smile at her. After a depressing ride through Vonra, we finally reach Central Command. It's a crummy looking building, gunshot holes in it, and pieces of it have completely fallen off. It's an all around damaged, sad building with a massive satellite on the roof. Leezol quickly hops out of his seat and takes our cuffs off. We all jump out of the craft and grab our bags and equipment, all of our guns and sidearms get strapped on as fast as possible. Leezol is standing by keeping watch, Sarge walks up to him and hands him a spare rife he had,

"Miner, you old fool, you have too much faith in me." Leezol says

"Probably, nonetheless, are you ready?"

Leezol nods and puts the rifle on his back. I also felt a strange urge to do an act of kindness for Leezol, I walk up to him,

"Sarge is crazy, but if he trusts you right now, then so do I, here." I say as I hand him some rounds of ammo.

"You melt my heart!!" he responds sarcastically.

Perhaps sarcasm is his twisted way of showing appreciation. I check on everyone to see if they need anything before the assault. I see PVT. Lane, Mitchell, grabbing his bags, but his protective vest looks twisted and crooked. I approach him and start fixing it for him,

"So, you and PVT. Juna, very nice." he says.

Slowly, everyone seems to be finding out about her and I on their own.

"Thanks, but focus on properly putting on equipment, that crooked vest could have slowed you down, right?"

"Yes, sir."

I pat his shoulder and walk towards my equipment. I kneel down and grab an old photo out of my bag, it's a photo of me and my parents from when I was about 7 years old. My parents always preferred good old fashioned film for photos. The photo is wrinkled and old, but I carry it with me everywhere. I look at the photo for a few more moments, when I see a pair of boots walk up to me,

"They are going be okay, Clark."

I look up and see Somma extending her hand to help me up, I grab her hand and kiss it before getting up. Somma still looks bothered by something, but smiles as I kiss her hand. I wish there was more time for me to find out what's wrong, but we only have a short amount of time to plant the bombs and prepare for the fight. We gather in front of the Central Command building and wait for Sarge to give the green light,

"Everyone ready? Weapons loaded, gear on tight, everything?" he asks.

We all nod with anticipation. I'd be lying if I said I wasn't nervous. Sarge gives us a thumbs up,

"Alright, we can do this, okay? Now go, go, go, go!"

I kick open the door, Blaine and I throw smoke bombs inside. We make our way in, quietly taking out all four guards in the room with our knives. Blaine chuckles,

"Two for each of us, very nice."

"I'm surprised you didn't need any help." I respond while putting my knife away.

We let everyone else know the room is clear, everyone quickly runs in and closes the door.

"PVT. Denza, go to the monitors, tell us what we're dealing with here." Sarge demands.

She runs to the monitors on the desk in the center of the room, taking a look at the cameras.

"Well, this doesn't look fun."

"I wouldn't think otherwise, what's going on?" I ask.

"From what I can tell, there are four levels with 10 rooms each, all filled with guards in the hallways and rooms."

"Sounds fun to me. Alright, squad, to me!" Sarge yells.

We all quickly approach him,

"Listen up, we have 4 floors we need to clear and fast. Leezol, Parson, Dillon and Mitchell- Martin and Reddina, you five clear the first two floors. Shuua, Denza, Juna, the other Martin kid and I, we'll go above you and clear the last two floors. Carlston, you plant the explosives, you pyromaniac. Keep your communicators on and give updates, Is that clear?"

With all of us yelling "Yes, sir!", we begin to head to the lifts up to the next levels. I stay behind and walk next to Somma

"Please be careful, okay?"

"I will, you be careful, too, please?" she says as she holds my hand tight.

Without realizing it, she and I are still holding hands as we enter the lift with everyone. The left begins to go up and Sarge sees us holding hands,

"Well, enjoy that while you can, you're both going to have to let go in a second."

That's what upsets us. We reach the first level and the door slowly opens. My group begins to leave the lift, but when I try to exit with them, Somma holds my arm,

"Come back to me." she says softly,
"Always."

She slowly lets go of me and I get off the lift and look back to see her eyes filling with tears, I quickly smile and blow a kiss to her. I see her smile, but I don't know if Vespins know what blowing a kiss means, I can only hope. My group approaches a corridor filled with soldiers, PVT. Dillon grabs a smoke bomb and throws it in, as soon as the smoke goes off, we all come out and open fire. In typical Specter fashion, our noise causes the soldiers in the rooms to come out and open fire. In this particular situation, it would be impossible to do this quietly. All of us get behind cover, despite us being pinned down, Leezol laughs,

"Well, we are doing better than I thought we would!"

I lean to my left and open fire, taking out a few soldiers, but nearly getting hit myself. Everyone else gets shots in, as well. PVT. Reddina and Dillon have definitely improved with using their guns, I've never seen such accuracy and focus from them, I'm assuming the others in the floor above us are showing improvement, too. I notice that most of the soldiers look pretty young, too young to be here at least, but it doesn't stop Leezol who grabs a grenade from my belt and stands up to throw it. Most of the soldiers stop shooting in shock of seeing their own, the great CPT. Auldin Leezol fighting with us, about to throw a grenade. Leezol throws the grenade, but no one runs away, they are probably still in shock. The grenade explodes taking out multiple troops, the rest of the soldiers start falling back.

"Let's push ahead, we got them running and hiding!" Leezoil exclaims.

It still doesn't feel good having him give orders, but I was already about to give the same order. We get out of hiding and make our way forward, I grab my communicator,

"Specter 2 to all Specter's, the 1st floor is almost clear. How's everyone else doing? Over."

"This is Specter 1. The 3rd floor is almost clear. Over." Sarge

says,

"This is fun, you guys should let me plant explosives more often!" Blaine exclaims.

Admittedly, he does have the most fun job. We hear yelling coming from a room at the end of the hall with the door closed, we approach the door and I use a playful knock, hoping the troops inside will surrender peacefully.

"Open up, please!" I ask playfully.

"Scum! Leave this building and you may live!" we hear from behind the door.

I tried to be nice. I kick down the door and we all aim our guns at the injured and defeated soldiers. They all raise their hands and look at Leezol with confusion,

"CPT. Auldin Leezol? I don't understand, what are you doing?" a young soldier asks,

"Well, to be honest, I have no idea what I am doing, all I know is, Xenem turned their back on me so that means I will stab them in *their* back, starting with this poor excuse for a Central Command."

Leezol starts squeezing the trigger of his gun, but I stop him,

"They've given up, we don't need to kill them, they're just kids!"

"They are Xenem soldiers, they will report this instantly if we let them live. I know them, remember, I used to fight with them?"

The young troops shake their heads in panic, promising they won't report anything.

"Fine, they can go," Leezol turns to the soldiers, "Now, remember this, Xenem will burn, whether you all burn with it is up to you, now go!"

The soldiers run out of the room as I shove Leezol in anger. I should've figured he'd be an issue. I'm worried enough about Somma and the rest of Specter without having to also worry about him killing everyone and everything so needlessly. I get it, he was betrayed by his own, that would piss me off, too, but I figured, as a soldier, he would understand that there's a job to do and killing everyone is not a part of it. I grab my communicator,

"Specter 1 to all Specter's, the 1st level is clear, heading to the 2nd level now, over."

"*You're slow! We are being lifted to the 4th floor as we speak.*" Sarge responds.

Considering we were delayed by a bloodthirsty Leezol, it's understandable why we took longer than we should have. Before we head into the lift, I have us reload and do whatever we need to do before storming the next level. PVT. Dillon reloads his rifle and PVT. Reddina pulls out his canteen and takes a sip of his water. Leezol is standing by the lift door, shaking with anticipation. He clearly isn't feeling any fatigue, it worries me. I really have to watch him like a child and keep him in check so he doesn't go off the rails? It's just another worry for me.

We head in the lift going to the next floor. It's a quick trip upwards, the doors open and it seems like this floor has more guards than the first one. The soldiers open fire on us so fast that we don't even get to really do anything, we immediately jump for cover. Pieces of the walls around us explode near us with every gunshot, it's almost blinding. On my communicator, I hear Sarge,

"*Specter 1 here. The 4th floor is clear, how's the 2nd floor coming along? Over.*"

I grab the communicator,

"We're completely pinned down here, we need backup, now! Over."

"*On our way, hold on! Over.*"

"Should I head up there? Over." Blaine asks,

"*Negative, Specter 3, we're on our way down, keep planting the explosives! Over and out.*"

Somehow, we are managing not to get hit. I peek out to see if I can get a shot or two in, but I end up nearly getting hit. Luckily, I only get grazed. The lift doors open and Sarge's unit comes out, guns blazing, taking out multiple soldiers. Their cover fire allows me and my unit to get out of hiding and finally get some shots in ourselves. The soldiers on the first level were a lot easier to scare into running away, probably because they were mainly kids and young adults, but the soldiers on this level are much older, seasoned and seemingly have no fear, ferociously fighting back with all they have. The good news, just as I thought, everyone has improved with their weapons, it's amazing to see. More and more soldiers go down one by one until there is one left. We cease fire and walk towards him. He stays behind cover, but quickly pops out with his handgun aimed at Somma,

"No!" I yell as I quickly pull out my handgun, shooting his gun out of his hand.

The soldier trips over himself trying to run, Sarge picks him up and slams him against the wall,

"Now, why would you try and do a thing like that?"

"You cannot win, Xenem and all of the Confederacy will rule all!"

"Oh, I can tell you'll be an issue." Sarge says before he headbutts the soldier, causing him to fall unconscious.

"Well, let's go check on Mr. Pyro down below"

After checking all the rooms for any more soldiers, Sarge grabs his communicator,

"Specter 1 to Specter 3, we are all finished up here, how are things looking down there? Over."

"*Specter 3 here. I think we are all set down here, I'm ready when you guys are. Over.*"

"Great, we're on our way down. Over and out."

Sarge begins laughing as he walks away. The group walks towards the lift behind him, but I stay behind and look at the bodies on the floor. It's always a depressing sight to see the result of such a useless war. Somma comes up to me and hugs me.

"I am so happy you are okay! When you said you needed us to come down, I tried to get everyone together to go as fast as possible, I feared you and everyone else wasn't going to make it."

"I told you, you can't get rid of me that easily."

Somma sighs in relief as she lets go. She holds my hand tight as we walk to the lift,

"You and everyone did such a great job, I'm really proud of you all!" I say while swinging her arm back and forth playfully.

"Well, we had a great teacher and-" Somma abruptly stops and looks at the graze on my arm, "Wait, what Is this?"

"It's just a graze from the first level, I hardly felt it."

Somma looks at the graze mark some more and rubs it with her thumb,

"You need to be more careful, my love."

"Well, that's no fun!" I say playfully as we continue walking to the lift.

Somma chuckles,

"Of course, I fall for such a reckless man!"

"You know I always come back, though." I respond as we enter the lift.

Somma smiles at me and rubs my arm. Whether she is still bothered by something like she was before is a mystery to me, it's been on my mind all day, but I'm just glad she is safe. The lift down is pretty quiet, the only noise is the sound of everyone reloading their weapons and adjusting their equipment. The doors open and we walk into the main floor we entered from, we see red blinking lights on every column and wall we see, it's the handiwork of Blaine Carlston. He approaches us with a smug smile on his face,

"What do you think? Do we need more?"

All of these explosives will certainly tear this building down, I just hope we'll be a safe distance away, but still close enough to the ships for a quick getaway. We make our way to the airstrip heading towards the ships. We reach a few ships and seem to be far enough from the building, we all get behind cover,

"So, the bombs go off, then what?" I ask,

Sarge chuckles.

"Well, what happens is we have another fight on our hands, we'll lay down fire for Leezol who will get into a ship and fire it up. Once we are safe inside, we can use these big ol' guns on the ship to wipe out what's left of the soldiers."

"I must say, I am rather impressed by you all." Leezol continued, "Most of you are essentially children, brats, but you all handled yourselves like true soldiers. If there is one thing I respect no matter what, it's those who can get the job done, and so far, you have done that. Very impressive."

"Come on, Leezol, look at them, you're gonna make them cry!" Sarge responds.

Leezol's words oddly mean a lot, to me, at least. We may hate him, but we turned someone who saw us as an incapable team of kids with no order or focus into someone who now sees us as warriors who can get the job done. Blaine takes out the detonator from his bag,

"So," he continued, "who would like to do the honors?"

Sarge looks at the squad,

"We all should, everyone, put your thumb on that big, shiny red button!"

We are all taught to avoid pushing big, red buttons, but I think right now, we can make an exception. We put our thumbs on the button, we all can't help but smile. I realize the job is not done yet, more soldiers will be flooding in after the explosion, but the confidence in the team is soaring.

"Alright, ladies and gentlemen, are we ready?" Sarge asks.

We nod our heads.

"Okay on three- for Geb, for Tanli and all of Kana. Three...Two...One!"

We all press down on the button and within an instant, the building gets demolished, swallowed by flames reaching high up in the clouds. I almost wish we had a camera to replay the explosion in slow-motion. Despite the debris falling down everywhere, we can't look away. I tend to not care or focus on destruction as a result of war and fighting, but I have to admit, this felt good, for all of us. Good riddance.

THE GREAT ESCAPE

The sound of the explosion is deafening. The Central Command in Vonra has been a symbol of everlasting darkness and oppression to the people of Tanli for a long time, it feels great helping them take steps towards being free and possibly allies to the USC. The celebration does not last long, though. We hear yelling from a distance and vehicles approaching. We quickly get back behind our cover, Sarge pushes Leezol towards the ships,

"Get on a ship, don't be picky, we're getting out of here!"

Soldiers begin flooding the airstrip, yelling and questioning what happened. Not long after, they see Leezol making his way into a ship and start opening fire. After a few moments, we return fire.

"They have taken away my clearance!" Leezol exclaims, "I am going to have to break in, just keep covering me!" Leezol yells.

I fire a few shots out of my cover, I'm lucky enough to get one soldier before quickly being forced back into cover. I look to my right and see Somma behind cover shaking and trying to replace her ammo clip. Her skin is piercing through her covers, she looks completely lost out here, but to be fair, we all do. While trembling, she drops her clip on the ground which bounces outside of her cover. She sighs and begins to reach for it. I decide to do something foolish or heroic, maybe both, and stop her as she slowly tries to grab the clip.

"Stay down." I say while pulling her back.

"Carlston! Get over there and cover Parson!" Sarge yells.

Blaine makes his way to us and starts firing multiple shots, giving me just enough time to jump out and grab her clip, but as I try to make my way back, I hear a single gunshot and before I know it, I am hit.

I hit the floor, if I had to guess, I would say we are also dealing with a sniper. Blaine and PVT. Shuua quickly make their way to me and drag me behind cover. Sarge goes to me,

"Oh, damn, your thigh! Reddina, we need medical assistance now!"

PVT. Reddina hurries his way to me and sees the wound in my left thigh, he starts getting self-healing bandages out of his bag. As the name implies, they are bandages one puts on a wound and the wrap starts applying fast healing gels and medicine to the area, it's a quick way to start healing a wound if one isn't able to access any standard medicine. It's a very underappreciated advancement in technology.

"It will be okay, sir. I will get you wrapped up." he says.

PVT. Reddina has always been the unofficial medic of the squad. Typically, we all carry medical equipment, but he is usually the first one who steps up when medical attention is needed. I'm down on the ground in pain, he is busy working on my leg and Somma is frozen, looking at me in shock and horror, so it has become seven against hundreds. Somma crawls to me, I hand her the ammo clips that was still in my hand,

"You have to be more careful, Ms. Juna." I try to say as calmly and as playfully I can, despite me being in a mass amount of pain.

She slowly grabs the clip and shakes her head,

"This is all my fault. I am sorry," she continues while shaking her head, "I am so sorry, it should have been me-"

"I'll be okay," I interupt, "put the clip in your gun and focus. Don't focus on me, focus on the people attacking us."

Somma nods her head and quickly hugs me tight,

"My hero." she whispers.

Somma quickly returns to cover. I'm starting to get the sense that being a hero tends to hurt like hell. PVT. Reddina finishes wrapping my thigh and helps me get behind more cover before he returns to his position. He did a solid job, it's a tight wrap, good amount of pressure on the wound. Most people as young as him wouldn't have done such a good job and stayed as calm as he did. As time goes on, I really see the potential Sarge saw in him, in everyone for that matter.

Finally, Leezol breaks into a ship and opens the hatch, he runs in and tries to start the ship. We hear him call us on our communicators,

"I made it into a ship, but I still have to get it up and running, it will take me a few minutes, just keep shooting!"

I feel useless laying behind cover while everyone is fighting. Next to me, I see a small space and I begin to wonder, can the barrel of Sarge's old sniper rifle fit through it? It's the same rifle he used to stop Leezol and his men when we first met. I call to Sarge and he looks at me, I point at his rifle on his back. He smiles as he figures out what I am trying to do,

"Good thinking, kid! Careful with her, she may be old, but she still has some kick." he says while handing me the rifle.

I reposition myself the best I can without hurting my leg further. It takes some doing, but I am able to make the barrel of the gun work its way through the space and still be able to move it around and look through the scope. I haven't used a sniper in a while, I'll probably be a little rusty, but I'm sure it's like riding a bicycle, it just takes a few minutes for it to come back to me.

I look through the scope, you can see it has definitely tell it's been through a lot by the rust and scratch marks alone. All the advancements in weaponry over the years, yet Sarge decides to use a rifle that has been in his family for centuries, it's a miracle it's still functional. Much to Sarge's dismay, he did have to update it a bit to use against the Confederacy's more advanced armor and technology. From what I heard, back when the war started, he had to get the fire power upgraded to match the power of what everyone else was using. He was stubborn and didn't want a single thing changed, but if he wanted to use it, he knew it needed to be done. The engineers on Vespis were able to keep the gun looking the same, but still upgrade the mechanics inside the gun, it's been so long that Sarge doesn't even remember that being done.

Through the scope, I try to spot the sniper who shot my leg. I have no idea where it came from, though. I see the white flash of a scope come from the tower on the left and go after it. I rush the process, trying to finish off the sniper quickly. My first shot to the sniper misses, Sarge was right, this really does have some kick. My missed shot ends up alerting the sniper and making my job harder now. I exhale in frustration and reload the round. I look back into the scope and look for him again. He pokes his head out slowly, I close my eyes and inhale, holding my breath. With the crosshairs on his head, I exhale and squeeze the trigger, killing the sniper. It's lucky there isn't much wind at all, or else that would have made my job even more frustrating. I look back into the scope and am alarmed to count three more flashes up in the other towers, another one on the left then one in towers on the right and center. I have no idea if I killed the one who shot my leg or not. I reload and go to work taking out the rest of them. Luckily, after the first soldier, using Sarge's sniper became easier for me. Using the same method, I hit the sniper in the middle tower in the chest, then move to the right. I spotted him instantly and was able to hit him in the head. A shot I must say I am proud of. I move to the left tower, this one was harder to find, though.

The flashes have completely disappeared. I keep looking and find no one, but seemingly out of nowhere, someone picks me up and throws me across the ground. PVT. Dillon and Denza look and try to attack him, but I hold my hand up,

"No! Keep firing, I can handle this!"

They reluctantly return to their position. Being thrown and landing on my thigh was not ideal, but with the help of adrenaline, I was able to barely stand back up, but it was all too easy for the soldier to tackle me. If I had to guess, this is the soldier who I assume was the sniper who not only escaped my sight, but also was the one to hit me in the thigh. After tackling me, he starts punching me in the ribs and face, I gain enough strength to push him off me and start attacking him. I crawl over to him and do my best to get up and drop my elbow on his chest and start hitting him in the face, but not for long. He overpowers me and now is back to beating me while I'm down. After what seems like a thousand punches to the face, he wraps his hands around my throat and starts choking me.

It's a painful mix of being tired, shot, and beaten that causes me to not be able to get him off of me. Everything starts going black for me, I begin to hear Somma's voice in my head, all I hear are her pleas, begging me to stay, to not go anywhere. If the last thing I hear in my head is her voice, I would not complain. Life slowly begins to fade from me, when I hear a voice yell,

"No!"

Somma tackles the soldier. I gasp for air, I try to look at what's going on, but my vision is blurry. All I hear are hits being landed and both of them grunting. I shake my head trying to clear my vision, when everything becomes a bit clearer, I look to my right and see the soldier on top of Somma with what looks like a knife in his hand. As I crawl to them, I rub my eyes to see more clearly and I was right, it's a knife. I try to get up and run to them, but I immediately collapse to the ground. I look up and see the knife go into Somma's left side. She lets out a pained, agonizing cry as the knife enters her body and her silver and red blood pours out like a flowing river.

"No! No!" I cry.

Fueled by pure rage and adrenaline, I grab a piece of sharp debris from the explosion of the Central Command building, a broken piece of a pipe with a sharp pointed end to be specific. I get up with all the strength and adrenaline I have and charge at the soldier. I tackle him off of her, getting on top of him and driving the broken pipe into his chest, he lets out a scream in pain, but something dark and vengeful comes over me. I begin stabbing him over and over again in the chest, yelling in anger and frustration each time I drive the pipe into his chest. Each stab filled with more hate and bloodlust than the last. I start to blackout, I can't hear or see anything other than the green blood of the soldier going all over my face, hands and clothes. Everything goes black, until I feel someone pick me up and drag me away. I can tell by the lack of care with how I am being dragged away it's Blaine. From what I can make out, he takes me into a ship and lays me down on the floor and wipes the blood out of my eyes with a rag before walking away.

I feel my heart beating out of my chest, to my left I see someone else get laid down next to me, I reach my hand out trying to find out who it is.

"Clark, I am sorry." Somma says weakly, as she grabs my hand with the little strength she has.

I was truly hoping I was just hallucinating or imagining Somma being stabbed. I figured the blood loss and pain was making me see things, but I don't think that's the case.

"Somma, no." I respond with my voice breaking,

I slowly crawl and lay my head on her chest and place my arm over her. Everything begins to become too much for me, I feel tears running down my face as I lay with Somma, from what I can tell, she is crying too.

"I'm sorry, I was supposed to keep you safe, I'm sorry-I'm so sorry." I say, with my face soaked with tears, feeling her weakening heartbeat.

She is too weak to say anything, but I feel her gently place her hand on my head. Sadly, not even that stops me from crying. What a disaster this became. I see a pair of boots stand next to us, it's PVT. Reddina,

"Excuse me, CPL. Parson? I need to tend to PVT. Juna."

"It's my fault, it's all my fault, I let this happen." I respond in a crying, bloody mess.

"Sir, I need to tend to her wounds then I will go to you."

"I'm sorry. I'm so sorry"

I hear Sarge sigh,

"Carlston, Dillon, get him away." he says with a defeated tone in his voice.

The two of them gently pick me up and lay me back

down next to her, I look over to see her, her eyes are closed and she is barely moving, I see her slowly reach her hand to me, but Blaine and Bradley put me too far from her, she is just out of reach. I see PVT. Reddina place down the ship's medical box on the ground next to Somma, he opens it and starts pulling out various medical tools and equipment, but before I see him do anything, my eyes start to close, soon enough, I pass out.

When I wake back up, I slowly sit up and look around. We are currently in the ship flying back to Tanli with Leezol driving the ship. It's quiet, I look to my side and see Somma laying down with her face uncovered, sleeping. I slowly make my way to her and gently rub her cheek with my thumb. It's bittersweet for me, I can see she is breathing and alive, but I remember what happened and how it happened.

"Let her rest, son."

I look up and it's Sarge extending his hand to me, I grab his hand and he helps me up, my legs wobble a bit as I stand up, but Sarge holds on to me so I don't fall.

"How do you feel?"

"I'm sorry, sir."

"Kid, I asked 'How do you feel?'"

"I'm okay, sir. Thank you," I continued, "how is everyone else?"

Sarge shrugs,

"Bumps and bruises, but we're alright, Ms. Juna received a nasty stab wound, but Reddina was able to patch her up and tend to your thigh some more, make sure to thank him, he stayed with you both for a while in case anything went wrong. We're almost back in Tanli, so do what you need to do."

I nod my head, I walk back to Somma who is still resting. I slowly take my arrow and feather necklace off and open her hand, I put the necklace in her hand and close it before kissing her hand. Using the help of a nearby seat, I stand up and look at everyone else. Blaine is asleep and everyone else is silent, I limp my way towards them. They all smile at me as I approach them. PVT. Shuua stands up to offer me her seat, but I put my hand up and shake my head,

"That's not necessary, thank you." I say before I pull up a seat next to them and sit down,

"SSG. Miner won't say this, not yet, at least, but we are extremely proud of you all."

Their faces light up, as if they have been waiting to hear those words for a long time.

"I saw you all fight," I continued, "compared to where we started, you all have improved to levels beyond what we thought was possible. You were focused, kept your eyes open and shot with a level of precision and accuracy that many soldiers that share the same rank as you don't even possess yet. You had each other's backs and helped where you could, we worked as a team and those Xenem troops got a small glimpse of what the *REAL* Specter looks like and how we operate. Great job, all of you. You all have earned my admiration and respect. I'm sure SSG. Miner will tell you the same things soon enough, but I will make sure to tell him what I saw today. We're near Tanli, so get ready."

They thank me and smile at each other, I turn to PVT. Reddina,

"May I speak with you for a moment?" I ask,

He gets up out of his seat and helps me out of my chair, he puts my arm around him and walks me to another area of the ship. We stop when we reach the back of the ship, he moves my arm off of him and he looks at me,

"Yes, sir?"

I sigh and immediately hug him.

"Thank you, not just for tending to me but to PVT. Juna as well, I'm sure that stab wound was rough and hard to deal with, but you came through for me and her and the rest of your squad. She means more to me than you realize, if you couldn't tell, she and I are in a relationship and I can't let something like this happen, but I messed up. Luckily, you worked your magic, and she is okay, so thank you, if you ever need a favor from me, you got it. Thank you, *Carden*."

He is noticeably shocked, but soon enough, he slowly hugs me back.

"Thank you, sir. It was no problem at all." he continued as the hug ends, "Also, I did know about you and PVT. Juna"

"Well, I appreciate that you didn't ask me about it or say anything."

"It was none of my business, sir."

I smile and pat his shoulder,

"We're landing soon, get ready."

Carden and Kierra were the only two to not mention my relationship with Somma, like Carden, I'm sure Kierra knew it wasn't her business or concern. They were smart enough to know better. I limp my way to Leezol driving the ship, we're flying over the colored sands, the view is incredible, seeing the sands from up above is a whole other experience. Leezol look behind him,

"Oh, look, it is the brave, possibly foolish, CPL. Parson. I see your leg is still in rough shape, I for one suggested we amputate your leg, but I was outvoted. Oh, well, there's always next time."

I scoff and walk back to Somma, I grab a cloth and pour some water from my cantine on it. I carefully sit down on the floor next to her and dab her forehead with it. A few minutes pass, when her eyes slowly open. She sees me and smiles,

"'Why can I not always wake up and see you?'" she asks softly while grabbing my hand.

I kiss her cheek, she smiles while slowly closing her eyes, I let her rest because quite frankly, she needs it after what happened. I don't think I'll ever get the image of her being stabbed out of my head. I don't even know what happened afterwards, obviously we all made it out, but how? I passed out then woke up in the ship flying.

"Hey, Sarge, how did we make it out of Vonra?" I ask.

"Oh, after we got you and Juna on the ship, the rest of us hurried onto the ship, Leezol got the ship up and running and shot everyone in sight. Typical, Leezol, no survivors, that's the

Xenem blood in him! After there was no one left, we flew away and slowly made our way back. We can't go fast, we don't want to attract attention, so that takes us to now. Quite a day!"

I find it completely believable that Leezol left no survivors, this ship must have been like a toy or game to him. We finally reach Tanli, Leezol lands right outside the village, where a crowd of people are cheering and awaiting us. The ship's door opens and we hear a roar from the crowd, as we walk out of the ship, the villagers approach us, hugging and patting us on the backs and arms. The squad and I form a path through the villagers so we can move Somma to a safe location. I make my way back inside the ship and slowly pick up Somma. I limp out holding her, the crowd goes silent as they see her in my arms. They all stare at me and her as I walk through the crowd. We walk to the outpost we stayed at with Geb, I gently place her down on a cot and cover her with blankets.

We are all resting at the outpost when after a while, we hear footsteps run up to us,

"My friends! You have done it," Geb exclaims, "I heard you returned, but I needed to see it for myself!"

Geb walks to each of us and gives us a hug, except Leezol, he knew better not to try to hug him, but instead bowed his head to him in appreciation. Geb looks at my thigh,

"No, Clark! What happened?"

"I'm okay. It was a sniper, he did a number on PVT. Juna and I."

"Somma, too?" he asks while looking for her, he looks around and sees her laying down on a cot. He runs to her and takes a look at her.

"What happened?"

"She saved my life, one of the soldiers attacked me by surprise, nearly killed me, until Somma stopped him, but got stabbed in the side doing so."

"Vespins are truly one of a kind. Well, my friend, you rest, I will take care of her!"

I pat Geb on the back and head to a cot nearby so I can

keep an eye on Somma. I trust Geb will take good care of her, but I don't want to leave her side. All things considered, we all feel pretty happy. For so long we were so fixated on taking out Xenem, we became so focused that we forgot what Specter was made for, quietly and secretly **infiltrate the Chelorian Confederacy Systems and take out their leaders, factories, bases, everything** and end the war. We haven't ended anything, yet, but we are closer to doing so, thanks to the fall of Xenem controlled Vonra. There's still so much to do after we finally hit Xenem, but it's nice to get one step closer to completing that task.

It was a long, painful, stressful day for all of us so we all have an early night. Geb stays by Somma's side all night and lets me rest. I wanted to stay by her side, but Geb insisted I need to sleep. I wake up in the morning around the same time as everyone else. I get up and limp to a barrel with water in it nearby. I wash my face and wash off my war paint since I was too tired and worn out to even think about it last night. After the paint is off, I lean over the barrel and close my eyes, taking deep breaths, trying to not focus on everything that happened, but I can't get it out of my mind.

After a few deep breaths, my eyes stay shut, until I feel something get placed around my neck. I open my eyes and look down. I see a silver arrow and feather hanging off of a brown Leather cord around my neck. I grab the pendants with a confused expression on my face, I turn around and see Somma standing behind me smiling with her hands behind her back. I am overcome with joy, I quickly wrap her in a hug, not squeezing too tight, though. I don't want to hurt her side, but that doesn't stop her from holding me tight. I was optimistic she was going to survive, but at times, things really did seem bleak. A stab to the side could be fatal, I feared the worst when it all happened.

Somma giggles, while hugging me, I never want to let go. I'm filled with so many different emotions, but mainly relieved. I eventually let go and help her sit down on a chair near us, I pull up a chair and sit in front of her,

"How do you feel?"

"My side is sore, but I am okay. I am glad everything else went well, though!"

I smile and nod while looking down, Somma slowly reaches for my face and lifts it up to see the cuts and bruises on it.

"I am relieved you are okay. I do not want you to get hurt. Not again." she says,

The smile fades away from my face, I lower my head and nod in response. I don't have a response. She is right, my recklessness not only caused me to get hurt, but Somma, too. She isn't too bothered by it, though. She picks my face up again and kisses my cheek multiple times,

"Where is that handsome smile?" she playfully asks while rubbing my cheek with her thumb.

That "handsome" smile disappeared for a long time while she was out, I think I'm still in shock that she is okay and not mad at me. I eventually give in and give her what she wants, I smile, but it's a forced smile and she could tell.

"I am okay, my love. I am safe, everything is okay." she says,

Every time I look at her, all I see are flashes of her getting stabbed. She says she is okay, but that sight haunts me. Without even realizing, a few tears run down my face,

"Somma, I am so sorry, it's all my fault." I say as tears fall down my face. "I wasn't paying attention to my surroundings and I ended up getting in that mess with that soldier. I never wanted you to get hurt, too. I'm sorry."

Somma, who is still rubbing my cheek, wipes my tears,

"I love you, Clark, you know I would do anything to keep you safe, just like you would do the same for me, but my love for you was not the only reason I did it. You told us to watch out for each other, even if it was not you being attacked by that soldier, I still would have taken action and ended up getting stabbed. I truly wish it was not you who was attacked," tears start running down her face, "it is an absolutely horrible sight, seeing someone you love nearly get their life choked out of them. I tried looking for you behind the cover, but when you were not there, I got worried and started looking around. I looked behind me and I saw you, the man I love, my hero, being choked and no matter how hard you tried to fight, that soldier kept going, I had to get in the way. Yes, getting stabbed hurt, but if it keeps you safe, I would get stabbed every day."

Funny how she calls me a hero, her hero, when she has truly saved my life. While I wish she never got hurt, I am grateful to be alive and forever grateful for her. There are no words I could say that would show how grateful I am for her and how much she means to me, so I do the next best thing, I gently pull her close and kiss her on the lips.

"I love you, thank you." I whisper to her while hugging her,

"I love you, too, I will always keep you safe, remember that."

We hear footsteps walk up to us,

"If you two can manage to stop hugging and being annoying, Miner wants us all to meet him by the fire." Leezol says.

I help Somma up out of her chair and we walk to the fire where we meet everyone else. Miner walks in front of all of us while clapping,

"Well done, everyone. You all showed those Xenem dogs what a problem Specter can be, as well as how badly they screwed up by turning on old Leezol! Unfortunately, it didn't all go without any slip ups or injuries, we all got scratches, bruises, and even shot and stabbed. Either way, we all came out alive and the people of Tanli owe you all their thanks."

We all look at each other and smile, even Leezol gives a little smirk. Somma grabs my hand and smiles at me, despite the injuries we sustained, we are happy with how we did.

"Now, before you all run off, our good friend, Mr. Tawin, wishes to say something." Sarge says before stepping out of the way.

Geb walks in front of us all and bows his head,

"My friends, you have done a wonderful thing. Because of you, my people can return to Vonra and begin to rebuild, hopefully with the help of the Coalition. I cannot speak for the rest of Kana, but as far as Tanli Village and Vonra are concerned, you will always have a home and ally with us! Oh! I nearly forgot!" Geb pulls out a pouch and opens it, taking out necklaces, "During your mission, I finished working on something special for you all."

The necklaces have a thin, brown rope with a piece of rainbow Noli on it, but it's carved into the shape of what looks like a raven skull.

"I started working on these after Clark told us about Ravens, I made one for each of you and polished them myself!"

He begins handing each of us a necklace, they're incredible. He nailed the way a Raven skull looks, all the right curves and details, a long beak with a thin line carved into where the mouth is, hollow eyes, not to mention the smooth, polished pieces of Noli he used are beautiful. They're all different colors, each piece looking more magical than the last.

"A beautiful blue flash for Clark! On Kana, blue represents bravery and respect and you, my friend, are certainly brave and present ever lasting respect and kindness!" he says as he hands me a necklace, "For Somma, a pink flash. Pink represents kindness and compassion, very fitting for you, my dear! Now, Blaine, orange flash, for power and strength, perfect for a towering man such as yourself! Kierra and Carden, you two are so alike, so smart, so creative, I hope you do not mind that both of yours share the same color. Red flash for intelligence and creativity. The Martin twins! You both do not say much, but whenever we spoke, you both were respectful and kind, once again, your two pieces will also share the same color, green flash for the calm and collected. Bradley, you are a very confident young man. From what I heard from your squad, you used to be entitled and filled with a large ego, but over time have turned into a brave soldier. You have a yellow piece for change and growth. Rachel, being who you truly are can be hard, there's a fire in you, a fire that pushes you to not change for anyone, you get a purple flash, for grounding and perseverance. Now, you all carry a piece of Kana and protection from the gods, it is the least I can do for you all."

We are left speechless, we all look at our necklaces in amazement. but Geb isn't done yet. He slowly walks up to Leezol,

"We did not have the greatest friendship when you first arrived, but I feel that, just like Bradley, you have grown, so you also have a yellow flash Noli."

Leezol slowly grabs the necklace and looks at it then looks at Geb,

"Thank you, Geb, it is a very kind gift."

Geb bows his head and lets Sarge come back to finish what he was saying before. Sarge walks up in front of us all, but Geb holds up his finger,

"Not yet, Richard, I did not forget about you!" Geb pulls out one more necklace, "A white flash for you. I know I said the white flash is more dangerous, but it is customary for the chief or leader of a group or tribe to adorn the white flash Noli, I didn't mention this when I first taught you all about Noli pieces with a white flash, but it symbolizes their connection to the power and leadership of the gods. Richard, you lead a strong and kind team and I could not think of a man more deserving to carry the white flash with safety and protection like you, my friend. I did my best to drain most of the energy while keeping the white flash, so it should not be too dangerous. I still ask that you be cautious with it, my friend!"

Sarge grabs the necklace and laughs,

"I hope this doesn't blow up on me!" he continued, "Thank you Geb, you and your friends here can always count on us if you need help in the future."

Geb smiles before walking away. We all put on the necklace, now wearing one with a silver arrow and feather pendant and another with a piece of rainbow Noli carved into the shape of a raven skull. I like it. A random design with both items pops into my head, I grab a nearby stick and start drawing in the dirt an arrow with a single feather hanging off of it and a Raven skull crossed together. It's not the best drawing, but I can make out what it is, I really like it. Sarge walks up to me,

"That's good, I was thinking we need a logo, maybe this could be it. Like you said, arrow for purpose, ravens for wisdom and feather for spirit. Purpose, spirit and wisdom, what a combination! What do you think, kid?"

"I love it, sir."

"Great, I'll speak with the others and ask them what they think. How do you feel, by the way?"

"Still limping and sore, but I'll be okay."

"Well, I'm waiting for GEN. Juna to give us an update on when we can attack Xenem, if all goes well, the USC may help us. Xenem already knows about us, so it's not like we are much of a secret to them anymore, so the USC may agree to help us fight their blockade. Still no word from him yet, so you and the rest of the squad can take a break until then. Dismissed."

I have been waiting for Xenem for months now, we are so close to finishing this job and I can't wait. I guess for now, I just need to rest. From a relaxed and relieved feeling, I randomly start feeling light headed and my thigh starts to really bother me, I limp my way to a chair and collapse onto it. My hands shaking, I move my wrap and see that my wound has seemingly gotten worse. I have no idea what it is, but black surrounds the wound. I've never seen anything like it. Bradley walks past me and notices it,

"What the hell? Reddina, get over here!"

Carden runs over with a confused expression, he sees me in the chair sweating and pale.

"What is the matter -" he says as he sees the wound, "Oh, no, what is that? I'll grab the others, stay there, sir!"

It's not like I can go anywhere even if I wanted to.

Bradley looks around,

"I'll go get something that might help."

I didn't want this to be a whole scene with everyone involved, but at this point, I don't even care. I hear Somma's voice behind me from a distance,

"Where are you taking me? What is going on?"

Bradley is quickly pulling her by the arm towards me. He gets Somma in front of me.

"Clark, what is wrong?"

"Hey there, Ms. Juna." I say weakly with a faint smile, trying my best not to worry her.

Despite my best efforts to make it seem like everything is okay, I think it had the opposite effect. I don't think Somma was happy to see me looking like death. Although, Bradley was right, seeing Somma did help, but I start to doze off and lose focus. Somma gently puts her hands on my face to try to get me to focus on her,

"Clark, look at me. What is going on?" she asks before I slowly move my wrap to show her the wound.

She gasps after seeing it, covering her mouth.

"Reddina looked at it already," Bradley continued, "he has no idea what it is, he's getting everyone to see if they can help."

Somma sighs and shakes her head,

"Please get him some water, I will stay with him." she says while sitting down next to me.

She holds my hand tight as Bradley runs off to get water.

"Recently, it seems we never have a moment of peace, my love." she says.

I give a soft chuckle because she is right, it's one thing after another.

"We live exciting lives, don't we?" I say to her weakly.

She chuckles and kisses my cheek. Being by her side almost makes me forget that there is a black mass in my thigh, the pain gets worse, but luckily, everyone else has arrived, including Bradley with a cup of water.

"What the hell?" Sarge exclaims as he walks up to me.

Everyone's face is in shock and disbelief, we've never seen anything like this before. Leezol pushes everyone aside and takes a look.

"Oh, no."

"What is it?" I ask,

"This wound, you were hit by a Kenva rifle. They shoot rounds that poison people from the inside, creating a black mark around the wound. Only the Black Guard use these rounds, fitting for their name."

"Well, what can we do?"

"I do not know," he continued, "I do not know if any medical equipment can stop the spread, no matter how good. The bullet can be taken out, but the poison stays. I'd say, we need to amputate it."

"Not funny."

Leezol looks down and shakes his head,

"Parson, I was not joking."

CELEBRATION OF HEROES

Leg amputation, fun. That was something I never thought I'd have to deal with when going into this war. Maybe, it's the shock of it all, but I don't have much of a reaction to what Leezol said. Everyone else starts yelling at him,

"No, there has to be another way!-"

"We can figure something out!-"

"Do not say that!"

"Enough!" Kierra interjects, "I have an idea, Vespin blood has healing properties, I have read cases of their blood being used to cure the most hopeless and bloody wounds for other people who are not even from Vespis. If all that is true, PVT. Juna may be able to save his leg."

We all look at Somma, she nods her head,

"It is true, we do not do it often, but it works. I never understood how it worked exactly, but I think it can help him."

Magical blood, I always thought it was just a legend. If Somma doesn't understand how it works, then it must really be a mystery. Even with the legend confirmed to be true, I remain skeptical. Carden steps forward and takes a closer look at the wound.

"Even if this does work, he needs a lot of blood. PVT. Juna has already lost a massive amount of blood from being stabbed, she has not even fully healed yet. The little blood she has is slowly healing her, but it is not enough to let her give any extra to others, not yet at least. This could kill her." he says while fixing the bandage, hoping it will do something to stop or slow the spread, even a little.

The options, at the moment, are either I lose my leg

or Somma gives more blood than she has and probably dies. There has to be other options. Carden and Kierra are some of the smartest people I have ever met. Surely they can think of something.

"Absolutely not, we are not risking her life. Take my leg!" I demand.

Somma sighs and looks at me with tears in her eyes,

"Is it okay if I have a moment alone with him?" she asks everyone.

Everyone slowly walks away, talking amongst themselves about what to do.

Somma and I and sit together in silence, her hand gripping my hand tight. After a few moments, she turns to me,

"I will do it."

"No, we are not risking your life. I can't lose you, we can't lose you."

"Let me do this, my love, I am the reason you were shot, let me save you."

"You already saved me and you paid the price, I can't let you be in more danger, they can take my leg."

Somma looks down and wipes her tears, she gets up and kisses my cheek then walks away. I'm left sitting alone thinking about what a mess all this is. Obviously, I appreciate Somma's willingness to help me, but I can't let her risk dying. Not for me or anyone else here. If losing a leg keeps her safe. I'll gladly do it. Besides, prosthetics will make it seem like nothing ever happened. Carden walks up to me,

"So, what are you going to do?"

"Are you able to amputate my leg?" I ask, knowing it's a near impossible task for a Private, but he's the best shot I have at the moment.

"I will need some help, but I think I can, sir."

"Get everything you need, I want to get this done today."

Carden nods his head and walks off. I usually wouldn't be so hasty to amputate my leg, but I fear the longer we wait, the more it will spread. I don't know where Somma went, but if she needs to be alone, I understand, I just hope she understands that I can't risk losing her. It wasn't guaranteed she would die, but if there's even a small chance of it happening, I'm still not taking the risk. Geb slowly walks up to me,

"I heard how you got that wound protecting Somma, it seems you have a desire to help others no matter the cost, even if it means you getting hurt in the process." he says while escalating my leg.

"I just don't want anyone to get hurt. It's a small price to pay."

"A price nonetheless. We all admire your bravery, Clark, but Somma truly loves you and wants to help, it is beautiful, really. I spoke with her just now and she would not stop crying, she wants to save you. Do not think of it as someone saving your leg or your life, you have a team willing to do what it takes to help you just like how you help them. I wish you luck, my friend, may the gods protect you."

I grab the Noli necklace he made for me and look at it. I didn't get a chance to actually look at the colors, it really is something. We didn't ask for a reward to take out Vonra. Life threatening injuries aside, it felt good taking out Xenem's rule over Kana, the reward was weakening their hold on not just them, but the rest of the galaxy, even if it is a little, it makes our job moving forward easier.

I wish I could go find Somma, but I don't think I'm in any state to be walking around. I don't know if she's mad at me or thinks I'm an idiot, to be honest, she wouldn't be wrong. Either way, I am sticking with my decision, I have faith in Carden and whoever he gets to help him. I wonder how my parents will react to seeing me with a prosthetic leg, not too thrilled I'd imagine. Like me, in time, they'll get used to it.

I sit by myself staring off into the desert for about an hour and a half, as boring as that seems, it was pretty peaceful, despite the pain. Carden walks up to me holding a bag filled with everything he needs with Kierra and Leezol of all people following behind him. Kierra I understand, she's brilliant, but Leezol? Carden puts down the bag,

"Ready when you are, sir?"

"Bringing PVT. Shuua was smart, but Leezol? Why?"

"He understands the poison and what it does better than us, we could use his assistance on where it has spread or where it is going because I am unsure of where exactly I need to cut. Also, he kept demanding we bring him, it got frustrating, we thought he found it funny and wanted to watch, but he started mentioning how he can actually help, it made sense to include him, I hope it is alright."

I nod my head and ask them to help me to the makeshift operating table away from the others so they don't have to see anything. On the ship flying back to Tanli, Leezol made a joke telling me he voted for my leg to be amputated, perhaps he was not joking, it looked like he was making the right call in hindsight. I lay down on the table and everyone starts setting up equipment. We still use Anesthesia and all the old-fashioned tools for knocking me out, I am sure Leezol would rather just hit me across the head, though. Carden grabs the mask to put over my face, he reaches to put it on but stops,

"Oh, PVT. Juna wanted us to tell you she loves you."

"Thank you, now, let's get this over with." I respond while shutting my eyes.

Carden puts the mask on me and turns on the gas, I slowly start passing out. Before I go unconscious, I think about Somma, which calms me down, but within seconds I'm out like light. During my sleep, I saw a mixture of images. My parents, Somma, the squad, the Heleai Fields, the stars, I have no idea if some of those images mean anything, but it was comforting. I hear something that I've been hearing for a while now, "*Come back to me.*" in Somma's voice. I wish she was here, having her in my arms as she sleeps always keeps me calm and has even helped me sleep many times. I hope she's doing okay.

I slowly open my eyes to what I assume was a successful surgery. It's silent, the only sound I hear are the howling winds of the desert. I prepare myself to look down and see a missing leg, but something feels off. I look down and see I still have both legs, confused, I sit up and see the wound, it's practically fully healed and the black that surrounded it is completely gone. This feels like a dream, I have no idea what's going on.

I feel something in my hand and open it, it's the arrow and feather necklace. My vision is blurry, but I can feel the shape of it and everything. If I had to guess, it's Somma's. I gave her my necklace when she was unconscious and it seems she was returning the favor. I bring the necklace closer to me, after closely looking at it and smiling, I see a tube hanging off my arm connected to a needle in my vein. I'm still a little disoriented to see clearly, but I follow the tube to a clear bag on a metal rack. I rub my eyes and see the bag is filled with a liquid silver and red like substance being put into my body. Then it hits me, that's Somma's blood.

I'm filled with a range of emotions, confusion, anger, fear, frustration among other things. I begin to fear the worst, the idea of Somma being dead after donating what little blood she had left to keep her alive and heal her wound causes me to freak out on the table. I start sweating and panicking, holding her necklace to my lips with my eyes closed, trying to hold back tears. Fear completely takes over, pain filled tears fall down my face, I kiss the pendants on the necklace,

"Come back to me." I say with my voice breaking.

I feel someone gently touch my cheek,

"Always." a calming voice responds.

I open my eyes and see Somma standing in front of me smiling, her face fully unwrapped and shimmering. I go back to thinking I am dreaming again for a moment, but this is definitely real. I have no idea what to do or say, I'm frozen sitting on the table looking at Somma with a shocked and confused expression on my face. Somma starts giggling and wraps me in a tight hug, it snaps me out of my shocked trance, I immediately hug her back.

I let go and look at her wound, it's still healing but looks a lot better, a part of me wants to be mad that she risked dying for me again, despite me telling her I don't want that, but seeing her standing in front of me alive and well, still able to give blood makes me put that anger to the side. That being said, I am still confused about how it all happened.

"It's good to see you up, kid." Sarge says.

Somma helps me off the table, still holding onto me around my body, I laugh in disbelief,

"What happened?"

Sarge chuckles,

"That's a long story, the squad wants to say hi to you, come with me and we'll tell you."

"Just one moment, sir."

I turn to Somma passionately kiss her on the lips, as if I haven't seen her in years, it feels that way, at least. I put her arrow and feather necklace back on her, then turn to Sarge,

"Now we can go, sir."

Sarge laughs and leads us to everyone else. I really thought I lost her, it was scary, but I should've known. People always tell me Vespins are strong. Everyone is together by a fire talking, they all see me at the same time and run up to me to say hi. They all shake my hand, except Leezol who bows his head at me. I sit down with everyone, I'm next to Somma who's holding onto my hand and it doesn't seem like either of us wanted to let go.

"So, what happened? I went in thinking I would wake up with one less leg, but clearly that didn't happen." I say, still in disbelief.

"Well, when I was gathering my things," Carden continued, "PVT. Juna came up to me, telling me I cannot go through with the amputation and begged me to extract her blood, I had no idea what to do."

Leezol steps forward,

"That is where I came in. Parson, hunting you all for so long, I learned a lot about all of you. For instance, Vespin's do have healing blood and they can be put inside others to heal them, but Vespin's do not need all Vespin blood in their veins to stay alive. Really, any type of blood can be put in them and still work its magic. Granted, your blood has no healing properties, but it still flows through and keeps the girl alive. Once I told Reddina and Shuua all this, we devised a way to extract your blood and safely put it inside Juna's bloodstream while also being able to take her blood and put it inside your bloodstream, thus saving Juna's life and your leg. So, to put it plainly, you both share each other's blood. Juna was so grateful, she even smiled at me a little, that is when I knew things were off."

"And, is this completely safe? For both of us?" I ask

Leezol nods his head,

"It is safe, Juna was afraid you would be mad, but I told her, I have never seen you get mad or yell at her, it confuses me. I do not understand how you can do that with her."

It's brilliant, I was sure there was no way around either me losing my leg or us losing Somma.

"Thank you. Thank you all, I don't know what else to say, all the support and work, it all helped. You guys did an amazing job." I tell everyone while pulling Somma closer to me.

Geb told me I have a team who's willing to do whatever it takes to help me. I was blinded by panic and fear to see that he was right, I was a fool. Leezol telling Carden and Kierra that information is shocking, for so long he wanted to kill us all, but now helped save Somma and I. Geb steps forward, asking for everyone's attention,

"Excuse me, my friends? As you know, all of us in Tanli, and probably all of Kana, are grateful for what you have done ever since you arrived here. From Clark stopping that thief and the rest of you helping around the village where you can, always showing us kindness, respect and appreciation, and of course, freeing Vonra. You have all earned our admiration and respect, but also our eternal friendship. No amount of Noli jewelry or praise will ever be enough to pay you back for your sacrifices, but we are having a celebration in the village tonight and we would be honored if you all came. There will be music and dancing and art and so much more!"

Sarge looks at all of us, we nod at him and he looks back at Geb,

"Your people don't need to celebrate or thank us, but we will gladly attend, thank you."

"Excellent, I will bring you all traditional Tanli ceremonial clothing for the event!"

As Geb walks away to run his errands for the event, everyone gets up and goes their separate ways. Somma and I say seated by the fire, Somma is still holding onto my hand, but I see no issue with that.

"So, a celebration," I continued, "that's fun."

"It is!" she responds, "I have not been to any events like that since before the war. We would have parties and celebrations all the time in Felv, it was always so much fun to go with my father. He would go off and talk to his friends from the military while I went off to dance and talk with others. Did you ever do anything like that when you were younger?"

"Well, in High School, we had dances with music, food, and different activities. I never really went, though."

"Why is that?"

"I wasn't a social kid, I hated big gatherings and still do, also, no one ever asked me to go with them, but that doesn't matter now. Tonight should be fun for you guys."

Somma frowns then quickly smiles, she gets up from next to me, facing me and smiles while holding both of my hands,

"Clark Parson, my hero, man of my dreams, Hero of Tanli, will you go to the dance with me?"

I must admit, I'm still as quiet, shy and antisocial as I was when I was a kid. So, when Somma asked me to go with her with such majesty and grandeur, I felt shy. All I could do is smile like a fool and nod my head, but Somma shook her head, she wouldn't take it,

"Well, I need a yes or a no, my love!"

Trying to top her wonderful question, I slowly kneel

160

down on the ground, doing my best Prince Charming pose. Despite the pain it put me in to kneel, it was worth it seeing her smile,

"Somma Juna, the girl I love, my Jewel, my beautiful Diamond Queen of Vespis, my savior and hero, I will be honored to take you to the dance!"

Somma giggles and wraps me in a classic big Somma hug. Earlier she mentioned how she and I can never have a moment of peace, to an extent, she is right, so moments like this, we have to cherish. Somma lets go and takes a look at my wound,

"I have never given blood before.

"I really do appreciate it, thank you."

"I am sorry for going behind your back and talking to Carden, I thought you would be mad, but I did not want you to lose your leg."

"If I knew, you could have given blood and be safe, I never would have fought you on it, it seemed it was either your death or me losing a leg. Your life means more than my leg."

"So, you are not mad?"

"Everyone said you cried, that's my fault, so the only person I am truly mad at is myself, so if anything. I'm sorry."

"My blood is in you and your blood is in me, we carry a piece of each other now. To me, that is true love and I am happy to share a piece of me with someone I love, but if you are truly sorry," Somma smiled with a playful grin, "I suppose you can make it up to me by wearing something extra fancy for the celebration tonight!"

"Ms. Juna, you are cruel, but you have a deal!"

I get up off the ground and help Somma up,

"I guess I need to go get some things for my outfit tonight."

"Yes, I hope you do not disappoint, I want to see my handsome Prince of Tanli!" Somma jokes before kissing my cheek and walking away to get ready for the party.

She wants something fancy, and Geb is already bringing

us ceremonial outfits, so I decide to go to the markets and pick up a few things for my special outfit. Once I reach the Tanli shops, the people there greet me and thank me for what Specter did for them. I already see some decorations were put up, so far it looks great, very festive. The first piece of my majestic outfit will be a wig, I'll look ridiculous, but that's the point. I enter a dress store and upon entering, I immediately see a shelf filled with wigs. It's hard to find one I like because I hate them all, but again, that's the point. I pick out a big white wig with a ponytail on it with a red ribbon, it looks the least ridiculous on me, so I decide to go with the ponytail wig. Afterwards, I find a pair of white gloves to match the wig. I approach the shopkeeper in shame and embarrassment, the shopkeeper looks at me and laughs,

"I am sure you will look wonderful!"

I smile and nod my head while pulling out the coins Geb gave us all,

"No, I will not take that, Geb Tawin told us about you and your team. We can return to Vonra soon, you have done enough."

I bow my head and put down a few coins on the counter for the shopkeeper. Now that I have gloves and a wig, I'll need other over-the-top items. I stop at a small shop that sells random items, I spot a black cane with a silver ball handle on it, I actually like it. I point to the cane and the shopkeeper grabs it and bring it to me,

"You can have it, thank you for everything, my friend."

It's hard to find any faults or problems with free stuff, but I can't keep taking things for free from these people, they barely get by as it is. Just like what I did with the last store with the wig, I put down a few coins for the shopkeeper and bow my head. This time, the shopkeeper accepts the coins. So, I have a wig, gloves and a cane, paired with the ceremonial outfit, I think I will definitely be the most stylish man at the event.

I return to the outpost and see an outfit on a cot near my things, I pick up the outfit and it's ceremonial for sure. It's a long tail coat that's navy blue with a gold swirl pattern on the sleeves, torso and back with a pair of pants that are white with blue swirl patterns on each leg, the same pattern as the sleeves. I wonder if my outfit is the only one that's so extravagant, or if everyone has a similar outfit.

The sun begins to set as I reluctantly put on the outfit. The suit itself looks pretty good on me, but putting on the wig and gloves with the cane takes it to another level, I don't even recognize myself. Blaine walks past me and starts laughing uncontrollably, which I knew would happen. Luckily, everyone's outfits do look similar. The same suits as me with white shoes for the men. Sleeveless dresses, white leather strap sandals and a white ribbon to put their hair up in a bun or a ponytail for the women. I haven't seen Somma yet, but everyone else looks great. Each of us has a swirl pattern, it looks like our outfits are the same color of our Noli stones. Carden and Kierra wear red, Blaine in orange, the Martin twins in green, Rachel in Purple, Bradley and Leezol in yellow and Sarge in white. Most of us have never dressed so formal before, Sarge even combed his hair. Leezol walks past me and also laughs, but I laugh back at him, seeing a bloodthirsty former Xenem captain wearing a bright yellow outfit is something you just don't see. Leezol grunts and quickly walks away, I'll never get that image out of my head.

It's time for us to go, I go to get Somma and when I see her, I am completely flustered. No wraps on her anywhere, her sparkling hair is straight and in a ponytail with pieces of her hair down by her face. Her dress is the same style as Kierra's and Rachel's, sleeveless with a swirl pattern, but her dress is pink. She is absolutely stunning.

"Good evening, my lady, may I escort you to the ceremony?" I ask while bowing and extending my hand to her.

Somma turns around and sees me, within a second she starts laughing,

"A handsome prince all to myself!" she exclaimed as she takes my hand

"What do you think? Am I forgiven?"

"Hmm, not yet! I need a magical night with my prince first!"

You'd think I'd be mad that I'm not able to take off the wig yet, but Somma is having so much fun with it that I decide to tough it out, it's the least I could do after all she has done for me. Geb walks up to us to take us to the ceremony, he's wearing an old gray suit with tears in it, it looks like he has had it for years and it's been through a lot.

"You all look wonderful!" Geb continued, "Clark, you look like royalty, very good! Are you all ready? I will walk you there."

Walking with Somma, being with someone so beautiful, I can't help but wonder how did I get so lucky? As we continue to follow Geb, we link our arms together like in Fairy Tales, I'm really trying to sell this whole Prince look. Geb fixes his suit as he walks,

"Apologies for the suit, I've had it with me for years and cannot seem to throw it away."

"No problem, Geb," Sarge responds, "we didn't expect others to dress up for us, it's not necessary."

"Of course we dress up, it is a celebration! Now, we are almost there."

After a few minutes, we are back in the center of Tanli Village. It looks completely different, almost unrecognizable. There are colorful decorations everywhere, torches have been lit all over the village, there's a banner that reads *"Layen!"*, there's even a place for dancing and a stage where local village musicians are playing music on interesting looking instruments I have never seen before, but they sound great. Geb sees us trying to read the banner, he laughs,

"Yes, that means 'Thank you!' You will be hearing that a lot tonight." he says as we walk through Tanli.

People begin to cheer as we make our way through the village. Back on Nesturu, people would call me a "Killer" or "Murderer" and all sorts of names, going from that to being called a "Hero" is overwhelming. I never have been crazy about being called a Hero for killing others, but it still is much appreciated. Geb leads us to their stage as the band finishes their song. Geb walks on stage in front of the musicians and raises his hands to get everyone's attention,

"Excuse me, my friends? We are here to celebrate the incredible, brave men and women from all over the galaxies who have risked their lives for us. We were all skeptical when they first arrived, but I think I speak for all of us when I say we are blessed and grateful to have met them and given them a home because now, *we* have a home to return to!" Geb continued as the crowd cheers, "Their bravery, strength, intelligence, and kindness has inspired us all and I am happy to call them friends. Once we return to Vonra and rebuild it back to the once glorious capital city it once was, I know we will do our best to find a loyal, kind leader. A leader who shall have Kana join the United Starlight Coalition, forming a strong alliance, thanks to these incredible warriors. I would like to bring up their wonderful leader," he points at Sarge, "SSG. Richard Miner! Do not worry, I will translate."

Geb steps back as Sarge reluctantly walks on stage, the crowd cheers as he thinks of what to say.

"Well, this is all too much!" Sarge continues as Geb translates, "Thank you, thank you all. All of you have been thanking us all week, but we should be thanking you. When we first got here, we were hurt, beaten and tired, and understandably, you were all skeptical of us, but I am happy that my team and I were able to prove ourselves to you all. We live dangerous, hard lives. As many of you know, two of us got wounded during our assault on Vonra, but they both have survived and are here tonight. We don't get to enjoy celebrations or hear such kind words so often, so on behalf of my squad and myself, thank you all for everything and I hope you all enjoy the party!"

The crowd cheers as Sarge signals us to join him on stage. We all walk up next to Sarge in front of the crowd and hear them cheer, we all smile and bow our heads at them, I do hear laughing, I assume that is for me.

After a few moments of standing on stage, we decide to walk off and join the celebration. The band starts playing a slow melody, people start slow dancing on their makeshift dance floor. Everyone in the squad is being approached by villagers to thank them, except me. I step away to the side, away from the crowd and watch people dance to the music, I still have pretty bad social anxiety. Large crowds are hard for me, but it's nice seeing everyone have so much fun. I look at Somma smiling and laughing as everyone thanks her, her beauty never ceases to amaze me. It's supposed to be a fun celebration, but my heart starts racing from the crowds. I'd hate to ruin everyone's time, staying away from everyone seems the best way for me to still be at the party without being surrounded, so I walk away. I hate to be rude, but all this just isn't me.

I turn around while walking away, everyone seems to be having a good time, it makes me smile as I take a seat at a nearby bench. I have no problem sitting away from the crowd and watching, but after a few minutes I feel my heart beating faster and faster again. I stand up and lean on a nearby wooden post, placing my hand on my heart and feeling my heart racing. I quickly turn to face away from the party, looking at the desert sunset, it calms me down a bit.

"There you are, my love!"

I turn around and see Somma smiling and walking towards me with the wind blowing through her shimmering hair, I smile at her, but she can tell something is wrong,

"What is wrong?" she asks,

"It's nothing, I-" I stop and shrug my shoulders.

I didn't know what to say. I'm someone who has social anxiety and can't seem to function at parties with someone who has been to thousands of parties and ceremonies and loves them. How do I say I can't celebrate with her and everyone else without making her upset?

"Do you not like the party?" she asks while rubbing my arm,

"I like it, it looks great and everyone is so kind, I just-" I stop myself again and look down.

Somma takes my hand,

"We can go, if you want, I am sure they will be okay if we go for a little."

"It's okay, don't let me ruin your night, I'll be okay over here."

"I wanted a magical night with my Prince," she continues as she fixes my wig, "I cannot do that if my Prince is not there. We can go anywhere, as long as you are with me, I will be happy."

I smile and walk with her away from the party. We don't go far, we stop a little outside of the village, near the Heleia Fields, but we can still hear music. Things are a lot calmer for me now, but I see Somma looking at the party and moving her shoulders to the music. It's a slow tune, very melodic, I like it. It's been playing for a while now, but I'm not complaining. I fix my wig and adjust my outfit before stepping in front of Somma,

"May I have this dance, miss?" I ask while bowing and extending my hand again,

Somma giggles while nodding and takes my hand.

"I must admit, I don't know how to dance." I say as we get close together,

"It is okay, my love, I will teach you."

Somma grabs my left hand and places it on her hip, she places her right hand on my arm and with her left hand, she grabs my right hand,

"Now, just listen to the music and follow the rhythm, I will lead." she says while pulling me in closer.

Somma takes a step to the left and I do my best to follow her. I nearly trip over myself, but I stay up.

"Geb told me this piece of music is called 'Flower in Rain'. I love it, it is very beautiful!" Somma exclaims.

I smile and nod, I love it too. Somma takes a step to the right and I follow a lot better this time. Somma gives a mischievous smile and takes a step back, I tumble over a bit, but recover before I fall. Somma laughs,

"I am sorry, that was mean!" she continued while taking off my wig and fixing my hair, which I'm sure looks like a sweaty mess, "So handsome. You are doing great! We will go slower, though."

We go back to moving left to right slowly. I am keeping up with her the best I can and it feels nice. A wave of confidence hits me and I twirl Somma with my right hand, once she holds onto me again as we continue dancing, she looks at me with a shocked expression,

"What was that? Have you known how to dance this whole time, Mr. Parson?"

I shake my head and smile, Somma goes on her toes and kisses my lips. She puts her head against my chest as we continue to dance. I hear her sigh,

"I wish I had met you before all this. We could have danced every day."

"It doesn't matter where, when or how we met, I consider myself lucky to have met you in general. I promise, after all this, I will be happy to dance with you every day."

Somma smiles and passionately kisses me on the lips. We continue dancing for a little while longer, but I see something approaching Tanli, it's a ship. As it gets closer, I recognize the ship's colors, it's Xenem. Before I could say anything, the ship fires at Tanli and we hear an explosion. Somma and I quickly let go of each other and run towards Tanli. As we enter the village, we see some of the squad helping everyone leave the village, the only people who weren't there getting people out was Sarge, Blaine and Leezol.

"We got some uninvited guests!" Bradley yells as we run past him.

The village has been lit on fire and there are Xenem soldiers everywhere that are being dropped from ships above us. We find the others fighting the Xenem soldiers, Somma quickly removes her sandals and rips the bottom of her dress to give her legs more room to move. We run to their side and start fighting with them, a soldier runs up to me, but I am able to use his momentum against him and take him to the ground as I knock him out with a few punches to the face. To no surprise, Somma is handling herself perfectly fine, even in a dress, attacking the soldiers legs to get them lower so she could fully take them down.

"What the hell is going on?" I ask Sarge,

"We were dancing when all of a sudden, we got hit with a damn missile, it's Xenem, no doubt getting revenge for us taking down Vonra, such scum! Keep fighting, we can't let them destroy Tanli!"

The soldiers keep coming, but we are handling them well enough, until a ship gets closer and shines a light on us. The light is blinding, I look away and see a few soldiers grab Somma and start pulling her into a nearby ship. We see the soldiers take her and try to run for her, but the airborne ship fires a missile at us and blows us away. I hear Somma struggle,

"No! Let go of me!"

With all my energy, I look up as I crawl towards her, Somma is using all of her strength and energy to fight off the soldiers. Her hair has come out of its ponytail due to her intense struggle as her skin starts shining brighter to a near blinding light appearance, she looks over at me as our eyes meet one last time before a soldier quickly covers her with a blanket. Even the blanket doesn't fully dampen her light, but it works well enough for the soldiers to see. I try to get up, but the blast was too much for me. I collapse onto the ground. I weakly lift my head up, the last thing I see before it all goes black, is Somma trying to push the soldiers off of her, but with no success. She gets pulled into a ship that quickly takes off and flies away.

TAKE TWO

"*Recently, it seems we never have a moment of peace, my love.*" is the first thing I hear in my head as I wake up. Somma was not wrong at all when she told me that. Waking up from the blast, it looks like I'm somewhere completely different. Buildings and structures are burnt down, bodies on the floor, some of them are Xenem soldiers, the others are men, women and children. Innocent villagers. It was foolish to think that attacking Vonra wouldn't cause Xenem to seek revenge. We exposed our location by doing so, and now Tanli paid the price and Somma is gone. I slowly get up and take off my bloodied white gloves and coat. I see Somma's white ribbon on the ground, I pick it up and put it in my pocket as I look around more and see the squad helping the surviving villagers. Sarge brings them cups of water while everyone else is cleaning up the mess and bringing the survivors blankets. I hear Leezol behind me muttering something.

"Are you okay?" I ask.

"I suppose, I can't say the same for everyone else. We pissed Xenem off, hitting Vonra caught their attention. I am assuming they figured who else would create such chaos for them, certainly not some poor villagers. Remember, Parson, Xenem knows about Specter, I was just the first to find you all."

I hate it when he's right. The good news is Xenem didn't try to take back Vonra, they did this purely for revenge, so the surviving members of Tanli still have a home to go back to. Why did they take Somma, though? They didn't try to take anyone else, so what do they want with her? Either way, I'm sure they're taking her back to Xenem, probably where my parents are, so this rescue mission just got more difficult and a lot more personal. My agreement with Sarge was he helps me get my parents back and hit Xenem in exchange for me joining the squad. I've held up my end of the deal, now is the time to hit Xenem. I walk up to Sarge who's still helping the villagers,

"Sir, they took-"

"I know," he interrupts, "I have no clue why. I just know her father is going to be furious, but he'll be more likely to give us the green light to head to Xenem and give us assistance through the blockade. Help these villagers, I'll contact him."

Sarge storms off and grabs his communicator. I turn to the villagers, they look completely defeated and in pain. I roll up my blood and dirt covered sleeves as I grab a bucket of water. I quickly bring it to them, some of them have empty cups and I refill them. They nod their heads in appreciation, but don't say anything. The people here are usually talkative, but this attack has taken a lot from them. I meet with the rest of the squad who are still in the village helping. I walk up to Carden who is wrapping villagers with bandages to heal their burn wounds.

"How is everyone?" I ask,

"Almost everyone needs medical attention, but they are lacking supplies, especially after the attack."

"I'm sure the Central Command in Vonra had medical supplies. We could have taken them and given them to these people, but instead, we blew it up. What were we thinking?"

"We wanted to get in and get out quickly, but I understand what you are saying. Either way, Xenem still would have attacked Tanli. It was only a matter of time"

Carden is right and there is no point in dwelling on the past, what's done is done, as frustrating as it is. I leave Carden and try to find Sarge to see if he spoke with GEN. Juna. He already disapproved of Somma being a part of Specter, her being taken will just make him feel stronger about it. Not to mention, I'm dating his daughter and he doesn't even like me, which is an entirely different issue that I will still need to deal with. I doubt he'll kill me.

Sarge is standing outside of Tanli Village staring off into the desert, he finds it peaceful, like me. He turns around and sees me walking towards him.

"Well, he isn't thrilled that his daughter was taken." he says,

"I'm not thrilled either, so what's the plan?"

"Luckily, the timing is on our side. GEN. Juna was waiting for clearance to aid us in reaching Xenem and he finally got the green light to help us. Gear up, son. Xenem awaits."

Sarge grabs his communicator, switching to our channel,

"Specter 1, calling all Specters, report to the outpost."

Sarge and I walk back to the outpost where we meet everyone. They all stand at attention once they see Sarge. Leezol shoves Carden and Mitchell aside and approaches him

"What are we doing, Miner? Are we burning down Xenem?"

"We sure are, my old friend!" Sarge exclaims,

Leezol and everyone else looks shocked, they weren't expecting Sarge to be thinking the same thing as Leezol, that never happens. Sarge walks past Leezol and approaches the rest of the squad.

"Listen up, GEN. Juna has given us the go ahead to attack Xenem, but this time, he and the USC will help us get through the blockade. Xenem's attack last night was cowardly and by taking PVT. Juna, they went too far. So, it's time we say goodbye to Tanli and finish what we started. Get loaded up, we leave in an hour. Dismissed!"

We begin to walk way, when Geb, who looks beaten and exhausted, runs in front of us to stop us,

"Wait! Tanli Village and myself want you all to know, we do not blame this attack on any of you. We still appreciate you all, which is why me and some friends in Tanli made something for your squad, it's on your uniforms. We hope you like it. Now, go save the galaxy and come back soon!" he says before bowing his head and walking away, he stops and turns back to us, "One more thing I wish to say. Before you all go, I feel it's time you all know the truth, especially Richard and CPT, Leezol."

We all look at Leezol and Sarge, they walk towards Geb with confused expressions.

"I was hoping you both would notice sooner." Geb says,

Sarge and Leezol look even more confused,

"I suppose I do look different compared to the last time you both saw me-"

"Wait-" Sarge interrupts and looks closer at Geb with Leezol.

"It cannot be-" Leezol continued, "Ben?"

Geb, or I guess I should say Ben, gives a small smile and nods his head. I've only heard Sarge and Leezol mention someone named Ben a couple times. I guessed he was an old friend who died a long time ago, but if he is that same Ben, then this is truly shocking, more so for Sarge and Leezol.

"Geb Tawin, it's an anagram. It's really you. Ben Gawti, I don't believe it!" Sarge exclaims as he hugs Ben, "Where have you been? What happened to your leg? Did you really lose it in a mining accident?"

"Well," Ben continued as he sits down, "it was no accident. Back when the war started, Auldin and I were flying back to our homes after leaving a meeting with Chancellor Tyro. He had tried to recruit me to join his ranks, but I refused. He wanted you too, Richard, but he had told us you refused him. Auldin was the only one who agreed to join. On our way home, we noticed Xenem ships following us. They did not know Auldin was on board with me and fired at us. We did not react fast enough and they took us down. We made our way into Kana and crashed to the ground, the ship caught on fire. I tried to get up, but my leg was trapped under a piece of the ship. I asked Auldin for help, but what did you say, Auldin?"

Leezol shakes his head in shame,

"'You chose the wrong side.'" he quietly responds.

"That is right, that is the last he said to me before leaving me to die. He did not leave unharmed, as you can see, the fire and destruction burnt his face. I consider it a form of punishment, some form of justice. In such a dire situation, the only choice I had was to either die or cut off my leg and escape. That day I found out, if I was to break down Auldin Leezol, I would find all dirt, no value."

Sarge's face goes pale, he turns to Leezol, who gently touches his burn, remembering that day.

"You told me Ben died in an accident. You left him to die! You damn coward!" Sarge yells as he punches Leezol in the face.

Leezol falls to the ground and stays there shaking his head in disbelief.

"Ben, I am truly sorry, what I did was wrong, I have regretted my actions ever since then. It killed me to leave you like that!

"Just like it killed me to watch you leave." Ben responds

From the moment we met Leezol, he was evil, we all wanted to kill him, so hearing this doesn't surprise us at all. Early on in our time at Tanli, Sarge noticed many things about "Geb" that were similar to his old friend. I figure Ben was waiting for them to catch on and I'm sure he didn't want to wait all this time. I wonder if he recognized them right away, though.

"What did you do after you escaped the crash?" Rachel asks,

"My leg was off, so I had to bandage it myself to try to stop the bleeding as much as I could. After that ordeal, I had to crawl for miles to the nearest village. The people there were kind enough to give me a place to rest and they even wrapped my leg properly. This of course was Tanli, this was not long after Xenem took control of Vonra. Tanli was still new. I decided to make Tanli my home and stay away from the war, the people welcomed me and I have been here ever since. I never thought I would see my old friends again, until you all showed up. I recognized them immediately, it is part of the reason I offered to help." he turns to Sarge and Leezool, "Richard, you are still the same as you were when I met you and Auldin, you are still a bitter, cruel man, but like I said when I gave you the piece of Noli, you have changed and grown into someone better, a somewhat respectable person."

We're all shocked, but no more than Sarge and Leezol. I could see they were working towards being friends again, but hearing what Leezol did to Ben might have ended those chances. Sarge still looks perplexed,

"Why didn't you try to find me?" he asks.

"If I told you what happened, you would have been furious and done something foolish. You always acted too quickly without rational thought."

"You're damn right. I would've burnt Xenem to the ground years ago!"

"Exactly, you would have gotten killed. This was the best option."

We all collectively wanted to weigh in and possibly deescalate the situation, but we know better than to not get in the way of Sarge when he's mad. Luckily, he brings his focus back on the mission.

"Alright, enough! Ben I'm thrilled you're okay, but we don't have time to get into more details. Leezol, get up and get packed, GEN. Juna is waiting for us outside of the Xenem blockade."

After a couple moments of awkward silence, we all thank Ben for the gifts and kindness he has shown us over time before we go to put on our gear. Our uniforms are on our cot's, I pick mine up and see something stitched on the left sleeve. I grab the sleeve to take a look, it's a sewn black and white patch with a raven skull and an arrow with a feather hanging off of it crossed over each other making an X shape, on top it says "Specter ", at the bottom it has our motto, "Unseen. Unheard. Unbreakable."

I love it, something I did that started as some sketch in

dirt is now our logo, I'm truly honored. How will the rest of the USC feel about it? I'm not too sure nor do I care right now. I put on the uniform, my warpaint and wrap Somma's white ribbon around my right wrist. My bag is packed, I put Somma's uniform with the new patch inside to give to her when we break her out. I'm the first one that finishes getting ready, I'm eager to get going and finish this mess. Half an hour later, everyone is ready. We all grab our bags and head towards the ship we stole from Vonra. There are villagers that await us by the ship, we walk past them as they bow their heads and say thank you. We bow our heads back at them as we enter the ship, we stop at the entrance and wave goodbye to everyone, we owe a lot to these people, we appreciate them as much as they appreciate us, we'll miss them.

Leezol gets in the pilot seat and Sarge sits in the co-pilot seat,

"Don't abandon us, Leezol." Sarge says with malice and distrust in his voice.

Sarge has every right to be mad and not trust Leezol after what we found out, but he needs to put all that aside for now. Leezol starts the ship and takes off, leaving the atmosphere. It's pretty quiet, Sarge and Leezol say nothing to each other, they don't say anything to the rest of us. I roll up my right sleeve and look at Somma's white ribbon wrapped around my wrist and think back to last night. One of the last things we did before she taken was dance, well, she danced, I followed like a fawn learning to walk. I was never a fan of dancing, but when it was with her, I could've done it for hours.

If Sarge isn't going to rally us together, then I will. I'm not in the right mood or mindset to be giving a speech either, but someone has to. I reluctantly stand up and go in front of the squad,

"Alright, listen up. I know we're all feeling down, that attack on Tanli took us all by surprise and we did what we could to save everyone. Don't let that deter you all, they did it because they are scared. They took PVT. Juna, our friend, a member of this squad and we are going to get her back then, we will tear down Xenem and if we are lucky, finally get rid of Valkis Tyro once and for all. This will be a crushing blow to the Confederacy and get us one step closer to ending the war. We can do this, we are one person down, but we treat this the same as any other operation. Getting in will be loud and dangerous, but once we get through the blockade, we breach Xenem's capital unseen and unheard, is that clear?"

After a not so convincing "Yes, sir." from the squad, I sit back down. It wasn't my best speech, but my head is all over the place. It's an hour long flight to Xenem without using hyper-speed to avoid detection. Once we arrive, there is nothing there, no blockade, no patrolling ships and no GEN. Juna with the USC. All of us immediately think something is off. Sarge grabs his communicator,

"This is SSG. Richard Miner calling for GEN. Pyren Juna. We have reached Xenem, but there is no blockade, it's empty out here. Where is everyone? Over."

"This is GEN. Juna, we received new intel that Xenem has gotten rid of their blockade. If I had to guess, they were spread too thin all over the galaxy and sent their pilots and soldiers to help elsewhere. You are clear to proceed with extreme caution. Over and out."

Even with GEN. Juna giving us a reason why there is no blockade, something still feels off.

"That does not make sense." Leezol says,

"I agree," Sarge responds, "this is still a clear entry into Xenem, probably the only one we will ever have so, like he said, proceed with extreme caution."

Leezol waits a moment before reluctantly beginning his descent. Entering Xenem, we are met with thick green and black clouds filled with green lighting flashes all around, nearly striking us, it's impossible to see anything, but Leezol stays focused and makes it out. All the stories we were told of this place are true, it's a nightmare here. Nothing but destroyed buildings, military camps, outposts, prisons, factories and of course a black and green tower in the center of the capital city, Kitexa. It's massive, surrounded by a river that appears to be turned red, green and many other colors. I can't imagine all the horrors that went down by that river with all that blood. If I had to guess, Tyro is at the top of the tower, and my parents and Somma are being held in the prison right next to it. Air defenses spot us and take aim, but after a moment, they disengage, worrying us even more.

Worried, Leezol speeds up and we quickly land a mile away from the prison by the tower. Prisoners and hostages get out first, then we burn Xenem to the ground, starting with Tyro and Kitexa. We all grab our gear and run off the ship, I put on my old coat over my uniform with the mindset that it will provide extra padding of some sort. I run out with everyone else, we can breathe outside, but barely. The air is thick with ash and smoke from the factories, burning buildings and bodies. We make our way to the prison and huddle by the entrance,

"Okay, just like Vonra, Parson and Carlston will enter first and clear the room, then we follow behind, got it?" Sarge asks us.

We nod our heads, Blaine and I make our way to the door. He goes to the left side of the door and I go to the right. Before we enter, we nod at each other. We kick the doors open, but it's an empty room. No guards or soldiers in sight. All of this feels really strange, I'd leave if the task wasn't so important. The rest of the squad enters the deserted room, they're as baffled as we are.

"This isn't right," Sarge continued, "keep your guard up and-"

He is quickly interrupted by the door slamming shut behind us all. Within seconds, Xenem soldiers flood into the room pointing their guns at us. We look at Sarge who looks furious, he nods at us and puts his hands up and we do the same. It was a trap. The soldiers take our guns and explosives before cuffing us, they lead us to a large room with over a hundred prison cells, all filled with people from all over the galaxy. Men, women and children were put in these cells, truly horrifying. The soldiers open a cell while other soldiers uncuff us before pushing us all inside and slam the door shut behind us. This isn't ideal, but we've gotten out of worse situations. Sarge sits down on the floor against the cell and shakes his head,

"What were we thinking? We should've left as soon as the air defenses didn't attack us. It was all too good to be true."

"They knew we were coming." Leezol responds.

It's safe to assume Leezol is right, no blockade, no air or ground defenses and an unguarded prison? A trap for sure. I walk around our cell trying to find my parents and Somma. It's hard to see or move around with so many people crowded in the cell. Our cell is large and I've already worked my way through most of it, all hope seems lost until I hear familiar voices,

"Clark? Is that you?"

"It is him!"

It's my parents. I'm filled with relief and joy, I make my way to them and hug them both tight. After all this time, it seems like a dream getting to see them again.

"Are you guys okay?" I ask while holding onto them

"We're okay, the food needs some work, though!" my Dad jokes.

My Dad has always been able to stay positive and find a way to have fun in any situation and prison is no exception for him.

"Why are you here?" my Mom asks while fixing my hair and uniform, as if prison is a place to look presentable.

"I'm here for you, me and my squad, I'll introduce you!"

I lead my parents back to the squad by the entrance of the cell. Sarge stands up and looks at us.

"Mom, Dad this is SSG. Richard Miner, he leads the squad."

Sarge shakes hands with my Mom and Dad,

"Nice to meet you both. Your kid is one of the bravest soldiers I've ever met and a hell of a warrior, you both should be very proud."

My Mom rubs my shoulder while my Dad pats my back. I introduce them to the rest of the squad, which goes perfectly fine, but I wonder how my parents will feel about the incredibly kind and pleasant man known as CPT. Auldin Leezol, formerly of the Xenem military.

"So, this is Captain Auldin Leezol, he's our- associate." I say with an unsure voice.

My parents try to shake his hand, but Leezol instead bows his head to them, which is still kinder than I thought he'd be.

"Mr. and Mrs. Parson, your boy is kind, caring and a natural leader, and like Miner said, a great warrior. I may not like him and his friends, but I respect him, so I congratulate you both on raising him well." Leezol says.

"Thank you, CPT. Leezol. You're a Xenem soldier, why are you locked up with Clark and his squad?" my father asks,

"Yes, well, we have a mutual enemy in Xenem, I am helping them take down Valkis Tyro and Xenem as a whole after what they did to me."

My parents nod, knowing better not to dive deeper into Leezol's situation. A few guards enter the room and open our cell door, they cuff the squad and I and start dragging us out. The urge to fight back is strong, but I didn't want to cause any trouble, especially in front of my parents. They watch as I get dragged out,

"It'll be okay." I quickly say to them before I'm out of the cell.

They take us to the tower where we get put on a lift, a soldier presses a button and we head up towards the top of the Tower.

"Where are you taking us?" Sarge asks,

"Shut your mouth!" a soldier yells before hitting Sarge in the back with his gun.

We finally reach the top of the tower where we get escorted to the middle of an office overlooking Kitexa, the office has no window which lets the thick air surround us. After a few minutes, a door opens and Valkis Tyro walks out, wearing a long black and green robe, he certainly looks like Xenem royalty, not exactly what I expected him to look like, though. He walks up to each of us and looks us in the eyes. After he finishes, he goes in front of all of us and sighs,

"So, this is Specter. Very impressive, so diverse! How exciting! Now, which one of you is Richard Miner?"

"That's *SSG.* Richard Miner to you." Sarge says while stepping forward.

"I have found my answer, *SSG.* Richard Miner. You live up to the legends. I recall wanting to recruit you for my military, but you refused, a shame."

"I'd never serve under you, Tyro."

Tyro scoffs and walks to the ledge of his view of the city,

"You all would do wonders here. If only you all would stop being such a nuisance, but I suppose I should expect that, *he* warned me you were all tiresome fools."

"Who?" Sarge asks,

"We will get to that soon, I want to meet my new prisoners. Which of you is Clark Parson?"

I step forward,

"You took our friend, where is she?" I ask while staring Tyro down,

"My men take a lot of people's friends, you have to be specific."

"Somma Terra Juna! Where is she?" I yell trying to charge at him, but I get yanked back by guards.

"Settle down. I will kill you where you stand if you do not behave, boy! I tire of you, get him back in line!" Tyro yells before guards pull me back.

Tyro walks down the line to every member of the squad. After me, he moves to Carden and laughs,

"Carden Reddina, Folin's fascinate me, teeth sharp

enough to kill and quite clever. They could easily take over anywhere they choose, yet you all choose to be slaves to the USC, sad. Perhaps, if you are still alive at the end of all this, I could use you as a guard dog."

Carden stares down Tyro with an anger in his eyes I have never seen. Tyro moves further down the line, stopping at Kierra,

"Who is next? Yes, Kierra Shuua! Ever so wise, just like everyone from your home. Answer me this, what happened to your eye? Some blue worked its way in, very unsettling, do not look at me. I do not understand it. Speaking of not understanding, " Tyro points at Blaine, "Blaine Carlston, how you have not blown up your meaty hands baffles me, just like everything baffles you, yes? Feel free to clap once for yes and two for no. Do not feel too bad, I get confused, too, like with these two. Damn twins. The Lane Brothers, do forgive me if I mistake you both for each other and kill one of you thinking you are a different twin."

Tyro cackles, but we remain silent, not letting him get to us.

"Bradley Dillon, a handsome young man, maybe we will cut off that face soon, it would make a wonderful decoration. Well, look who we have here," he steps towards Leezol, "old Auldin Leezol! How the mighty have fallen. Do you see now how going off on your own, and ignoring my orders can be rather foolish? You were dead weight anyways, my only regret was not killing you sooner. Last and very well the least, Rachel Denza, but that is not your name, is it? Richard, yes, *sir*?"

Rachel grinds her teeth and throws a kick, she's lucky enough to hit Tyro in the stomach and he falls to the floor, the guards hit her in the back and drag her back in line. Tyro coughs while laughing as he slowly gets up,

"How lady-like!" he exclaims.

Tyro and the guards erupt in laughter filling Rachel with more rage. Tyro makes Leezol look like a saint, I have never seen anyone make a group of people so angry in such a short amount of time. Our tolerance is already low, between falling into a trap and still not knowing where Somma is, getting us all pissed off was all too easy for him. After Tyro finishes laughing, he begins walking away from us,

"I would love to talk with all of you, but another time perhaps, assuming we do not kill you all."

Sarge steps forward,

"Who were you talking about earlier?" he asks,

"Oh, yes, *him*. He is a new friend, send him in!" Tyro yells at a couple guards.

Doors to his office open, a few soldiers enter with none other than GEN. Pyren Juna following behind them wearing a Xenem uniform. Our faces go pale, we are completely speechless and bewildered. This can't be real, there is absolutely no way GEN. Pyren Juna, a legend on the battlefield, is a traitor. It isn't possible.

"Hello, Miner, Specter, Leezol." Juna says with a smug smile on his face.

We are completely stunned silent, even Sarge and Leezol are silent. Juna nods his head,

"I understand, you are confused. I know it is hard for you all to think logically, but just try. Ladies and gentlemen, for most of my life, I fought for what is right, I fought to protect my home and my family, but sometimes when you fight for too long, you look for other ways to protect what you love. Chancellor Tyro snuck into my home a while back, I was ready to kill him where he stood, but he stopped me, he said he was there to talk. I thought he wanted to talk about a way to have Xenem join the USC, but he opened my eyes. My friends, the USC is dying, the Confederacy is getting stronger every day and Xenem is creating more powerful and deadly weapons than ever before. My best chance of survival was to join the winning side of this war, which is what Chancellor Tyro offered me. I was reluctant to do it, but I knew not even an 'unknown' unit of children could save the day. It was the only choice I had."

Hearing someone of Juna's stature speak so dismissively

of the USC is another shocking blow, he wasn't always the friendliest person, but he was loyal, or so we thought. Tyro being able to break through Juna's tough exterior is a true testament to his ability to manipulate others. Just like before Juna showed up, he almost got us all to attack him so he would have more of an excuse to kill us, not that he even needed an excuse. Sarge shakes his head in disbelief,

"Juna, what is going on in your head? This is crazy!"

"You shut your mouth you old fool! I am doing what it takes to survive, I suggest you do the same!" Juna responds.

Tyro raises his hand,

"Quiet! Both of you. I am giving Specter one chance, the same chance I gave to GEN. Juna. Leave the USC, join the Confederacy, fight for Xenem. Your talents are wasted being a hidden unit who's restricted by the lunacy of the Coalition. They all may not know of your existence, but those who do shall restrict you more and more until you will not be able to move at all. With us, you will be free and together. We will rule everything, everywhere, as equals!"

Sarge looks at all of us and smiles then looks back at Tyro and Juna,

"A tempting offer for weaker men, like Juna, but we will have to decline. I've never been an 'evil lord ruling over all' type of person, none of us are. So, you both can piss off!"

Tyro sighs and nods his head as he turns to Juna,

"You tried to tell me, my friend, I did not listen, my mistake, I had to try." Tyro shrugs his shoulders, "Oh, well, GEN. Juna, please remove the moronic filth, he bores me."

Without flinching, Juna pulls out his handgun from his holster and shoots Sarge in the head. His body falls limp, the shock and horror on all of our faces was evident. The urge to attack not only Tyro, but Juna, too, was becoming overwhelming. Some guards run up to Sarge's corpse and drag him to the edge of the office overlooking the city. They throw him off into the river, leaving a blood trail behind him.

"He was always a damn fool." Juna says while holstering

his gun.

Tyro walks to the edge and looks down,

"Having a space to drop dead bodies makes my life so much easier, not as messy as leaving them in my office, of course that blood trail is not a great example. but someone will clean that. Blood of cowards tends to stain."

We are all pale and silent, including Leezol. We are not sure what we just witnessed or if any of this is real or some hallucination. Tyro stands in front of us and waves his hand,

"Hello? Why so silent? Is it the blood? You are soldiers, yes? You have seen blood before, relax. You are free now, you can join us without worrying about some old relic."

"Juna, Tyro, you twisted brain dead fools, you both will pay!" Leezol yells.

Sound begins to leave my ear, I can't even hear what anyone is saying anymore, all I hear is ringing. As it gets louder, the image of Sarge getting shot keeps replaying in my head. It plays over and over again, Juna pulling the trigger, blood exiting Sarge's body through his head then falling to the floor. Now, I start to wonder if we're next if we don't do what he says or question him? Juna was so quick to listen to Tyro and shoot not only an ally, but an old friend. There's no telling where all this is headed for us.

The ringing begins to fade away and I hear Tyro finish with a speech he was giving. I didn't hear it, but I am sure it was disagreeable on all fronts. I shake my head and feel the rage built up inside me begin to boil over. I know I'm probably going to get shot, but I can't stay silent any longer.

"Juna, you damn coward!" I yell.

"Excuse me, Parson? Me, a coward? You have mistaken me with your dead friend. I am a fighter, a survivor. I will not let anyone stand in my way of survival and greatness, not Miner, not you, not anyone!"

"What about Somma? Xenem troops took her and I'm sure she would be sick to her stomach seeing what her father became!"

"You know nothing of my daughter, even if you are romantic with her, which sickens me, so you shut your mouth before I-"

"We know your daughter better than you do!" I interupt, "You just killed the man who's been more of a father to her than you ever were, she's here somewhere and we are going to get her and burn this place to the ground, then you'll see who the losing side really is, you sad, weak, pathetic excuse for a man!"

Juna tries to respond but Tyro laughs and claps interrupting him,

"I like you, Parson! You are angry, passionate, determined, not to mention no fear! If your squad is anything like you, then we will all get along, assuming you do not do something foolish."

Juna scoffs,

"Everything they do is foolish, look how they got here."

"Hush, Juna, they were determined to save their friend and take out an enemy, they just got sloppy, but we can fix that. What do you all say? Specter fights for Xenem?"

Nothing anyone has said has tempted me even a little to switch sides, I'm sure the rest of us feel the same. We loved Sarge, he was a father figure to all of us, and killing him was the wrong way to go about recruiting us. The squad stays silent, but they shake their heads, their eyes filled with rage and hate. We almost feel trapped, we just watched Sarge get killed and if we do anything in retaliation we die, so we have to stand there and listen to Tyro and Juna spew their nonsense and not say anything. I tend to be a quiet person, but all of this is taking things too far. I owe so much to Sarge, I know I used to think he was crazy for putting a team together of mainly rookies, but Sarge knew exactly what he was doing. Everyone has proven themselves over time, he wasn't always there, but when he was, he always filled us with confidence and pushed us to be more, to be better. He had his flaws, but he truly was a legend and didn't deserve to get betrayed like this. We could have avoided this if we had planned better. We paid the ultimate price and lost our friend and leader, SSG. Richard Miner. A legend.

"Tyro, when we blow your head off," I continued, "I think we will come to find you truly have no brain, we will never fight for you. Juna, you traitorous snake, you will pay. Once we find Somma, she will see the coward you are and will have you face what you have coming."

Tyro and Juna erupt in laughter,

"He does not know!" Tyro says,

"You have to feel bad for them!"

I tilt my head in confusion trying to figure out what they mean,

"Parson, as strong of a soldier you are, you still have no clue what is really going on here." Juna says,

"What are you talking about?"

"I told you all, I would do anything to protect myself and my family. I refuse to let anything happen to them, they will be safe, I swear on that. That being said, I suppose it is time to show you all what we mean, bring out our newest recruit, men!"

The office doors open again with more soldiers walking out with a glowing white light following behind them. Just like with GEN. Juna, it's a horrific, shocking discovery to see Somma slowly walking out, also wearing a Xenem uniform.

NEW FRIENDS, NEW HOPE

It seems the apple doesn't fall far from the tree. If I had to guess, we are still hallucinating. At first, seeing Somma filled me with relief, but not for long once I saw her uniform. Seeing her in a green and black uniform is sickening, seeing GEN. Juna was bad, but this makes it all become much worse. Somma makes her way down the stairs and stands next to her father. She is fully covered, only showering her eyes. She'd usually only cover herself up like that if she was doing something that requires stealth, but she's out in the open. I suppose Tyro didn't want to deal with Somma's shine, so he probably forced her to cover up. GEN. Juna's skin is barely shining. Nothing about this is bothering him. Somma's skin is glowing bright, I could see she is stressed, but Juna doesn't seem to care or even notice. She still wears her arrow, feather and Noli raven skull necklace, though. I feel myself become light headed, my legs buckle inward and I fall to the floor breathing heavily. Blaine picks me up and with some luck, I am able to stay standing.

"Come, now, Clark, you look weak!" Tyro continued while clapping and laughing, "Your friend, your Somma is safe, rejoice! Specter is reunited!"

Somma and GEN. Juna, traitors? This has to be a nightmare of some sort. Leezol of all people is as shocked as all of us, if not more.

"You see, my Somma is safe." GEN. Juna continued, "Those soldiers took her and brought her to me here. When I first told her about what I had done before your attack on Vonra, she was understandably hurt, angry and in disbelief. Once she arrived here, she was still angry and wanted to go back to Specter, but when I told her about the USC dying and us guaranteeing our safety here, she agreed to join Xenem. She wanted none of you to get hurt, that is why you all still draw breath. We are giving you one last chance here. Somma can come back to you all, be a part of Specter, but under Confederation rule, Xenem rule. Do not be fools."

The only part of that offer that sounds tempting is Somma coming back, but we would never join them, especially after killing Sarge. I do my best to stay up and take a step forward. Looking at Somma, I see she's worried, stressed and confused. The way she looks at me and shakes her head as I step forward, I know she doesn't want me to say anything, but I have no choice.

"We will never fight for you, you can keep me in prison, but let everyone else go, they were following orders. They don't deserve to be kept here."

"If you wanted your squad's freedom, perhaps you should have taken my offer, you all would have been free. What fools you are. Well, GEN. Juna, what should we do with our new friends?" Tyro asks.

Juna looks at Somma then looks back at me with a devilish grin.

"I think we should give them a fighting chance, my Somma will face off against your new leader, Mr. Parson, in hand-to-hand combat. If Somma wins, you all go back to your cells with the other filth, if Parson wins, we let all of you, including Somma and Parson's parents go free, free to go back to your weak Coalition."

There has to be another way to get us all out. I am not going to fight Somma, I'm not sure what's going on with her, but she is still a member of this team, I still love her and want her out of here. I don't think anyone in the squad wants me to fight her, at one point in time Blaine and Leezol would've jumped at the opportunity to fight her, but they don't even want that anymore.

"I am not going to fight Somma, I will gladly fight you

two, but not her."

"So many tempting offers today!" Tyro exclaims, "I must decline, though. I would rather see Ms. Juna fight, GEN. Juna has been talking about her for a while. I'd like to see if she lives up to his praise."

He leads Somma in front of me. In my time with her, I've been able to pick up on how she feels by just looking at her eyes, and what I see is panic and fear, not to mention her skin is shining even brighter. We stand in front of each other staring into each other's eyes, under different circumstances, this would be romantic. Somma subtly shakes her head,

"I cannot, I-" I hear her whisper to herself,

Usually, I'd say something back, but she is on a path she needs to figure out on her own. A path which unfortunately leads her to having to attack me, not because she wants to, but because she feels she has to.

"Wait!" Tyro exclaims, he walks up to me, "I am not a cruel man, let me make this fair."

He begins uncuffing me, expecting me to attack her back. He is sorely mistaken, if we weren't surrounded by armed guards, I would attack Tyro instead in an instant after getting uncuffed. As he walks back to GEN. Juna, Somma looks down and sees her white ribbon on my wrist, she gently grabs my wrist and brings it closer to her and looks at it then looks at me with tears in her eyes.

"Somma, what are you doing? Snap his wrist, do something, anything. Beat him!" GEN. Juna yells,

Somma looks at me again while holding my wrist, a tear rolls down her cheek, she shuts her eyes,

"I am so sorry." she whispers.

She immediately twists my wrist. She has me in a painful wrist lock. I was taught early on in my time as a Private how to get out of a lock like this, but I won't do it. The squad gets pulled back by guards, they can't help, it's better that way, though. I don't want them involved. I can't help myself and release a pained grunt, Somma sweeps my leg and I hit the ground, I hear Tyro and Juna laughing, cheering and clapping. Somma takes the time to quickly kneel down next to me,

"Clark, please you have to fight me, I do not want to hurt you."

I groan in pain and shake my head. I slowly get up, beginning to walk towards Tyro and Juna,

"Uh oh! Ms. Juna, your friend does not understand the game!" Tyro exclaims,

Somma grabs my arm and pulls me back towards her before throwing a kick to my leg. I manage to stay up but she throws a second kick and causes me to collapse onto the floor again. I get up to my knees and stay there shaking my head as my hair falls in my face. Hearing Juna and Tyro laughing, Somma standing in front of me, my squad at gunpoint and being yelled at, I always try to keep my emotions in check, but living this nightmare gets to me. I cover my face with my hands and let out a yell filled with so much pain, anger, frustration and sadness, it causes the room to go silent for a moment. Somma sniffles and walks back to her father,

"He will not fight back, you both wanted a fair fight. There is nothing I can do."

"There is something you can do," Juna continued, "Finish him."

The squad erupts in anger,

"No!"

"Let him go!"

"Cowards!"

The guards throw them to the floor and prepare to fire on them, Tyro lifts his hand,

"Wait!" he exclaims as he walks up to me on the floor, "You truly love her, is that it?"

With my hair in my face, and tears in my eyes, I say nothing. I hear Juna groan in disgust, but Tyro laughs,

"I would say that is a yes. GEN. Juna thought so, but I disregarded it. How sweet, but also unfortunate."

He quickly pulls out Somma's knife from her belt. It's the

knife she kept from Leezol when we first met him. He grabs Somma by the throat and points the knife at her.

"Either you fight or I kill her where she stands and you all die with her!"

I look at GEN. Juna, at first, he looks concerned, but somehow relaxes after a moment. Somma's eyes are filled with fear as she gasps for breath, Tyro begins laughing and brings the knife closer to her. Something snaps in me, I realize there is no way out of this, I shoot up from my knees and tackle Tyro and wrestle the knife from him, after I finally snatch it away, his guards open fire on me, luckily, their aim needs work, which allows me to quickly run towards the end of the office and jump off. I hear the squad, including Somma, yell "No!". Jumping out, I look out into the sky and see the black clouds, green lighting striking near me. It strikes a few times during my jump, sometimes near me, sometimes further away. The strikes are the last thing I hear. It is a far fall. I land in the river below the office, it hurt like hell, but somehow, I'm alive. Whether everyone in the office thinks I died is a mystery to me, but I hope they do think that, that way I can get the drop on them without them expecting it.

Truth be told, I did think I was going to die. I felt dying was the only way to satisfy Tyro and hopefully give everyone a chance to live, albeit in a prison, but alive nonetheless. Now, I just have to figure out a way to make it back. I'm mentally and physically drained, from Somma attacking me to falling into the river, my body is in complete pain. I feel myself go unconscious floating down the river, it's oddly relaxing, despite the fact I'm floating in a river of blood and other liquids I don't want to even think about. I close my eyes and pass out, thinking about everyone I left behind back at the tower. My parents, the squad, Somma. What happened to her? It's clear she's not okay with betraying us, so why is she doing this? To be honest, the answer seems obvious, it's her father. She has always tried to live up to his expectations and prove herself to be a good soldier for her family's legacy. She's always been a good soldier, but a better person. Juna once told Sarge and I he pushed to prepare for the horrors of war. He cares about her, but he cares more about his legacy and the war.

My eyes open, I wash up on a small piece of land, covered in mud. I slowly sit up and look around. I've never been to Xenem, so I have no idea where I am. I see something on the ground near me, I get closer and see it's Sarge's corpse. The river ended up washing him up at the same spot as me, which is lucky because he deserves a proper burial. I have to bring his body back to the USC so they can bury him. Seeing his corpse fills me with anger and regret, I bow my head and shed a few tears over his body, I pick up his body and carry it with me as I try to find safety. Carrying around a dead body isn't the best look nor does it make my journey any easier, but there is no way I am leaving him in Xenem of all places. Admittedly, it is hard to carry him. I'm weak from what happened and carrying a full grown man through slippery and rough terrain is hard on me.

The squad only got so far when researching Xenem, they weren't able to discover much in the amount of time that was given, so I have no idea what awaits me in the wilds of Xenem. The only weapon I have is Somma's knife that I grabbed from Tyro. As sharp as it is, I doubt it'll be much help. The wilds of Xenem, as expected, are dark and dreary. The ground is uneven making it hard to walk through, each painful step feels slippery and disgusting, I don't know what I am stepping on and to be honest, I don't want to know. Night begins to fall, but I don't know where I could possibly rest in this wasteland. I wish I could lay down anywhere and sleep peacefully, but something tells me the ground should not be laid on. I reluctantly choose to keep walking while still holding Sarge's body, my arms grow tired and weak, but I can't drop him.

I push and keep walking for a few more hours, until I see a small camp in the distance. There are tents and a fireplace, it's nothing fancy, but it looks like a place to rest. I can't trust anyone, but I'm also in no position to be picky. I slowly approach the people in the camp, they see me and quickly pick up their guns and aim them at me. One of them slowly approaches me,

"Who are you? What do you want?"

"I'm sorry, I don't mean to intrude. I just need a place to rest for the night."

"Why are you carrying that body?"

"He's a friend of mine who was killed."

The man slowly moves my coat to the side, showing the USC logo,

"Your uniform, I recognize it. Come with me. My name is Fesio."

They lower their guns and lead me into the camp. People come out of their tents and stare at me, I'm led to a big tent, two armed guards opens the flaps,

"Stay in here, put the body down on the table. Vai will be in shortly." Fesio says before leaving me alone in the tent.

I gently place Sarge's body on an empty table near me, I take my coat off and place it over his body. Usually, I wouldn't sit down before being told I could, but my legs are too weak to care at this point, I collapse on a chair and nearly fall asleep immediately, but I wake myself up. It wouldn't look great meeting someone new and the first they see is a body on the table and a filthy stranger asleep in their tent. A few minutes pass and the tent flaps open, I quickly stand up as a woman walks in holding a rifle. She drops it on the table next to Sarge. She's from Xenem, a young woman, but carries herself like she's seen a lifetime of battle. Long wavy red hair, wears a dark green shirt with the sleeves torn off and black pants with black eye makeup and two red lines going downward on both cheeks, she looks like a real warrior. She pulls out a cup from her bag and fills it with water. She hands it to me,

"Drink this. It is clean, do not worry."

I slowly grab the cup and take a sip, it doesn't taste odd in any way. I begin chugging the water. After I finish, I hand the cup back to her.

"Thank you, ma'am."

"My name is Vai Vianti. Now, who are you?" she asks, ignoring my thanks.

"A pleasure to meet you. I am sorry to intrude. I just need a place to rest for the night."

"I asked for your name."

"I'm afraid that's confidential."

Vai scoffs,

"Alright, fine. I know you are from that United Starlight Coalition, though. That is how I know you will not try anything foolish, for your sake, I hope I am right about that. So rest, but tomorrow, I have questions, like who is this dead body on my table. I will have someone escort you to a tent."

A man walks in to take me to a tent, I pick up Sarge's body and follow him. He leads me to a tent nearby where I place down Sarge's body outside, I hope it'll be safe out here. I enter the tent and see a long, tattered piece of cloth on the ground, I assume that's my "bed". Like I said, I can't be picky. I lay down on the cloth and it may be because I am exhausted, but it is incredibly comfortable. I quickly fall asleep. I'm not sure how I'm even able to sleep after everything that happened.

The next morning, I see light peak through my tent, I hear footsteps approaching,

"Get up."

I assume it's my gracious host greeting me. I make my way out of the tent, I'm relieved to see that Sarge's body is still where I left it and safe. Vai helps me up and takes me to her tent,

"Sit down." she demands,

I slowly sit down and look around her tent, it looks old fashioned, no screens or technology anywhere, it's covered with paper maps of different parts of Xenem and blueprints for random buildings. The table we sit at has a large map of Kitexa with a red circle around where Tyro's tower is.

"How did you find us?" Vai asks,

"I was washed ashore by the river with my friend who

got killed, I carried him for hours trying to find a place to rest and lay low, that's when I came across your camp."

"What were you doing in the river?"

"Would you believe me if I told you I jumped out of Chancellor Tyro's office to escape certain death."

"I would. What were you doing in his office?"

"Trying to kill Tyro and free Xenem of his grasp. In doing so, *we* hoped to bring this war closer to an end."

Vai tilts her head in confusion,

"'We'?"

I probably shouldn't have that. People aren't supposed to know about Specter and our existence, but I'm getting the sense I can trust Vai not to go running to Tyro with information of me surviving or about Specter.

"Oh, yes. I'm part of a unit. We were trying to save some people and take out Tyro."

"I saw on your sleeve 'Specter', that's your squad's name?"

"It is, I hope I still have a squad to go back to, they got captured."

"And what is with the number on your chest?"

"That's my codename, 'Specter 2'"

"Who is 'Specter 1'?"

"The man lying dead outside. Our squad leader, SSG. Richard Miner, or 'Sarge' as we liked to call him."

"I am sorry to hear that. I suppose that makes you 'Specter 1' now?"

I haven't even thought of how things are going to be with Sarge gone, am I the new leader of Specter? Either way, my main priority is getting back to the tower.

"I'm not sure who the new leader is, but can you help me get back to the tower? If I'm not mistaken, it seems you are trying to accomplish the same thing as us. Together we can end Tyro's rule."

Vai stands up and looks at the map of Kitexa,

"Maybe, if I can trust you. We are planning the same

thing, so lucky you and possibly lucky us. Do something for me, then maybe I can help. We were planning on laying bombs down around the tower, but we lack explosives. I was going to send my brother, Teni, and some other people to rob a transport carrying explosives and other weapons, they will need an experienced soldier who can lead them. I would go myself, but I need to stay here and plan. Will you do it?"

"When is the transport coming through?"

"Later today. I have mapped it out, it should not be too difficult. The map has instructions on how to go about it. Assuming everything goes well, you will all return safely, then we will talk about working together."

Seeing as I don't really have a choice, I agree to help them. Vai gives me a tattered bag carrying an old rifle, shoddy medical equipment and a nearly dull knife. She walks me to a group of men and women,

"Listen up, this is our new friend, I guess you can call him 'Specter 2'-"

"Clark," I interrupt, "You may call me Clark."

"Right, this is Clark, he will be leading the charge on your raid. You listen to him, hopefully he does not get you all killed. The transport will be passing through Kitexa in a couple hours, its path to its next drop is nearby. I will give Clark the map with directions. Get going!"

Vai hands me a crumbled map before leading me with the group to a pile of bushes and plants that's hiding a Ranna, it looks similar to the one we took to Vonra, except newer. It's been a while since I worked with new people. It may seem rude, but the only thing I need and want to know about them is their names. Vai walks back to the camp as we board the craft and everyone sits down, I hand the map to the women who will be driving the Ranna,

"Before we go, what are your names?" I ask as I take a seat.

"Fesio."

"Teni."

"Grolo."

"Cinniya."

"Mezza."

"Thiani."

They're a group of three men and three women, all from Xenem. Teni is the brother of Vai, so I oddly feel like keeping him safe would bode well for me, even though I am sure he can handle himself. I'm hoping they know how to fight. I recognize Fesio from when I arrived at Vai's camp, I guess it's a friendly face. Vai said this job shouldn't be too difficult, but we must always be ready for the possibility of people fighting back, especially if they're from Xenem. My warpaint has fully washed off after everything I went through, doing something like this without it feels off. It may be silly, but I'll need some paint for when we make our way back to the tower. I'm sure Vai can spare some.

Our Ranna makes its way to the main road, I get to see a proper tour of Xenem and it's as I thought, a wasteland. It's nothing but burnt down ships, buildings, dead bodies and nature. Somma once said that Xenem in the past was beautiful, but I can't see it. The photos she found made it seem like a completely different planet.

"What is the white ribbon for?" Fesio asks,

"It belongs to someone close to me, they're one of the people I am trying to save from Tyro."

"A girl?" Thiani asks.

I look down, which seems to give them their answer without me saying anything. The group looks at each other in confusion. We don't say much else during our ride to the transport, which is just as well, I didn't feel like talking. I can't stop thinking of the look Somma gave me before she was essentially forced to attack me. I know she doesn't want to be here or work for Tyro and her father, but she'll never say it to them. In a way, she's a prisoner, too. Even if she betrayed us, whether it was by force or not, I still love her and want her to come back to us. To me.

After a couple hours of driving through the "beautiful" scenery of Xenem, we reach the main road the transport will be coming in through. We get off the road and hide, waiting for the transport to come through. A few minutes pass by and we see our target. It's a small land craft with a few soldiers guarding it. Thiani begins driving towards the transport at full speed. The soldiers spot us and open fire, we take cover and open fire back. Thiani pulls up next to the transport, doing her best to evade the gunfire. The rest of us hops on, I order Grolo and Teni to start picking up crates and moving them to the Ranna. The rest of us fight the guards. There's about twenty crates to move and these guards aren't keen on letting us take them. It's hard getting a shot in at them making our job a bit more difficult.

Despite the soldiers being somewhat difficult to deal with, Grolo and Teni are moving the crates with ease and are almost finished. Things take a turn when we hear a craft approaching us from above. More Xenem troops get dropped onto the craft and open fire. I take cover and think to myself, "We already have plenty of crates, should we get out of here now?" Then I realize, getting all these explosives will not only help Vai's cause, but mine too. We have a common enemy who would not be too happy finding out his explosives were stolen then used against him. Despite the troops ferocity, they don't have the best aim. We take out multiple guards and are almost finished with the crates when one last person jumps onto the craft.

I'm hiding behind cover and can't see who's left or who jumped on, but the soldiers stop firing. The group is hiding behind cover with me, we look at each other in confusion. I look to my right and see a pair of boots stop in front of me, slowly, I look up. It's Somma, who's still shining brighter than usual. I wish I could do something to help her calm down, but this is the price she's paying for allowing herself to be controlled by her father and Tyro. The last time I saw her, it ended painfully, so I don't see why this time should be any different. Her and I are stunned silent. I slowly stand up in front of her while the rest of the group charges at the remaining soldiers. I remain silent as I stand up, there is so much I want to say, but I don't know where to begin.

"Clark, I thought you died." she says.

"Are you going to kill me?"

"No, never. We can get out of here right now and just run away." she says while reaching for my face.

I gently grab her hand, stopping it from getting closer,

"You know why I can't do that. I will save the others, I want to save you, too, but if I'm going to do that, you need to decide who you're going to be." I respond while quickly taking the white ribbon off my wrist and tying it on her wrist.

I back away from her slowly when quickly after, soldiers shoot at me, one of them hits me in the right arm and another soldier hits Fesio in the ribs, he falls off the transport which pushes Somma out of the way and causes her to fall over. I try to grab Fesio, but I'm not fast enough. Teni runs up to me and grabs my arm,

"There is nothing we can do for him, we have to get out of here!"

I don't respond and keep looking at Fesio in the distance on the ground. Another soldier charges at me. I evade his attack while grabbing his uniform and throwing him off the moving transport. The damage to the transport craft causes it to slow down to a near stop. Somma was too distracted by what was going on from the attacking soldiers to the transport slowing down, it allowed the group and I to quickly jump back to the Ranna. Thiani quickly accelerates ahead and we make our escape. I look back and see the remaining soldiers running around trying to fix the transport, Somma is still standing in the same spot watching us escape. It truly killed me to not be able to hug her or kiss her, stopping her hand took an incredible amount of strength. I hope I never have to be in that position again. Could it be she is trying to use my emotions against me to make me fall into a trap or does she genuinely still love me and wants this all to end? Impossible to tell at this point.

On the way back to the camp, everyone is cheering and laughing, celebrating the successful heist. I remain silent, I'm too distracted to celebrate. Mezza turns to me and notices my silence,

"So, Clark, what was going on with that girl on the transport?" she asks,

"Oh, don't worry about it."

The group looks at each other in shock.

"You are trying to help a Xenem soldier?"

"She's not a soldier of Xenem. It's complicated, don't worry about it."

The group stays silent, hopefully knowing they shouldn't keep questioning me about the matter. It'd be a smart move, I will not stand for people who are essentially strangers questioning me about the people I know and love. I get that Somma is on the wrong path and she doesn't look that great to strangers at the moment, but they don't know her history or who she really is. I've always had the philosophy of if you know nothing, then say nothing.

The Ranna makes its way back into the camp, I jump off the side and make my way to Vai's tent while the others remove the crates. I pass by my tent and see Sarge's body is gone. In a fit of rage and panic, I storm into Vai's tent, set on demanding answers. When I enter her tent I see Sarge's body on her table with a small pile of plants spread out on him. Vai walks in a few minutes after me holding more of the same plants,

"Oh, Clark, I see you and the others made out okay, good work."

"Thank you, what's on Sarge?"

"Gaveau plants, they can keep anything fresh and preserved for weeks if applied correctly. It secretes an adhesive that sticks to anything you put it on for a few days."

It's an interesting looking plant. green with purple accents. A purple liquid secretes from the plant, which I'm assuming has the healing and preserving properties that Vai was mentioning. At last, Xenem has something useful to offer.

"That's amazing, thank you." I respond,

"It was no problem, he was starting to smell so I was going to have to do it either way. Did you run into any issues with the transport?"

"A little, a reinforcement of Xenem troops showed up unexpectedly, but we handled it. Sadly, we lost Fesio."

"Damn, how did they know to send others? Either way, good work. You should rest, when you are ready, we can talk about getting into the tower."

I leave her and go to my tent to sleep. It was a long and stressful day, so I definitely need the rest. I take off my old coat and Specter uniform, both are filthy. It feels good to be out of those clothes. I am a bit cold, wearing only pants and a tank top, but it beats being covered in dirty clothes. Night falls and everyone in camp is asleep, besides those keeping watch. I've been asleep for hours, but suddenly, I hear someone enter my tent quietly, with my eyes closed, I see a white light. I feel someone gently rub my hair. Despite it being gentle, it's enough to wake me up. I open my eyes and see a mellow white blur in front of me, I rub my eyes and sit up, I open my eyes again and see Somma kneeling in front of me. It seems like a dream, but something tells me this is real.

"Please do not send me away, I just needed to see you." she whispers.

"How did you even find me?"

"After you and your friends left the transport, I tracked you all back here."

"Are you here to kill me?"

"Is that what you think of me now?"

"I don't know, but if you're here to kill me then go ahead, I'm unarmed. Your father already killed Sarge the same way, so go ahead, follow his lead."

Somma uncovers her face, other than her skin shining brighter than usual, I can see the stress she's been under. Her eyes look tired and it seems like all she has done is cry. Even as she sits in front of me, tears start falling down her face.

"Sarge is dead? None of this was supposed to happen, I was told no one would die or get hurt. Clark, you do not understand. I-" Somma stops herself.

She really has no idea what to say, but I am eager to hear what she came all this way to tell me.

"What is going on?" I ask, "You and your father betray the USC and you track me down for what? If you're not going to kill me, then tell me what's going on."

"I did not want any of this," she continued while sitting down, "When I arrived on Xenem, I did not know my father was going to be there waiting. He made me join Xenem, he threatened to kill all of you if I did not listen to him. He told me I would be happier and safer by his side and a part of Xenem, but I feel more alone and scared than ever. I almost had to execute some prisoners, it was awful. When I refused to kill anyone, Tyro beat me. All of this kills me."

I rub my eyes in confusion, I figured Juna had a lot to do with her random turn, but forcing her to join them and threatening to kill us is a surprise.

"You have to help me, Clark." she says with his voice breaking.

"They could have sent you, you could just be saying all this to get me to lower my guard. How can I trust you?" I respond, keeping my guard up.

More tears start falling from Somma's face,

"It is me, it is Somma, your Jewel, your 'beautiful Diamond Queen'. I may be wearing different colors, but I am the same girl from Vespis. You may not believe it, but I still love you and I know you still love me. I need my hero."

I stay silent and look down, deep down, in my heart, I know she's still the same girl I fell in love with, but after Juna's turn, it's hard to trust anyone, especially his daughter. In the silence, something occurs to me,

"Before we attacked Vonra, your father called you, when

you finished speaking with him, you were so distracted and upset all day. Was he calling to tell you he turned?" I ask.

"Yes, at that time he did not try to make me join him, but he told me his turn was for my safety. I was so furious and upset with him. I knew he was going to end up being our enemy and it hurt. I was so worried about everyone that day. I wanted to tell you all, but I did not want my father to be executed for treason. I went down the wrong path and it seems we are all paying the price."

To be honest, she walks free opposed to the others in cages, so some of us paid a higher price. I decide to change the subject to get her mind off the call.

"When you attacked me in the tower, you were pulling your hits, it still hurt, but I know you could have hit harder." I respond.

"I did not want to hurt you, but I knew if I did not attack you, my father and Tyro would have killed you all. Why did you not attack me back?"

"I don't know what's going on with you, but you're right, I still love you and care about you. I was never going to hurt you and I'm not going to hurt you."

Somma smiles and unwraps her hand before extending it to me. I know I was skeptical of her and to some extent, I still am. I slowly reach for her hand, she could possibly twist or snap my wrist in an instant, so I have to be careful. Somma watches my hand slowly go to her, but she decides to extend her hand further and grabs my hand. I flinch expecting her to break my hand or wrist. Somma was visibly hurt by my reaction,

"I am not going to hurt you, again. That is not who I am." she says looking down,

"I'm sorry, it's hard to trust anyone right now."

"Please trust me, I am still your Somma, I need help to get out of here, to get us all out of here. I do not want to hurt anyone else. Especially you."

"I'm planning a way to get us all out, Specter, you, my

parents, everyone."

Somma smiles and rubs my hand,

"Always a hero."

I sigh and look down in silence. After a moment I look back up at her,

"Always." I respond.

Her worried shine dies down as more tears fill her eyes, but tears of joy. She hasn't heard me say that in a long time. She smiles while tears fall, she slowly gets closer to me and kisses me on the lips. That was another moment where she could have killed me, so maybe I should start trusting her. After she kisses me, she wraps me in a hug.

"I have to get back, but thank you for not giving up on me. I will help get us all out when the time comes. I love you."

"I love you, too. Please stay safe. Be careful getting out of here."

Somma kisses my cheek and puts her face mask back on quickly before leaving my tent. It's nice to see that so far, she's not a traitorous snake like her father. As she leaves, a sudden urge rises inside of me, wanting her to stay.

"Wait." I say as I grab her arm,

Somma looks back at me, the sparkle in her eyes seemed to have returned in her short time with me.

"It's dangerous out there and I don't want to risk the lookouts seeing you. If you want, you can stay with me tonight."

Somma moves back into my tent and sits down,

"Are you sure?" she asks while uncovering herself.

Her skin isn't as bright, for once in what I assume is a long time, she's calm. I move over to make space for her. She smiles and slowly lays down next to me. I'm still sitting up, I guess I'm keeping my guard up, for whatever reason, I'm not even sure anymore, but I feel the need to be ready for anything. I grab the blanket and put it over her. It's a small blanket that didn't even fit me, but it fits Somma perfectly fine. Having her next to me again feels nice. It makes things seem normal again.

How I miss normal. Many things can happen as the night goes on, I must be cautious, but then again, it's Somma. I will have to wait and see what will happen, but my mind remains open going forward, as open as it can be right now. I'd be lying if I didn't feel somewhat afraid. I feel completely isolated and though I know it's Somma, I don't know her true intentions here. Perhaps she really did just want to see me. I think she knows that a part of me wants her here with me. A big part. There is always a chance that I was right being skeptical, if she attacks me again, I wouldn't know what to do. No matter what she could do to me, mentally or physically, I could never harm her. I will remain fully alert for whatever may come.

A NIGHT WITH THE ENEMY

At first, when Somma woke me up, a part of me wanted her to go. It came from the side that doesn't trust easily, now more than ever, but another part of me just wanted her with me. Ever since she was taken at the celebration in Tanli, I've felt alone. Even with the rest of the squad by my side, I felt alone. I thought when I saw her for the first time that would all change, but seeing her in that Xenem uniform made me feel worse, more alone. An hour has passed of Somma trying to sleep with me sitting, keeping my guard up. Somma opens her eyes,

"Are you going to lay down?" she asks, looking up at me.
"Don't worry about me."
Somma grabs my hand and looks off in the distance,
"I miss laying with you at the Heleia Fields. Can you please lay down with me?"
I think to myself "If she wanted to kill me, she would've done it by now." I lowered my guard a lot in the past hour with her, I'd be dead if she was anyone else. I've missed laying down with her, too. Somma moves over, I slowly lay down next to her. She tries to put the blanket over both of us, but there is no way it was going to work, it's too small. I chuckle and grab the blanket, putting it back over her.

"I'll be okay, you need to stay warm." I say while covering myself with my old coat.

Somma moves closer to me and wraps her arm around me. I slowly place my hand on her back, the memories really start flooding back to me of all the amazing time spent with her in Tanli. Not that I ever forgot, but after everything that happened, those memories didn't pop-up much in my mind. Somma grabs the arm sleeve of my coat with the new hole from when I got shot on the transport. She sighs,

"Are you okay?" I ask.

"I am sorry I distracted you at the transport, if I was never sent to help, you probably would not have been shot."

"You know me, I'm reckless and foolish. Something was bound to happen."

"Too reckless, my love." she responds as she holds me tighter.

Maybe it's all that time spent with Blaine that made me so reckless. I try to be a smarter person, but sometimes I lose focus and injuries happen. Turns out, seeing the girl you love turned traitor messes with your mind and has a lasting effect. I look at my arm and the wound is almost fully healed. It hurt like hell when I got it, but I don't know how it healed so fast.

"It is healed?" Somma asks,

"How did you know?"

"You carry Vespin blood, the blood I gave you stays inside of you, your wounds heal faster now and you can take more damage, I suppose that is why you did not die when you jumped from the tower."

I'm not sure what this means going forward. Am I part Vespin now? Is my skin going to glow from now on? I'd feel foolish and ignorant asking Somma those questions, I already feel foolish asking myself those questions in general. We were told it was safe, but who knows if something happens soon after? I'm still alive and seemingly healthy, physically at least, so no complaints or anything negative to report at the moment.

Things being normal between Somma and I is something I have missed. Not trusting her was a hard time for me, I felt bad about it. At the time, I felt I had no choice but to not trust her, I just hated how it hurt her.

"I'm sorry, Somma." I quietly say,

Somma looks up at me with concern in her sparkling

eyes.

"I know you're having a hard time with everything." I continued, "I didn't make it easier with my lack of trust and I'm sorry."

"I understand. When I entered the office and saw everyone's faces, I knew I hurt you all. If I was to ever get out, I know I would need to earn everyone's trust back. The moment I saw you, and the white ribbon on your wrist, I just wanted to hold you and have you take me away. Instead, I attacked you, making things worse."

I figured she didn't want to hurt me, I saw it in her eyes. When the leader of Xenem and your war hero father is watching, I imagine it's hard to not do what you're told.

"All I did was hurt you," Somma continued, "Tyro almost killed me when he found out you loved me, but you still saved me. When you took the knife and jumped out the tower, I was devastated, the last thing I did to you was hurt you. I am so sorry, I wish-" she stops and starts breathing heavily. Tears fall as her skin shines brighter.

I know that feeling all too well, she is having a panic attack. I hold her tighter,

"It's okay. We're okay. Just breathe."

"I am sorry, I am sorry-" she keeps muttering while losing breath while sitting back up.

When I had my panic attack by the Heleia Fields, Somma comforted me in a magical way no one has done for me before, it's time I return the favor.

"Look at me." I say while sitting up next to her,

I gently grab her face and move it in front of me, I smile at her and rub my thumb on her cheek. She says nothing but smiles back while her breathing slows down. It was gratifying helping her calm down just like she did with me. I gently put my forehead against hers with our eyes closed, as if this time it was I who was absorbing her pain and her worries.

"'I am here, be calm, I am with you.'" I say softly, quoting what she told me.

I gently lay her down and cover her with the blanket. She still breathes heavily, but she is calming down. I rub her cheek and watch her, even in panic she is still the most beautiful girl I've ever seen. I kiss her lips and lay down next to her, she immediately puts her arm over me and holds me tight. Her heavy breathing starts to calm as she squeezes me. Panic attacks feel terrible, I had hoped to never see her have one. Her shine dimmers as she finally calms down and rests her head on my chest. Luckily, I have news that'll break the tension and take her mind off of everything.

"We found something out before we came to Xenem, it's pretty shocking." I continued, "Apparently, Geb Tawin is a long lost friend of Sarge and Leezol's. Unsurprisingly, Leezol left him to die after some trouble a long time ago, but Geb cut his leg off to escape. His real name is Ben Gawti. He recognized Sarge and Leezol, that's why he offered to help us when we got to Tanli."

Somma looks up at me in amazement,

"Fascinating! It's an anagram. That is sad, though. I hope he was able to find some sort of peace. He was always so kind to us, I hope we see him again after all this."

"We'll go back to the Heleia Fields, I'm sure we will see him again."

Somma giggles and holds me tighter, I can tell she is starting to feel better about everything.

"I don't think your father approves of me." I joke trying to break the tension again,

Somma chuckles,

"I do not think your parents will approve of me either, but if they got to really know me, I think they would like me!"

"Well, your dad wants to kill me so I think you'll be fine with my parents."

Somma squeezes me tighter,

"Do not worry, I will not let him hurt you."

"Look who's the hero now."

"You will always be the hero, my love. Sometimes the

hero needs saving, though." she responds.

It's true, I'd definitely be dead by now if it wasn't for Somma and the squad. I still have her knife that I took from Tyro. Vai's bag came with a rusty, dull knife, but it is still useful. I have no need for Somma's knife.

"I believe this belongs to you," I pull out her knife from my belt, "make sure no one else takes it from you."

Somma slowly grabs the knife, she looks up at me and kisses me on the cheek,

"Thank you, but I cannot help but feel bad. You do not deserve any of this." she continued, "All this violence, death and chaos that surrounds you, people betraying you and hurting you, like me, you do not deserve it. Behind your quiet and reserved demeanor, I know you are a kind, thoughtful, strong, brave man, I see it in your eyes and I truly wish you peace. I am sorry chaos surrounds you and I am sorry that I hurt you. I hope you never change who you are, that is the man I fell in love with. It is who I will always love. I think I lost who I was, I hate it. How do you stay who you are through everything?"

I've seen many people who have become cold, rude and completely dead inside from this war, it's hard not to become that way, especially after what I've been through, not just recently, but my whole life. It's so easy to lose sight of who you are when going through so much pain and anger. At any point I could just stop caring, treat others poorly, only do things for myself leaving others to fend for themselves. I can't do that, though. I enjoy helping others and working with a team. Specter, Somma, my parents, they keep me human.

"The truth is, I don't know." I continued, "Do I get urges to do the wrong thing or give up, of course, it's easy. I could have easily left Xenem after the tower, leaving you, the squad and my parents to find your own way out while I run away, avoiding possible death or capture. That's just not who I am, though. I can't leave, not without all of you. You all are how I stay who I am. The possibility of you truly being a traitor, ending our relationship, that drove me close to giving up on all of this, but I knew somewhere inside was the real you. I can't give up on what I love, whether it is you, the squad or my parents, I won't give up on keeping you all safe. Even though I can't really keep anyone safe recently. Either way, nothing will stop me from fighting for you all."

I hear Somma sniffle as she wipes away tears and squeezes me tight,

"Thank you. We do not deserve you."

"You deserve better."

Somma gets up and gives me a long kiss on the lips, holding my face with both hands, when she stops kissing me, she still holds on to my face gently,

"Do not ever think that." she continued, "I would have died long ago if you were not with us. You protect all of us and taught us how to be warriors. Sarge was not around much to teach us much, but I will always remember that day, when you and SPC. Carlston had us practice shooting and the advice you gave us about always keeping our eyes open. What you told me when I told you I was scared, I was sure you would dismiss me like my father or anyone else would have, but you treated me with kindness and respect like no one ever has. I knew from then on you were a true leader. They may not show it, but Specter loves you, I love you and we need you."

"I've never been so in love with someone in a Xenem uniform." I joked.

Somma smiles and kisses me on the cheek. She lays back down with her head on my chest. I don't understand how someone so sweet can be raised by someone like GEN. Juna. Even before his betrayal, he was rude, arrogant, and condescending. Somma has never been open about her family, but I figure after all this time together, she could maybe open up to me. It doesn't seem like either of us are going to get much sleep tonight, so this is as good of a time as any to ask.

"Can you tell me about your family?"

"My love, you do not want to know about my family." she

responds,

"It's not going to change how I feel about you."

"I hope not."

"I promise. You know I'll always love you no matter what."

Somma sits up and pulls me up with her, she looks me in the eyes as she holds my hands tight,

"You would be the only one in the squad to know, my father and I do not tell anyone about our family." she continued while squeezing my hands. "The 'Great' Juna legacy took everything away from me. I had a mother, brother and sisters. They are gone now."

Tears fall from her eyes and land on my hands. Even Vespin tears sparkle like diamonds.

"What happened to them?" I ask,

"The Juna legacy happened." she continued, " As many people know, my ancestors were kind and generous, but also great military leaders. They passed down the same teachings and lessons through generations, but one has been the most prominent, 'Protect the House of Juna, always'. Protecting the family and its legacy meant everything to us. It is a kind and caring sentiment, until it drove my family mad. Over time, my father became overprotective of everyone in my family, obsessed with our safety and ensuring the Juna bloodline and its legacy. Years before I joined the war, Xenem attacked Vespis, my mother, Tala and my brother and two sisters, Tomlen, Ramsi, Deya and I were at home with our father. We wanted to evacuate and leave the city, but my father stopped us, he handed my mother a gun, with a crazed look in his eyes he told her 'Stay and fight, protect the House of Juna!' He left shortly after to go fight. My mother had never used a gun before. My father spoke to her like she was a soldier under his command. After he left, we tried to leave, but we heard explosions go off near our house. My mother had us hide under a table, before we knew it, a missile hit our house. The roof collapsed, killing my mother and two sisters. Tomlen and I barely survived, we made our way out of the wreckage and saw the ruin our house was in. Our father returned and broke down in tears with us. Now, he is working for the people who killed our family and is forcing me to do the same. After their deaths, Tomlen and I had to be strong for him, he was driven deeper into madness, we were the only ones keeping him from going completely insane. When Tomlen was old enough, he enlisted in the war under my father's command. He was so broken by what he saw and went through, plus my father putting the pressure of the family legacy on him made things too unbearable. He killed himself a year after joining the war. My father and I are what is left of our family. That is why he has been so protective over me and critical of what I do, because when he is gone, I will be all that is left. The same pressure he put on Tomlen, he puts on me, I hate it and wish it would all stop, but I cannot kill myself. I cannot do anything, I am trapped in this legacy. Clark, you do not know how badly I wish I could die and just end this, this legacy stained with blood and tears. I could not save my family, I can barely save you. I feel like I cannot do anything."

Somma breaks down in tears. Her family history is so tragic, I can see why she kept it to herself all this time. You wouldn't even expect someone like Somma to have such a dark past filled with so much loss and ruin. It doesn't surprise me that her father caused her family to perish, he has shown little to no affection towards Somma. He told us he treated her like a soldier to prepare her for this life, but even then, there is a line and at this point, he has crossed it. Betraying the USC and forcing Somma to join him is too far. I have to believe that in some twisted way, he loves her, but from what I see, he has completely lost it. A part of me regrets asking her about her family, talking about it devastated her. She suppressed it for what I imagine was a long time. There is a lot I want to say. I have more questions, but I don't want to make her more upset. Right now, I need to comfort her.

"You can't blame yourself for what happened." I say while wiping her tears.

"I could have saved them. I could have gotten them out before the missile, had I been more brave. I failed them."

I've never had to help someone through this sort of issue. I was lucky enough to have a normal family life. My parents were always good to me and if Kent was still us, I'm sure they still would've treated him as well as they treated me. Somma is still weeping, I know I need to try to help her feel better.

"Your father lost his way, but the way I see it, protecting the 'House of Juna' isn't about fighting in wars or being soldiers. To me, it seems the 'House of Juna' is built on how you treat others. It could be possible your ancestors wanted their descendants to protect the kind nature of the Juna's name, not their legacy in battle. You're a great soldier, but a better person. The moment I met you, you were incredibly kind and respectful to me, to everyone. Those qualities might have been one of the only things your father taught you that I agree with. Your kindness and positive spirit has helped all of us, especially me, so in that sense, you truly keep the legacy alive. Besides, your kindness is one of the reasons I fell in love with you."

Somma wipes her tears and smiles. She wraps her around me and hugs me tight,

"Thank you, Clark."

Somma doesn't let go. She still cries, but not as much.

"Do you know where Sarge's body is?" she asks,

"I found his body nearby when I woke up after jumping from the tower. I carried his body for miles until I found this rebel camp whose goal is to end Tyro's reign, they agreed to let me stay and keep Sarge with me. He's currently in the large tent that belongs to the leader of this rebellion, Vai. She has him in the tent with her with some sort of plants on him that'll preserve his body. When we get out of here, I want to give him a proper burial."

"May I see him?"

"I'm not sure, if Vai's asleep we might be able to sneak in

for a little."

Somma nods and starts covering herself up while I put on my coat. When she's ready, we slowly exit my tent. There are a few people roaming around keeping a lookout. I have no idea how Somma was able to sneak her way in. I go in front of her, I hold her hand and lead her to the tent, Somma squeezes my hand tight as we sneak through the camp. We usually don't hold hands during our stealth operations, but I can make an exception. We reach Vai's tent, I enter first to see if it's clear. Vai is on a cot sleeping, Sarge is still on her table. It's a good thing she doesn't mind sleeping with a dead body in her space. I open the tent flaps and Somma slowly walks in looking around. She looks at the table and stops moving. Tears form in her eyes as she approaches the table. She moves a piece of the plant from his face, she quietly gasps as she sees his face,

"I am so sorry, sir." she whispers with her voice breaking.

She grabs his hand,

"Thank you for giving me a chance. Thank you for everything. I will never forget you."

Somma stands by him for a few minutes while I keep watch.

"Sarge and my father did not always get along, but there was mutual respect between them. I cannot believe my father killed him."

"He didn't even hesitate," I continued, "when they asked Specter to join the Confederacy, Sarge declined, Tyro demanded that your father get rid of Sarge. Without any thinking or contemplation, your father pulled out his gun and shot him. It was horrifying."

Somma shakes her head,

"He told me he would not hurt him or any of you. Hurting others was never part of protecting the family or its legacy. I do not believe it." she slowly lets go of Sarge's hand and puts the plant back over him, "Goodbye, sir. Rest well."

Somma and I quickly leave and reach my tent, we go inside and Somma begins uncovering herself.

"Are you okay?" I ask,

"I cannot believe you carried him all this way."

"I wasn't going to leave him in mud in the middle of Xenem, I had to save his body for a proper burial, it's what he deserves."

"He made the right choice putting you in Specter. I am sure he was proud of you."

"I hope so. It really should've been me who died."

"Do not say that, he would not have wanted that. Keeping us safe was always a priority to him, despite what has happened, everyone is okay and that is what he wanted."

I nod my head, but Somma could tell I was still hurt. Somma holds my hands,

"It is okay, my love. He would want us to not dwell on his death, we will be okay." she says before kissing my cheek.

I give a shy smile and hug her, after a few moments, I start laying her down gently,

"You should sleep."

"What about you? Are you going to lay down?"

"I'll be okay, don't worry about me."

Within an instant, Somma gives a playful smirk and grabs my arm, pulling me to the ground next to her. I go to the ground, not realizing what just happened, Somma gets on top of me and laughs,

"My, my, you really thought I would sleep without you next to me?" Somma jokes before kissing me on the lips, "You should know better, my love!"

"How foolish of me."

"Very foolish."

Somma kisses me on the lips again,

"I have missed kissing you." she says softly.

She rubs my face with her hand while still on top of me, her eyes sparkle as she looks at me, there is so much I want to say,

"I am madly in love with you." I blurt out without thinking.

Somma giggles,

"I will always love you, Clark."

She hugs me tight while on top of me, everything feels like a dream whenever she holds me. Life seems normal, no war or people trying to kill us. I wish everyday was like this. Somma is still hugging me, but I hear her whisper,

"Can you tell me about your family now?"

Despite my home life not having many issues, it's something I never talk about, I'm not sure why to be honest. It always did feel odd not knowing Somma's family story, so I imagine she feels the same way,

"You really want to know? There's not much to tell." I respond,

"I do! On Vespis, I would be called your *Telani*- your Queen Lover. On your planet, I would be called your 'Girlfriend', yes? As your girlfriend, I want to know about your family."

"*Telani*, I like that. On Earth, I would be called your boyfriend, what would I be called on Vespis?"

"My *Relani*- my King Lover!"

I did feel it's about time she and I actually discussed what we are. I know it sounds childish and like we're still in school, but after a while, you begin to really wonder what you're called in our situation. Somma seems thrilled to find out, too, she looks at me and smiles, it's enough to make me lose focus as I am trying to think of what to say about my family. She knows what looking at me does, she laughs,

"Should I cover my face?" she jokes,

"No, no, I'll focus!"

Somma laughs and kisses my cheek,

"Start with your father, I imagine he taught you to be kind and brave or was it your mother?"

"It was both my parents that taught me that. Although my father, he was a professor of Earth's history on Vespis. He was the one to introduce me to superheroes. I'm named after one."

Somma tilts her head in confusion,

"What are 'superheroes'?" she asks,

"Their fictional characters or creatures with powers, like flying or super-strength. I was named after someone named Clark Kent, whose alter ego was someone named Superman, who had a lot of abilities and always helped those around him, saving them from danger and fighting off villains. My dad named me and my brother after him because he thought we would do incredible things and save the world. I guess I haven't lived up to his expectations."

"My love, that is not true. I am sure your parents are proud of you. If they knew everything you have done for me, Specter and the entire USC, it would bring them to tears."

Sarge and even Leezol told my parents such kind things about me. They seemed proud, but they don't know the full story. I have messed up quite a bit. The pressure of having to live up to my father's expectations of me being some sort of Superman has stressed me out for some time. It's not the same level as Somma's stress and expectations, so I guess I should consider myself lucky. It seems I let myself get in crazy and dangerous situations to prove I can truly be the hero my parents know I can be.

"What about your mother?" Somma asks,

"My mother is one of the most kind-hearted people I have ever met. While my father taught me to be brave, my mother taught me the value of kindness and helping others. She would always volunteer at health clinics and help the homeless, she told me 'Showing kindness costs nothing, but can change everything.' I never forgot that. I miss them every day. They're in that Xenem prison with the rest of the squad and I need to get them all out. All of us need to leave, they're counting on me, assuming they don't think I'm dead."

Somma rubs my face,

"You are a lot like this 'Superman' person, my love. I knew you were a hero, but I can see you are a superhero!"

I chuckle and shake my head, I've always wanted powers

like the Man of Steel, I wouldn't have gotten my ass kicked so much, that's for sure.

"I did not know you had a brother." she says.

"I had a twin brother, but he died when we were younger. I don't really like talking about what happened, not yet. My mother always told me he is always by my side."

"I am sorry to hear that, but she is right, he is still with you and your family, in here." she gently touches my heart, which brings me to tears.

"His name was Kent." I continued, "My father wanted both of us, his sons, Clark and Kent, to change the world, but all he has is me. Even with Kent by my side, I feel weaker every day with the more we go through."

"My love, you carry the strength of not just Kent, but thousands. You have to stay strong. I know you can. You are the strongest person I have ever met, you cannot let this war or what has happened make you feel weak. Your parents need you to be strong, as do I." she responds while rubbing my cheek with her thumb.

Somma kisses my cheek, she has been on top of me for so long, I've gotten used to the feeling of it. I don't mind it at all, I think it's cute. Somma grabs my left hand looks at my Nordic tattoos,

"Who taught about the gods and giants you tell us about?" she asks before kissing my hand and holding onto it.

"That was me. Growing up, I was bullied in school for the way I dressed and looked. To avoid people, I spent my days in libraries, reading stories and learning new things. One book I found had stories about those gods and giants, I immediately connected to it. I couldn't stop reading about it. I was fascinated by the stories, so I studied more of it and live my life based on its teachings. Those stories, combined with what my mother and father taught me, shaped me into who I am today. Although I am not sure who exactly I really am."

Somma hugs me,

"I know who you really are and I love you always. Thank

you for telling me all this."

I kiss her cheek and hold her. It feels bittersweet, I'm holding Somma and the world around us seems to disappear, an incredible feeling, but I know that she can't stay and will have to sneak back to the tower soon. Somma gets off of me and lays down, but still holds onto me. I can see now that she's tired and is falling asleep, as am I. It's been so long since I have stayed up so late, I guess Somma and I were trying to make up for lost time. Somma looks up at me,

"My love?" she asks while placing her hand on my heart., "Can you tell me another story from the World Tree?"

Luckily, I'm awake enough to think of a story.

"On Earth, the Sun, Moon and the day and night sky were people, gods and giants. When Earth was created. Odin and his brothers, Vili and Ve, threw sparks up into the sky, sparks from the fire realm Muspelheim, those sparks became the Sun, Moon and the stars in the night sky. The Sun is pulled by a horse drawn chariot, a horse is a four-legged animal from Earth with a mane of hair. The chariot is steered by a woman named Sól, who rides around the world every day. The Moon, also pulled by a horse drawn chariot, is steered by a man named Máni. They are brother and sister who ride around the world. They ride through the sky, but the sky itself is alive, too. When the Sun has risen, the god Dagr rides through Earth in the air on his horse whose mane shines so bright that it lights up the sky. His mother, the giantess Nótt, rides in after him when the Moon is up, her long hair is pitch-black and covers the sky, which is why the night is dark. They all help the world tell time, but the Sun and Moon are constantly being chased. Two sibling wolves, another animal from Earth, named Sköll and Hati, chase the Sun and Moon. Their chariots must always stay moving so they don't get caught and eaten by the wolves, but they always manage to escape danger. Sounds like us."

Somma smiles,

"I could listen to you talk forever." she says softly with her eyes closed,

She holds me tighter as she falls asleep, I do the same shortly after. I really don't know what tomorrow is going to bring, where Somma will stand or what will happen. She knows her father is a bad person, but it's still her family and she doesn't want to lose him, emotionally or physically, she has lost everyone else in her family already.

I wake up the next morning, Somma is unfortunately gone. I look down and see the white ribbon wrapped back on my wrist and a piece of paper next to me. It's always odd seeing paper, but my pad is currently in Xenem's hands which doesn't exactly thrill me. I pick up the piece of paper and read it,

"*My love,*

I am sure you wanted to wake up to me like how I woke up to you. You looked so handsome and peaceful as you slept, I did not want to wake you. I could not resist and kissed your lips before I left, it is probably the last time I will be able to do that for a while, which kills me. I had to leave and go back to my father and Tyro or else they would be suspicious. You told me I need to decide who I am going to be and you are right. I truly love you with all my heart, but I do not know what to do in such a complicated situation. Until I figure everything out, I unfortunately have to fight for Xenem with my father and defend Kitexa. I do not want any of this, but I cannot abandon my father or hurt him, he is not a good man, not anymore, but he is still the only family I have left. I hope you understand. I wish no one would get hurt from all this, most of all you. I am sure you will be upset with me and I am sorry, but I wanted to tell you, spending a night with you again helped me find the joy I once had. You are an incredible man who I am forever grateful for, thank you. No matter what happens, I love you, always. I hope to see you again soon and be in your arms once more. I will miss you and think of you every day, my Relani.

Love, Somma, your Telani"

I figured she couldn't stay, but it still hurts that she's gone again. Last night felt like a dream. We were in a small, filthy tent in the Xenem wilderness, but being with Somma made it seem like paradise. I gently fold the letter and put it in my coat pocket. I really do wish I woke up to her, instead, I woke up to the sound of people arguing and running around.

"Clark, get out here." I hear Vai say,

I leave the tent, Vai is standing there smiling with her arms crossed.

"What's going on?" I ask,

"In the mood to blow something up?"

BOMBS FOR THE WICKED

A few days of planning with Vai have passed. If I understand her correctly, it sounds like she has a plan to tear down Tyro's tower using bombs. It doesn't seem like she knows about Somma spending the night, I want to keep it that way. I don't think Vai would take too kindly to a "Xenem" soldier sleeping in her camp. She leads me to her tent and shows me a hand drawn map of Kitexa with a big circle around Tyro's tower.

"How are you with explosives?" Vai asks,

"I'm no stranger to using them, my squad and I just blew up the Central Command in Vonra a while back."

"That was you guys?" Vai exclaims, she looks like she's meeting a celebrity.

I nod my head, but thinking about it brings back memories of Somma getting stabbed, such a horrible time.

"When I heard about that I did not believe it, I did not think someone would be foolish enough to pull something like that off."

"Foolish suicide missions is our specialty." I joked.

Vai is visibly impressed, hearing about what Specter accomplished in Vonra fills her with confidence. If we never attacked Vonra, Somma wouldn't have been dragged into this mess, but I'm still glad we broke Xenem's rule over all of Kana. The same people who I helped steal explosives with walk in the tent, they line up in front of Vai. She approaches them,

"You all remember Clark? Well, he will be assisting you all again with our little plan."

They look at each other with concern,

"Is there a problem?" Vai asks,

The group shakes their heads, before I get on the Ranna, I go up to Vai,

"I was wondering if you had black paint I could borrow?"

Vai smiles and grabs black paint from her beat-up side satchel and tosses it to me,

"I like a soldier with warpaint, have fun!"

It may sound odd, but I feel off without any war paint. I quickly put the paint around my eyes and the lines on my cheeks before heading to the Ranna. After my warpaint is applied, Vai sends us out to head for Kitexa. The group leads me to the same Ranna we used during our last job. It's a silent walk to the craft, it seems like there's some tension between everyone. Personally, I don't care if my group has a problem with me. I don't know what issue they could have, but I'm not here to make friends. We get on the Ranna and head for Kitexa. Just like the walk to the Ranna, the ride to is silent. For most of the trip, I'm trying to sharpen the dull knife I was given the best I could, making barely any improvement.

"We need to be smart about this," I say to the group, "There will be guards around the perimeter of the tower, we have to take them out quietly. No one else needs to die if we are careful. We have to move quickly and quietly, understood?"

Everyone nods their heads, they don't seem to have a problem with being quiet. That being said, we need communication for something like this,

"Is there a problem?" I ask,

"No problem at all." Teni responds sarcastically.

Usually, I would try to get the problem out of them so we don't have any animosity going into something like this, but I just want to get this done as fast as possible. As long as they have my back and do their jobs, I don't care how they feel about me. The Ranna stops a mile out of Kitexa, we jump out carrying the explosives in our bags. The bags are heavy, but we have to move quickly. If I had to guess, everyone in my group used to be soldiers. The way they move and carry themselves, how they handled themselves during the transport robbery, it seems like they've been part of a unit before. It makes working with them easier, besides the silent treatment they're giving me.

We reach the tower and hide behind a broken down aircraft to take a look at the guards. To no one's surprise, it's heavily guarded. There are soldiers constantly walking around the tower on the look-out. Cinniya takes out her sniper,

"I will cover you all while you go ahead, take out the guards quietly and set the bombs. Once you go around the tower, I will not be able to cover you, so be careful." she says while adjusting her scope.

We wait a few moments for a small gap for the rest of us to silently make our way to the tower. After a few seconds, a gap opens and we quickly run towards the tower. A guard walks around the corner, but before he could react, Cinniya takes him out. Another guard comes from the left, but Cinniya, once again, has our backs. We plant a few bombs along the tower as fast as possible. I know if Blaine knew what we were doing, he would be incredibly jealous. After planting the explosives on the back of the tower, we move to the part of the tower where Cinniya won't be able to cover us, we really have to be careful now. We stop running and quietly walk to the sites we will be planting the explosives. Quietly taking out guards along the way, we plant explosives at various points around the tower's foundation for maximum damage. It's difficult for me to use such a dull knife on the guards, I really have to put in force which is not fun.

So far, everything is going okay. No one has gotten hurt and Cinniya hasn't spotted anything unusual. Our luck doesn't last long, though. A few bombs we carry have clipped and damaged wires. Grolo opens his bag and brings out tools to try to repair the wires. A few moments after he begins working on the wires, we hear footsteps approaching us from the left and right.

"Cover me, I need a few minutes!" Grolo exclaims while

moving faster.

We get behind cover as Xenem soldiers close in on us. I have no idea how they knew we were here, but I guess we lost the element of surprise. The soldiers open fire at us, I move to the ground and peek out and fire a few shots taking out a couple of soldiers. Everyone else starts firing, too. A few shots nearly hit Grolo, causing him to jolt and mess up his progress on the repairs. Obviously, we want him to move fast, but we can't focus on everything all at once, the soldiers coming from both sides are causing us to panic. We decide to split into teams and take both sides doing our best to fight off the soldiers. So far, it's working out, I'm not sure why it took us this long to think to do this. Even with this plan seemingly working out, A soldier manages to hit Grolo in the left arm, Mezza goes to Grolo to wrap his arm, but he stops her,

"No, I am fine, keep firing, I am almost done!"

It's respectable, but foolish. I admire it either way. After what seems like hours of fighting an unlimited supply of soldiers, there's finally a break where there are no more soldiers approaching us. The timing is perfect, Grolo finishes the repairs and begins planting the bombs.

After some more time, we finally plant all the explosives and start to head back to Cinniya. While making our way back, I look up and spot multiple cameras along the walls. Before I could say anything, a few soldiers rush out of the tower and aim their guns at us, they begin to search us and throw us around. How could I be so foolish? I should have figured there would be cameras, my group should have figured that, too. Now, it makes sense why we got ambushed. There aren't that many guards, but it's enough to not want to make me do something that'll get us killed. The same can't be said for Teni, though. In the chaos of all the shouting, he slowly stands and reaches for a gun in his back pocket when someone comes up behind him and puts a unique looking knife to his throat.

"Not a smart idea." I hear a woman's voice say,

With all the noise and being thrown around, I can't see

who it is, but I recognize the voice and the knife.

"Stand them up!" she demands.

The guards pick us up and turn us to the woman, it's Somma holding her knife to Teni's throat. Somma looks down the line with ferocity in her eyes, but when she sees me, her eyes turn to a look of worry and panic. Somma shakes her head,

"No, please no."

The group looks confused, they already questioned who she was and our relationship, but this doesn't help. One of the soldiers hits me in the back of my head with his gun, he looks at Somma,

"What should we do with them?"

Somma remains silent, but shakes her head. It's obvious she had no idea I would be here, nor did I know she'd be someone I have to worry about going into this.

"Dammit." I whisper to myself with my hands up, recovering from the hit.

Somma is still holding Teni with a knife to his throat, but seeing me caused her to loosen her grip and lose focus. Teni quickly elbows Somma's side. He grabs the knife, preparing to attack her, the rest of the group turns around and starts fighting the guards. As Teni pulls back to stab Somma, I make my out of the fight behind me and quickly run towards them,

"Teni, stop!" I exclaim while holding his arm back.

Teni looks back in frustration, realizing I cost him an opportunity to kill a "Xenem" soldier. He shoves me away, he growls as he backhands Somma on the right side of her face and slashes the knife towards her, giving her a deep cut in her right arm and cutting off her arrow and feather necklace. She lets out a pained cry, I run up to Teni and snatch the knife away from him and throw it to the ground, I grab his coat collar and throw him towards the rest of the group,

"Go help them take care of the guards!" I yell at Teni who looks at me with hate in his eyes,

"Now I see, you wish to die with Xenem scum?" he asks,

"Get the hell away from me, I will kill you where you stand, I don't care what you tell Vai. Go help them!"

Teni reluctantly goes to the group who are still fighting the guards. I quickly pick up the knife and turn to Somma. I lead her to a secluded area nearby and sit her down behind some crates so she's out of sight and away from danger. I look at her arm, it's a nasty wound. Teni went too far.

"I'm sorry." I say to Somma as I inspect her wound,

Somma looks at me with the same worry in her eyes, but this time, her eyes are also filled with tears.

"I am happy to see you, but what are you doing here? Why are you with them?" she asks,

"They're part of a group who's helping me destroy the tower and get rid of Tyro, they're helping me free everyone."

"I should have recognized the camp you were staying at. My father and Tyro both expect me to fight people like them, you cannot be with them, Clark. I will not fight you again."

I look down and shake my head, all of this is such a complicated situation, I hate it. I decide to not think about it much at the moment, seeing as Somma has an open wound. I open my bag and grab bandages,

"Give me your arm, please."

She says nothing as she moves her arm towards me, I take her coat off gently and start wrapping her wound. They're basic bandages, not like the ones Specter or the USC usually carries, but I shouldn't expect much from a bag with random old weapons and equipment in it that was given to me late notice. I hear everyone is still fighting, guaranteed they will be mad at me for leaving them to help what they assume is an enemy, but I couldn't care less at the moment. Somma stops me from wrapping her arm and gently touches my face and lifts it up to her. I look up at her with confusion.

"You have to get out of here, my love. Please." she says as she rubs my cheek with her thumb.

"I'm not leaving you with this wound."

I continue wrapping her arm quickly, once I finish, I rub

her arm gently and smile,

"I didn't do that bad, did I?" I joke.

Somma smiles with her eyes. She uncovers her face and kisses me on the cheek,

"Thank you. You have to leave now, I will be fine."

"How's your face?" I ask, ignoring her request.

It sounds like an odd question, but Teni struck her pretty hard, leaving a red mark.

"I barely felt anything."

"You sure can take a hit."

"I will teach you how I do it, my love." Somma jokes.

I smile and kiss the red mark on her face, it's the best I could do for that particular injury, but Somma didn't mind at all. Realizing I need to go, I grab her hand and give her knife back before grabbing my bag and getting up,

"I'm getting you out of here, get somewhere safe." I respond while standing back up.

Somma nods at me with sadness in her eyes, I kneel back down and take off the white ribbon from my wrist and put it on hers. Somma smiles and wraps me in a tight hug, It seems like all her hugs are tight hug. I feel her put something in my pocket,

"This will help you when the time comes." she continued, "Please, be careful. I do not want them to hurt you. I've seen what this rebellion can do. I need you to come back to me, Specter needs you. Please, come back."

"Don't worry, I always come back. I'm pretty hard to kill, I guess."

"How lucky for me. I love you." Somma responds before kissing my cheek and letting go.

"I love you, too. Stay safe, please." I respond as I stand back up and reluctantly turn and run back to the group.

It was hard leaving her crying and in pain, but she's right, we need to leave. I return to my group who is about done beating the guards down, impressive work, if I'm being honest. I find Somma's arrow necklace on the ground and pick it up. As

I am putting it in my pocket, I hear Teni stomp towards me,

"You! What was that?"

"What part of 'no one else needs to die' did you not get? You were going to kill her."

"I care little for Xenem scum, but it appears you may have a soft spot for them. A weakness!"

Teni and I lock eyes in fury, I can tell Teni wants to attack me, but Grolo runs up to us,

"We must go!"

Teni scoffs as he walks away, but turns back to me, pulling his knife out and pointing it at me,

"I do not know who exactly it is you are protecting, but I will not hesitate to kill them if they get in our way."

I slowly walk towards him, locking eyes with him once again. Once I'm close enough, I quickly grab the knife out of his hand and point it back at him,

"And *I* will not hesitate to kill you, don't do anything stupid. Get moving." I respond while giving him his knife back.

Teni snatches the knife back from me and stomps away. I look back over to where I put Somma and she is still sitting there, she was watching what just happened between Teni and I. I look down in shame knowing I put a target on her back by stopping Teni. I look back up and Somma smiles and blows me a kiss, just like how I did during the Vonra assault. I can't help but smile and blow her a kiss back before running off back to the group and the Ranna.

I regroup with everyone and we make our way back to the Ranna. Thiani starts it up and gets moving,

"How did it go?" she asks,

"We had some- complications." Grolo responds while wrapping his arm.

"What do you mean?"

Everyone stays silent, ignoring the question. By simply looking at Grolo, she would know exactly what we meant. Thiani swats her hand at us in annoyance. I'm surprised Teni didn't say anything to the others yet. Teni is Vai's brother, so maybe it wasn't wise to threaten him. It was the heat of the moment, he nearly killed Somma, I don't care who you are, you do not threaten her or anyone in Specter. If it wasn't Somma, I probably would have even helped Teni with his attack. It's just another unfortunate result of GEN. Juna forcing Somma into this mess. Everyone was too preoccupied with the guards to notice what Teni and I were arguing about, but they have been skeptical of me for a while now and I am sure Teni will tell them what happened later on. Despite the job being a success, the mood in the Ranna feels that of defeat, anger and bitterness. In general, they're a quiet group of people, but this feels like they're intentionally not talking to me. It's going to be a long ride back.

After a few hours, we reach the camp. Once we stop, Teni quickly gets up and leaves the Ranna. The rest of us get up slowly and grab our equipment and make our way off of the Ranna without saying anything to each other. I turn to the group and look down,

"Good job, all of you. You should be proud."

They all give a small smile and bow of appreciation. My problem was never with them, despite the fact that Teni almost went too far, he did good, too. He just doesn't want to be near me, though. Walking back to my tent, I see Teni storm into Vai's tent, I can only imagine what he is telling her. Usually, I would try to clear my name, but I'm not ashamed of what I did or feel the need to explain myself. I go back into my tent and place my bag and rifle against the side of my tent. I take off my knife from my belt and put it on the ground next to me before I lay down and close my eyes, it's been another long day. Every day since I've arrived in Xenem has been a long day. Even though I only spent one night with Somma in this tent, it feels weird not having her here. I wish she was here, it's so lonely, especially now that most people here are skeptical of me. I open my eyes and pull out Somma's broken necklace to take a look at the damage, Teni cut the leather in half. Somehow, I am going to have to put the arrow pendant on a new string.

It doesn't seem like anyone here has any spare leather cords they can give me. I look through my bag to see if it has anything in it that can be used as a necklace, but no luck. I throw my bag to the side in frustration which causes my rifle to fall over, but as my rifle fell, I felt something gently whip my arm. I grab my rifle and see a piece of brown leather is wrapped around the barrel of the gun. I've never noticed it before, I don't even know why it is there, for design, I guess. It's not the exact same color and look of the original piece of leather, but it is close enough. I unwrap it from the barrel and cut it to the right size before putting the arrow and feather pendants on it. I tie the ends and hold the fixed necklace up in front of me, it looks solid and seems sturdy. It looks close enough to the original to not make much of a difference, so I can't be too upset about how it turned out. I don't know when I'll be able to give this back to Somma, but I hope she is not too upset about it.

I put the necklace back in my pocket as I hear footsteps approach my tent.

"Clark, get out here." I hear Vai say calmly.

I leave the tent and see her rubbing her eyes in frustration. She waves her hand towards herself, telling me to follow her. She leads me to her tent where Sarge's body is still on her table.

"Teni is not too happy with you." she says while sitting down,

"All due respect, I do not care about him or how he feels about me."

Vai clenches her fist, her eyes are filled with fury and locked onto me,

"Watch your mouth, he is my family. You disrespect him, you disrespect me."

"He acted foolish, he nearly killed more people than we needed to!"

"Yes, he told me all about that Xenem soldier. I spoke with him about disobeying an order like that, but tell me, why did you help the Xenem soldier?"

"*She* wasn't a Xenem soldier, it's complicated."

"'*She*'?"

This is the second time I slipped up like that in front of Vai exposing information I should not have. I should have figured she'd catch the key word again.

"There is a lot more going on than you realize, you don't need to worry about me." I continued, "Once Tyro is gone, you all won't have to hear from me again."

I begin to walk out, but Vai stops me.

"Whoever you are protecting will not survive what we have planned, especially if they fight for Xenem. Teni told me what she looked like, from what he could tell at least, and it was a lot. There is nowhere she can hide, even with her face covered."

I stop walking, fury fills my body. I quickly turn back to Vai and approach her. I drag a seat to me and sit in front of her, leaning in close,

"You, Teni or anyone here will not lay a hand on her. I appreciate you letting me stay in your camp, but if any of you touches her, I will kill them. I will fight with you, but you leave her alone." I calmly tell her before getting up.

Vai's face is visibly shocked, she probably isn't used to people talking to her like that. I usually don't speak like that to anyone, but threatening people I love won't stand.

"I let your dead friend stay in my tent, collect Gaveau plants and put it on his body and give you a place to rest and equipment which is scarce for us. This is how you want to handle this?"

"And I thank you, but you, as well as your brother, have no say when it comes to how to handle things. Goodnight, Vai."

Her face goes from confusion to anger,

"Traitors have their lives taken!" she exclaims,

I stop again,

"And fools die every day. Don't do anything stupid, the same goes for Teni or anyone else here. Just stay out of my way."

I storm out of her tent. I'm in no mood to hear more empty threats. I've proven myself to them more than once, yet they still do not fully trust me. Nothing I say or do works, so I'm better off just keeping to myself and getting this partnership over with. I go back to my tent and lay back down, Vai and Teni really got under my skin, so I figure sleeping is the best thing for me to do right now. It takes me a while to fall asleep, but eventually, I'm able to sleep a little. A few hours pass when I hear rustling outside of my tent. The sound isn't enough to fully wake me up, so I ignore it. I stay on alert, though, which is a good thing because I hear someone enter my tent. My eyes are still closed, but I feel a presence near me, someone kneeling over me.

To keep the element of surprise, I keep my eyes closed and lay still. I hear a knife slowly be taken out of a sheath,

"Traitors have their lives taken." I hear a voice say quietly.

I recognize the voice, it's Teni. I should have figured he would try something like this. I hear him breath heavily, but after a few moments of silence I hear him grunt like he is lifting his arms up to stab me while I am down. How cowardly. Before he does anything, my eyes shoot open and Teni's face goes pale. I quickly grab my knife next to me and stab him in the heart. Teni looks down at the knife in his body in shock, he looks back up at me with a mixture of anger, confusion and pain in his eyes. He suddenly collapses to the ground. I get up and kneel next to him watching as he breathes faster and faster on the ground.

"I knew we could not trust you." he says while his voice shakes.

"I didn't want any of this, but I told you I would not hesitate to kill you if you did something stupid. Trying to kill someone who was never your enemy is more than idiotic and now you paid the price. I hope you rest peacefully. Smile knowing your work with your sister will not go unfinished.

I'm still taking out Tyro. A shame you won't be here to see it with Vai and everyone else."

Teni scoffs and shakes his head,

"Vai will come for you. She will know who killed me and there will be nowhere you can hide, you traitorous fool! We should have killed you when we had the chance."

"I'm not a traitor, I am just trying to save my friends, my family, my loved ones. Just like you."

"You dare compare us? We are not the same. Why Vai trusted you remains a mystery I now see I will never figure out. She made a mistake with you, but she will avenge me." he says as his eyes slowly close and his breathing stops.

I take the knife out and lower my head. I wasn't lying when I told him I didn't want this. There's been enough bloodshed and Teni didn't need to die, but he left me no choice. I don't take his words lightly, I'm sure Vai will come for me, so bombs or no bombs, I need to get to the tower and get everyone out. I put my knife and sheath on my belt and grab my bag and rifle. I quietly leave my tent, before I leave, I have to get Sarge. I quietly enter Vai's tent, she's asleep. I approach Sarge's body and slowly pick it up. The Gaveau plants fall off him as I pick him up going all over the floor. I guess the adhesives have worn off. I am not looking forward to having to carry him around again, but I will not leave him here, especially after what I've done.

A part of me wants to wake Vai up and admit to what happened, but I know that'll end badly, it ends bad for us either way, but at least if I leave now, I have a better chance of survival. I slowly back out of her tent holding Sarge and leave the camp avoiding the patrols. I head into the trees around the camp so I am harder to spot. Once again, I am on the run. My bag and rifle naturally adds more weight for me to carry, making it harder for me to move, but like last time, I have to keep moving. Holding Sarge again brings back images of him being killed in my head. With everything going on, I nearly forgot GEN. Juna betrayed us all and killed Sarge. I can't kill him, though. For some reason, Somma is devoted to keeping him alive. She doesn't even like him, but it's her father and he is all she has left from her family. Everyone can see he deserves to die after what he has done, I just wish Somma would see it. Maybe she does see it, just does not want to admit it. I still haven't forgotten the tragic story of Somma's family. At one point in time, I'm sure Juna was a great father but a lifetime of war and paranoia seems to have completely broken his mind in half. Who he was seems to be lost. Things seemed so simple in Tanli, we got a taste of what civilian life was like. The war barely affected Kana. Besides Vonra, life in Tanli Village made us forget about everything.

    I know it's probably unsafe, but after a while, I figure I am far enough away from the camp to sleep. I'm not too thrilled about having to sleep on the ground in the wilds of Xenem, but I don't think I'll find another camp to sleep at. I find the cleanest looking tree and place to lay down, I place Sarge's body down gently, I sit down against the tree and take a look around. Maybe at one time the wilds here were majestic, but now it seems like some wasteland. I put my hands in my pockets and I feel the item Somma put in it. I take it out to see it, it's a recorder. I never knew she had one of these, what could she possibly use one for? I turn it on and it lights up blue, the screen shows me a recording that was recent. I decide to play the recording to hopefully see why Somma gave me this.

    "*Log 319.*" I hear Somma's voice say,

    I guess she used this to log information of some sort.

    "*I am constantly being filled with panic and fear. I think the only reason Tyro has not killed me yet is because he knows my father would be furious. There has been talk of killing off some more of the prisoners, including Specter. I feel worse knowing I helped put people in that prison and will probably be the one to execute them all. I have to believe that everything will be okay, though. I know Clark is out there working on a way to get us all out. Luckily, Tyro and my father thinks he died when he jumped off the tower, so he will be able to surprise them. As for his new 'friends', Tyro knows about them already, ruthless rebels. I support them trying to take down Tyro, but they are violent, ruthless and cannot be trusted, no matter what their cause is. They better not hurt Clark, I do not trust them at all, but I trust him with my life. He has saved me and Specter multiple times. I wish I was with him right now at the Heleia Fields. How I miss sleeping in his arms with the desert winds blowing past us, kissing his lips and feeling him holding me tight. Spending the night with him again was the first time I was happy and felt safe in a long time, I always feel safe with him. I truly love him with all my heart, it kills me knowing everything he has been through, including me attacking him, which I will always regret. He deserves love and peace, he really is a hero who has done so much already. As much of a hero that he is, what Tyro has planned is too much for anyone to handle. The tower's defenses have been doubled, making it nearly impenetrable to enter. More guards around the tower and new security systems, but at least with the new systems in place, I can try to sabotage them day by day. Either way, Clark will find a way to tear it down, he has always been very clever. I do not know when I will see him again, but when I do, I will have to stop myself from running up to him and jumping in his arms, which seems easier said than done. I hope I make it to that day. I hope Clark will make it to that day, too. I guess I will have to wait and see what my reckless hero has planned. I cannot wait to see him again, hopefully freeing us all."*

I put the recorder in my pant pocket as I sigh thinking about Somma. She's such a sweet girl, I really don't deserve her, but the information in the recording is definitely going to help moving forward. The fact I am alone now, makes things harder. I was supposed to have an entire rebellion behind me, but it seems that I've become a new target for them. I hope their hate for Tyro will overpower their hate for me, or more specially, Vai's newfound hatred for me. It's not a question of if she goes after me or if she will be mad, it's certain, Teni knew it and I know it. Her loyal followers seems to do whatever she wants, they might not even know why they'll be going after me, but they won't question it. They can try to do whatever they want to me once this is over, but if they go after Somma, I'll have to put them all down, essentially doing Tyro's job for him. The situation keeps getting more and more complicated. I'll get some sleep, but tomorrow, I'll have to march to the tower and fight my way in and get out with everyone. Limited ammo, worn out supplies and a sleep deprived soldier, what a powerful mix, but if I am to die, at least it will be getting everyone out. Somma is right, I am reckless, but perhaps I can use that to my advantage. Going stealth probably won't work that well, so making some noise, or as Sarge would say "Creating some smoke" might benefit me, benefit us all. Either way, alive or dead, doing whatever it takes, no matter what is just who I am. What a damn fool I am.

I surprisingly slept pretty well, as well as I could have on the ground in the delightful Xenem wilds. I thought I would have been killed or captured while I slept, who knows if Vai knows about Teni and sent out a search party already. She didn't speak about it much, but I'm sure she loved him and wanted him to be safe. I feel terrible about it, she offered me shelter and I did my best to repay her and work with everyone, but instead I killed her brother. He tried to attack me first, but she probably won't see it like that. To make matters worse, I took the bag she gave me with the equipment inside and I doubt she gave it to me as a gift. There's not much inside the bag, some ammo and medical equipment, but not much of either, not since I used most of it during my time with Vai's group and wrapping Somma's arm.

I can't stay in one place for too long, not with Vai presumably chasing after me. I get up and pick up my bag and Sarge and get moving. I have no idea where I am, everything looks the same, burnt down trees and bushes, dead plants and decomposed bodies, the usual. It's a grim scene, but I have to push through it all. I walk a mile before I hear what sounds like a stream or river, I move closer to the sound and to my surprise I see a river of what appears to be water. Whether it is clean or not is questionable, but I'm glad to see something normal here. I gently put Sarge and my bag down and approach the water to take a closer look. It looks clean, it seems being so far away from the blood, trash and toxic sludge from Kitexa and Tyro tower has caused the portion of the river to remain clean. If I had to guess, there is probably some sort of natural filtration system somewhere. It's certainly odd for Xenem to have something like that, but I wouldn't complain.

While I am still a bit skeptical of the water, I decide to wash my hair and face, since spending a night in the wilds of Xenem is truly disgusting. There's a small bit of fear that makes me think my face will melt if I wash my face with this mysterious water, but I move past it and throw the water on my face. It seems to be clean, I quickly put my head in the water to wash my hair and I must admit, it feels amazing. You wouldn't think this water was on Xenem, it hasn't been touched by anything toxic which is a major surprise to me. Everywhere I have been so far has been a barren wasteland from the war, so seeing something like this is truly a spectacle. After my hair, I take off my coat, uniform and shirt to run it through the water. Before I put the coat in, I take out Somma's folded letter and put it in my pant pocket. I can't lose it, especially if it's from her.

I run my shirt, uniform and coat through the water and watch as all the dirt, dried blood and loose fibers wash away from them. I can't remember the last time the coat was washed, I used to wear it all the time. The river washes off a fair bit of the filth, they are not fully clean by any means, but there's definitely a difference. I take everything out and place them on the ground to dry for a bit. I know it is unwise to stay in one place for too long, but I want to enjoy this seemingly magical river for a bit longer, especially while everything dries. I grab my canteen and fill it with the water from the river, praying I can drink it. After the canteen is filled, I sit down next to the coat and put my wet hair in a ponytail while looking around. It's an interesting view. The river seems to be the only thing that looks clean and normal while everything else that surrounds it is dead and has decayed. There's a strange beauty to it that I am able to enjoy. After a few minutes pass, I hear rustling in the bushes behind me, I fear it's Vai or one of her soldiers who found me. I quickly stand up and pull out my knife, ready for someone to jump out and attack me. I currently have no top on, only wearing pants, so I really feel exposed and unprepared for what's to come. To my surprise, it's a man stumbling out of the forest, with tattered bandages around his Abdomen. It's Fesio.

THE DEAD WALK

Fesio looks like a mess. Other than his wound, he looks like he has been through hell. Last I saw of him, he was shot off the transport. I thought he died. He looks just as shocked to see me, we don't say anything to each other for a few moments, I imagine it is due to shock, for both of us. No one has seen me with my shirt off before. Somma has seen me in a tank top during our time in Tanli, but Fesio is the first to see me shirtless. I'm a bit self-conscious about my scars and don't like people, most of all people who are essentially strangers, seeing them. Fesio slowly approaches me with a pained expression on his face, once he is close enough to me, his pained expression turns to a small smile. He playfully pushes me,

"You look terrible." he jokes,

It may be a joke, but I'm sure I really do look terrible.

"I think we both look terrible. Take a seat." I respond while helping him down.

I grab the cantine out of my bag and put water from the river and hand it to him,

"Drink, it looks like you need it." I say to Fesio while handing him the cantine.

To be honest, I didn't know Fesio that well, if at all, but I still feel somewhat responsible for him. I feel like I could have done more to help him when he was shot. Maybe I couldn't have caught him, but we could have gone back to pick up his body during our escape from the transport had I tried harder to go back. Teni rushed us out. I suppose I am partially to blame, too. Somma showing up really did distract me and I was not in the right mindset. What's really confusing me is how he survived and where has he been?

"What happened to you after you were hit?" I ask.

It takes Fesio a while to respond due to him chugging the water I gave him. He nearly empties the cantine before finally stopping. He takes a few more moments to gather himself. After another minute he sighs and looks up,

"When I was hit, I thought I was dead," he continued, "it is all a blur to me, but I remember hitting the ground and losing consciousness. As my eyes started to close, I recall seeing the transport and our Ranna keep moving, leaving me behind. I was too weak to stand up and chase after you all. I figured I was a dead man anyways. When I woke up, I was in incredible pain, not to mention dehydrated and overheated. I had to force myself up and stumble away. After that, I was barely surviving with a limited medical, food and water supply, but after I spotted you here, I did not believe it. I thought I was going crazy."

I'm all for the concept of no man left behind, it's how my squad is run. It's clear that no one on that team was familiar with that concept, though. I feel terrible, I can't imagine how hopeless all that feels. I'm not sure if Fesio is mad at me. For all I know, he thinks we all forgot about him and left him to die. My trust for anyone is at a low point, not that I ever really trusted Vai or anyone from her camp, but I was still almost killed by one of them. That's enough for me to be wary. In general, there are very few people I trust, my parents, Somma, Sarge and the rest of the squad. Trusting Fesio is going to be tough, but perhaps I don't need to fully trust him. My hope is that he will help me reach the tower, I'm sure he still wants to take it down. By helping Fesio properly fix his wounds and letting him heal safely, I don't see why he wouldn't help.

Fesio looks around, taking in the view, but looks back at me,

"What are you doing out here?"

"After we stole the explosives, we went to plant the bombs on the tower, but someone I knew showed up and complicated the plan and caused me to lower my guard. Teni began to question my loyalty. He became unsure of me during the heist where we lost you, but what happened at the tower furthered his suspicions. That night, he tried to kill me in my sleep, but I woke up right before he did anything and ended up killing him. I didn't want to, but I had no choice. I knew Vai would be furious, I had to run and so I ended up here."

Fesio scoffs,

"Teni was always quick to anger, he was a damn fool."

I don't give a response before nodding my head and looking down. After Fesio takes a few more sips from the already half-empty canteen, he hands it back to me and slowly lays down,

"Thank you." he says quietly while closing his eyes,

I still have more questions for him, but he needs to rest, so I let him fall asleep. As much of a rush I am in to get everyone out of prison and save Somma as well as my parents, a beat up, tired Fesio won't be much use to me. He quickly falls asleep, not minding at all that he is laying on dirt, but who am I to talk? That's how I've been sleeping for a while now. I shake the canteen and feel how empty it is. In a matter of less than 5 minutes, Fesio drained the entire canteen. I get up and approach the river to fill the canteen again, I look back at Fesio who's covered with filth and decide to grab a rag out of my bag and run it through the water after filling the canteen back up. I walk back to him with the filled canteen and wet rag and sit down next to him. I figure while he sleeps, I can clean his face a little.

The dirt and filth from Fesio's face comes off almost immediately. He's from this wretched planet, I imagine everyone from Xenem knows that clean water is nearly impossible to come by, I don't know if he already knew of this river and was intending to come here to clean up or if I was the one to discover it, but either way, Fesio arrived in bad shape. It was lucky we crossed paths here. As far as Xenems go, Fesio doesn't look like most of them, which is lucky for him. People from Xenem look like demons out of a nightmare, especially with their piercing green eyes and wrinkled pale skin, Leezol is the spitting image of a Xenem, inside and out. What I noticed about Fesio upon meeting him for the first time was his eyes, while green, lacked the killer and heartless look that you see everywhere else on this planet. Everyone in Vai's rebellion looked almost identical, but Fesio looks to be on the younger side. He was a lot easier to identify, it's a shame what happened to him on the transport.

I did the best I could to clean up Fesio. Other than his face, I cleaned his hands which were covered in dirt and dried up blood, I even cleaned and rebandaged his wounds. He looks a lot better now than he did when we first encountered each other here. He's still sleeping, probably the first decent sleep he has gotten in a while, I know how that feels. There's not much else I can do at the moment. With Fesio asleep and cleaned up, mostly, at least, all I can do is wait for him to wake up so we can figure out a plan. Thoughts of Somma begin to flood my mind. Through everything that has happened, thoughts of her beauty and kindness and images of her smile have been the only thing keeping me from going insane in this incessant turmoil. I pull out the letter she left me and read it again, though what she wrote was bittersweet, it came from her nonetheless and I will always cherish it and the words she put down. After reading the letter, I grab the recorder and listen to her last entry again. Hearing her voice brings me comfort, even if she is not really with me. I can't help but smile hearing her voice again. Somma always had a soft and calming voice, you wouldn't expect her to be a soldier just by looking at her and hearing her voice. After hearing her recording again, I start feeling tired. Her voice seemed to have soothed me. Before I try to get some sleep as I wait for Fesio, I decide to record a message of my own for her when I give the recorder back. After I record my message, I quickly fall asleep.

I wake up about an hour later, I don't remember exactly what I said in my message. I was too tired when I recorded it, but either way, I hope I said the right words. Even if words have never been my specialty. I look next to me to see that Fesio is still asleep. He's so still, if I didn't know any better, I'd think he's dead. I wouldn't be surprised, especially after seeing the condition he was in. I let him rest for long enough, but he needs to wake up and we need to think of some way we can get out of this mess. Fesio is left better off, he has a group to go back to with open arms, assuming he still wants to go back, but I don't have that luxury. Sure, I have a team waiting for me, but the path to them is suicide. According to Somma, Tyro has everyone on high-alert, getting anywhere close to Specter is going to be a nightmare. Fesio has studied Tyro and Kitexa with Vai, so any knowledge he could give me would be more than helpful, so it is time to wake him up.

I gently grab his shoulder and shake him a little to see if he wakes with no success. The pessimist in me starts to think I might have two bodies on my hands now. I shake a little harder and his eyes quickly open and he sits up with almost superhuman speed while looking around, his hand on his knife, prepared to attack any possible threat. He is in complete survival mode. I raise my hands knowing better not to try to wrestle his hand away from the knife on his belt. In his state, I could've been an easier kill than fish in a barrel. After Fesio comes back to reality he quickly looks at me with primal rage in his eyes,

"You could not let me sleep?"

"Sorry, Sleeping Beauty, but I think I let you sleep long enough."

"I am not beautiful when I sleep, I do not think so, at least." he responds while shoving me.

I forget that sarcasm is lost on most of the people on Xenem, I got so used to Leezol's and Tyro's crass and sarcastic nature that I assumed sarcasm was a universal concept, especially on Xenem. Fesio's shove put me to the floor, he's stronger than he looks. I could definitely use him to help me reach the tower. I'm sure even he realizes it's a suicide mission,

246

so I don't think giving him water and a place to rest is enough to have him help me. I had to jump through hoops with Vai and her team and all I got in return was a near death experience at the hands of Vai's brother. Killing Teni really put me deeper in this hole, so here's hoping all of this will not end up in vain.

"How's your wound?" I ask Fesio as I get up off the ground and dust myself off,

"I am alive."

My kind of answer. His wound certainly looks a bit better, as good as it can given the limited medical supplies we had to work with. The past couple of hours, the only question that has been running through my head is how to ask Fesio for help. I suppose the best way to do it is to flat out ask and hope for the best. Both of us aren't exactly in pristine condition, we've been through hell. We do have a common enemy, though. That appears to be the only hope I have for gaining his help. I hear Fesio muttering something under his breath with anger in his voice, I can't make out what he is saying exactly. The only words I hear are,

"Fools... Traitors... Bastards..."

I imagine he is thinking about the Transport robbery and how he was left behind, or more appropriately, left for dead. I really want to ask for his help, so I'm hoping by asking him what is bothering him, it will open up the conversation.

"Fesio," I say while nudging him, "What's going on?"

"Years I have devoted to Vai and her damned rebellion. She never went looking for me, nor has she sent anyone. I hid away off the trail for days, waiting and watching to see if anyone had come for me. Not one sign of anyone from the camp! Now, I am stuck in the middle of nowhere. What do I do now?"

"We can blow something up." I respond, trying to move the conversation.

I do feel for Fesio, it is truly terrible what he has been through, but we can't dwell too much on what happened. I'm sure he wants out of this situations just as much as

I do, moving the conversation was the only way to further the process. He doesn't seem too bothered by the shift in conversation, almost as if he knew I was going to say something like that sooner or later.

"What exactly did you have in mind?" Fesio asks,

"After the Transport robbery, we planted bombs all around Tyro's tower, if we can detonate the bombs before Vai and her team does, we can avoid a confrontation with them and if we are lucky, take out Tyro and free my squad."

"What if I want a confrontation?"

"After I am gone, you can fight whoever you want, but right now, our main problem is Tyro."

Fesio shrugs his shoulders. He stands up and points East. Looking at where he is pointing, I can see the tower in the distance. Even miles away, it can still be seen, I suppose Tyro planned for that. Hoping his power can be seen for miles. Fesio's point turns into a clenched fist, shaking with anger,

"How I have wanted to tear that monstrosity down. That is why I joined Vai, but we are just two people. Even if we did set off the bombs, we are still two, ill-equipped, exhausted, beaten and broken fools."

Obviously, I am aware of our condition, nonetheless, we do not have much of a choice. We have nothing to go back to if we don't attack. It appears all Fesio has left is vengeance, I know that can fuel anyone for days. While vengeance is also on my mind, there is so much more. My parents, Specter, Somma, the entire USC, I need to get them all out and end Tyro once and for all. I take a moment to formulate a response to Fesio who is still staring off at the tower with both fists clenched. I walk next to him and look at the tower again,

"You're right. We are not in good shape, but we're soldiers. You want revenge, right? There is no doubt that Vai and your old friends will hear the explosion and come rushing to see what is going on. After we get inside, you can fight whoever you want from her rebellion. I already took care of one of them for you, so it makes your plan easier."

Fesio cracks a smile and starts pacing back and forth, it seems like a million thoughts are running through his head, but seemingly happier thoughts, filled with hope, which is something that has been lacking between both of us. The muttering resumes while he paces, could it be he is formulating some sort of plan? Either way, I remain silent so I don't distract what I am assuming and hoping to be the formation of a solid plan.

"I have an idea, it is mad, but it just might work." Fesio continued with a devilish grin, "We go to the tower, we fire a couple shots at the bombs, they explode, we march in and fight."

Calling his plan "Mad" is an understatement. I'd assume Fesio was joking, but from what I've learned, most people from Xenem lack the ability to joke.

"That's all well and good, but you are forgetting that even with the bombs set off, we have an army to deal with." I respond,

"Clark, what is next to the tower?"

"The prison."

"Exactly!" he continued while grabbing my shoulder, "The bombs will surely destroy a part of the prison, if not all of it. People will be escaping, causing the army to not only deal with a bombing, but also escaping prisoners as well as our assault. They will not know what hit them. We kill everyone in that tower, kill them all!"

The plan does not sound any less crazy, if anything, it sounds even more crazy than before. That being said, it's the only plan that could possibly work. There is something Fesio said that concerns me, though. "We kill everyone in that tower, kill them all." We can kill all of them in the tower, all but one, Somma. I'm not too keen on telling people about her, seeing as the last time the truth came out, I was almost killed in my sleep. In no way am I embarrassed of her, but she's still technically fighting for Xenem and that makes her an enemy to anyone involved with Vai. Despite Fesio's mad ramblings and ideas, I do feel he can handle who Somma is better than Teni or Vai.

"You can kill whoever you want in that tower, besides one person." I say to Fesio while grabbing him by the shirt, ensuring he is listening closely, "There is a girl in that tower from Vespis, her name is Somma, even though she may fight you and defend the tower, know that she is truly on our side and you will not lay a hand on her, understood?"

"I do not understand, if she is going to fight us, why are you defending her?"

"She is there by force, her scum of a father, GEN. Pyren Juna, betrayed the USC and forced her to fight by his side with Tyro, but she hates it just as much as I do. No matter what happens, she survives. Got it?"

Fesio still looks baffled, but he slowly nods in agreement. I don't care if he does not fully understand the situation, if at all, but as long as he remembers not to touch Somma, then there won't be a problem. I let go of his shirt and walk towards the tower, I stop and look at it while contemplating the best way to go about the plan. It may seem simple to just set off a bomb and start firing, but even with the distractions, we can easily get killed. I hear a dry chuckle behind me,

"I see." Fesio continued while standing nexting to me, "It was that girl on the transport. I knew she was not born of Xenem, we all knew. I sensed you both knew eachother, you did not try to kill each other. She did not really try to kill any of us, but more so, she just tried to stop us from taking the bombs. Even then, she did not do anything. She was distracted by you. Who is she exactly?"

"She's a part of a squad I'm in, but even more, someone I love, we're together. Her and the rest of my squad as well as my parents are being held in the tower and in the prison. We need to get them all out, they will help us."

Fesio looks down and pulls something out of his pocket, it's a necklace with a green crystal pendant. He smiles while looking at it. It certainly is a beautiful piece, but I'm not sure why he brought it out.

"How lucky you are, Clark." Fesio says softly, "You can still fight for those you love. I lost that luxury. My Tavia wore this necklace. I gifted it to her, she never took it off. I had to take it off her when she died. A Xenem soldier killed her for believing she stood against Tyro. Of course, she did, but it was still wrong. I was not with her in her final moments, I was working in Kitexa dumping waste into the river for a factory I worked for. When I returned, I was in shock and horror to see they left her body on the ground like trash. I took it off her before burying her, swearing vengeance. Soon after her murder, I joined Vai, in hopes of finding her killer and ending Tyro's reign. It will all be torn down in her honor. I will get my revenge one day and avenge her murder. There is nowhere he can hide from me once we are in."

I should have figured a Xenem soldier killed Tavia. Fesio still has fire inside of him, a burning vengeance towards all who stand by Tyro. It's probably the only thing keeping him going. As tired and beaten down as we are, I want to get going as fast as possible. We've already wasted so much time resting, who knows if my squad is still alive at this point?

"I'm truly sorry to hear what happened," I say to Fesio, "but you have the chance to do something great for her. Like you said, 'It will all be torn down in her honor.' I'm sure she would be happy to know you helped bring down Tyro. Are you ready to go? I think we've rested long enough."

Fesio inhales deeply and rubs his eyes before slowly grabbing his bag. He puts the necklace on and begins walking. He stops and turns to me,

"Are you going to drag your friend all the way to the tower?"

It may sound rude or improper, but I am getting tired of carrying around Sarge's corpse. I still refuse to bury him on Xenem and I really don't think Fesio and I can trade off shifts carrying him. I look at Sarge's body on the ground covered with rags, I approach his body, but Fesio stops me.

"If you are going to carry him around," Fesio continued while opening his bag, "Then use these for his body, it will slow the decay process." Fesio grabs Gaveau plants out of his bag and hands them to me.

I recognize them from when Vai used them on Sarge a while back. A very unique looking plant, it did wonders.

"Thank you, where did you find these?" I ask Fesio while gently placing the plants on Sarge.

"Who do you think told Vai about these plants and where to find them? I know this land better than most."

Fesio comes up behind and nudges me to the side as he finishes up covering Sarge properly as I wasn't too sure on how to properly cover and wrap him. There isn't too much I know about Fesio, other than he's bright and a survivor. The journey back to Kitexa will be long, so I figure I can talk with him more about who he really is, assuming he is okay with it. After he properly wraps Sarge, he picks him up and hands the body to me. We begin walking, but not before I give him a smile and nod of appreciation. The leaves don't make Sarge any lighter, but if they keep him from decaying, I'll take it. The easiest path back to the tower seems to be mostly along the path of the river, despite it being out in the open, it does give up a water supply and the river itself seems well hidden.

For the first few minutes of the walk, we remain silent, with only the sound of our footsteps on the dirt, the stream of water and the cold winds blowing. Fesio and I are both quiet by nature, but someone had to say something.

"How did you learn about Gaveau plants?" I ask Fesio as we're walking.

"My mother, Kritisi, studied plant life. She taught me everything I know about plants. She raised me and my siblings all alone after my father, Noltev, died in prison after trying to spread a message of hope and positivity on the streets. Tyro saw it as propaganda against him and had him locked away where they killed him. He was a great man, a great father who always looked out for us. My mother wanted us to leave

Xenem, but my father refused, he wanted to stay and give people hope. After Tavia died, I did not want Tyro and his men to take anyone else from me. My sister and brothers left home when they got the chance. Truth be told, I was never close with them and did not care when they left. Despite all that happened, my mom stayed. I went to my childhood home to gather a few things and try to convince my mother to leave Xenem once and for all, I had to get her out. I rushed to the house to collect my things and begged her to get out while she could. At this time, Tyro began making it impossible to leave or enter Xenem, but if she acted fast enough, she would be able to catch one last transport out. She wanted me to go with her, but I could not leave Xenem in the hands of evil men like Tyro. Before reluctantly leaving, she gave me her book of plants. A parting gift, so I never forget her and always have something to read. I escorted her to the transport, but were caught by soldiers who immediately opened fire and killed my mother in front of me. I held her in my arms and watched the life leave her eyes. The soldier ran to me and picked me up to arrest me, but I grabbed one of their guns from their holster and opened fire on all of them. At that point, I knew I had to run and not look back. Tyro's reign has taken everything from me, everything, but not my life. I assure you, on the life of my father, my mother and Tavia, he will not get that."

I couldn't think of much to say after hearing such a tragic story,

"I'm sorry." I respond, it's the only thing I can think to say.

Fesio spoke with such passion and anger, as if talking about his past made him relive his tragic losses all over again. He has lived a life that would break most people, no matter where they come from. I'm no stranger to Tyro's cruelty, he forced the girl I love to attack me and enjoyed every second of it. Fesio got it worse, though. I try to push the conversation forward so he doesn't think about his losses. It's safe to assume the study of plants was a passion carried over from his mother, seeing as I still don't know much about Gaveau plants or the extent of his botanical knowledge, it makes me want to know more about him.

"So, Gaveau plants," I continued, "what else can they do?" I say with a brighter tone in voice, trying to lighten the mood.

"They are edible, safe to eat if you have nothing else. Lucky for us, they are everywhere if you know where to look."

There were times before I stumbled into Vai's camp where I recall seeing plants that fit the description of Gaveau, if I knew what they were at the time, I would have bags full of it. So far, Fesio is proving to be a great travel companion. He's quiet, he reminds me of Carden. An odd question pops into my mind, though. Undoubtedly, Vai hates me and wants to kill me, she probably has inspired her soldiers to want the same thing as her, but if Fesio was never left behind, would he want me dead, too?

"Fesio, may I ask you something?" I ask him while walking up next to him, Fesio nods and grunts while looking ahead.

"If the group never left you behind, would you be a part of the hunting party that is looking for me?"

Fesio shrugs his shoulders,

"I suppose not, your death serves no purpose to me. You did not kill anyone of value to me."

Not that the question really mattered, especially now, but it is relieving to hear that. As far as he knows, I left him to die, just like the rest of the group, so I'm a little shocked that he doesn't want to kill me. I didn't want to bring up what happened, but for my own sake, I want to clear my name with him.

"I'm just letting you know, I tried to save you when you fell, but everyone held me back. If you still feel I left you behind and if it'd help you feel better or more at peace, you can take a shot at me."

Fesio chuckles and shakes his head,

"Clark, I know you had nothing to do with it, if I did, you would have been in the dirt hours ago. If you still want me to hit you, though, that is okay with me."

I crack a smile and give a quiet sigh of relief, I believe him when he says I'd already be dead if he thought I had anything to do with that mess. Fesio stops walking and looks at the river, I walk past him, but stop right after.

"Is everything okay?" I ask Fesio while slowly approaching him, like he is a wild animal.

"I was thinking about something. You said the girl, Somma, would attack me. I understand she would be following orders that she does not agree with nor like, but even then, I cannot let her attack me without defending myself. I respect your wishes, but if I have to, I would have to kill her."

Any other time a threat would be made on Somma's life would end poorly, but in Fesio's case, I see his point and understand what he is saying. That being said, I can't let him kill, or even hurt her. Not her or anyone I'm trying to get out.

"You've been through hell, I get that," I continued while standing next to him, "but if she attacks you, I am asking that you do not harm her in any way. If she throws a punch, you block. If she shoots at you, jump for cover. If she runs after you, run faster. That being said, she's not someone who lets her aggression take hold, but still, try to avoid her and let me handle it. Do not under any circumstances hurt her, please."

Fesio lets out a long sigh and nods before walking away continuing on our path. Usually, I'd demand a response, a verbal confirmation he heard me, but that's only if I was with Specter. I am not his leader. I can't act like he is under my control, so all I can do is hope he heard me and won't mess up. I truly do not want to harm Fesio, especially after all he has been through and he's a great help to me, but if he hurts Somma or anyone in Specter, I can't let that go unpunished.

"She sounds special." Fesio continued while walking along the stream, "How did you meet her?"

It seems like forever ago when I met her, but it's one of

those moments you don't forget. Talking about Somma usually brightens my mood, so I let my guard down and decide to tell him the story, a rather funny, but embarrassing story in my opinion. Pretty much embarrassing for everyone involved.

"I met her when my squad was formed. I had already met some of them beforehand and made my introductions, but when it came to Somma, I should have figured she would be special right from the start. My departed friend we have been carrying around was the leader of my squad, Specter. He introduced us. His name was SSG. Richard Miner, we called him 'Sarge'. He was a great man. He brought me to Vespis, her home planet, to meet her. Truth be told, I don't think she was aware she was being tasked to be a part of our squad. Sarge took me into the USC Headquarters in Felv, we walked down a corridor to a room at the end, he stopped me from entering, though. I had no idea what was going on, Sarge had his classic grin, but said nothing else to me. I asked what was going on, but he kept smiling and held up a finger, telling me to wait. I put my hands in my coat pockets and started leaning on the wall waiting for whatever it was Sarge had planned. I heard people talking behind the door, I couldn't make out what they were saying, but I could hear the people speaking were a man and a young woman. I was still confused and waiting for the big reveal, until I heard the man say something. The next thing I knew, the woman's voice became clear through the door. After the man said something to her, I heard the woman start laughing excitedly and repeating the same phrase over and over again, 'Thank you! Thank you! Thank you!', now, something you need to know, Vespins have shining, sparkling skin that gets brighter if they get too stressed or even excited, sometimes to blinding levels. The young girl was so excited, her skin started glowing brighter and brighter. Her light was piercing through the crack of the doors hitting Sarge and I in the eyes. From what little vision I had, I saw the light quickly go out and heard the man say something in a firm tone. Sarge laughed and he turned to me and said 'She sounds rather excited.' It was my first time being hit in the eyes with Vespin light without any sort of eye protection. I was still feeling the effects of the lights hitting me, I couldn't stop rubbing my eyes trying to regain vision, that's when I heard the door open and heard people walk towards us. I felt and looked like a fool rubbing my eyes like a madman. I felt Sarge elbow my arm trying to get my attention, I blinked quickly a few times as a last effort to try to fix my sight, which worked a little bit. I turned to Sarge and his eyes darted towards the people in front of us. I looked and saw a man standing in front of me, he was a General for the USC. Feeling like a complete idiot, I quickly stood at attention. The General scoffed and turned to Sarge, 'You expect my daughter to work with this Earthling who cannot keep his eyes open?' he asked. Hearing that pissed me off, but I knew better not to talk back, especially to a General. Sarge felt my anger and tried to deescalate the situation, 'C'mon, Juna,' he said 'the kid was blinded by a burst of light without warning, give him a break.' That's when I heard the woman enter the conversation. 'My apologies, sir.', I was still regaining vision, but I could tell she was young. I quickly apologized to GEN. Juna before I turned away and rubbed my eyes one more time. I turned back around and with my vision back to normal I was able to see everyone. To the right of the General, I saw a woman, an incredibly beautiful woman. I was right about the young part, she looked a little younger than me, at least. As soon as I looked at her, she gave me a smile, a smile I would come to love later on. 'Are you okay?' she asked me with concern and a touch of embarrassment in her voice. I'll admit, I didn't handle the introduction too well. I was still getting my vision back and was taken aback by her beauty and didn't want to say the wrong thing in front of the General who already did not seem to like me. I tried to tell her I was okay, but I kept stumbling over my words. I was a mess, my hair was in my face after violently trying to regain my vision, so I kept trying to move it away from my face to look presentable, pair that with me forgetting how to speak, it was a disaster on my end. I decided to just cut my losses and stop talking. I looked down in shame and heard the General sigh, 'You are a fool." he told Sarge before storming off. I felt completely ashamed of myself, I couldn't seem to lift my head up. Sarge was just as annoyed with me as the General was and I felt it. After a moment of silence and me looking down in defeat, I saw a pair of boots step in front of me, 'Hello!' she said 'I apologize for my father, he can be hard to deal with. Are your eyes okay?" I gain the confidence to look back up at her, but this time I'm able to speak, 'I'm okay, thank you, ma'am.' I responded, I got to see her smile again, it was enough to calm me down. Sarge walked up to us for proper introductions. 'CPL. Clark Parson, this is PVT. Somma Juna, it was time you both met each other.' Somma smiles again and grabs my hand and starts shaking it, 'It is so nice to meet you, I have heard so much about you both! I promise, I will not disappoint either of you!', my hand nearly fell off from her shaking it so much. After she let go of my hand, she saw how messy my hair was, men weren't supposed to have long hair in the USC military, but Sarge didn't mind. After she saw my hair, she giggled and grabbed a hair tie out of her pocket and handed it to me. It was an interesting design, with lots of different symbols colored blue, black and Red. I fixed my hair and put in a hair style people from Earth call a 'ponytail', I've been using that tie ever since, I don't think she notices it, though. Anyways, her father was the legendary GEN. Pyren Juna. He never liked me or the idea of Specter. He didn't want Somma anywhere near us, but I guess Sarge spoke with her in the past and the idea excited her. I suppose GEN. Juna let her join as some sort of way to show her she could do better, luckily, she hasn't realized that yet. From then on, Somma and I became closer over time and now we can't imagine our lives without each other. That's why I have to get her and the rest of my team out unharmed. When I planted the bombs for Vai, I saw her again and she looked so stressed and scared. Not to mention filled with worry and panic for me. I told her I would return and right now, I just hope Somma, my parents and the rest of my squad are okay."

I can't remember the last time I spoke so much, it felt off.

"Interesting." Fesio responds.

His blunt responce made me feel a bit foolish telling him all that just for a one worded response. Fesio, by nature, is quiet, so I shouldn't be too surprised that was his response. I'd probably respond the same way, too. I didn't respond to Fesio's insightful comment, but he let out a chuckle,

"Sounds to me like she had feelings for you the moment she met you."

He could be right. Somma is a very friendly person, she could have easily been acting kind because that's just who she is, but I hope she felt something in that moment. I didn't realize it either, but looking back, I felt something for her, too. I suppose for the first few months I was too focused on the mission and training everyone with Blaine. There's not much time for romance in our particular situation, but either way, I'm happy things between us turned out how they did. That being said, my love for her makes her an easy target for people trying to get to me. It already happened, by none other than Tyro and the man who didn't like me right from the start, her damn father. For all I care, Fesio can do what he wants with him. As long as Somma, my parents and Specter runs free with me, the tower goes down and Tyro with it, I'll be happy. It's about damn time something goes my way.

After a mile of walking, Fesio and I hear rustling in the bushes to our right, we both stop and look at the same time. The rustling continues as we slowly approach, our only defense, our knives and my old my Rifle from Vai. The rustling suddenly stops, when two men jump out of the forest and tackle Fesio and I. I didn't recognize either of them, but they clearly knew who we were.

"Hello, Fesio!" the man on top of Fesio says.

"Hello, Marzen."

As for the man on top of me, I haven't had the pleasure of meeting him yet. He's just someone else that wants me dead.

Both of the men are trying to choke us, but Fesio and I keep fighting their hands off of us. Fesio grabs a nearby rock and strikes Marzen in the head, effectively knocking him to the ground. Fesio quickly gets up and throws the man off of me, the man grunts as he hit the ground, he quickly looks back and laughs,

"You were always my favorite, Fesio!"

"Devka, what are you both doing here?" Fesio broadly asks as he marches towards him.

I still have no idea who these men are or what they want with us. Fesio handled them rather fast, it's no secret he knows them both, but from where? There is still not a whole lot that I know about him. I stand back up and take a look at the two men. Marzen is tall, too tall to move so quietly and be unseen. He has long greasy brown hair, dirt marks all over his face. Devka is shorter, but he covers his mouth with a bandana and wears a hood. One thing was certain, they were both from Xenem. Both of them wear disheveled clothes with tears and rips in them. It seems like they've lived in the forest for years. Fesio grabs both of them by their shirts,

"How did you find us?"

"Fesio! Is this how you say hello to us?" Marzen playfully asks, "We grew up together!"

"Answer the question. What are you doing here?"

Devka tries to fight free, but I come up behind him and elbow the back of his head. He grunts in pain and watches me as I walk in front of him standing next to Fesio.

"Who is your pet?" he asks.

Fesio is visibly losing his patience, he throws them to the ground and pulls out his knife,

"Who shall I start with first?" he asks me,

I put my hand on the knife and lower it, before he does anything to them, I need to know what's going on.

"Who are you?" I ask them both.

Both of them look at each other and stare me down with violent intent behind their piercing green eyes, but they do not respond. Fesio sighs and walks up next to me,

"Devka and Marzen Vianti. Vai's brothers. They do not stay at her camp, they prefer the wild, like the animals they are."

It's safe to assume that they heard about Teni and are seeking revenge just like Vai, but why attack Fesio? Marzen slowly gets up and points at me,

"You owe us blood! Vai told us what happened, we leave with your head!"

"Your business is with me, why attack Fesio?" I ask.

Devka chuckles as he gets up,

"Let us call it a loose end. Vai knew he survived and counted on him seeking revenge, she cannot have that."

Vai seemed so kind and like a good leader at first, but I was clearly mistaken. Fesio wasn't lying when he called them animals, they look like wild beasts. They act like it, too. Both begin to slowly approach us looking like they're ready to pounce.

"Stay back, don't do anything stupid!" I exclaim.

"Stupid, like how you killed Teni and betrayed Vai? Lots of stupid going around!" Marzen responds.

Fesio steps closer to them,

"Teni tried to kill Clark, he had every right to defend himself!"

They ignore Fesio and start to get closer, but the sound of their footsteps calls the attention of Fesio and I, we look down at the dirt then look back at each other. Seconds before Marzen and Devka launch at us, Fesio and I quickly grab dirt from the ground and throw it in their face, they both yell in pain and cover their face which gives us our chance to tackle them both, we grab the rope from their belts and tie their hands behind their backs and sit them up on a rock. Fesio takes both of their knives as Marzen violently moves his body around trying to get as much rope off as possible. He looks around and sees Devka is tied up next to him. Marzen laughs,

"Same old, Fesio. We never could beat you. Not in the

past and clearly not now."

"Not without his pet, at least." Devka adds.

Marzen kicks Devka's leg,

"Oh, shut it!" he exclaims before he continued, "You both realize once we tell Vai what happened, there is nowhere you can hide, yes? We already know Clark is heading towards the tower, Vai will see him and go in for the kill. Once we are out of these ropes and run off, there will be nothing you can do to stop it!"

At that moment, somehow, they both get out of the restraints and lunge towards us, but Fesio was ready and extended both of his arms out, holding their knives that go into both of their chests. Marzen and Devka slowly look down then look at each other. Fesio lets go of the knives and they both fall back onto the rock. Marzen laughs weakly,

"Fesio, always filled with surprises." he says as he takes his last breaths with Devka.

Fesio pulls the knives out,

"It looks like Vai has no brothers now."

That's all he said before walking away. It was another situation where I didn't want to kill anyone or have people die, but I am starting to see I can't always control that. This proves I was right, Vai is coming after me. I can't afford to stop or slow down, Vai will send more people, I have to reach the tower and free everyone. After that, Vai can try her best to kill me herself, but I have proven I am not easy to kill.

Fesio and I pick up our things, including Sarge who was dropped when Fesio was tackled. I look around then turn to Fesio,

"Does Vai have any more relatives I should know about?" I joke,

Fesio sighs,

"Me."

TONIGHT, WE RIDE

It's shocking to say the least, why wouldn't he tell me? Could he possibly fear I want to kill everyone close to Vai? He seems too smart to think something like that.

"Fesio, why didn't you tell me? Why didn't you say you're Vai's brother?" I ask.

Fesio stops and quickly turns to me.

"I am not!" he snaps, but quickly lowers his voice, "Not anymore."

Fesio sits down near the river and looks at the flowing water. He knows the rush we are in, but he doesn't seem bothered by it at the moment.

"I told you I was not close with my relatives, they left home together without me. Days after I ran off, I found Vai in the forest. She was not too happy to see me nor did she want me to be a part of anything she had planned, but she lacked followers other than Devka and Marzen. She knew I hated Tyro just as much as she did and reluctantly let me stay. It was not ideal, for either of us, but it gave me a place to sleep and have some sort of way of getting revenge. We barely spoke with eachother, I stopped considering them my family long ago. I kept my family's name, Telkit, in honor of my parents. Vai, Teni, Marzen and Devka changed their last name to Vianti. Their new name comes from an ancient dialect once used in our world many years ago called Ullenweld, Vianti is its word for 'Vengeance', I refused to use that name. Despite all that, I never wanted to kill any of them. I wanted to fight Vai at the tower so her followers see that she is not a goddess who will lead them to glory, she would have to submit to me, only then,

I would let her run free in shame, but I never wanted to kill any of them, but I had to. I gave up on the concept of family long ago. That idea died with my mother. When you told me you killed Teni, I suppose I should have felt something like anger or hatred, but all I could feel was relief. Call me what you will, but it will not change what he did leaving me behind. They are not my family."

Here I thought Somma's family life was complicated, I can't help but feel bad for Fesio, even when he had a home with his sister, he felt alone. He never seemed to mind. In my time at Vai's camp, Fesio would always be in his tent and barely spoke with anyone, least of all Vai and Teni. I often wished I grew up with siblings, but now, I'm not too sure that would've been a good thing. Fesio is a private person, but I still find it frustrating he kept this from me. Even if he doesn't consider them family, he knows Vai is after me, he could've given insight on how she operates or to elude her, but he never said a word about it. I sit down next to him and shake my head,

"I'm sorry, I am, but you didn't think to tell me that the person who is after me, who wants to kill me, is your sister. That would've definitely helped."

Fesio laughs,

"Why do you think I am here? I could have easily left you at any time to follow my own plan, but I know how Vai works. I figured she would send Marzen and Devka, how do you think I was able to predict everything they did, for all their time spent in the wild, they never knew how to use their surroundings like we did, rocks, dirt, anything. Vai and her followers typically work in the shadows, that is why I don't have us go through the forest. They are not going to step out of the shadows, not unless it makes a statement. Blowing up a tower gives her an audience, but we are too small to be made an example, they would much rather kill us in the dark, so we stay in the light. It was bold of Marzen and Devka to jump out like that, that is the one thing that caught me off guard, but you will not see that with Vai and her followers, not while you stick with me and stay in the light. I am sorry I did not tell you, Clark, but you of all people know that keeping problems inside is our only way of living. It is who we are."

I thought I was so clever, ending up where I am, but Fesio has a point. I truly do not know what I am dealing with. I figured I was far enough where no one would find me, Fesio finding me I considered a fluke, but if Marzen and Devka can find me, then who knows how easy it will be for others to do the same. Fesio is also a target now, it'd be all too easy for Vai and her people to kill two birds with one stone if they were to find us again, but I now see we have to stay out of the forest.

I don't respond to Fesio, but I pat his back and stand up, extending my hand to help him up. He grabs my hand and stands up. I begin to walk, but faster than how we used to. Without question, Fesio follows my lead. Unsurprisingly, the walk back to the tower has already taken its toll on Fesio and myself. Through all the walking, harsh weather and the slight inconvenience of his now departed brothers attacking us on the orders of his sister, Fesio has not complained once. It's a rare occurrence that he makes a sound at all. The only thing powering me through all this is the thought of everyone being free and getting rid of Tyro. As for Fesio, the only thing that seems to fuel him is revenge. I hear him sigh, from what I have noticed, anytime Fesio sighs, it is usually a sign he is about to speak. Almost as if it's a chore to him. After the sigh, he slightly turns his head to me,

"All your questions about me and my family, I have a question for you." he continued, "I have heard Vespins are beautiful, is it true?"

"I guess. It's hard to tell at times. Somma's father has been a soldier for years, under all his scars, there's a possibility he was much better looking. Most of the people from Vespis who have fought in their military for a long time come back in worse shape, so it's never easy to truly tell with them, but with people like Somma, it's different. Somma is incredibly beautiful, others from Vespis are generally beautiful, too. Yet, no one comes close to Somma, I don't know what she ever saw in me, but I'm very lucky. You'll see for yourself."

Fesio chuckles,

"If she was not going to try to kill me, I might see the beauty."

To be fair, even when Somma fought me in a Xenem uniform, she looked beautiful, so I'm not worried about Fesio not seeing what I'm talking about. Any time Fesio speaks, it seems like he only asks questions. I'm no better, there's not much else to say with someone who's still a mystery to me besides questions. We both realize asking too many questions would get tiresome for both of us, so opting out of speaking seemed like our only options. Fesio, who's been walking ahead of me, slows down to walk next to me,

"Thank you for not killing me while I slept, Clark." he says while grabbing Sarge off my arms and starts carrying him.

It was oddly worded, but I expect nothing less from Fesio. Nonetheless, I appreciate it.

"Just like you said, 'your death serves no purpose to me'." I respond.

Fesio chuckles as he checks his bandages, it's the first time he looked at them since he woke up,

"I suppose you changed my bandages, too?" he asks.

"I did."

"I can see why your team sticks with you, you are a good leader."

I can't help but smile a little, but the feeling of pride quickly turns to a feeling of bittersweetness. Through this entire journey with Specter, Sarge has been the leader. Now that he's gone, who's going to lead us? Vai was the first person to raise that question, but speculated it was me. To be honest, I don't feel much like a leader. I was always a second-in-command to Sarge, I suppose. Even then, I feel like I failed. I can only imagine how pissed off everyone is at me. Somma may not say it, but she's probably disappointed in me. I could have fought her at the tower and maybe given Specter a better chance at survival. Instead, I jumped off the tower, probably making the situation worse. At the time, I felt it was the best way out, literally. Seems cowardly in hindsight, I did think I would die, though. At times, I wish I did. Never have I felt so defeated than in that moment, who knows, though? Maybe I'll die freeing everyone, so everything I've done will mean something.

"I'm not a good leader, but thank you." I respond to Fesio.

Within an instant, Fesio sticks his arm out in front of me stopping me in my path.

"In the short time I have known you, you have proven to be a better leader than Vai and anyone else I have followed whether it was in my pursuit of vengeance or anything else. You think I do not know the burden you carry? You have remained calm and determined to free your team from a fortress, while carrying a corpse. You also let me rest and tended to my wounds when you barely knew me."

"Again, thank you, but I was just trying to do the right thing."

"Exactly." Fesio responds before walking.

Everything he said is true, but I can't help feel like I failed. That feeling is what's making me fear how the others will react to seeing me. I imagine shock at first, then anger for presumably abandoning them. Either way, I have to get them out, regardless of how they will react.

The sound of the river gives us a sense of calmness, it still shocks me that something like this is on Xenem, even Fesio looks at it in amazement from time to time. The sound of the river gets interrupted by the sound of an explosion. Fesio and I quickly turn to each other in panic and look at the tower. We see it engulfed with flames and crumbling. We're still a couple miles away, so we start rushing the best we can to the tower. Vai detonated the bombs earlier than I thought, throwing our plan off course. Fesio is still carrying Sarge while sprinting, I would have us stop to trade off holding him, but we can't stop. Fesio looks to the right into the forest,

"Screw it! Follow me! I will hold onto your friend, just keep up." he yells as he quickly turns right into the forest.

I'm hesitant to follow him, he did tell me Vai's soldiers would be in the forest for us, but I have to trust Fesio. If he feels we should run through, then I have to follow. As we enter the forest, we hear more explosions and gunshots in the distance. The noise causes the wildlife to scatter and nearly trample us, but Fesio doesn't let it bother him. I'm surprised I haven't run into any wildlife yet, or even been attacked. I have no idea what any of these animals are. If I follow Fesio's lead, I'm hoping I will be okay.

As the chaos escalates, a group of animals run next to us. They're strange looking to say the least. Six legs, all gray, teeth like a Sabertooth, but no eyes. That's what it looks like at least, the top of their heads have long pieces of hair that covers the eyes. If all that wasn't crazy enough, they have razor sharp tusks coming out of their cheeks curving upwards. I wouldn't dare touch one, especially with tusks and teeth like that. Fesio looks at one and starts running towards it,

"Jump onto one!" he yells while mounting one of the beasts.

Every instinct in my body is telling me to do the opposite. So many things can go wrong, but I do my best to ignore the fear and jump onto one. I barely make it on and hang off its side as it sprints through the forest. Fesio's mount was much more graceful. It's a good thing he has Sarge, I'd be dragging him if he was with me. My legs are being dragged against the floor as I hang off the beast trying to get on top, but the faster we go, the more frantic the animal gets, making it more difficult to get on. I'm eventually thrown off and hit a tree which causes me to get painful cuts and scrapes on my palms and arms. Luckily, the cuts are not too bad. It takes me a while to get up, I hit my head on the tree then landed hard on the ground. I sit up and lean against the tree trying to catch my breath when I realize in all the madness, I lost Fesio.

The sounds of the running animals, explosions and gunfire in the distance cause me to freeze for a moment in panic. I hear movement in the branches above me when someone who looks like they're with Vai jumps down in front of me with a knife,

"You look lost, boy!" he says mockingly.

He grabs me by the throat and brings the knife closer to me. I grab onto his hands trying to get them off of me, but I'm too weak from the fall. The knife is inches from me when the animal I was trying to mount plunges its tusks into the man while roaring. It sounds like the roar of a bear and a panther mixed, a truly terrifying animal to be on the wrong side of. The beast throws him off of its tusks, instantly killing him. It turns to me and slowly approaches, I start to think to myself "Am I its next victim?"

I slowly extend my hand out towards it trying to calm it down. It tilts its head and starts sniffing my hand, it growls, but something comes over me and I move forward, gently placing my hand on its face. It stops growling and slowly bows its head to me. I chuckle and rub his head, I never wanted to hurt it and it seems like it sensed that. The beast backs up which allows me to slowly get up. I cautiously walk towards my bag and pick it up. I wipe the blood from my palms on my coat while slowly approaching the side of the animal. I place my hand on it,

"It'll be okay, I won't hurt you."

The beast looks still enough, I slowly climb on top and take a seat on its back. I can't help but feel accomplished for being able to finally mount one. I hear something galloping coming towards me, I see Fesio on top of his beast,

"There you are! I see you finally mounted a Lipund, well done." Fesio continued as he tosses me some rope, "You come from Earth, I believe this is just like riding those animals you call a 'horse'. Wrap the rope around him like mine and use it to steer, kick its sides with your heels to get it moving. Now, keep up and follow me!"

Fesio kicks the sides of his Lipund and immediately takes off. I don't have too much experience riding a horse. I think for my 4th birthday party my parents rented a pony for me to ride, but I think this is a little different. I look down at the Lipund,

"Okay, buddy," I continued while rubbing its side, "Work with me here."

I kick its sides with my heels and the Lipund bolts towards Fesio and his Lipund. At first, the speed takes me by surprise and nearly caused me to fall off. I remain determined and focused to not fall, not again. I eventually catch up with Fesio and the other Lipunds, he looks like he has ridden these for a while, but compared to me, that's easy. We try to make our way out of the forest, but men and women from Vai's camp jump out of the trees trying to attack us. The first few miss us, hitting the ground and immediately being trampled by running Lipunds. More of Vai's troops jump out of the trees around us as if they were falling from the sky. Fesio was right, the forest would have easily been our end had we gone through it from the start, which I would have, as ashamed I am to admit that. More troops miss us and get trampled, but others make it onto Lipunds, quickly wrapping ropes around them and start chasing us.

As if riding these things wasn't hard enough, now I have to worry about not letting anyone get close to me. I look back and see about twenty troops on Lipunds chasing us. I try to go faster while grabbing my bag and rifle, I grab a handgun from the bag and toss it to Fesio. With my rifle, Fesio and I turn and fire at the troops behind us. It's hard to get a good shot in, we don't want to hit any Lipunds, but doing this on the back of a wild animal seemingly going a million miles an hour makes it almost impossible. We miss the first few shots, but a small window opens when Lipund behind us moves off to the side allowing Fesio to get a shot in, hitting the troop in the chest, he instantly falls off and gets trampled. It seems like the Lipunds are working with us to attack Vai's troops. As more people jump out of the trees, the Lipunds move out of their way so they miss while some even throw their heads up, impaling the falling troops with their tusks. It becomes increasingly easier for Fesio and I to get good shots in at everyone. Only ten troops remain, but they are not so easy to fight off. The ten start jumping to different Lipunds trying to get closer to us while evading every shot we fire. It's something I wouldn't ever try. They eventually make it close enough to bring their new Lipunds next to Fesio and I. Luckily for us, having them so close makes it easier to shoot them, but the same applies for us, too. Five troops stay on me while the other five go towards Fesio. He is able to shoot three troops close to him, but two remain and get close enough and fire at Fesio. In an act of desperation, Fesio hangs off the side of his Lipund and with his left arm alone, he grabs the leg of a soldier and drags it down off of the Lipund and to the ground, but he has one last soldier to deal with.

Fesio is handling his last pursuer better than I am. I'm only able to shoot one off his Lipund, but everyone else, I've either grazed or completely missed. I've been grazed a few times, but nothing serious. Like Fesio, I need to be creative to get rid of them. Shooting at them like this doesn't cut it anymore. Despite the risk and my body telling me not to, I need to pull on the reins of the Lipund to slow down, it might give me a chance to get behind them and fire a good shot at them. Fesio claims it's just like riding a horse, so in theory, this should work. I take a deep breath and pull on the makeshift reins, my Lipund immediately slows down. As I hoped, I ended up behind the now bewildered troops and was able to fire five shots at the people in front of me, but I only hit four. Just like Fesio, one remained for me.

He turned around and brought out a knife, he growled before jumping off towards me. I fire at him but miss. At the last second, my Lipund raises its head and impales the soldier. He was inches away, had I not been on this incredible creature, I would be dead. With his last few breaths, he raises his arms and tries to slash at me, I catch his hand and grab his knife from hand, I quickly impale it into his throat. The Lipund flings its head and throws him off his tusks. Fesio is struggling with his last pursuer, they look like they are wrestling each other trying to get the other thrown off his animal. I kick the sides of my Lipund and head to them, but the soldier punches Fesios bandaged wound. He wallows in pain and allows the soldier to grab him. As the soldier is about to throw Fesio off, I ride up next to them trying to help. I grab my knife and jam it into the soldier's left thigh, the soldier yells and turns to me which allows Fesio to grab him by the throat and with all his might, lifts him off his Lipund and spikes him to the ground to be trampled.

Thinking we were in the clear, we run towards the closest exit from the forest. Just as we are about to leave the forest, one more person jumps from a tree. It looks like a woman, but her face is covered. My Lipund tries to flings his head up to impale her, but she spins like a corkscrew, gracefully evading the tusks. What she does baffles me, but she ends up tackling Fesio off his Lipund. I stop my Lipund and climb to help Fesio, but the woman throws a type of smoke bomb at me, the smoke is like nothing I've experienced before. It burns my eyes and completely blocks my respiratory system. I'm sure I look like a chicken with its head cut off trying to run out of the smoke. After a while of running around trying to escape the effect of the smoke, I finally begin to feel my senses come back. I rub my eyes and look around to see the woman on top of Fesio trying to drive her knife into him. My vision is not the best at the moment, I scramble on the floor trying to find something to throw at her since I don't have my rifle and Fesio still has my handgun. I feel around until I find a rock, I pick it up and even with blurry vision, I throw the rock at her and by some miracle, I hit her in the back of her head. She yells in pain and frustration, she furiously looks at me, which gives Fesio his opening to kick her off of him and grab the knife from her hands and point it at her.

"Enough! Who are you?" Fesio asks while bringing the knife closer to her.

All the other troops were unmasked, so why is she masked? I approach them while rubbing my eyes, I violently rip her face cover off and despite my vision still recovering, I can see it's Cinniya. She looks at me and her eyes are filled with rage, I'd guess that she saw this going differently. She turns her gaze to Fesio who still has her knife pointed at her,

"You both are becoming a problem."

"The same could be said about you all. Stand up!" Fesio responds.

Cinniya slowly stand up and turns to me,

"Teni was right about you. If only Vai saw through you sooner, he would still be alive. Now, she wants to take someone from you. We had someone special in mind that she was happy to accept as a target."

Fesio shakes his head and moves away, we knew exactly who she was talking about and he knew to move out of the way. I march towards Cinniya, my eyes become the ones filled with rage, I grab her by the throat and push her against a tree,

"You stay the hell away from her or you will all end up dead." I say with my teeth clenched,

I didn't want to kill Cinniya, but she asked for it by saying that. She chuckles,

"I knew something was off between you and her, we all did. Maybe Vai will let me take care of her, that is if she has not gotten to her already."

Fesio steps forward next to us,

"Vai has clouded your minds. You all seek violence only Tyro would wish for. You are becoming what we all once fought to destroy."

Cinniya growls at Fesio, she instantly pulls out a smoke canister and uncaps it in my face causing Fesio and I to be blinded and has me let go of her. We hear her laughing as she runs away. The smoke begins to clear, we're lucky it wasn't whatever the hell Cinniya threw at me earlier. Instead, it seems to be regular smoke, other than the temporary blindness and coughing, we got off easy. Fesio rubs his eyes and looks around in every direction,

"We lost her!" he yells,

As if I didn't have enough reasons to rush to the tower, I have to get there in time before Vai or Cinniya finds Somma. I am more than confident that Somma can handle herself against either of them, but I don't want to risk anything. Vai's bloodshed wouldn't stop with her, though. She knows about Specter and what our uniforms look like, she will probably kill them all if given the chance. I quickly rush to my bag and rifle and pick them up. I look to my left and see our Lipund's off in the distance who scattered after Cinniya attacked us. Fesio picks up Sarge's body and we rush to the Lipunds and climb on. We kick their sides and race to the tower. We were so close to making it out of the forest, I thought we were in the clear, but Vai's followers were so well hidden. It makes me wonder if the same thing will happen again as we try to leave for the second time. The Lipunds are running so fast, it feels like we're flying. We manage to leave the forest and find a road that looks to lead to the tower. At this speed, it seems we will reach the tower in minutes. All roads in Xenem look the same, everywhere you look, destruction. It's the same as when I went with Fesio and Vai's group to rob the transport, the view saddened me then and it still does. I thought we'd see patrols everywhere, but it seems like the tower is drawing everyone's attention. We pass by a few dead bodies on the ground, but they look fresh. It's safe to assume that Vai's followers had some fun while heading to the tower. The good news, it looks like we aren't too far behind.

More pieces of the tower start crumbling down, it's only a matter of time before the entire structure comes down. As long as Somma leaves the tower in time, I don't care who goes down with it. The bombs going off put us in a tough position, we wanted to set them off at the right time and Fesio wanted Vai to come to us, but we're playing her game now. It's almost as if she knew our plan. We are close enough to hear people shouting, Fesio and I make our Lipund's run faster, but as we get closer, the sounds of the gunfire and explosions cause the Lipunds to get scared and make us fly off them. We land on the ground, as we get up, we see them run off. It's a shame to see them go, but luckily, we're close enough to use our feet. Fesio and I see bodies on the floor, both from Vai's side and Tyro's.

"Here. Grab whatever you can from them. They do not need it anymore." Fesio says while placing Sarge's body behind a large fallen piece of the tower.

I follow behind him and place my coat over the body. I have been wearing my old coat over my Specter uniform for a while now, it feels weird taking it off. Fesio approaches the body of a Xenem soldier who was shot in the chest and abdomen. He pats the body down, looking for items to grab. It's a good chance to grab ammo and any sort of weapons we may need. We begin to loot the bodies for anything else we can find and grab the guns that belonged to the Xenem soldiers. Compared to Vai's guns, they're far superior. Fesio and I also grab whatever sidearm they had and their ammo before we continue to charge towards the tower. I didn't particularly like looting dead bodies. It was my first time doing something like that and it felt wrong, but Fesio didn't seem phased by it at all. After retrieving Sarge's body, we reach the tower and hide behind another piece of the tower that came off, we slowly peek at what's going on and it is utter madness. Nothing but chaos and violence everywhere you look. No one on either side is showing any kind of mercy.

The tower looks different, massive steel barriers are around the entire building, making it nearly impossible to get to. A hole was dug by Vai's group to try to dig their way in, but who knows if they made it far enough to reach inside? As if the violence couldn't get any worse, I look up and notice a massive turret at the top of the tower. A soldier grabs onto it and starts firing at Vai's troops. That turret wasn't there before, neither were the barriers, Somma was right, they raised the defense systems of the tower. I don't know if there's more awaiting us moving forward, but I have to push forward no matter what. After the turret mows down Vai's troops, the remaining Xenem soldiers run off to try to secure the tower elsewhere. The soldier leaves the turret which allows us to approach the tower. I put Sarge down behind our cover. Fesio and I leave our cover cautiously and go into the hole that was dug. They seem to have gotten through but the hole was closed up by falling debris. We try to break through, but we have no luck.

We leave the hole and approach the barrier. I place my hand on it and I've never felt steel or really anything this thick. I look up, the barrier is too high and we have no way to climb it, but to my left, I see a camera looking at us. The lens of the camera zooms in closer to us, but Fesio picks up a rock and throws it at the camera, disabling it completely. Whoever was looking at us is most likely alerting Tyro, but we can't do anything as long as the barrier is up. I would just let the tower crumble down, but Somma is still in there. I pace back and forth trying to formulate a plan while Fesio tries to find random things to try to climb the wall with. We both stop and look at each other in desperation, but we have no ideas. Just as it seemed hopeless, we hear gears in the barrier turning, the portion of the barrier we are standing in front of comes down into the ground, leaving a cloud of thick dust. We cough and clear the dust with our hands, but I couldn't believe what I saw, Somma.

She stands in front of the tower, her face and hair fully uncovered. The wind causing her hair to fly around, she looks beautiful, like a goddess. Her eyes tear up, she smiles as she runs to me and jumps in my arms. She gives me the tightest hug I think she has ever given me, I even start to tear up. I lift her up and spin her around, I had no idea if I would ever be able to hug her again. A huge weight is lifted off me now that I know she's okay. She grabs my face and kisses me on the lips passionately before hugging me tight again. I put her down and she looks at me and smiles.

"If you knew what I went through just to see you again." I say while wiping her tears.

"I knew you would come back."

Somma grabs my hands and looks at the bloody bandages on them, she looks up at me,

"What happened?"

"Don't worry, I'm okay."

Somma turns her head to Fesio and her eyes go from tears of joy to a flash of anger. She lets go of my hands and storms towards him,

"I recognize you. Did you do this? Did you hurt him?"

Her fists are clenched, ready to strike. Fesio's eyes widen as he lifts his hand up while backing away. I run in front of Somma and gently put my hands on her face. Her eyes become less angry and the light dies down as she sees me,

"He didn't do this. It's okay. This is Fesio."

"I saw him with you and the other rebels when you raided those bombs, I saw him die. He is dangerous!"

"He didn't hurt me and he won't. I wouldn't be alive if it wasn't for him. You can trust him. I do."

I slowly step out of the way, Somma slowly walks towards Fesio,

"You saved his life?"

Fesio nods. Somma looks at me and I nod my head, too. She looks back at him and extends her hand, as does Fesio and they both shake hands.

"Thank you, Fesio." Somma says.

Fesio bows his head,

"I hope you know, Clark saved my life." he continued, "I was only returning the favor, but I found he is an incredibly brave and dedicated warrior who fought through the wilds of Xenem to get back to you and your squad. I am not used to seeing such bravery, he is a great man. Also, Clark was right, you truly are beautiful, if you do not mind me saying so."

I've never heard Fesio give such compliments to anyone. As far as what he said about me, I truly do appreciate it and I feel the same way about him. I would be dead somewhere in the middle of nowhere if we didn't cross paths. Somma smiles and puts her hand on my arm,

"He said that I was beautiful?" she playfully asks before kissing my cheek, "That is very kind, thank you, Fesio. I know how brave Clark is. That does not surprise me. I have always known the kind of man he is, but what happened to you?"

"It is a long story and we should get moving, but I can try to tell it quickly if you really want to know, if that is okay?" he turns and asks me.

I nod my head and sit down on a nearby rock while holding Somma's hand. With Somma out of the tower, I feel more at ease with waiting out here.

"Well, during the transport, what you saw was partly true." Fesio continued, "I was hit and almost died, but I was just badly wounded. Everyone could have turned back to get me, but they did not. Clark wanted to, but no one would listen to him. I felt betrayed and did not want to return to our camp. I went off on my own and did my best to heal my wounds and survive, but it came to a point where I could not go on much longer. I was aimlessly wandering around in a forest when I heard a stream of water. I kept walking and saw it was a river. I then saw Clark washing his coat in the water. I saw all the dirt and blood from his coat wash away, but Clark looked like had not slept for days. His eyes were filled with pain, he looked hurt and broken, physically and mentally."

Somma looks at me with tears in her eyes, she kisses me on the cheek and rests her head on my shoulder while holding me tight.

"A part of me did not want to go to him." Fesio continued, "I did not want to because I did not think there was anything he could offer that could help me because he looked like he needed all the help he could get. Something inside of me told me to go to him and when I walked out of the forest, at first, he had his knife out ready to attack whatever he thought was coming for him, but once he saw me, he put the knife away and greeted me like an old friend. He offered me all he had, water, a place to rest and his company, he even cleaned my face and rebandaged my wound while I slept. I could have left after I rested. I could have left at any time, but after learning more about him and hearing how he spoke about you, his team, about anything in general, I wanted to help. A lesser man would leave under the conditions he was under, but Clark never once thought of leaving without everyone. Besides, we both wanted Tyro eliminated and I wanted to have my revenge against those who abandoned me, so it was mutually beneficial. Clark has earned my respect, though. He is a true leader and a fierce warrior. Not even death could stop him from getting back to you, Somma."

I can't help but smile and look down. Somma wipes her tears and kisses me on the lips. She looks around on the ground,

"Where is Sarge's body?" she asks.

I get up and lead her to his body and take my coat off of him and the Gaveau plants. Those plants are miracles, Sarge's body doesn't look any different. Somma kneels next to him and puts her hand on his chest,

"I will not let you down, sir." she whispers.

She puts the leaves back on him and I place my coat back over him.

"When we leave, someone has to get his body from over here. We're going to give him a proper burial." I say as we walk back to the tower.

Somma begins grabbing bandages from her belt, she turns to Fesio

"Can you check the prison to see if you can find a quick and easy way to get everyone out? Just be careful. Your old friends and Xenem soldiers are still everywhere. I need to rebandage Clark."

Fesio nods and runs to the prison. Somma turns back to me and smiles,

"I've missed that smile." I say while moving her hair out

of her face.

Like a viper, Somma quickly launches at me and kisses me on the lips for what seems like several amazing hours. It's the longest she has ever kissed me. Somma moves back and laughs,

"I am sorry, I have missed you." she continued, "Fesio was right, most people would have quit or ran away dealing with what you went through, but not you. You always come back. Thank you, my love."

I hold her hands,

"So many things tried to kill me on my way here, but I couldn't let them take my life, not while you and everyone else was trapped here. At times, it seemed hopeless. I sometimes hoped someone would have killed me-"

"You are here now," Somma interrupts, "I will not let anyone hurt you while I am around if I can help it. You cannot always be the one saving me in this relationship, my love."

She wipes the dried blood from my palms, but I see around her coat collar she has a bruise, I lift it down and see how bad it was, it was a large bruise and it looked painful as hell.

"Who did it?" I ask,

Somma looks down, ignoring my question and lifts her collar back up, she grabs bandages and tries to put them of me, but I grab her hand,

"Who?"

Somma sighs,

"My father."

GEN. Juna keeps finding new ways to make me sick. I truly didn't want to kill him. He means a lot to Somma, somehow, but I won't let anyone hurt her like that. Not even her father. I have to find him. It's not too surprising that he would hurt Somma like this. For someone who claims to care so deeply for family, he has a funny way of showing it. Understandably, Somma is the only one who wants him alive. She still loves him despite all he has done. I suppose it makes sense when it's the only family you have left. Somma can feel the anger filling my body. My fists clenched, I'm breathing heavily, I'm truly pissed off and she can tell. I looked at the tower to try to figure out where he could be, but she quickly put the bandages down. She gently grabs my hands, redirecting my focus back to her,

"It was my fault. I was not listening and -" she stops herself after seeing anger fill up inside of me. She gently grabs my face with both hands, "Look at me, my love. I am okay. We will worry about him later, let me bandage your hands."

Somma sits me down and unwraps the dirty bandages from my hands. She looks at the cuts I got from when the Lipund threw me off,

"You seem to have a new wound every time I see you." she jokes.

I chuckle through my nose and look down at her hands holding mine, it makes me think about how long it took me to get back. Somma wouldn't have been under so much stress for as long or gotten hurt if I got here sooner and didn't let so many things get in my way. I close my hands, hiding my wounds,

"I'm sorry." I say softly.

Somma sighs and grabs a rag from her bag, dampens it with some water before she opens my hands and starts cleaning my wounds, gently wiping them with the rag,

"I wish I could have been with you. I let all this happen. I understand if you are still mad at me."

At first when this all happened, I was mad. I genuinely thought Somma betrayed the USC and was okay with everything her father did and what she did, but deep down I knew it wasn't her. I didn't stay mad for too long. Somma begins wrapping my right hand, I look up and see a tear rolling down her cheek.

"I'm not mad at you. You *were* with me, in here." I say while placing her hand on my heart, causing her to tear up more.

I'd like to think my father taught me how to talk to girls. I have him to thank for that line, despite the fact I truly meant it. With tears still in her eyes, Somma smiles and grabs my hand, placing it on her heart. I've been away from her for so long, something about feeling her heartbeat again made something come over me. I was feeling a range of emotions, but there was only one thing I was able to say,

"I love you, Somma."

She smiles and leans in, kissing me on the lips with our hands still on each other's hearts. She smiles and rubs my cheek with her thumb,

"And I love you." she responds with tears still in her eyes.

She finishes wrapping my right hand and moves to the left, I move her hair out of her face and put my hand on her thigh,

"I think I still owe you a magical night, don't I?"

Somma giggles,

"Absolutely, you think I forgot?" she playfully asks.

She finishes wrapping my hands before putting the bandages away. She looks up at me while smiling, I look back at her and smile.

"Thank you very much, beautiful." I say before kissing her hand.

Somma giggles and looks down shily while blushing, she looks back up at me and sees my smile again. A smile I had thought I lost.

"Since the day we met, I have always loved your smile." she says.

I kiss her cheek, which in turn, causes her to smile more. While we wait for Fesio to finish up with his scouting of the prison, Somma tries to fix my hair, which is a complete mess. After she does her best to fix it, I decide to put it in a ponytail. I pull out of my pocket the hair tie she gave me when we first met. She chuckles and looks closer at it,

"After all this time, you still have it?"

"I always have it with me."

Somma looks down and blushes as she holds my hand,

"You are a romantic, Mr. Parson." she jokes,

I smile and nod, I can't deny at heart it's true, I am a bit of a romantic. Somma kisses my lips,

"I hope you can smile for me every day. It brings me so much joy, my love." she says.

"I don't think I've smiled since the last time I saw you. I was so worried about you and everyone."

"I was worried, too. I did not sleep much most nights. I kept wanting to sneak out and find you, just so I could see that you are okay and lay next to you in your arms and finally be able to sleep." Somma continued, "We stick together now, okay? We get everyone and do what we need to do. We finally leave this place, together. For Sarge."

I couldn't agree more. Just like she said, for Sarge.

CHOICES

There was something comforting about the bandages Somma put on me. They weren't the ones that the USC use. She was using basic bandages provided to her by the Xenem military when she got to the tower, but for a while I've been bandaging my own wounds with the same bandages in dirty environments. What made it comforting was that it was Somma wrapping my hands. I knew she wouldn't take any shortcuts or mess up. Anyone could have done it and I still would have appreciated it, but it's different when someone you love does it.

Fesio hasn't returned from the prison. A part of me is worried, but I've learned Fesio is great at getting out of trouble. Somma and I are sitting on a rock waiting for him. She lays her head on my shoulder and grabs onto my arm, from what I can tell, it's been a long day for her so far,

"You can sleep if you want, I'll wake you when Fesio comes back." I say while putting my arm around her.

"I will sleep when we are out of this place."

I can tell that she's focusing on what's ahead, but I know from experience, that can mess with your mind. Sarge knew this, too. Whenever he thought I was looking too far ahead or focusing too much on something, he'd distract me. Sometimes with a joke or a story. It's my turn to distract Somma. She is jittery, I can feel her getting more riled up.

"Have you been practicing your dancing? Last time we danced you kept falling over." I joked.

Somma playfully hits my arms and laughs,

"That sounds like you!"

"Are you sure? I thought I did amazing."

She giggles,

"Yes, my *Relani*, you were perfect."

"Don't feel bad, I'll teach you my secrets when we're out of here."

"Promise?"

"I promise, we'll dance all night."

Somma kisses my cheek then puts her head back on my shoulder,

"I would love that."

I hold Somma tighter, I can feel her calm down. Sarge was unorthodox, but his methods worked. We finally see Fesio running back to us, Somma and I stand up and meet him in front of the barrier,

"Is everything okay?" I ask,

"Yes, I had to deal with some rather annoying soldiers, but they are taken care of." he continued, "Most of the guards are scattered dealing with Vai's attack, so it should not be too difficult."

Fesio may have a different view of what "too difficult" is, but either way, three of us against the tower are not great odds. I really don't want us to separate, but it seems to be the only way to do what we need to do.

"Fesio and I will go inside the tower. He has some business he needs to take care of and I will try to find Tyro. Somma, please go to the prison and try to free the rest of the squad, including Leezol and everyone else. Hopefully everyone will want to fight once given the chance."

"They do not trust me." Somma continued, "I have tried speaking to everyone in Specter, they do not trust me or want anything to do with me. Everyone in there hates me, they will not believe I am trying to help."

I figured that would be an issue, but I need her to try. I hold Somma's hand tight, I turn to Fesio,

"Head inside the tower, clear out anyone you see, but don't go anywhere else without me."

Fesio nods his head and runs inside, Somma starts breathing heavier and heavier, her skin begins to shine brighter, I place my other hand on her heart, it's racing. It begins to slow down a little after my hand makes contact with her. I take her to the rock we were sitting on before and I sit her down, I kneel in front of her and hold her hands drawing her attention to me.

"Somma, listen to me. I know it's going to be tough and maybe even scary, but I know you can do it. You've known them for a while, they know you're not some evil traitor. They just need time and some convincing."

Her skin is still shining brighter than usual, something else is bothering her.

"What's going on?"

Somma looks up at me, she goes to the ground in front of me and wraps me in a tight hug like she can't let go of me,

"Do not go in there! I do not want something to happen, I just got you back. I cannot lose you again. Please, come with me, I can protect you."

"I'll be okay, I promise. I'll have Fesio with me and-"

"The tower is crumbling faster and faster, it is too dangerous!" she interrupts, "Even if Tyro and my father make it out, we will find them again and handle it. Just come with me. I need you, Clark. Please, do not go."

She still holds onto me, I really don't know what to say or do. I'd love to go with her, but I can't let Fesio go in alone or risk losing Tyro. Somma may be right, we could find him again, but that could take months or longer, we have him right here. As much as it kills me to break Somma's heart right now, we need to follow the plan. Nothing I could say would change her mind, but I still have her recorder she gave me last time I saw her. It's the same one where I recorded my message for her. If I give it back to her, it might give her some comfort. Somma slowly lets go of me and she looks down to the ground in defeat with tears running down her face, possibly because she knows in her heart that we need to do the plan my way.

"Look at me." I say while gently moving her face up to me, I kiss her on the lips and wipe her tears, "You are the most brilliant person I've ever met. I think you know this is how it has to happen. You know I always return to you no matter what. I am more than confident you can free everyone and make peace with Specter, after that, you all can join me in the tower and we finish this together. It'll be okay, I promise."

Somma nods her head, I did the best I could trying to make things seem better, but it didn't seem to work. I grab the recorder from my pocket and put it in her pocket,

"Here," I continued, "I recorded something for you, if you ever feel alone, play it and I'll be there."

She doesn't say anything back, but she gives a small smile. I hold her hands and help her up. We hold hands as we approach the tower,

"Remember, get everyone out then meet us inside, okay?" I say.

Somma looks down and nods her head, I try to walk forward, but she holds onto my hand and pulls me back. She puts her hand on my heart and kisses me on the lips,

"Be careful. I love you." she says with her hand still on my heart.

I place my hand over her hand,

"I love you, too. You be careful, also."

Somma reluctantly lets my hand go and heads to the prison as I enter the tower. I look around and it's a bloodbath. Bodies everywhere, both from Vai's side and Xenem's. I look to the left and see Fesio leaning on the wall with his arms crossed,

"She will be okay." he says as we enter a corridor.

I nod my head, I don't really feel like talking much at the moment. We have to hurry, it's a miracle the tower hasn't completely collapsed, yet. From what I remember, there were enough explosives around the tower to turn it to dust, but it's only crumbling bit by bit. It's a risk taking any elevators, but we're running out of time. Tyro and Vai are probably on the higher levels, Fesio will be occupied fighting her, but Tyro is all mine. We cautiously walk onto an elevator, the first place we decide to check is Tyro's office. As the elevator begins to go up, I notice it is going slower than the last time I was on it. If I had to guess, the damage to the tower is worse than we thought. I check the ammo on my guns, but I remain silent. I didn't have to say anything for Fesio to pick up that something was bothering me and he knew what it was.

"You must not worry so much." Fesio says.

"I should be with her."

"She survived this long on her own. Have faith."

Faith was never the issue. I know Somma can handle herself. I guess the real issue is I wish we left on a better note. I wish we left filled with confidence and assurance that we would see each other again. Instead, I left her when she begged me to go with her and truth be told, I don't know if I am going to make it out of here alive. Fesio didn't need me to say anything, my face said it all.

"She may be upset now, but once she sees you again, she will completely forget about what happened. I have never seen someone so in love with another person before. You are a lucky man. "

"Thank you." I respond as the elevator doors open.

We slowly step off and take a look around. I don't have the greatest memories of this place. Flashes of what happened here play in my head. Sarge getting shot, GEN. Juna walking out in a Xenem uniform and of course, Somma being forced to attack me or else Specter would die. All of that, ultimately leading me to jumping out of the tower. This is by far my least favorite place to be. The room is empty, there's a disturbing aura. You can feel death with each step. Fesio approaches Tyro's desk. Admittedly, it looks nice up close, I barely took a look at it last time I was here. It looks to be made of what looks like black marble with intricate carvings in it. Fesio places his hand on the desk,

"I never thought I would ever step foot in here."

"It's not as glamorous as it seems, is it?" I respond.

There is a door at the back of the office, it could be an entrance to some sort of panic room, but I need a passkey to open it. Times like these I'd get Kierra to hack into it, but she is currently unavailable for now. I have to find another way through, but looking around the office some more I notice a hologram pad is on the desk Fesio is looking at. If it belongs to Tyro, there could be vital information we don't know about, possibly in relation to the entire Chelorian Confederacy. I grab the pad and everything is in Xenem, I don't know any words or phrases in Xenem. I'd be completely lost, luckily, I have Fesio. He walks up next to me and looks at the pad,

"Why would he leave this here?" he continued as he points at the top left of the screen, "Here he has his files and access to the cameras. Everything else looks like random nonsense for running Xenem. I really want to see what is in his files, but we need a passcode. Perhaps your friends can hack into it."

Guaranteed Kierra can hack into it, too, but that'll have to wait. I feel the sudden urge to look at the cameras. I open the camera section and scroll back to see if I can find any more dirt on Tyro. We see a clip with Tyro, GEN. Juna, and Somma from a few days ago. Fesio taps on it and it shows a conversation between them,

"You begged me to bring your daughter along, Juna, but she has proven to be a waste of time and resources!" Tyro yells while pointing at Somma.

Juna steps forward,

"Give her time. The USC made her weak, but I can change that. We can-"

Tyro held his hand up interrupting him,

"No need, she can prove herself right now, yes, Ms. Juna?"

Somma slowly nods her head in defeat. I've never seen Somma's skin shine this bright for this long. Even under all of her coverage, her fear was beyond obvious. She was in a constant state of stress and panic. Tyro signals his guards to bring in a man who is being dragged in by his arms with his bloodied knees dragging on the floor. The guards drop the man in front of Tyro's desk. He looks beaten to hell, Tyro chuckles,

"Forgive me, friend, but I never caught your name. No matter," Tyro turns to Somma, "Execute him."

Somma looks at Tyro in confusion,

"What did he do?"

"Does it matter?" he responds while grabbing the knife from Somma's belt. He hands it to her.

"Take this and execute him, now!"

Somma slowly grabs the knife and approaches the man. He shook his head as fast as he could, he was too weak to say anything. Tyro and Juna both yell at her to do it, but Somma can't bring herself to do it. She backs away and lowers her head. Tyro growls, snatching the knife from her hand and stabbing it into the man's throat. He drives the knife in deeper before twisting it. Blood squirts out of the wound. Tyro violently rips the knife out of the man's throat before he throws it to the floor. He waves his hand signaling his guards to throw the corpse off the ledge. He marches towards Somma,

"You see how easy that was? It is so simple, you dumb, weak, pathetic child!" he yells before trying to backhand Somma in the face, but she evades.

Tyro chuckles and grabs her by the throat and slams her to the ground,

"You do not ever do that again. I do not care who your father is. I will kill you if you step out of line again. Like I said, 'dumb, weak, pathetic child.' I expected more from a Juna."

Tyro moves away from Somma and walks away. She is left on the floor, slowly getting up. Her father walks up to her, she looks up at him, but he shakes his head in disappointment and follows Tyro out, leaving Somma on the floor alone in the office. She slowly gets up and walks to the edge of the office where the man was thrown off. She looks down in defeat.

It's no secret that Tyro is a cruel person, but it's still

shocking to see. We have no idea what that man did to deserve to be killed or punished like he was and I feel like Tyro didn't know either. It's just another body to him. We scroll through the list of other footage, we see multiple videos that contain people getting murdered or tortured, nothing out of the ordinary. We keep looking and Fesio looks closer at the screen,

"Is that you?" he asks.

He's right. It's the moment where I jumped out of the tower. I had no idea what happened after the jump. I slowly tap on the clip and watch with Fesio. It's almost impossible to see anything with Somma's skin shining through her clothes, it was definitely brighter in person, though. Her shine causes static and interference with the cameras. It's painful watching this and reliving it from what we can see looking past the effect Somma's shine had on the cameras. I change the angle to the camera by the edge of the tower. It's the moment where Somma put me to the ground again, the moment I nearly gave up and would have let Tyro kill me right then and there. Zooming in, I can see tears running down Somma's face. It was hard for me to see it in person, but she was crying her eyes out. Even with her face covered like it was, it's clear to see on camera. I look away from the screen, it's too hard to watch. It was one of my lowest points.

Fesio continues to watch, he remains silent, most likely due to shock. I remember everything that happened. I can hear Tyro in the video, Fesio is watching the moment I jumped. Naturally, I didn't see what happened after I jumped. I didn't want to watch any more of the video, but curiosity got the better of me. I look back and see Tyro with Leezol's knife to Somma. We watch as I get up and snatch the knife from his hand. Fesio, still watching in shock, watches me jump off the tower, he quietly gasps,

"No!" he exclaims as if he was there.

I continue watching to see what happened afterwards. The moment I jumped, Tyro and GEN. Juna started laughing to a point of near fainting. Everyone in Specter tried to run to the ledge, freaking out, but were pulled back by guards. Leezol lowered his head in defeat. Somma slowly walked to the ledge, she fell to her knees and clenched her heart with tears running down her face. Her light began to shine so bright it caused the camera to go blurry again. A few seconds later, the camera goes back to normal, GEN. Juna covered her with his coat, dampening the light.

"Get up. He means nothing to us." he says to Somma while picking her up off the floor.

He walks her back to Tyro, who is still laughing. Somma doesn't move, she covers her face with her hands, I can hear her weeping, trying to be as silent as possible. Admittedly, the audio on these cameras are great, we could hear every little thing. While weeping and looking towards the edge of the tower, we hear her whisper,

"I am sorry, Clark. I am so sorry. What did I do? I am sorry. Come back to me. I am so sorry I-"

Her father interrupts her by grabbing her by the arm and walked with her out of the office with Tyro while the guards drag Specter to the elevator to be taken to the prison. Everyone in Specter, including Leezol, tries fighting the guards, but couldn't escape. After everyone is out of the office, it's left in deafening silence. As if nothing just happened. Fesio grabs the pad from me and turns off the video. He puts it in my bag and sighs,

"I am sorry."

I nod and walk to the edge of the tower. Looking down, it doesn't seem as high now that I know how it feels to jump from here to the bottom. The view of Xenem is naturally depressing, more than usual. Everything seems to be on fire or crumbled down. The sounds of yelling and gunfire fills the silence. I suppose this is what Vai wanted to lead up to Tyro's demise, utter violence and chaos. Fesio walks up next to me,

"Forgive me, but Somma has spent so long waiting for you. She thought you were dead once. Then you came back to her then left again, she probably thought you were dead for a second time. Now you are back to her and left her to pursue your enemy and once again, she has no idea if you will die or not. She begged you to go with her, if I were you, I would have gone. You can all find Tyro together with your freed squad."

What he's saying is all true. I feel like such an idiot. I was so blinded by my hatred for Tyro and GEN. Juna, getting rid of them became my goal. The tower is going down by the second, I don't know how much time we have, but Fesio is right. I need to go with Somma and help her free everyone. I sigh and walk to the elevator, Fesio follows me,

"You are a good man, Clark. I will walk you out, then I search for Vai. Do not worry about me."

"Thank you, Fesio, for everything." I respond.

We approach the elevator and the doors open. We're shocked to see that standing in front of us is GEN. Juna.

"Hello, Parson." he says in a cold tone that causes a shiver to go up my spine.

He punches me in the face, Fesio charges at him, but Juna dodges and punches him in the ribs before throwing him into a wall hard enough to knock him out. Juna sighs and chuckles,

"I did not believe it was you. That jump would have killed almost anyone." he continued as he walked up to me on the ground, "You are a survivor, a fighter, like me! I may not like you, but I do respect you."

He picks me up and grabs me by my shirt collar,

"Looking past your bravery, my Somma sees something more in you that I do not. She has always seen the beauty in everything, even in the most tragic, filthy things or people and sometimes I would see it. Not with you, though." he throws a knee to my stomach and begins punching me in the face multiple times, "You should not have come back! You and that pathetic rebellion will die here. It is time for you-"

I interupt him with a headbutt to the face. He speaks too much, it's my only opening. He is stunned by my attack, I throw him against a wall and charge at him. I begin throwing punches of my own at him, I have to admit, it felt good. Somma told me not to kill him, but she said nothing about hurting him. Juna tries to move out of the way, but I grab him and shove him back against the wall and continue my attack, going for his ribs. I want to save some energy for Tyro, but this has been a long time coming. For the first time, his skin begins to shine brighter. Now I know he's worried, so I can't stop now. I grab him by his hair and pull him to a bookshelf by Tyro's desk and throw Juna into it, causing books to fall and the shelves to break in half. It's a shame, it's a beautiful bookcase, it looks to be made out of the same wood Leezol's knife handle is made out of. Juna falls to the floor in a bloody mess. I kneel down and grab his throat,

"You goddamn snake! I've been waiting to do this for a long time!" I say while punching him in the face multiple times.

I stop, pulling him up and throwing him into another wall. I grab him by the throat,

"You hurt her, you sick bastard, why?"

He knew exactly who I was talking about.

"As if I have to answer you, but she does not listen. She is weak and will not do what needs to be done. She would not kill you, she would not threaten or kill anyone else. She gets this kindness, this weakness from her mother. I can change that, she just needs correcting, if hurting her is what it takes, so be it. After that, I will watch her kill you myself!" he responds with blood coming out of his mouth.

He spits blood at me, anger gets the better of me. Despite being able to dodge him spitting blood at me, it still enrages me. I start throwing a flurry of punches everywhere. His face, body, sides. After a few moments, I wasn't focusing and Juna dropped to the ground, evading a punch. He grabs a piece of wood from the broken bookshelf and stabs me in the thigh. I fall to the floor in agony. Juna laughs as he grabs me by the hair, ripping the hair tie out of my hair and throwing it on the floor. He repeatedly punches me in the face. Each strike is harder than the last. It's hard for me to block anything, Juna drags me by the hair and takes me close to edge of the room overlooking Kitexa,

"A familiar sight, no?" he continued while getting on top of me, "I will not throw you off, though. That has proven to be ineffective. I have to do something you will not come back from. Just like I did to that old fool, Miner. I will finally be rid of you then soon your entire weak excuse for a squad. Somma will be free of all of you and will become the soldier she needs to be."

Juna pulls out his serrated knife and jabs it into my left side, twisting it deeper. I scream out in pain which amuses Juna. He violently pulls the knife out and hovers it over my heart,

"Shame. You would have been such a fine soldier for me and Chancellor Tyro, you have a lot of heart. You put on a good fight, but you could not have expected to beat me. You are nothing, boy. Goodbye, Parson."

I try to push him off, but fail as Juna swats my hands away. Juna raises his knife in the air preparing to finish me off. I close my eyes and see images of Somma which brings me some sort of peace in my final moments. I quickly whisper to myself, "I'm sorry, Somma."

With my eyes still closed, I hear a gunshot. I open my eyes and see the knife getting shot out of Juna's hand, getting launched across the room. Juna looks back, I do my best and weakly look up to see who it is. We see Somma standing at the door of the elevator pointing her smoking handgun at him, with all of Specter and Leezol behind her also aiming their guns. They all look like they've been beaten every day, cuts and bruises all over their faces, but they're alive, that's all that matters. Juna is frozen in shock and Somma makes her way to him,

"Get off of him, now!" Somma demands.

Juna stays where he is on top of me, unable to move due to shock. Blaine and Bradley run to him and pick him up off of me, throwing him to the ground. Somma runs to me and kneels next to me. She grabs my hand, I try to speak, but she stops me.

"My love, do not speak. It will be okay, I am right here." she says with tears coming out of her eyes, she kisses my hand and looks around,

"Someone help him!" she exclaims,

"I tried to go back, I'm sorry. I tried." I say weakly.

Somma squeezes my hand tight,

"It is okay, I know my love, it will be okay. Just keep breathing for me."

I smile and look up at her, she gets more beautiful every time I see her. I reach for her face, she grabs my hand and places it on her cheek, unfortunately getting blood on her face. I slowly grab from my pocket her arrow and feather necklace I fixed.

"I tried to fix it. I'm sorry."

Somma looks shocked,

"I thought I lost this after it was cut in half, I did not know where it went, I felt terrible. It looks perfect, thank you so much, my love."

Somma kisses me on the lips and holds my hand while holding onto the necklace in her other hand.

"You got them all out. I knew you could do it, my brave girl." I say as she holds onto me.

Somma smiles and kisses my hand before moving to the side for Carden. He runs to my side, opening his bag of medical equipment,

"Glad to see you are okay, sir. Well, partially." he says while getting badges out.

I weakly pat his arm. It almost doesn't feel real. Seeing everyone again is a sight I fought so hard to see again. Despite Specter being reunited putting me in a better mood, my thigh and side are bleeding profusely making me feel weak. Not even the Vespin blood in me could work its magic fast enough to stop the blood loss. Carden unbuttons my uniform and inspects both wounds. He slowly looks up at Somma,

"He is losing too much blood, I am not sure if I can stop it."

Juna laughs while being pinned on the floor,

"Just let him die, you are all dead anyways!"

Blaine picks Juna up, Bradley hits him in the face with his gun so hard he knocks him out. Somma sighs and turns to Kierra,

"Help Carden, please. Work on stopping the bleeding."

Kierra runs to my side next to Carden and puts pressure on my thigh while Carden tries to stop the bleeding from my side. I feel Somma grab my face and place her head against mine, her tears fall on me.

"Clark, just hang on. Please hang on." she pleads while crying, "You still owe me a magical night, we can go anywhere and dance all night. We can go back to the Heleia fields and lay there forever. Just hang on, I need you. Do not go. Please do not go, my love. Please, just hang on!"

I try my absolute hardest to keep my eyes open, but the pain and blood loss is too much for me to handle, my eyes begin to close slowly despite my best efforts. Somma kisses me on the lips while crying,

"I love you, please just hold on. We can be happy and safe. Please hang on for me."

There was a time I'd kill to die, but now I'd give anything to live. Somma's voice begins to fade, the last thing I hear is Carden and Keirra doing their best to save me and Somma crying,

"Please do not go, Clark." she says with her voice breaking.

She has begged me to not leave her before, I seem to always disappoint her. If I had left the office earlier or not gone at all, I'd be with her. While it was nice beating the hell out of Juna, look where it got me, beaten and stabbed. Despite my hands shaking and covered in blood, I grab the recorder from Somma's pocket and hand it to her. She grabs it from me and hits play on my message. I can't really hear much from everyone else, I can only hear Somma and the sound of my voice from the recorder.

"Log number 1, I guess.

Well, let's see what has happened so far. First off, I failed. There is nothing else to it. Sarge is gone and I should really be dead, but I suppose all this is some kind of sick joke. What a mess this all is. I have no idea what I am going to do. I don't know how much longer I have out here, I'm pretty sure, I am being hunted. I'm hurt, tired and filthy. Xenem is the last place I want to be stranded. It's not too bad. I was lucky enough to find the one clean river where I can actually drink water from it, it's not a bad sight either. I've reunited with someone from my time with that rebellion, Fesio. He's in rough shape, I don't know if I can trust him, though. I always have to be on guard here and admittedly, it's scary and I'm worried. I have to keep going, though. Specter is waiting, as are my parents and so is Somma, it was amazing seeing her again, despite the circumstances. Naturally, she looked beautiful. My parents have been waiting in that filthy prison cell for a long time. I joined Specter to get them out. I never thought I'd disappoint them like this. Hopefully Tyro won't hurt any of them, especially since he thinks I am dead. Truth be told, I just miss Specter. A part of me wishes they were with me right now, but then again, I wouldn't want them to deal with this place anymore than they have to, the wilds of Xenem would only make things worse for all of them. Of course, I miss Somma, too. What I wouldn't give to see her smile, feel her kiss me or wrap me in one of her tight hugs. I love her so damn much, I need to get her out, everyone out. They're fighters, they won't give up. Once we are out of here, I'll make sure nothing bad ever comes for us ever again. I'm sure Sarge would be so disappointed in me. I just ran away. I left my parents, Specter and Somma there to rot. I couldn't think of any other way to save them. If only they knew how sorry I am. I imagine Somma has some resentment towards me, I can't blame her. Tyro wanted me dead, jumping was my only way. I'll happily die in shame once all this is over. If I manage to survive this, I can't screw up again. I hope

Somma knows that I didn't want to abandon her or Specter. All I have is her fixed necklace, hopefully that makes up for me being an idiot in some way, maybe she will forgive me, even a little. Once I am with her again, I swear I'll be the man she deserves. I'll protect her always and dance with her even if I can't stand anymore, after all, our magical night got interrupted. Every night with her is a magic night for me, though. The moment she kissed me for the first time, the dark clouds above me cleared. From then on, she has consistently been my beautiful, guiding light, but how do I find her? I can only dream of her now. She doesn't deserve any of this. She deserves better. Even with me, she deserves better. Who am I compared to a Vespin as beautiful as her? I don't know what she sees in me to be honest, but there isn't a single day when I am not thankful for her. She means everything to me. Thoughts of her are the only thing keeping me going. One day, we will be together, safe and happy. I guess I should say something to Somma if she ever gets this. If you're hearing this Somma, I love you. I don't know if I'm going to make it back to you, if I don't, just know the last thing I'll be thinking of is you. Your smile, your voice, everything. That is all I could ever want in my final moments. I couldn't imagine my life without you, you mean everything to me. I know if I don't make it back, you will carry on and be brave because that's the kind of person you are. You'll stay strong and fight. We'll see, though, maybe death won't even stop me from getting back to you. I'll see you soon. Stay safe. I'm gonna get you all out. Even if I die trying. I love you, my Telani. Always."

At the time, I really didn't think I'd be dying as she listened to it. I forgot what I even said, it hurts to listen to. I really wanted to make it out with everyone, but at least they still have a chance. Somma cries as she puts the recorder back in her pocket and kisses my cheek while moving the hair out of my face,

"I love you, Clark. Always." she whispers.

She has not stopped crying, it's a painful sight, one that I never want to see, especially as my last moments pass by. The world around me goes blurry, I can't hear Somma or anyone else. For what seems like a few moments, the world goes black, but I open my eyes and the office is empty. My wounds are gone and the office is back to pristine condition, as if nothing ever happened. I'm not used to silence in this room. Usually there are screams, cries and the sounds of factories deafening everyone, but it's silent. I sit up and look around, I see a figure standing at the edge of the office overlooking Kitexa. I get up and walk to him,

"Not your finest moment, is it, kid?"

The figure turns around and it's Sarge.

SECOND LIFE

It is evidently clear that I died. I must have. Sarge is up and about and my wounds have disappeared. Despite all that, I didn't want to believe that I actually died. I slowly approach Sarge, I feel foolish, I want to poke him to see if he's really there or just some sort of spirit or hallucination. I slowly reach my hand out to him while his back is turned, he turns to to me,

"Hey, lookin' is free, but touching will cost you." he jokes.

I have truly missed his jokes. I have no idea what to do or say. I extend my hand for a handshake, that's the only thing I think is appropriate. Even in death, I see him as my superior. Sarge looks at my hand and smacks it away,

"What's with that handshake? Get over here, kid!"

Sarge gives me a tight hug. I think this is the first time he has given me a hug. He looks great. Clean and no bullet hole in his head. That's how I want to remember him. He lets go of me and walks me to a chair and has me sit down. I take a seat and look up at Sarge,

"Sir, I am so sorry. I wish that I-"

"Shut up with that!" he interrupts, "It ain't all bad."

It's on brand for Sarge to be so unphased by being dead, it makes me wonder how he reacted when he first got here. Sarge looks around and chuckles while pulling up another chair,

"By the way, thanks for carrying me around everywhere you went, if dying was all it took for one of you to carry me, I would've died much sooner!"

Sarge's dark humor has always been one of my favorite things about him, but I don't respond to what he said. I guess I'm still in shock and disbelief. Sarge sighs as he sits down next to me,

"I think I made the right choice picking you for Specter, you've become everything I knew you could be, son."

"Thank you, sir, but I failed. No other way to put it. Other than the fact I died. I didn't free Xenem, Tyro is still alive and GEN. Juna's fate is unknown. I even failed the people I love." I respond, lowering my head in shame.

"That's not failure, that's the job. Listen, you knew this wouldn't be easy. We all did. You messed up, too bad, try again. You're young. When I was your age, people would be worried if I *didn't* mess up. I failed, disappointed people and even hurt others, but I grew and I learned from my mistakes. I led a life I can be proud of. I'm not crazy about how things ended for me, but I fought for what was right and did my best. At the end of the day, that's all that could truly be asked of you."

I was letting what Sarge said sink in. Sarge wasn't perfect and he knew it. He didn't care what others thought of him. If he messed up, he would laugh it off, but he learned. He's right, he led a great life. We all respected Sarge, everyone in the USC did. Some people may not have liked him, but can respect the work he has done. Now I wonder if I led a life I could be proud of, especially now that I am dead.

"Sir, I don't know if I am proud of my legacy. I didn't really do anything." I say while rubbing my eyes,

Sarge smacks my head, it's something he would do if we said anything out of line or something completely ridiculous.

"You're smarter than that, kid! There's an entire room filled with highly trained, newly hardened soldiers, your friends, who are crying their eyes out over your corpse as we speak. That right there is legacy. Where I failed with those kids, you succeeded. You taught them how to be fearless, courageous and above all, kind soldiers. Somma loves you with all her shining heart because of your impact on her life. You even helped that Fesio kid. Damn near saved his life when you barely knew him. You channeled your crazy, idiotic side and jumped out of a tower to avoid hurting anyone, you carried me around for days, fought and clawed through hell just to save everyone, you never gave up. Oh, did you think I forgot you're the Hero of Tanli? Beaten half to death just to retrieve some stolen items from a shop plus helping us free Vonra. If that snake, Juna, didn't kill you, who knows what kind of legacy you would have left behind. Whether you died at a hundred years old or stay dead right here, right now, know that we are all proud of you. Me, Specter, your parents, Vonra, the USC, you fought for each of us and we appreciate all you have done. You're the best of us, Clark. So, go be the best."

I focused on everything bad that happened. All my failures and defeats. I never stopped to think about the good I've done. It's going to be hard to "go be the best" now that I'm dead, though. I doubt there is much to do in the afterlife except wait for those who have passed on.

"How do I be the best? Not only am I dead, but I also have no idea what else I could have done. I'm not like you, sir." I say.

"That's a damn good thing, if you were, we would all be dead! You're young, you will learn, but you're already a better man than I was at your age."

Sarge gets up out of your chair and extends his hand, he pulls me up and walks me to the elevator.

"So, kid, you want to continue the fight?"

The elevator doors open, I'm not sure I understand what he is asking,

"Continue, sir?"

"It's not your time yet. Just as well, I just got here. I don't need you taking up space crying and moping around. You got some more work to do, kid."

I slowly approach the elevator. I turn back to Sarge and stare at him blankly. I don't believe what I'm hearing. Sarge laughs,

"Look, I hate elevators, too, I never trusted them! That being said, that's the only way out of here. Next time I see you, you better bring some stories. I'd expect nothing less from the future legendary Clark Parson. Go be a hero, kid. Folks are waiting for you."

Tears fill my eyes, I hug Sarge goodbye,

"Thank you for everything, sir." I say with tears falling down my face.

"No, thank you, son. Now get out of here! I'm gonna slip on your tears and die again!"

I let go of Sarge and laugh. I walk towards the elevator, but Sarge stops me,

"Hey, tell everyone I'm real proud of them, even Leezol and Ben. They probably don't believe in ghosts or an afterlife, but just tell them for me. Tell them to always fight for what is right. Fight forever. That goes for you, too, Parson. Can you do that, Corporal?"

"Yes, sir."

I walk in the elevator and turn around,

"Till I see you again, kid." Sarge says with his classic devilish grin as the doors close.

There's a second of darkness, then all of a sudden, my eyes open and I am back in the land of the living, surrounded by everyone. Downside, I have my wounds again. It takes me a second to adjust, I feel Somma laying her head on my chest, crying more than she ever has since I've known her. Everyone else is either silent or crying, like Kierra and Rachel. What do you say after coming back from the dead? I can't stay silent, I know that. I decide to just say the only thing I could possibly think of,

"Hello."

Somma quickly lifts her head up and smiles, she launches at me and kisses me on the lips. She hugs me incredibly tight while crying,

"Thank you. Thank you. Thank you."

The rest of Specter, including Fesio, who's now awake, kneels next to me, they all give me a hug, even Blaine and Bradley. They have to work around Somma who isn't letting go of me, but they all manage to find a way. Leezol walks up to me and kneels down,

"Mr. Parson, you are just filled with surprises. It makes me glad I never tried to kill you more than once, I see how difficult that would have been. That being said, I am glad you are okay. You are a true warrior." he extends his hand and helps me stand up.

"Thank you, Leezol, it feels odd, but I'm strangely glad to see you're okay."

"Oh, shut your mouth." he responds while passing me off to Bradley to hold me up.

"Look at us, the two best looking guys in the squad, right?" he jokes,

I'm in an immense amount of pain, Bradley helps me walk to a chair at another end of the office away from everyone. He sets me down on the chair gently. I wince in pain, Bradley pats my shoulder,

"It's cool to have a zombie in the squad. I'm glad you're okay, though."

"Thanks, I need to be alone for a second. Stand guard at the elevator."

Bradley nods and walks to the elevator. I rub my eyes and sigh, I didn't think coming back from the dead would feel like such crap. I hear ringing in my ears, similar to what I heard when I passed on. The ringing gets louder, causing me to panic, my trembling hands cover my face and run through my hair. I start breathing heavier. I feel my heart racing as thoughts of Juna stabbing me flood my mind. Each image of him stabbing me I can feel like it is happening all over again. My head shaking, I begin muttering to myself,

"No. No. No. No." trying to push away those images.

I start to heat up and feel worse by the second. My eyes stay closed as if I can't open them anymore, I guess I know what that's like now. As the panic and fear get worse, I start feeling like I'm all alone, but I suddenly feel someone's soft and cooling hands gently touch my face, the ringing starts to fade away. I begin to hear a soft, kind and beautiful voice,

"It is okay. I am right here. It will be okay. Look at me, my love, I am right here."

I open my eyes and see Somma smiling at me, I immediately begin to calm down. My heart rate gets slower, Somma kisses my cheek which brings me back to a calm state.

"Are you okay?" she asks.

I nod my head with a faint smile,

"Can I hear your voice, my love?"

"I'm okay. Thank you." I respond while smiling and grabbing her hand,

Somma smiles back and places her other hand on my heart,

"I should have known you would fight death itself. I thought I lost you."

I don't respond with any words. Instead, despite the pain, I lean over and kiss her on the lips, she grabs my face and it keeps going. Kissing her is probably the best thing for me to do after coming back from the dead. I still feel regret for never listening to her pleas. She was right about everything. About Vai being dangerous, about me going in the tower, everything. I slowly move away and look at her, even though she has been crying for what seems like hours, she looks beautiful, it makes me tear up. Somma wipes a tear rolling down my cheek and smiles at me.

"I'm so sorry. I should've listened to you-"

"It is okay." she interrupts, "Do not worry about that."

"No, I am sorry. You told me Vai and her team were dangerous and I still went back to them. You told me to go with you instead of the tower, I didn't listen and I died. You were right about everything and I didn't listen. I'm so sorry. I understand if you're mad, but I was scared. I just don't want to lose you or anyone here. I can't lose you."

Somma kisses my cheek,

"I am never mad at you, I am always going to worry about you, though. Just like how you always worry about me. You will never lose me, Clark. I love you, always."

"I'm sorry I died." I joke,

"As long as you do not make a habit of it, I forgive you. You owe me many magical nights now." Somma holds my hand and continued, "How do you feel?"

"Not that great, but I guess I deserve it. I had it coming."

She grabs my other hand.

"You do not deserve any of this. It kills me seeing you like this because I know you do not deserve it. I feel helpless because I do not know how to help you. I watched you die in my arms and I did not know what to do. All I did was cry. You have done so much for all of us, for me, but I cannot seem to do anything right when it comes to helping you. I just hope I can be by your side the next time you need me, hopefully I will be of some help." she says while lowering her head in shame.

Seeing someone you love die is never easy, Somma is taking it extremely hard, which is to be expected. I can't let her blame herself for what has happened to me. She does more for me than she knows. I try to stand up, but I wince in pain. Somma looks up and quickly stands, she puts my arm around her and helps me stand up. I smile at her, she wipes her tears,

"What are you smiling about, handsome?" she asks while rubbing my cheek with her thumb.

"It looks like you helped me when I needed it. You're not so helpless, Ms. Juna. I'll always need you, I'm too reckless."

Somma smiles and wraps me in a hug. There was never a moment where she wasn't helpful. I just wish she knew that more. From what I've seen, GEN. Juna is most to blame. I've never once seen him thank her or treat her like she's his daughter. To him, she's another soldier he doesn't respect. It takes a lot for me to wish death upon someone, but I wish I did kill him.

"What do you want to do with your father?" I ask Somma, who's still hugging me.

She slowly moves away. She looks at Juna on the floor and stays silent for a moment.

"We need to take him to the USC and show them he is a traitor. I am not sure what they will do to him exactly. I cannot let him get away, but I will not have him die."

"I didn't mean to fight him, but he attacked me first. I almost killed him. I'm sorry."

Somma looks up at me with sadness in her eyes, it's enough to make me regret what I did, despite how good it felt.

"I have access to all the cameras, I saw what happened. I know you tried to come for me and he stopped you. I saw the entire thing while we were going to you. Everything he said to you was so awful, I know that you had to fight him. I knew you would not kill him, though."

"I became so blinded by rage and hate, I wanted to kill him. I almost did it."

"He is a killer, you are not." she continued while placing her hand on my heart, "I know who you are, my love. You are not a killer, you are a good person who knows what is right and wrong. I will handle my father, just rest, okay?"

I nod and lower my head, Somma gently lifts my head up and kisses me on the lips.

"Do not worry about what happened. It will be okay, we are all here now, it is almost over."

"Are my parents okay?"

"Yes, but they are hiding with the others somewhere safe. They are a bit shaken, but they will be okay after they leave."

"Thank you."

"Of course, my love. All of Specter protected them during their time with them both. I did my best to help them while you were gone, but there was not much I could do. They were not too trusting with me, but their faces lit up when they found out you are okay. They cannot wait to see you!"

I truly wish we could leave Xenem right now, but I get the feeling we don't want to leave empty handed. Sure, we're bringing in a traitor, but we came here to bring Somma and my parents home and to witness the end of Tyro and his reign. I'm not leaving without doing all 3 of those tasks. So, unfortunately it is not over. Not yet.

"Can you help walk to everyone?" I ask Somma,

"You stay seated, I will get everyone."

Somma kisses my cheek and walks to the rest of Specter. It's a relief I didn't need to get up. Moving around isn't exactly easy. Specter, Leezol and Fesio approach me.

"First, I just want to say I'm glad you're all okay. Thank you all for looking after my parents, I'm sure they appreciate all of you. A special thank you to PVT. Reddina and Shuua for bringing me back to life. You guys did great." I stop and look down trying to hold back tears, "I know that if Sarge was here, he'd be proud of all of you."

Everyone bows their head in silence. Sarge truly meant a lot to us. I didn't see it at first, but he really brought together the best squad anyone could ask for. He knew what he was doing.

"I wonder where his body ended up, I doubt it lasted long in the middle of nowhere." Leezol says.

"His body is right outside. I found his body and did my best to preserve it so we can give him a proper burial."

"You carried him the entire way back to us?" Mitchell asks.

I nod my head and everyone, including Somma smiles. I'd like to think everyone would have done the same if they were in my position. We've been in the tower too long now. The fact it hasn't completely crumbled to the ground is concerning. I've never seen so many bombs on one building before, I really thought it would go down. I doubt we have much time, we have to make a choice between getting out while we still can or finding Tyro. Personally, I think we should leave. Not only am I in excruciating pain, but I got what I came for, Somma, my parents and Specter. I can't let them risk more than they already have by being in this tower or anywhere near it any longer. Plus, who knows what else Tyro has up his sleeve. The tower shakes causing everyone to fall over, naturally, I get hurt the most out of it. Somma quickly gets up and runs to me,

"Are you okay?" she asks as she helps me get back in the

chair.

I nod my head as I struggle to get on.

"What's the plan?" Blaine asks,

"We have two choices," I continued, "we can leave right now and let this tower come crumbling down, but we'd also be risking losing Tyro, assuming he gets out alive. Or we go find him and end this. Personally, I'm fine with leaving. I don't want anyone else to get hurt or be put in any more danger. We can find Tyro again. It's not up to me, though, so we vote. Those in favor of getting out of here, raise your hand."

Everyone looks at each other, not a single person's hand goes up. I look down and sigh,

"Those in favor of fighting?"

Everyone's hands go up. Figures, if I was wrongfully imprisoned for this long, I'd want to fight whoever was in charge, too.

"You do not have to go with us." Fesio continued, "You are in no condition to fight. You can stay outside with someone else here and watch Juna, make sure he does not do anything moronic, like run off."

Specter now realizes that Fesio is with us and they have no idea who he is. Rachel steps forward,

"I'm sorry, but who is he?"

"My name is Fesio Telkit. Clark and I fought our way back here for our own reasons, but I am still willing to help you all if I can, especially if it includes getting rid of Tyro."

I can tell no one fully trusts him. Tyro and his men gave the people of Xenem such a bad reputation that just the sight of someone from Xenem makes everyone in Specter uneasy and distrustful. I hate to admit it, but Fesio is right. I'd only slow everyone down in the condition I'm in. Juna starts laughing,

"You idiotic children, you really think you can defeat Tyro on your own? Even with Parson, you are no match. He trapped you once, he will do it again. Whether the tower is crumbling or not, he is too smart for you all."

Blaine marches to him and hits him in the face with the butt of his gun,

"I have wanted to do that for a long time." he says as he walks back to us.

I have complete faith in Specter, but Juna may be right. It pains me to say it, but Tyro is extremely smart. Leezol searched for us after Tyro became the first person to discover the secret of Specter. Not to mention, he knew I wouldn't fight Somma when we found her, he just wanted to torture me before killing me. Everything he did, he knew would get a rise out of me, out of all of us. Everything he did to me would end up causing me to make a mistake. We can't underestimate his intelligence.

In my heart, I know Fesio is right. It feels wrong sending in the rest of Specter after Tyro without me. Granted, they will have Fesio with them, but he's still looking for Vai. Leezol will be of use, but I know Specter doesn't fully trust him. What Juna said didn't anger anyone too much. Maybe because deep down, they think he's right. Everyone is talking amongst themselves trying to figure out a plan of action. Usually, I'd be involved in those conversations, but I seem to have been benched. I look down at the floor listening to everyone throwing out ideas, they're all solid plans. I heard Kierra talking about disarming the door code that Fesio and I saw. I knew she could do it. Specter is a solid team with or without me. Even then, I hope it'll be enough. I was so invested in what was being said between everyone, I didn't even notice Somma walk up to me. I'm surprised when she kisses me on the cheek, the trance I was under is immediately broken. I look to my left and see Somma kneeling next to me smiling with her eyes shining while handing me the hair tie Juna tossed during our fight. I smile and slowly grab the tie,

"I thought I lost that. Thank you."

"Are you okay? I know I have asked you that a few times now, but I worry." she asks while rubbing my hand with her thumb,

"I'm okay, how are you?"

I tried my best to make some sort of quick, witty response. I can't have Somma thinking I'm not okay with me being left behind, but she sees right through me.

"It will be okay." she says,

"I know, but I can fight. I can still fight, I can go-"

I try to get up quickly to prove I can go with them, but my pain stops me from moving, I wince in pain and fall back into the chair. Like an idiot, I try getting up again, but Somma stops me, she rubs my cheek with her thumb before kissing it,

"It is okay, do not move. I know you can fight, my love. I know better than anyone you will always fight. I cannot let you, though. Not today. For me, please?"

She's right. I know it, inside I know it, but my body doesn't want me to stop. I nod my head, but Somma sees the conflict in my eyes, I'm not hiding it as well as I want to. She gently pulls my face towards her looking me in the eyes,

"All you have done is fight, my love." she continued while moving the hair out of my face, "It hurts me to think about it, but you had to fight for survival, fight to get back to me and everyone else. You had to fight my father and even fight me. You still want to fight, but I cannot let you. You are hurt and I would not be able to forgive myself if you got hurt more than you already are or even worse, killed. I already lost you once today, I refuse to let that happen again. If it was reversed, I know you would want me to stay behind. So, please do this for me. I promise I will come back to you. We will all make it out."

I'm disappointed, but I have to listen. I was given a second chance, I can't waste it. I sigh and hold her hand,

"Call me if you need anything, no matter what and I will be there as fast as I can, okay?"

Somma kisses my hand,

"I promise." she says while fixing the wrap on my hand.

The tower rumbles again. Everyone is still set on finding Tyro and I need to head out with Juna. Somma puts my arm around her and helps me out of the chair. She gently places her hand on the stab wound on my side, she sighs,

"I hope you know in a heartbeat I would stay with you outside, but I need to do this."

I pull her closer to me and rub her shoulder, she gives me a tight hug while cautiously avoiding my wounds. I'm not in much of a mood to talk, but I also hope she knows I'll be okay, even if I am disappointed. Despite not having much to say, I have the uncomfortable task of asking someone to stay behind with Juna and I. Like Fesio said, if he does anything idiotic like try to run off, I can't catch him, not without killing him. Everyone grabs their bags, Bradley grabs my bag from the corner of the office and puts it next to me, I haven't seen my USC bag for what seems like forever. Specter was kind enough to retrieve it before finding me.

"We brought your unstylish bag, everything is inside." Bradley says.

"We have the same exact bag." I continued, "I'm sure you're not going to like this, but how would you like to be the poor soul who stays with me and Juna outside?"

Bradley looks over at the rest of Specter, he shrugs his shoulders,

"Are you asking me because I brought your bag?"

"Absolutely."

Bradley sighs,

"Alright, fine. I could use a break anyways. Prison is rough for a guy like me." he jokes.

I need to get everyone's attention, there are so many things I want to say to everyone, but the longer we take, the more dangerous this will be.

"Listen, everyone, please?" I ask,

Everyone turns to me, Somma who is still holding me up, looks at me and smiles, momentarily making me lose focus. After a moment of looking in her eyes and thinking of what exactly to say, I finally piece it all together.

"If you guys knew how much I went through to see you all again, you wouldn't believe it. You all already know this, but you need to be extremely careful. I'd love to go with you guys and finish the job, but unfortunately, I can't. I'm putting SPC. Carlston in charge, you listen to him. Remember all your training, focus, be careful, look out for each other and follow orders. I'll be right outside with PVT. Dillon and Juna, if you guys need anything, you call PVT. Dillon or myself and we will be there as fast as possible, got it?"

"Yes, sir!" everyone in Specter yells out.

Somma walks me to the elevator, while Bradley picks up Juna off the ground and makes sure his cuffs are tight. He shoves him towards the elevator door. Somma gives me a long kiss on the lips and hugs me tight,

"I love you. I will see you soon." she says.

"I love you, too. Please be careful and watch out for each other." I continued while gently placing my hand on her face, looking into her diamond eyes, "Now, go be a hero."

Somma smiles at me, but her father groans and rolls his eyes. Bradley punches him in the gut and laughs,

"I'm sorry Somma, but I think we all can agree that he deserves it. Besides, I doubt you mind at this point."

Somma hands me off to Bradley, but is still holding my hand.

"Do what you must. Just do not kill him. Make sure-" she stops speaking for a moment, she tears up while placing her hand on my heart and continuing, "Make sure, no matter what, you keep him safe. If he falls you catch him, if he walks, you follow him, okay?"

Bradley nods his head. Somma kisses my hand before letting go and playfully tousling Bradley's somehow perfectly slicked back hair,

"Thank you, Mr. Dillon. Be careful!"

Somma goes on her toes and kisses me on the cheek before opening the elevator for us. As we walk in, I get some payback for Bradley and tousle Somma's hair, she laughs and does the same to me. As the doors close, I see her fixing her hair and smiling at me.

"Thanks for that," Bradley continued, "if she knew how

hard it is to get my hair just the way I want it, but we showed her. If you need gel, I have some in my bag."

A kind offer, but I have never once used hair gel in my life. Juna remains silent, which is unlike him, but at least it's better than him running his mouth again. The elevator begins to slowly go down. Behind Bradley's calm demeanor and carefree attitude, I can tell he's not too happy about missing out on finding Tyro with everyone else.

"I appreciate you staying back. I'm sure you want to go with them, so do I. I wish you could go, but everyone is right. It's safer with someone with me. So, thank you." I say to Brandley who's helping me stay upright.

"You're right, I want to find Tyro. What he and his men did to all the prisoners was truly awful. You've never seen such brutality and utter lack of humanity. We tried to stand up for ourselves and everyone else there, but we just got beaten time and time again. Sometimes they did it just for fun, to set an example to the others. Leezol got it worse than us. They really do not like traitors I guess."

"I'm really sorry you guys went through all that, but you're all stronger soldiers because of it."

Bradley shrugs his shoulders, it's understandable if he doesn't have much to say on the matter. I understand that feeling all too well, there is no reason to waste words and dwell on the past. I try not to.

The elevator doors open, we try to move as fast as possible to get out of the tower safely. Bradley is doing his best to hold me up while also pushing Juna, who keeps intentionally slowing down or stops walking completely. We finally make it outside and go to the area where Somma found Fesio and I. Bradley, while holding onto Juna's shirt collar, helps me sit down on a rock. He then goes behind Juna and kicks the back of his knee, causing him to fall down to his knees. Bradley sighs and approaches me,

"Where's Sarge?" he asks in the most serious tone I've ever heard him speak in.

I point to the debris where Sarge is laying, Bradley slowly walks to it. I turn and see him kneel down. He moves my coat, his head immediately lowers. He shakes his head in disbelief while wiping tears from his eyes. I see him place his hand on Sarge's chest and say something, but I can't hear what. At the end, I read his lips and see that he said "Thank you." to Sarge. We never hear Bradley speak so vulnerably, I wish I could've heard everything he said, but it's private and frankly, none of my business. Bradley stands up and looks back at Juna with fury in his eyes. He storms his way towards Juna, I put my hand up trying to stop him, but he completely ignores me and throws a right hook to Juna's face which knocks him to the ground.

"I may not be able to kill you, but I sure as hell can beat you into the dirt!" Bradley yells.

I would try to stop him, but I can't blame him for his reaction. Besides, beating the hell out of Juna's is oddly therapeutic. Even watching it brings me some sort of peace. He's the reason for all of this, I'm sure all of Specter is going to want to take turns throwing shots at him. Bradley has Juna by his collar, he's punching his face in over and over again. I let him continue with his beating for a few more seconds before tapping his arm,

"Alright, you got him. I hate him, too, but save your energy. He's not worth it. Just relax."

Bradley looks at me then looks back at Juna, he throws one more punch to his face before shoving him back to the ground and moving away. Bradley takes a seat next to me, he's completely out of breath and his knuckles are bleeding.

"You weren't there." Bradley continued, "Juna was always there to torture prisoners. Sometimes he watched, sometimes he joined in. He always had that damn grin on her face through it all. He tried to make Somma execute so many people or beat them, but she wouldn't. Watching him hit her every time she didn't comply pissed us all off. Sure, we hated her and thought she was a traitor, but she didn't deserve that.

Not to mention he killed Sarge. We should just kill him right now."

I'm on Bradley's side, despite the fact I think there is more than enough death and chaos going around. I try not to kill people if I don't have to, but Juna is almost as terrible as Tyro. Both of them deserve to die. What Bradley said angered me to my core, but I decided not to respond. If I did, it probably would have ended with us going through with killing him together. Juna passes out shortly after Bradley stops attacking him, as long as he doesn't die, I don't care how long he is out, Bradley really went after him, I'd be out cold, too. I'm only just scratching the surface of what everyone went through. If Bradley's experience was that horrible, I imagine everyone else's time was just as bad if not worse. The faster we get out of here, the better.

It now occurs to me, I have no idea how Somma even convinced everyone to trust her. It may have been as simple as her opening the cage door, but there has to be more to it.

"I know you all probably hated Somma or didn't trust her, but what did she say to convince you all?"

"For a long time, nothing she said, or at least tried to say mattered to us." Bradley continued, "She was just another traitor. She tried to protect us a lot which we did appreciate, but it didn't help her case much. You know we can all watch out for ourselves, but I put it upon myself to step up and protect anyone I could, whether it was ignoring someone we think of as enemy or getting in the way of a beating. No matter what, though, we ignored her, we didn't even look at her. I will admit, it was hard for us. Her turning was just as painful for us than it was for you, but we hated treating her like the enemy. Today was the same. We heard the chaos outside, Somma came running in and looked around. She tried to calm everyone down, but they were all scared of her. She ran to us and said she's there to help, naturally we didn't believe her, nor care. No matter how much she begged us to listen or say anything, we did nothing. She opened up all the cages, letting everyone free.

When she got to us and opened the gate, we were hesitant to move, but then she told us everything with her father and that you are alive and at the tower. Some of us still didn't believe her, but we put that aside. She could lie about anything, but we knew after a moment that she would never lie about you. We reluctantly followed her and were lucky to catch you in time before Juna gave you a killing blow. Personally, I don't fully trust her, yet. I will say, though, it's nice to have everyone together again. I guess you all grew on me."

I pat him on the shoulder, Geb was right, Bradley has changed from when I first met him. He now cares about something bigger than himself. I would say at this point, I can't be too mad at him or Specter for how they treated Somma all this time. I even treated her the same way before I figured out what was going on. Her relation to Juna didn't help either. It's as if he planned it out perfectly. It makes sense for father and daughter to team up, so turning on the USC seemed like a family decision. If you used your eyes, though, anyone could see she was never happy.

Juna begins to wake up after Bradley beat him unconscious. He spits blood out of his mouth towards us, nearly hitting our feet.

"How about you get these cuffs off of me and we can have a fair fight, Mr. Dillon?" he says, staring daggers at Bradley.

Undoubtedly, I have it worse than Juna, but he's been beaten to hell today, too. It makes me feel a little better about myself and what happened to me. Bradley ignores Juna, which is something easier said than done. I haven't had much of a chance to talk to anyone besides Somma and Bradley. Most of Specter are quiet people, you won't hear them talking or complaining much. I still want to talk to them about what they went through. I understand more than anyone how hard it is opening up to others and keeping things inside, but I don't want them to be like me, I want them to be better.

"How do you think it's going in there?" Bradley asks.

"It's been quiet, I'm not sure if I like that. You'd think we would be hearing gunshots or explosions. Even the tower is barely crumbling. I figured things would be more chaotic."

"Especially with SPC. Carlston in there. Do you want me to go inside and see if everything is okay?"

"No, we need to stay here. They'll be okay."

I have to trust that Blaine will act like a true leader while he is in there with everyone else. I've been so focused on what's going on around me, I haven't even figured out how I was able to come back from the dead. Sarge told me it's not my time, but I still wonder what Carden and Kierra did. I haven't even checked my wounds to see, either way, they hurt like hell.

"How was PVT. Reddina and Shuua able to bring me back?"

"It was impressive. You were bleeding out bad, we feared the worst. Even when your eyes closed, we felt defeated, but Reddina and Shuua dumped their bags on the floor and grabbed every piece of medical equipment available. Reddina found this weird looking gun. They forced your wounds closed on your leg and side and used the gun. It looked like it poured out a hot gel that helped them close your wounds and stop the bleeding. They had PVT. Juna do CPR on you while they worked, she eventually stopped and collapsed onto you while crying her eyes out fearing the worst, but luckily, it was all a success. "

I lift up my shirt and see the scar with the gel on it. Even with Vespin blood in me, I can tell this is going to take a while to heal. I wish I could tell Bradley and everyone else I saw Sarge, but they wouldn't believe me. It's just not the right time. He wanted me to tell them he's proud and I want to honor that wish, but how can I? I technically told them, but not in the way he would have wanted.

We start hearing gunshots and explosions within the tower. I begin to worry, but I can't do anything, neither can Bradley, even though I know he wants to storm in there. We sit and listen to all the chaos, it's dreadful, Juna remains silent with a small smirk on his bloodied face. I close my eyes, trying to block out the noise. I don't want to imagine what is going on inside. I am confident Specter can handle themselves, but I can't help fearing for the worst, especially here. I feel Bradly tap my knee, I open my eyes and uncover my ears and it is silent again.

"I have to go in." Bradley says while getting up off the ground,

I grab him by his uniform and pull him back. He throws his gun down and drops back to the ground in frustration. I completely understand his eagerness, but I can't be left with Juna alone. Odds are, he would try to kill me again and I don't think I would be able to stop it this time, I wasn't able to the first time. My communicator starts to static, I put it closer to my ear and hear slight laughter.

"*Oh, Mr. Parson, our game is not over yet.*"

The voice is Tyro. Sadly, he is right. Our game is far from over.

THE ULTIMATE SACRIFICE

Juna cackles hearing Tyro. Bradley and I sit frozen in shock and fury. Both of us wondering how he got one of our communicators. I can only assume Specter got captured and he took one. I have no idea what to say or if I should even respond. Bradley sticks his hand out trying to reach for the communicator, I'm sure he has a lot to say, but so do I. I pull away from Bradley and raise the communicator close to me. I look back at Bradley, he nods once. I press down the button to respond, though my heart is racing.

"You're damn right it's not over. What's going on? How do you have a communicator?"

"*It is truly fascinating. You all fail over and over, yet you keep trying to succeed where you are all clearly at a disadvantage and cannot win. Though I must say, I do respect the drive. Now, I feel it is time for us to have a little chat. If you can manage, go inside the tower and find me under the tower. There is a hole down the first hallway on the right that those damn rebels created. I will be down there, waiting for you to limp your way inside. Alone.*"

It's suicide going in there alone in my condition. I know Bradley would want to go with me, but we can't leave Juna out here alone. I try to stand up on my own, but Bradley stops me.

"Take it easy. You can't go in there, you're a walking corpse, you'll die for real if you go in there alone. Let Specter handle him."

If I was in any better condition, I'd sprint my way inside and find him. More static comes from the communicator,

"*Oh, one more thing. Did I mention your friends will be there? Better hurry, my friend.*"

I hear Specter shouting in the background, yelling threats at Tyro. He violently shushes them, we hear people hitting them, causing them to be quiet

"*Your squad lacks manners, Mr. Parson. Interrupting me like that would get most people killed, but right now, I am focussed on you. Speaking of someone focused on you, Ms. Juna, I have someone you might want to speak with!*"

I hear Tyro violently grabbing Somma and her grunts of pain,

"*Clark, you have to leave. Please, stay away. We will be fine. You need to get out of here-*"

I then hear Tyro smack her, interrupting her midsentence. I hear his gut-wrenching cackle,

"*Look at me, now I am the one interrupting people. Well, Mr. Parson, it looks like you have a choice. Wobble your way down here or I kill your entire squad, starting with GEN. Juna's weak daughter, a shame, she could have been so much more. You have five minutes. Now, get moving, if you can!*"

"Let them go, I will go to you, just don't hurt them."

"*Tick, tock. Get moving!*"

Bradley and I look at each other in shock, our faces go pale. I look up at the tower then look at Juna. He doesn't say anything, but I can see he is also in shock and filled with anger. He couldn't care less if the rest of Specter dies, but with Somma being a part of it, panic starts to fill inside of him. Some piece of him still loves her and thinks of her as his daughter, which is shocking to see.

"What choice do I have?" I ask Bradley.

"It looks like you don't have one." he responds while rubbing his eyes in frustration.

He's right. I like to believe there is always a choice, but right now, there is not. Bradley slowly stands up, realizing that this is probably the last time he is going to see me. We both know what Tyro intends on doing to me once I am inside. I've never feared death, but this time, it hits me. For the longest time, I knew I could die leaving nothing behind, besides my parents. Now, I have more. I have someone I love, an entire squad of people I respect and care about deeply. My demise is inside that tower, but if it will get everyone else to safety, then I will gladly give my life for theirs. Bradley helps me stand up and puts my bag on my back,

"I know we're in a rush, but thank you for everything. All due respect, but I used to think you were just another boring soldier telling me what to do, but you were more. You're crazy and maybe even stupid, but I've never seen someone fight as hard as you have. If this is my last time seeing you, then I want to say thank you and I am happy I got to serve under you." he says while extending his hand to me.

Tears fill his eyes, I smile and shake his hand,

"You didn't serve under me, you served *with* me, I'm proud of you. No matter what happens in there, I want you to keep growing and keep fighting for more than yourself. Specter is your family, treat them as such. Always look out for them, just like I did." I hand him my communicator, "Call as many people as you can in the USC, tell them to send a fleet to Xenem and attack. We came here to tear this place down, my final order to you, PVT. Dillon, watch Juna and make the call, finish the job. Got it?"

Bradley nods his head once before slowly letting go of me to stand alone. It takes me a moment to take a step towards the tower. Each step hurts tremendously, I nearly collapse in pain, but I can't stop.

"Parson!" I hear Juna yell behind me, "You may not like me, but I know you love my Somma. Get her out of there. Please."

I nod at him. Any other request, I'd ignore him, but this time I will make an exception. Getting Somma to safety was already a priority. She told me to stay away, but there is no way I was ever going to do that. It takes me a few minutes, but I eventually limp my way inside the tower. I've been inside of this now decrepit monstrosity before, but this time it feels different. A cold chill runs up my spine, I feel weaker than usual, my guess is it's the fact that I know my time runs short. It's nearly impossible to walk anywhere in the tower. Bodies and debris are all over the floor. No matter where you step, you are stepping in blood. The Xenem army and Vai's army have taken heavy casualties, who knows if I was still with Vai if I would be dead by now?

As I continue limping my way through the bloodied halls, glimpses of my life play in my head. From childhood to this very moment. Despite my best efforts, tears roll down my face as memories with Specter, Sarge, Somma and of course, my parents play in my head. I leave all that behind, it's painful, but it needs to be done for everyone's safety. I see the hole in the ground Tyro mentioned, it is literally a pit of despair. A makeshift ramp was made with thrown together materials from debris. It looks uneasy and close to collapsing, like me.

Under the tower, it's dark and cold. Fitting for Xenem. I hear the bone-chilling cackle of Tyro, I try to stay ready for anything or anyone to jump out at me assuming it's a trap.

"Welcome to the festivities, Mr. Parson." I hear Tyro's voice echo.

I try to move faster, I see dimly lit lanterns in the distance and a bunch of shadows moving around. I get closer to the lights and trip on something. I grab my light from my bag and point it down and see Fesio on the ground. His face is covered with cuts, bruises and blood. I can't bend down all the way to see if he still has a heartbeat, but luckily, I can hear him breathing, weakly. I hear a woman laughing next to me, I point the light to my left and see Vai and what is left of her team. She also looks beaten, but in better shape than Fesio. She has a vicious smile on her face and laughs,

"Fesio is strong, but foolish. He was never going to beat me, not even with your help. He had this beating coming and speaking of people who are owed a beating," Vai hits me in the head with a kick, causing me to fall over onto piled up debris, "I owe you a lot more than that for what you did. If there is anything left of you after this."

"Vai, what are you doing here? You hate Tyro, now you're working for him?"

"I am working *with* him, that includes capturing your precious squad. We could have killed your little friends, but Tyro wanted them alive. He is letting me do what I want with Fesio, I am still considering letting him live. As for Tyro, I do hate him, but I also like how he paid me and my army to back down. He even guaranteed me a position of power after he rebuilds. I cannot trust him, so if he backs out, then I shall kill him. If he keeps his word, then I will have the power I deserve. It works for me either way. Now, you have someone waiting for you."

Vai points at Fesio's body and one of her troops, grabs the body and drags him away to unknown fate, at least unknown to me. She picks me up from my shirt off the debris she kicked me onto and throws me further down the path. It's hard to pinpoint what hurts exactly, everything hurts. I can barely stand, let alone walk. I start getting closer to the end of the path where all the lights are. Two guards come out of the shadows and point their guns at me, I raise my hands as far as I can without putting me in excruciating pain. Both guards laugh, but are quickly silenced by Tyro's cackle,

"He has arrived! Bring him closer, you fools. No matter that he made us wait, he is here now. We can celebrate!"

The guards go behind me and push me forward where I see all of Specter and Leezol in a line on their knees with their hands cuffed behind their backs. They are covered with dirt and blood. Tyro emerges from another pile of debris,

"Mr. Parson, welcome! We have been waiting!"

All of Specter looks up at me, Leezol's head remains down as he shakes it in disbelief.

"I'm here now, let them all go." I demand.

"Not so fast, my weakened friend! I never agreed to that. I feel this is a perfect time to kill you all. Starting with Ms. Juna perhaps? Or perhaps that idiot Carlston? Gods know he's no use. He has been throwing empty threats at me ever since we caught him, most annoying. Shall I let you pick, Parson?"

Panic fills in the eyes of everyone, I try to approach Tyro, but the guards behind me pull me back,

"Tyro, she's GEN. Juna's daughter. Do you really want to kill the last remaining daughter of your General? He is going to kill you!"

"Just as well, I was going to kill him next. He has proven to be most useless, like his daughter. Might as well start with her then work my way down, ending with my old friend Auldin Leezol!"

Tyro pulls out his knife with a sadistic grin and approaches Somma, whose face and hair is uncovered, her skin getting brighter each second. She begins to try to move away, but a guard forces her to stay put. I try to step forward again, but the guard to my right hits me in the back with his gun causing me to go down to the ground. I look back up, watching him get closer to Somma,

"No! Wait!" I yell with all my power and strength, my voice echoes.

I haven't yelled like that since Somma turned on us. Tyro looks shocked, he turns to me and snaps his finger. The guards pick me back up and take me closer to Tyro,

"Is there something you need to say?" he asks mockingly,

"Tyro, I am begging you. Let them go and you can do whatever you want with me. You can force to me work, you can torture me, you can even kill me. Just please let them all go."

Tyro smiles, the room remains silent, besides the sounds of everyone trying to break free and Somma crying even more after what I just told Tyro. I hated begging to him, but if I have learned anything from the past hour, it's that I have no options left, no choices. Tyro steps back and looks up and down my body,

"A kind offer. Perhaps we can still use you. You are not in the best condition, though. Perhaps I need to check your medical history before we can work something out. My pad!"

A guard opens my bag and grabs Tyro's pad I took from

his desk. He hands it to Tyro, who begins to scroll through it.

"Smart move trying to take this from me. I foolishly left it behind when that rebellion attacked. It has all the information I have attained over time, including all of your medical records. Now, I see here, Parson, you have quite a history. This one in particular fascinates me. A self-inflicted gunshot wound. Suicide, Parson? Very cowardly."

I hate that my attempt to take my life is on my medical record. I never wanted anyone to know. The only one in Specter who knows about it is Somma. Everyone in Specter looks at each other in confusion and worry, Somma looks down.

"Remove your shirt." Tyro demands,

I stare blankly at him, shocked that he's demanding that.

"I want to see the wound. If you will not do it, then my men will do it."

Tyro points at my shirt, the two guards behind me forcefully remove my uniform and rip the shirt off my body. I look down in shame, but I hear Specter gasp. All of them, including Somma, have never seen me without my shirt. Tyro twirls his finger, a guard turns me around, exposing the scars on my back. Tyro chuckles and has them turn me back around.

"Scars front to back. Everywhere. It is nothing to be ashamed of. A good soldier always has scars. That being said, a weak soldier tries to take his own life." he says while poking the scar above my heart with his bony finger.

I can't say that I disagree with him. I was weak, but I could only stay strong for so long. It was a mistake.

"Parson, do you still wish to end your life?"

I weakly shake my head in shame, Tyro punches me across the face,

"You answer me when I ask you a question, boy! Do you wish to take your life? I can end it for you right now and feel nothing of it!"

"No, I do not want you to end my life. I just want you to let everyone go."

"I have a few more questions. I find it odd that in your

records it does not say anything about the slashes on your face."

In an instant, Tyro slashes his knife across my face twice, cutting both of my cheeks. The guards next to me hold me up, keeping me from falling down. Specter erupts in anger and tries harder to escape and stop Tyro, but they keep getting stopped. Tyro laughs as he grabs my face, bringing the knife closer to it,

"How about now? Do you wish to die? Because I also see it says nothing about your wound on your side, it looks painful."

Tyro throws a kick to the wound on my side, which causes the gel to break and blood starts to come out. The guards let go of me as the kick causes me to fall to the ground on all fours. I try to cover the wound with my hand, getting blood all over it. Tyro walks up to me and throws a kick to the wound on my thigh which causes me to fall completely flat on the ground. I start to feel the same way as I did when life was fading from me. While everyone in Specter is still trying to escape and yelling in anger and frustration, all I focus on is Somma. She can't stop crying, she is trying to fight free, but she's crying watching what Tyro is doing to me. If this is delaying their deaths then I will gladly take it, no matter how agonizingly painful all this feels. The guards begin laughing as Tyro kneels next to me. He grabs me by the hair and lifts my head up before punching me in the face and throwing my head back down to the ground.

"I know I seem like a bad person, but I am not completely heartless."

He gets up and uncuffs Somma. He grabs her from the line, by the back of her neck and leads her to me. He throws her to the ground next to me.

"See? I am not so bad! I will allow you both to say your goodbyes. Make it fast."

Somma quickly crawls to me and lifts my face up. I'm nearly blinded by her shining skin, but I've learned to see past her shine. Tears run down her face as she kisses me on the cheek,

"My love, you have to get up. You have to fight." she says while weeping, moving the hair out of my face.

"I-" I can barely speak, but I utter the two words I never wanted to say, "I can't."

Somma shakes her head in disbelief,

"Do not say that! Please, Clark, you have to get up. You have to fight. You always get up. Do not let him do this, I cannot lose you again."

"I tried," I say weakly, "but I just can't anymore. I love you, Somma. I'm getting you all out."

"No, Clark please, you need to-"

Tyro grabs her by the hair, interrupting her. He violently throws her back towards the line. Guards grab her and try to drag her back in line with everyone else, but Somma's arm slips out of the guard's hands. She elbows him and punches the other guard's ribcage. She runs back to me and kneels down. She quickly lifts my face up again,

"Please, get up. I need you! You have to-"

Tyro growls as he kicks Somma's side, interrupting her heartbreaking pleas. My head drops to the ground as she's hit, I hear the kick cause her to collapse on the ground in pain, the guards grab her and drag her away, cuffing her again. After a few moments, I physically feel myself die, I don't feel a heartbeat or feel control over any part of my body. I can only hear what is going on around me and I hate it. In my head, I hear Sarge's voice, something he told me in the afterlife, "It's not your time, yet."

Hearing that and the pained cries of Somma wakes something up inside of me, like a bolt of lighting or a fire being lit. I'm filled with fury, fury that gives me new life. I'll call it adrenaline. My eyes shoot open, I grab onto some debris and push myself up with all my strength. Tyro looks shocked. His shock turns to anger, he marches to me and punches my side. I keep myself up, though. Tyro laughs,

"My friend, you have spirit. I respect that, but it is a waste of time and energy. Do you not realize that with just one stab, I can end your life?"

I wave Tyro to come closer to me, he tilts his head in confusion and slowly walks to me. I smile and look up at him, a sight I am sure he is not happy to see.

"You should not have hurt her, or any of them." I lean closer and start to whisper softly, Tyro leans in closer, "What *you* don't realize is that with just one stab, I can end your life, too."

With a burst of energy and power, I grab his hand with the knife, I turn it towards him and jam it into his body with all my force, causing us both to fall over. Tyro yells in pain as we go down. The guards rush to me, but are stopped by a rumbling coming from outside. We hear ships flying over and around us, cannons firing and shouting. A hole gets blasted from the outside, giving us a way out. The explosions cause debris and rubble to fall from above us, creating a wall between all of us and Tyro who was still on the ground with his knife inside of him. We're all confused as to what's going on. We hear people running towards us, I fear it's Vai's troops storming in to finish us all off. To my surprise, storming in and opening fire is Bradley accompanied by LT. Serro, PVT. Charlie Kemper, and Fesio with medics. They're no match for the Xenem guards. After they quickly get rid of all the guards, Serro, Kemper and Fesio go to Specter to free them. Bradley runs to me,

"Good looks and daring heroics while saving the day, I'm the total package!" he says while helping me up. LT. Serro approaches me, holding Tyro's pad he dropped.

"To think, this could have been avoided if you were not listening in on a private matter. That being said, you have proven your bravery and strength. I am happy you are still with us. CPL. Parson. PVT. Dillon, get him medical attention immediately."

As Bradley helps me walk away, Serro places his hand on my shoulder, I look at him and he smiles while bowing his head at me. Serro never was that crazy about me. I guess risking my life for the USC has a way of gaining favor. Bradley sits me near the medics who are currently checking on everyone else. Bradley finds a medic who isn't busy whose nametag reads Donzly, he pulls him over to me. He is visibly shocked, but quickly begins cleaning me up. I sit still with a blank expression on my face, tears begin to run down my face. There are multiple reasons why that would happen, but in totality, I think it's because we are all safe. Pretty hard to believe.

"We're going to have to fix these wounds onboard, we need to hurry." Donzly says.

I nod my head, he helps me stand up and we begin to walk out of the tower. I hear a voice behind us,

"Wait!"

Somma runs up from behind me and wraps me in a hug. I stand still in shock for a moment, once I look down and see the shining, silver hair of the girl I love, I come back to reality. I put my arms around her tight, something comes over me and I begin crying with her in my arms. What started as a few tears running down my face has turned into both Somma and I crying.

"I knew you would get up. My hero." she says, holding me tighter.

It hurts, but I don't mind it at all.

"I apologize, but we need to get him onboard." Donzly says.

Somma kisses me on the lips before letting go,

"I will be with you soon, my love."

I smile at her as we walk away. Leaving the tower, I see USC ships flying around, destroying factories and ships. Freeing Xenem has never looked so close. We make our way inside a nearby ship. Donzly opens a door to the side of the ship and lays me down on a bed, it's the first real bed I've laid on in a long time. Donzly leaves to prepare his equipment and gather the other medics to help him. I lay in silence, looking up at the ceiling of the ship, eventually, I close my eyes. It's probably not the best idea to do that, but I'm exhausted. I hear a chuckle and a seat being pulled up next to me, I open my eyes and turn to the right and see Ben sitting down smiling at me,

"My friend, you have seen better days."

I chuckle and extend my hand to him, he remembers what I taught and shakes my hand with his classic smile.

"It's good to see you, Ben. What are you doing here?" I ask.

"I flew everyone here! I was quite the pilot years ago. I would always race Richard and Auldin to see who the fastest pilot was, whether they admit it or not, I usually won!"

Ben bringing up Sarge hurts. I don't know if Ben knows what happened. I hate to be the one to break the news to him, besides it does hurt to talk, but someone has to tell him.

"Ben, I'm really sorry, but-"

Ben holds his hand up,

"I know. He is on another ship on the way back to USC headquarters, along with your parents. LT. Serro wanted me to give you this." Ben hands me Sarge's arrow and feather necklace along with the Noli necklace Ben made, "You can do with these what you will. The young soldier, Kemper, is standing guard with your parents and the other survivors. As for Richard, he shall be properly buried. Bradley told me you carried him around for miles just so he could be honored properly, I am sure he would have appreciated that. Thank you, Clark."

"It was tough, but I knew it was the right thing to do. I know the three of you were close to rekindling your friendships, I wish you had more time with him." I say while looking down.

Ben smiles and pats my arm before getting up,

"I am going to see if anyone needs any help. I will be right back, my friend. You rest!"

I put Sarge's necklaces in my pocket and close my eyes again. I hear the rest of Specter approaching the ship, but I also hear someone run on the ship and gasp. The fast footsteps approach me. Soft, cold hands gently grab my face and from their touch, I can tell it's Somma. I feel her kiss me on the cheek. I open my eyes and see her smiling at me. She seems to have taken her Xenem uniform off and probably left it on the ground somewhere around the tower. I'm sure she was glad to leave it behind. She only has her gray tank top on her, I hope she doesn't get too cold during the trip back. I slowly reach for her face, she grabs my hand and places it on her cheek. Her skin is always cold, it causes my body to cool down. I see a cut near her right eye, I gently rub it with my thumb, wiping the blood away.

"It is just a scratch, my love. Are you okay?" she asks.

"I don't know. I hope I am. I just want to get out of here."

"I know, we are leaving soon. We will have our magical night."

I smile and close my eyes. I feel Somma gently hold onto me,

"I love you always, Clark." she whispers.

I would respond, but talking hurts at the moment, instead I smile and hold her hand. Somma stays by my side and holds my hand while the rest of Specter gets on the ship, I open my eyes and they all gather around me. Blaine and the Lane twins shake my hand, Kierra and Rachel both give me a hug. I couldn't be happier that everyone is okay. Their uniforms are all off, as I'm about to question it, Ben walks back onto the ships and laughs,

"The Legends of Tanli! You are all okay!" he playfully exclaims.

Everyone turns and approaches Ben in rejoice, they all give him a hug like they are seeing an old friend, which we are. After they move away, he lifts up his finger for everyone's attention,

"LT. Serro wanted me to tell you that he has taken your uniforms and will have them washed and cleaned back at your Headquarters. I wish he would clean my clothes too!"

After Ben finishes laughing at his own joke, he walks to

Somma, who refuses to let go of my hand, and gives her a hug. Ben was always so kind to us all, but there was slight tension when Leezol walks up to him.

"Ben, it is good to see you again. We lost Richard. I know you probably think I had something to do with it, but-"

Geb interrupts him by wrapping him in a hug,

"I know, Auldin. We lost our brother, I know you did not do it. We shall honor his memory soon."

Leezol stares blankly with his arms down, but after a few moments, he closes his eyes and hugs Ben back. For the longest time, we saw Leezol as someone who had no feelings, no sympathy, no remorse, no love or care for anyone, besides himself. Now we see, when it comes to those he used to call his friends, his brothers, it is the only time where we see him act like a decent person. Ever since we all found out what happened with Ben, Leezol has acted differently, more silent than usual. He spent years suppressing what he has done, now that he faced it, he is not the same. LT. Serro walks in and calls everyone's attention. Everyone stands at attention, I try to get up as fast as I can to the same, groaning in pain as I move, but Serro puts his hand up,

"Parson, do not move. Rest. PVT. Juna, help him down." Somma holds my hand and helps me get back in the bed, "We have taken the former GEN. Juna into custody. He will face trial and judgment for his crimes against the USC. PVT. Juna, I understand this is difficult for you, if you do not want to testify against your father in trial, you do not have to, but the rest of you, I request your attendance. You all saw first hand what he has done. I am heading back to Felv to give them the news of Xenem's fall, sadly I cannot give any of you credit, you are all still an unknown unit to most of the USC. As far as they will know, a random unit went on a suicide mission. I will do my best to cover up any more of your existence, but just know, you all have done SSG. Miner and myself proud, I am sure he would be happy to see this day. Dismissed."

Donzly and other medics come on the ship and begin to

work on my wounds. It's hard to feel like celebrating while the tower still stands. It's been a symbol of death and oppression to the people of Xenem for so long. Tyro's fate is unknown, but as long as this tower still stands, the blood stained history of his reign remains. Martin looks out the window of the ship, eyeing the tower, I can tell he feels the same way as I do.

"How has the tower not collapsed? Surely, one more blast has to do the trick. Could it be done?" he asks us all.

"I suppose." Carden responds, "During our stay in Tanli, PVT. Shuua and I completed the EMP that was requested, the only difference is it is no longer an EMP, but now a vastly powerful bomb. We did not need the EMP anymore, this was the next logical option. We figured we would need it at some point. If placed under the tower, where we held hostage to be exact, I would say the explosion would cause the tower to finally collapse."

"I say we do it. All in favor?" I ask everyone.

Everyone raises their hand, but Carden and Kierra look at each other with concern,

"There is one major issue," Kierra continued, "We did not get far enough to develop a detonator or any sort of timer. It would have to be manually blown up by someone standing next to it. Naturally, killing them instantly."

Our time in Xenem has taken a heavy toll on us. We can't lose anyone else, who would even volunteer? The ship goes silent, we look at each other, but after a few moments, we hear Leezol sigh,

"Give me the bomb."

Unless this is a trick or a joke, it sounds like Leezol is going to sacrifice himself. There was a time where I would have gladly accepted Leezol's sacrifice, but not anymore. He is not the crass, sadistic, hate fueled soldier he was when we met him. Whether he was driven by revenge against Sarge or not, he isn't the same. Ben saw it before any of us, and he even got screwed over by him the worst. I really do wish the bomb could detonate from a distance. I would do it myself, but I can't even move that much, besides, Somma wouldn't let me. At heart, he is a soldier. I was taught to always be willing to sacrifice it all, I'd assume the Xenem army preaches the same. The difference is, he is sacrificing himself for us, the people he spent months tracking and almost tortured for information on a man he wanted to kill while capturing us in the process. I'm not even sure if Somma has forgiven him in any sort of way for what he did, or almost did to her. Despite everyone's silence, I can see that no one wants Leezol to set off the bomb. No one is going to say it, but they're thinking it. I'm willing to actually say something, even if it hurts like hell to speak, or do anything in general.

"No." I whisper.

Somma looks back at me and gives a small frown as she rubs my cheek with her thumb. I can tell she is shocked and even saddened by the possibility of losing Leezol. Carden slowly brings the bomb out of his bag, it's an awkward looking device. For all their incredible intellect, both Carden and Kiera never had an eye for design. Not that it mattered too much, not to them, at least. The bomb is smaller than I imagined, the fact something so powerful and destructive can come from something of that size is shocking.

"Assuming no one has any objections, one of you, teach me how to set this thing off." Leezol says while walking off the ship.

Ben steps in front of him,

"Auldin, there is no need to do something like this. A building is not worth your life, time will destroy this tower. We can wait for that day to come, no need to lose your life to destroy what is left of this tower. I already lost one friend, do not do this and have me lose another."

"Life? I lost my life a while ago. I am sorry, Ben. For everything." Leezol responds before moving around Ben.

Carden slowly follows him and starts explaining the mechanisms of the bomb. Their voices fade as they leave the ship. Frustration starts to fill my body, staying still becomes a near impossible task for me. I want to stop him, but what can I do? I begin trying to get out of the bed, but the medics try to stop me from moving, Somma helps them. She gently places her hands on my face, directing my focus to her,

"Look at me, my love. It will be okay. Please calm down." she says while rubbing my cheek.

While that would usually work, something came over me where I didn't even register what she said. Moving like I am hurts, but even if it is Leezol, I don't want to lose anyone else. Despite Somma's and the medic's best efforts, I move around to the point where I fall off the bed and land on my wounded side. I yell in pain, the medics try to pick me up, but I push them away and help myself up by grabbing the railing of the bed.

"We can't lose anyone else." I say out of breath while slowly pulling myself up with tears in my eyes.

I start limping to the exit while wheezing. I feel awful, but if no one is going to stop Leezol, then I have to. I grab my side with my right hand as I power my way to the exit, Somma puts my arm around her and helps me walk. She says nothing as we leave the ship. We see Carden walking back towards the ship,

"He knows what to do, we should leave before the blast." he says with sadness in his eyes.

We walk back to under the tower where we see Leezol kneeling in front of the bomb, setting up the detonation. We quickly walk towards him, Leezol hears my grunts in pain and turns around,

"Parson, you fool, what are you doing?"

"Maybe I am a fool, I am killing myself standing here, but it is because I can't let you do this. There are other ways-"

"Enough!" Leezol interrupts, "It is my decision. Let me do this."

"We can figure something else out. You don't have to do this."

Leezol sighs and walks to the hole where we entered, looking at the city under siege,

"I used to not care much for this city. I found the people weak and lacked any intellect. I thought that by working my way up the ranks, I could rid Xenem of the simple minded, leaving those with a brain. I was no better than Tyro. As it turned out, those who opposed him had brains all along. It was I who lacked any sort of brain, I blindly followed the orders of Tyro, where did that get me? Betrayed, imprisoned, beaten. I suppose I deserve it. I apologize for what I have done to you and your squad. This is my way to set things right, for all I have done to the people here and Specter. It is only fitting I go down with the tower I fought so hard to enforce the power of."

"What about Ben? You betrayed him, but even after all that, he still considers you a friend, are you going to leave him especially after you both lost Sarge?"

"I came here with the intention of not making it out alive, I knew this would be it, so let this be it, Parson. Get out of here."

Leezol turns around and walks past me back to the bomb. I turn around and try to say something again, but Leezol quickly turns back towards me,

"Quit your whining!" he snaps, "We are soldiers, we make sacrifices! Do you think your squad was happy when you jumped out the tower? No! I had to listen to them weep for days in a cold and crowded prison cell, all of them wondering what they could have done differently, how they could have been better. I told them what I am telling you. Soldiers, great soldiers, make the ultimate sacrifices. Do not worry about me. Get back to that ship and leave Xenem. Your job is done, Parson."

I have no idea what else I could say, I look down at Somma, who has said nothing this whole time. She looks up at me and nods her head. With her nod, I could see this is hitting her hard too. With Somma's help, I walk towards Leezol, realizing there is nothing I could say or do to stop him from doing this. I take my arm off of Somma and limp a few steps towards Leezol on my own. I extend my hand to him. He looks at my hand then looks back at me. He slowly grabs my hand and shakes it.

"Thank you, *Auldin*." I say somberly.

"You are a good man. I see why Miner liked you. Take care of yourself and your squad. Farewell, *Clark*."

Our last moments together, we finally addressed each other with our first names. It felt odd, we always addressed each other by our last names. He wasn't always a good person, but in the end, he did what none of us wanted to do. Now, we see what Ben always saw, not some violent soldier from Xenem, but Auldin Leezol, the man who made the ultimate sacrifice.

I let go of our handshake and turn back to Somma who now has tears in her eyes. She helps me sit down on nearby debris and turns to Auldin. She slowly walks towards him, realizing that he has put her through more pain than any of us, he lowers his head in shame. Somma stands in front of him, pulls out his knife from her belt and points the blade at him,

"We have our history, Ms. Juna. For that I sincerely apologize, I know I was not a good man. No use in killing me now, though. Who else is going to set this bomb off?" Auldin asks.

Somma says nothing, she turns the knife around with the handle facing Leezol and hands it to him slowly,

"This belongs to you. Thank you, Auldin. You are forgiven."

That knife has been everywhere, in many different hands. It is finally back to its rightful owner. Auldin slowly grabs the knife and looks at it like he is seeing an old friend. He puts it in his sheath and bows his head in appreciation. Somma smiles and extends her hand. Auldin and Somma shake hands, a truly bittersweet moment. She walks back to me and slowly helps me up. Going as fast as we can, we walk out of the tower.

"Both of you, wait!" Leezol exclaims, "Tell Ben I am sorry, I should have been better. The same goes for your squad. Tell them all I am sorry and I bid them farewell. Keep them safe,

Clark, they look up to you. You must lead as Miner did. Make him proud. Now, get out of here. I will give you all a few minutes to leave."

We nod our heads and leave. I feel ashamed I could not stop him, but he did not want to be saved. I tried, that's all I could have done. Walking away, I try to hold back my emotions as I usually do, but I can't help it. A tear rolls down my cheek and falls on Somma. She looks up at me and stops walking. She hugs me tight,

"You have so much love and care inside of you. Sadly, you cannot save everyone, my love. I know you tried with everything inside of you. I am saddened by it, too but it will be okay, we must leave now."

Somma kisses my cheek and wipes my tears. She helps me walk into the ship and lays me back down. The medics slowly approach me and continue working on my wounds. Everyone, including Ben, gathers around me, wondering what happened and why isn't Auldin back on the ship. I look at them all and shake my head. Ben looks down in sadness. He lost both of his closest friends only after spending a short time reconnecting with them.

"He wanted me to apologize to you all for what he did in the past, especially to you, Ben." I continued, "He wishes us all farewell. The bomb will detonate at any moment, we need to move."

Ben wipes his tears as he walks to the pilot seat and takes off. A few moments after we take off, we hear a loud explosion. We look out the window of the ship and see the tower engulfed in flames, finally causing its collapse. Destroying every piece of it, with Auldin sadly included. Everyone bows their head in respect and takes a moment of silence, with their only sounds being heard are sniffles and tears hitting the floor. Someone who was once our enemy, became our fallen brother. I can now only hope he rests well.

THE WAY BACK HOME

After the explosion and our moment of silence, I felt weak and went to sleep, letting the medics finish up. I wake up about an hour later, I notice they moved me to the back of the ship with the door closed, away from everyone else. Looking out the window to my left, I see we are finally miles away from Xenem. It feels too good to be true. Normally, flying from the Dommis system to the Waylif system would take quite a while. We would usually jump to hyperspace which have us there within seconds, but the speed and motion could cause injuries and wounds to worsen, so I guess Ben decided to be cautious and take the scenic route.

Being off of Xenem, I feel a range of emotions, both positive and negative. I haven't seen my parents since I was in the Xenem prison cell with everyone else. I am relieved to hear they are okay. As for Sarge's memorial, the USC will be handling the preparations and undoubtedly fabricating some story of what happened. Personally, I don't care what they say about Xenem's fall, they can make up whatever story they want. I don't need praise. I do wish that the rest of Specter get the praise they deserve, being prisoners of Xenem under Tyro's control doesn't sound easy. It doesn't get much easier for Somma. If word got out she betrayed the USC with her father, she would be a massive target. She already regrets what she has done, she doesn't need any more trouble for what happened.

I stare blankly at the ceiling of the ship, still fully waking up. I look down and see Somma sitting next to my bed, but she's asleep, laying her head on my chest with her hand on my heart. I smile and gently place my hand on her back, with my other hand, I place it on top of Somma's hand that's on my heart. I look down and watch the shimmer of her hair, it still amazes me just like it did the day I met her. From what I can tell, the medics used the same hot gell Carden used on me and placed healing pads on my wounds. As for the cuts across both my cheeks, there wasn't much that the medics could do about it, besides clean the wound and close it as much as they could.

I am so enamored by Somma's hair, I don't even hear Fesio enter the room and pull up a chair next to me.

"She has been by your side this entire time. She refused to move." he says while sitting down.

I'm glad to see Fesio is okay, all things considered. Last I saw him, he was being dragged away unconscious by one of Vai's followers. He waited so long to face her, it's a shame he appeared to be on the losing side of their fight. I can't forget what Vai told me, Tyro paid her to stop her attack and offered her power. What I can't believe is that she took the offer. Someone so dedicated to seeing the fall of Tyro bowed to him as soon as money and power came into the mix. She can call it what she wants, but I call it weakness.

"You got them out. Just like you said you would. Impressive."Fesio says.

"I couldn't get them all out. It's bad enough we lost our leader, but I lost another person. I could have done more."

"Do you not see what you have done? Your leader is no longer here, you took charge and got everyone out. Yes, you lost someone else, but believe me, those who come from Xenem, especially soldiers, are terribly stubborn. You would have had to knock him out to stop him. His mind was already made up. Your job is done. No need to dwell on what has been, but rather what is."

I know all too well how stubborn Auldin was. If I was in any better condition, I would have knocked him out. Maybe even set the bomb off myself. Fesio is right, though. No point in focusing on the past. We never liked Auldin or fully trusted him, but in the end, he saved us all, for that I feel he earned my respect and my eternal gratitude. I have no idea how Fesio got away from Vai, he showed up with Bradley to get us out from under the tower. Vai had him beat, I'm not sure what went his way that seemingly spared him. I nod in agreement with what Fesio said. A part of me didn't want to ask what happened with him and Vai, but curiosity gets the better of me.

"I'm glad you're okay, how did you get away from Vai?"

"As I predicted, she wanted to make an example of me. She was always a fan of putting on a show. She took me outside in front of what was left of her followers and was ready to shoot me in the head, but when the USC fleet arrived, they fired shots everywhere. It distracted everyone. One ship came flying towards us, firing its guns around me, scaring off Vai and her followers. I did not move. I figured I was dead anyways. The ship landed, PVT. Dillion ran out and helped me to get on the ship. It seemed he recognized me. I met LT. Serro, Ben and PVT. Kemper, they did not treat me like a threat or a prisoner. I appreciated that and with the energy I had left, I knew I had to help them find you. It would seem I have fulfilled my mother's wishes, I am finally off of Xenem. I might return, but not for a while, not with Vai still there, trying to gain the power she was promised."

I was hoping with Tyro presumably gone, a new era of peace would be born in all of Xenem, bringing it back to how it used to look. Vai may think that her rise to power would bring peace, but she is no better than the people she once fought against. Maybe she was always like that. I feel foolish for helping her. I appreciate her taking care of Sarge and offering me a place to rest, but that was the extent of her kindness. Fesio looks at Somma, who is still sleeping,

"She is strong. All of your squad is strong, but you would be amazed by what I saw before their capture. Vai surrounded us inside the tower, I tried to approach her, but our old friends Grolo and Mezza stood in my way. I had to fight them at the same time. Through all the fighting and chaos, I saw Somma stand her ground against Vai and Cinniya. If she got hit, she would recover so quickly and strike back. Neither of them would admit it, but Somma had them beat, she and the rest of your squad fought so ferociously and bravely, I saw the worry on Vai's bloodied face as more of her followers went down. Her worry only increased as Somma fought her. Thiani helped them, though. After I took care of Grolo and Mezza, I saw Thiani picking up pieces of broken glass and debris. Soldiers got in my way again, but PVT. Denza tackled her and fought as hard as she could, but Thiani had other soldiers push her off. She ran up to Somma and threw the glass and debris at her, which gave her that cut on her face. With that distraction, Vai kicked her in the face, Cinniya threw a kick to her side and Somma went down. She was the last one standing. I tried to fight Vai, she cannot do anything without help, though. It is easy to beat an opponent when they are outnumbered. Vai did not beat me, her numbers beat me. Either way, I am sorry I could not do more."

Somma begins waking up, Fesio points at her,

"She is waking up, I will give you both space."

Fesio gets up and leaves the room, closing the door behind him. I appreciate everything he has done, he did all he could. Nothing about what he said about Vai and her friends surprised me. How they fight is cowardly and weak. Cheating to win is a sign of pure weakness. I wish no one fell to their tactics, but admittedly, cheating gets results. Somma lifts her head up, her hair is in her face. It looked like my hair whenever I woke up for school when I was younger. I move the hair out her face, even with her messy hair, cuts and dirt on her face, she is still the most beautiful person I've ever seen. The only thing in my mind I think to say is just how beautiful she is.

"Wow." I continued, "So beautiful." I say while rubbing her cheek with my thumb.

Somma smiles, she brings my hand to her lips and kisses it. After waking up I still felt off, but now that I've had time to reflect, I start feeling the relief of being off of Xenem and everyone in Specter is safe on board. I do feel self-conscious, though. Tyro had my shirt ripped off, I've never been shirtless for this long. I never wanted Somma or anyone to see my scars. I never wanted them to worry. I regret all of my scars. It's a reminder of the times where I was not paying attention, being foolish or in the case of my fight with Juna, too weak. Somma gently runs her hand along my body looking at the scars. Everywhere you look, whether it's my arms or torso, it's all gunshot wounds, stab wounds and slashes. Not a pretty sight.

"They could have easily taken my shirt off, they didn't need to rip it." I joke.

Somma looks back at me, sadness fills her eyes. She rubs my cuts on my cheeks with her thumb, she doesn't respond to me. I already feel self-conscious about the scars on my body and feel exposed, her not responding doesn't help. I break eye contact with her and look down. Somma lifts my head up back to her, I look her in the eyes. She tilts her head as she looks into my eyes.

"You have been through so much pain."

"Like you wouldn't believe." I respond, moving my head away.

"I have seen it. You do not realize it, but when I look in your eyes, I see all your pain, stress, sadness, fury and fear. I feel these scars are because of that and everything you have been through over time, especially recently."

I start breathing heavier, my heart begins racing. Somma puts her hand on my heart and feels it beating faster. She gently picks up my hand and kisses it,

"In those same eyes, I also see love, strength, bravery, courage, kindness, loyalty, honor, wisdom, power and so many other incredible qualities that made me fall in love with you. Your scars and pain do not determine who you are. It hurt me seeing all of your scars, I wanted to break free from those guards and hold you tight, but what hurts me more is you hiding your scars from me and thinking of yourself as anything lesser than the amazing person we all know you are because of them."

"Thank you. I'm sorry you had to find out the way you did-"

Somma places her hands on my face, causing me to stop talking mid-sentence and kisses me passionately.

"I suppose I can forgive you if you were to give me another magical night." she says before kissing me on the cheek.

I see my chance and quickly pull her closer to me and start kissing her cheek multiple times playfully. She giggles as she hugs me,

"You are fast, my love!" she continued, "Oh, the medics wanted you to take these."

Somma hands me a tray with a few blue pills on it. I've seen them before, they help speed along serious injuries or wounds. I'm not sure how much good they'll be with Vespin blood inside of me doing their work at a faster rate, but at least it'll help. I swallow the pills and look around the room,

"Is there a shirt in here I can put on?"

"No. I would offer you my shirt, but I do not think it would fit, also I am sure you would not want me to take my shirt off here, my love. Another time, perhaps." she responds playfully with a flirtatious grin while rubbing my arm.

"Not here. Later on, when we're more alone on our magical night would be much better."

Somma looks down and gives a shy smile as she rubs my arm. Alone time with her is one of the things I've dreamed of happening for a long time. We haven't really been alone since she spent the night with me at Vai's camp. Even though the conditions were not ideal, I still loved every second of it, that is after I started trusting her again. It took a while for her to regain it, but I'm glad things are back to normal between us. As for Specter, I am not sure how long it will take them to trust her again.

"How is everyone else doing?"

"They are all okay. Everyone has come in to check on you, but you were asleep. They were worried about you like I was. I had to stay with you. They told me I had to leave and rest, but I could not leave you. I am sorry that I fell asleep on your chest. I hope I didn't hurt you." she says while placing her hand on my chest.

"You can fall asleep on my chest whenever you'd like. I was happy to wake up and see you like that. You needed to rest."

Somma smiles and lays her head on my chest again. I kiss her head and put my hand on her back, I feel Somma giggle. I look out the window and see nothing but black. I have no idea where we are. To be honest, I don't mind how long it is taking us to reach Vespis. I'm finally resting safely with Somma in my arms just like I had always wanted. Something Fesio said stuck with me. He mentioned how Somma handled fighting Vai and Cinniya. I knew Somma could take care of herself, but hearing how she fought filled me with such happiness. I'm saddened by how it ended, but I believe what Fesio said, she had them beat. I'm sure everyone fought with all they had and put up a hell of a fight, but Vai has an entire army at her disposal who are willing to do what it takes to win. I don't want anyone to feel ashamed. I gently tap her back to get her attention, she looks up at me and smiles. I gently rub her cheek with my thumb,

"I was told you fought two people at the same time, is that true?"

"I tried." she responds in a defeated tone, looking down as her smile fades.

"I was also told you almost beat them both. I'm really proud of you."

"You should not be. I lost, I could not beat them."

"Fesio told me what happened. A girl, Thianni, threw glass and debris at you which distracted you. Do you want to know what that tells me? You scared them. No matter what they did, you somehow found a way to dodge everything they threw at you and continued to fight. They're cowards and weak, if the glass wasn't thrown, I know you would have beat them both."

Somma smirks,

"Even the way she threw was weak. If it was not glass, I doubt I would have felt anything."

I can't help but laugh,

"I know. I'm proud of you."

You don't hear Somma insult people like that too often. I hope what happened doesn't affect her too much. Physically she has cuts and bruises from the fight and the glass, but mentally I know she's been under heavy stress, I don't want what happened to cause her to feel any worse than she already does.

"I can't even fight two people at once, I don't know how you did it. You have to teach me."

Somma places her hand on my heart,

"I am glad to teach you, but to be honest, what powered me was I had someone to fight for," she kisses my cheek, " I knew how much you wanted us to return. I had to fight with all I had. That is really how I was able to do it. I wish I was able to get away, but I did all I could. I wanted to come back to you, just like you did with me."

"You're too good for me, Ms. Juna." I respond with a shy smile.

Somma smiles as she grabs my hand. It could be the fact we are finally going home, for now at least, but it all makes me feel sentimental and grateful for Specter and Somma. I remember feeling so pissed off when I saw who was going to be in Specter, but now I couldn't imagine being with a group of better people. I want Somma to know how much she means to me, words have never been my strong suit. I'm usually quiet around her, but I hope she knows what she means to me. I hold her hand tight, I don't want to hurt her, but it's hard to not hold her tight. She seems to like it, though. I try to make eye-contact as best as I can which I was never good at with anyone, but I do my best with her,

"I'm really happy you're okay. I hope you know how

much you mean to me." I continued while rubbing her hand, "Meeting you is the only thing that happened during this war that means anything to me. I have never met anyone so kind, strong, beautiful, brave and caring. You make me strong and give me the power to keep moving, you give me something to fight for, you mean everything to me. I don't usually use this word, but you're perfect in my eyes. Thank you for everything and I hope you know no matter what happens, I will always love you. In life and death. I'm beyond happy to be with you and safely returning home by your side."

Somma starts crying tears of joy, she grabs my face and kisses me on the lips passionately. It seems I now have my Wonder Woman. She has cried so much, I'm glad this time it is due to happiness. Somma moves away and shyly moves her hair out of her face, she looks down and smiles,

"Do you remember when we first met?"

"You mean when I embarrassed myself in front of you and your father? How could I forget?"

"You did not embarrass yourself, my love! I always think about that day. I was so excited to be a part of Specter. I remember my light blinded you. I felt terrible about it, but as soon as your vision cleared and I looked into your eyes, all I could do was smile. When I shook your hand, I felt an immediate connection, I did not want to let go, but I knew I had to. You were so quiet and shy, you barely said a word, you are still just as shy and quiet. Unfortunately, my father hated that. He told me to stay away from you, but something about you kept drawing me closer. Your eyes, your voice and strength. Everything, to be honest. I was not going to listen to my father either way, I could not stay away. The night we first kissed at Ben's outpost, I knew from then on, you were the only man I would ever want to kiss. I fell in love with you long before then, but I knew I could not be with you, I thought you would not feel the same way about me. It killed me every day, seeing you stressed and filled with worry and I could do nothing to help you. I could not hold you or kiss you. You never noticed how I watched you from afar, wishing I could tell you how I feel. Everything that happened with us and crashing near Tanli made me realize how quickly things could end. I did not want to die without telling you how I feel. After we kissed, I knew I was truly in love. Being with you has been a journey I will always cherish. I am forever grateful to Sarge for introducing you to me. I am beyond happy you are safe, I nearly lost you so many times, I know you will always come back, but I never want to watch you die and suffer like that ever again. I will always protect you. I love you always, Clark." she responds before kissing my cheek and lays down on my chest.

All of this feels like a dream, I always get that feeling when I am with Somma. Our job isn't over, though. I'm not sure what will happen after Sarge's memorial, there are more planets and systems in need of my squad's reckless expertise. Who else is stupid enough to do what we do? We lost our leader, I doubt the USC will not allow us to operate without one. After all, this was Sarge and LT. Serro's idea. Somma and I lay together and hold each other in blissful silence, until we hear a loud banging on the door. Somma shoots up and opens the door to see Blaine. She politely puts her hands behind her back,

"Oh, hello, SPC. Carlston. Is everything okay?"

"Out of the way, I need to speak with the walking corpse. Alone."

"Oh, alright. One moment, please."

Somma quickly closes the door on Blaine and runs to me, she grabs my face and kisses me on the lips and all around my face multiple times seemingly at super-speed.

"Now I will go, I will come back soon, my handsome 'walking corpse'. I love you!" she says before kissing me on the cheek one more time.

"I love you, too. Make sure to dodge Blaine if he swings at you."

Somma laughs and opens the door to a seemingly fuming Blaine, she quickly walks past him with her head down, but I see a little smirk on her face. Blaine walks in and closes the door, he drops down on the chair Fesio was sitting on.

"I guess she has a thing for dead people." he says while nudging at my arm.

"Lucky for me. Is everything okay out there?"

"Hard to tell. No one is saying much. They're all worried about you. I tried to tell them you'll be okay. In boot camp, I remember, you would not stay down no matter what happened. Even when we were practicing combat and sparring, when I'd naturally beat you and get you on the ground, for some damn reason, you never stayed down. It frustrated the hell out of me, but I guess I respect that. It served you well recently. I tried to tell them that, but I think they just want to see you up and walking."

I can't be too shocked at their moods. Any time they saw me, I was either on the ground or getting beaten. If I could get up and walk around, I would. I'm just as worried about them, they all looked like they were in rough shape too. Other than Vai and her troops undoubtedly cheating to beat all of them, I'm sure Tyro and his soldiers beat them too. Blaine looks at all the scars on my body,

"I think I remember where you got some of these. I'm surprised you're not dead. People think I'm the idiot here, but I've known you a while. You do just as many reckless stunts as me, if not more. I do it for fun, but you do it to be some sort of hero. Maybe we should both be dead."

"How nice that would be."

Blaine chuckles as he stands up and looks out the window,

"You don't need to say it, by the way." he continued, "I messed up at the tower. I tried to lead like Sarge would, but I couldn't. That army attacked us like wild dogs. The numbers game got us beat. There was nothing I could have done. I knew you'd be pissed off, it almost got you killed again. I don't know how any of us are alive, I take full responsibility for what happened and I guess what I'm trying to say is, I'm sorry."

I never once thought to pin this all on Blaine, or anyone. Vai's ambush was one thing, but to beat them how she did, not many people would have gotten out of it. I'm surprised by Blaine's honesty and openness. He is usually brash and sometimes just unbearable, but I guess going through what they went through changes who you are.

"Don't apologize," I respond, "it wasn't anyone's fault. Even Sarge would have failed dealing with that ambush. I'm alive so don't worry about what happened, what's a few more scars?"

Blaine chuckles and sits back down,

"Are you going to testify against Juna? You should."

"I'm not sure. I want to, but he's Somma's dad. She wants him alive. I don't want her to hate me for speaking against him, ensuring his execution. She hates him too, but he's the only family she has left. She is okay with his imprisonment, but I don't know if the USC will allow that. Even without my testimony, they have enough evidence and witnesses to prove he's a traitor and attacked me. Serro has Tyro's pad with all the video footage." I respond while looking down, knowing I should fight against him during the trial.

"Well, your girlfriend's dad killed you, I think you have a right to wish for his death. Look at you now, you're broken. Just think about it."

Blaine gets up and walks past the window,

"It looks like we made it to Vespis, put on your sunglasses." he jokes.

He opens the door to Somma patiently waiting on the outside.

"Hello, SPC. Carlston, may I enter now?" she asks with her hands behind her back again.

Blaine scoffs and walks past her. Somma smiles at him as she enters the room. She sits back down next to me and kisses my cheek.

"I think he is starting to like me!"

352

"He's probably going to try to take you from me." I joke.

Somma playfully hits my arm,

"No one is going to take me away from you, my love." Somma holds my hand and smiles as she looks out the window and sees Vespis, "I am home."

I look out the window and see the shining ball of light Somma calls home. The last time I was on Vespis was when I met Somma. I feel anxious as we approach Vespis, it has nothing to do with the people or anything like that, I always feel anxious when entering a different planet. I always think we are heading into a trap. Considering that is what ended up happening last time we entered a planet, my fears have not only been validated, but have also doubled. I am sure Vespis is safe, I just have to be ready for anything. Maybe Blaine is right, I am broken.

"I am home, but I have no one to go home to." Somma says while looking down.

"If it helps at all, you have me."

Somma smiles and kisses my hand,

"I know, my love. That means everything to me" she looks back out the window, "At one time, I had an entire family to come home to. With my father under investigation, I come home to no family, besides Specter who do not see me the same anymore. I am beyond happy and grateful you are by my side, but it feels strange coming home with everything changed."

"Is there anything I can do to help?"

"You are here with me, that is all I need. Thank you." Somma gives me a long kiss on the lips before getting up, "We are about to land. Give me your hands, my love."

Somma takes both of my hands and helps me out of the bed. I stand in front of her with her holding in my hands to keep me up. I smile as I look down, Somma giggles,

"Why are you smiling?" she asks.

"Will you dance with me?" I ask, limping my way closer to her.

"It would hurt you."

"That is not what I asked."

With all my strength, I spin her around with my right hand. Once she twirls back to me, she looks shocked and amazed. Somma smiles and steps closer to me, she gently places her hands on my face and slowly moves the hair out of my face. She stares into my eyes,

"I will gladly dance with you. Always."

Somma kisses my cheek, I gently grab her waist, pulling her in closer and kiss her lips. Somma giggles and hugs me.

"We will dance later. We can dance all night once you feel better."

I hold her tight like I never wanted her to let go, which I didn't. After a few moments, the ship lands at the USC Headquarters in Felv on Vespis. We unfortunately let go of each other and she helps me walk to the door that leads to the main portion of the ship where everyone else is. The door opens and everyone is picking up their bags and the rest of their things. Kierra, who is usually the first one ready, walks up to me,

"It is good to see you moving. We were all worried." she says while handing me my bag.

I open it and place Sarge's necklaces inside.

"Thank you. I'm glad you're all okay too. Do you mind holding onto my bag until we're off, please?"

Kierra bows her head and walks to the door, waiting for everyone else. It seems that Serro went into my bag to retrieve Somma's updated Specter uniform to wash it. She never got to wear it, there's not much to wash. I suppose it doesn't matter, but I do hope she likes the new patch Ben sewed on. Everyone is finishing up getting ready, but Somma doesn't have her bag yet. I have Somma walk me to her things, I let go of her and try to grab her bag, doing my best to not sound in pain, but once I reach for her bag, I wince in pain. I try to do it again, but Somma stops me.

"You are too kind, my love. I will get it." Somma says as she grabs her things and looks around the ship, "Excuse me,

Ben? Can you help him, please?"

Ben smiles as he quickly walks to me. Somma kisses my cheek as she hands me to Ben.

"Clark, my friend, how are you feeling?" he asks as we both limp to the entrance.

"I feel okay. Thank you for flying us here. We needed the rest."

"It is the least I can do. It will be nice to visit Vespis again. Richard, Auldin and I always loved visiting Vespis, so much life and happiness! I hope he will be buried here. I am sure he would want that. Either here or at a Bar."

Vespis would be a great location for the burial. As great as Sarge was, he kept a lot of things close to the chest. He never told us his favorite places or where he is at his happiest. Thankfully, Ben knew Sarge better than any of us. We wouldn't know where to bury him. After everyone is ready, Blaine being the last one to gather his things, Kierra opens the hatch to the ship. We are nearly blinded by the light of Vespis, Somma looks at us and quietly laughs.

"You never get used to it!" Ben exclaims as he walks me off the ship.

Once my eyes adjust, I see Serro waiting for us with his arms crossed. We line up in front of him at attention. Serro looks at all of us, he turns to Ben,

"Mr. Tawin, once again, thank you for bringing them here. The USC is in your debt. I will bring everyone inside, someone will be here shortly to take you back to Kana. You all may say your goodbyes."

We all hug Ben goodbye, he hands me to a medic and we all follow Serro inside. Compared to Xenem, Vespis looks like a dream. It is almost as if it has gotten more beautiful since the last time I saw it. Pristine, clean, all white buildings and roads and art everywhere, Vespis has earned its name as a core planet of its system. It seems off having people as filthy as us anywhere near it. We enter the Headquarters, we try not to touch anything with our hands. Serro leads us to a hall with washrooms.

"While I appreciate and understand everything you all went through, you are filthy and look out of place. Your uniforms have been cleaned, Now, go clean yourselves up then meet me in the conference room. Mr. Telkit, you are also welcomed to wash up, I will have someone bring you clean clothes that should fit. Dismissed!"

Everyone walks in their own separate wash rooms. The medics sit me down on a bench and go retrieve items to keep my wounds dry while they help me wash up. It's going to be an awkward experience, but I don't really have a choice. I doubt the medics are thrilled about it either. Somma sits next to me and kisses my cheek,

"I would gladly go in there with you, but it seems the medics beat me to it. Lucky them." she jokes while placing her hand on my thigh.

"There is always next time." I respond while placing my hand on top of hers.

Somma giggles and kisses me on the lips before getting up and going into her washroom. I wait a few minutes, the medics came back holding wraps and other tools to help keep the wounds dry and not mess up the work that was done on the ship.

"Are you ready, sir?" one of them asks.

I sigh and nod my head. They help me up and take me into the washroom. I close my eyes and try to block out what is going on. Something inside me tempts me to open my eyes, I look down and see the water going down the drain is filled with dirt and blood. So much for not getting anything dirty. I found it to be a depressing sight, a reminder of all the hell we went through. I close my eyes again, about five minutes later, I hear the water turn off. The experience doesn't end there. They dry me off, which feels like an eternity. After the finish, I slowly open my eyes. They help me get into a pair of underwear,

"We will be right back, we will reapply your bandages."

The medics walk away and shut the door, leaving me in nothing but underwear. I limp to a small couch in the washroom and painfully sit down to wait. After a few moments I hear a soft knock on the door. Thinking it's the medics, I tell them to come in. I look down waiting for the medics to get get to work, but instead I see a now clean, sparkling hand on my thigh,

"May I help with anything, my love?"

I look up and see through my hair it's Somma leaning over with only a towel around her body, she looks beautiful. All the dirt and blood that once covered her are completely gone. Leaving only her shining skin and hair.

"What are you doing here, beautiful?" I ask, pulling her closer by her waist.

Somma sits down on my right thigh, I have my arm around her waist, with my other hand rubbing her smooth and sparkling thigh. I look at her, admiring her beauty. She runs her hand through my hair, moving it out of my face,

"I wanted to see if you needed any help. I see they already put some clothes on you, a shame."

"You need to be faster, Ms. Juna."

Somma giggles and kisses my head. She looks around and sees the blood and dirt slowly going down the drain. Somma sighs and kisses my head again,

"I am so happy you are safe." she says.

"I hope I'm safe, I still feel anxious."

"I think I know what will help, my love."

Unexpectedly, she begins slowly removing her towel while sitting on my lap, but is interrupted by the medics walking in. Sadly, I didn't see too much, the medics had horrible timing. She quickly covers herself again and stands up. The medics stop when they see her, having shocked and confused expressions on their faces. Somma looks at them and laughs,

"Well, I will let you both get to work, just know, he is my man, do not get any funny ideas!" she jokes, "You will see more next time, my love." she whispers to me.

Somma giggles as she walks away. The medics are seemingly frozen. Once Somma walks past them, they finally move. They walk to me and start putting new bandages on my side and thigh. They remain silent, as uncharacteristic it is of me, I try to strike up conversation to break the tension.

"I appreciate the help. It's been a while since I was clean."

"If I may, sir, how did you get so filthy and covered with all that blood?" the medic working on my thigh asks.

"Would you believe I died?"

The medics look at each other with confusion, they say nothing and quickly finish working on me. They help me put the rest of my uniform on. It's such a weird feeling being in a clean uniform. The medics take me outside and sit me down on the bench,

"Is there anything else we can do for you, sir?"

"No, thank you. I will have someone help me walk. I appreciate it." I say while bowing my head to them.

They bow their heads back and walk away. Most of the squad is out of their rooms. I pull off Somma's hair tie from my wrist and try to put my hair in a ponytail. It hurts too much to lift my left arm up, making it impossible to do anything with my hair. I lower my head and shake it in annoyance, my hair falls in my face, blocking my view around me. I fidget with the hair tie, for a few moments, when with the little vision I have, I see a sparkling hand grab the tie from me. My hair gets lifted and I see Somma smiling at me,

"Now may I help you?"

I smile and nod my head. Somma quickly puts my hair in a ponytail with pieces hanging off beside my face,

"All done!" she exclaims.

Somma looks beautiful. Other than her uniform being on, her hair is also tied in a side braid with pieces of hair also hanging off beside her face. She tied her hair with the white ribbon she wore at the celebration in Tanli. She fixes the collar on my uniform and smiles as she sits down next to me,

"I have forgotten how handsome you look in your uniform." she runs her hand along the new Specter patch Ben sewed on all of our coats, "This is the first time I am wearing the coat with the new patch, I love it!"

"The design was based on a drawing I did in some dirt at Ben's outpost, Sarge liked it and it became the logo of Specter. I think it looks good."

"I should have known you designed it, I love it more now."

Somma kisses my cheek and places her head on my shoulder. We wait a little longer for Bradley and Blaine to get ready. Bradley is undoubtedly getting his hair to look perfect and Blaine probably fell asleep. Everyone, except Somma and myself, leave the hall to wait for everyone else while we remain on the bench.

"You look beautiful." I say quietly to Somma, I'm still as shy as ever around her.

"Thank you! You have only ever seen me in uniforms. I hope I will look the same to you with normal clothes on."

"I know you will be just as beautiful if not more. I wish I could be with you every day to see how beautiful you look."

Somma goes to the floor, on her knees in front of me, and holds my hands,

"May I ask you a question, my love?"

I nod my head, Somma kisses my hand,

"If you do not want to, I understand. You know how much I love you and I know how much you love me. For a while I have been thinking about this, but after we meet with LT. Serro and after Sarge's memorial, we will probably be free to do whatever we want, until we have a new assignment or they find us a new leader." she stops and sighs, "I was wondering- well hoping, if you would want to live with me in our own place?"

Normally, a big decision like this would make me want to take a few days to think of the pros and cons, among other things, but something about this decision seems so easy, like I do not need to take time to think about it. I love Somma, I have never been more certain about anything before in my life, I will gladly live with her. I can see Somma is breathing heavily, she is blinking faster and faster while anticipating my answer. In my mind, not much time passes, but I guess in reality I took a while to answer. Somma tears up and looks down,

"I am sorry, that was foolish of me-"

I gently place my hands on her face, interrupting her. She looks up at me with tears rolling down her cheek, I smile at her and wipe a tear away with my thumb.

"The only foolish thing you said was thinking you know how much I love you, it's more than you can possibly imagine. Nothing would make me happier than to move in with you, my beautiful diamond queen."

Somma's face lights up. She launches herself up at me and kisses my lips. She wraps her arms around my neck and hugs me tight as she lets out a sigh of relief,

"Never scare me like that again, my love!" she jokes.

Somma giggles and hugs me tighter. We are interrupted by a door slamming open. We hear a loud, obnoxious yawn followed by Blaine stumbling out of his room, rubbing his eyes.

"Really cozy couch in there."

We decide we might as well wait for Bradley, Somma sits back down next to me and holds onto my arm. We sit in peaceful silence for a few moments, Bradley's door swings open and he walks out combing his hair. Both of them are too predictable. Bradley walks past us and points the comb at Somma,

"You stay away." he jokes.

Somma smirks and playfully reaches for his hair, Bradley quickly runs away, leaving only Somma and I left. It's now everyone who is waiting for us. Somma stands up and grabs my hands, helping me up. I stand in front of her and she smiles,

"Will you dance with me?" she asks while taking a step closer to me.

"I will gladly dance with you. Always."

Somma grabs my face and kisses me on the lips, she puts my arm around her as we walk to the rest of the group. It's great to see everyone looking clean and polished again, wearing the Noli and arrow and feather necklaces still. I'm amazed that all of our necklaces have survived Xenem. We see the rest of the group near the conference room. The room is filled with high ranking members of the USC and members of the media for Vespis and other planets. We wait outside the room for Serro, he walks out and takes us to the side,

"You all look much better. Remember, very few people in that room know about the existence of Specter. We have to have you all enter separately at different times. We have empty seats reserved at random spots for you all. PVT. Denza, you will enter first, take a seat anywhere that is open. I will let you all decide who goes after who. Be quick. Denza and Mr. Telkit, follow me in, but we do not know each other, got it? CPL. Parson, a medic will help you in when PVT. Juna is sent."

We all nod. Serro, Fesio and Rachel walk into the room. Serro walks up to the podium to speak with his associates. Rachel and Fesio find seats at random locations in the room. We all look at each other, wondering who will go next. I point at Martin, he nods his head. He enters the room and takes a seat. Carden is next, followed by Somma, Blaine, Mitchell, Kierra, Bradley, then finally, myself with the help of a medic who leaves after I am seated. We all sit in different seats apart from each other. We act as if we do not know each other. Once everyone else is seated, Serro goes to the podium. He looks at each of us then looks back at everyone else and smiles,

"Thank you all for coming. Let us begin." he continued, "My name is LT. Jovell Serro, I am happy to report that the planet responsible for countless deaths and primary weapons manufacturer for the Chelorian Confederacy, Xenem, has been liberated. Their factories have been destroyed and their prisoners freed. Without telling anyone in the USC, a squad of 10 soldiers went into Xenem with the intention to bring down the empire they had built. After spending days there and going through unspeakable horrors and injuries, the squadron successfully brought down Xenem, unfortunately losing their leader, SSG. Richard Miner." Serro looks down, then looks at all of us. He shakes his head, "The squad responsible for this is named Specter, a squadron created in secrecy by SSG. Richard Miner, myself and a few other members of the USC. The members include the departed SSG. Richard Miner, CPL. Clark Parson, SPC. Blaine Carlston, PVT. Carden Reddina, Rachel Denza, Bradley Dillon, Somma Juna, Kierra Shuua, Martin and Mitchell Lane. I now invite them up to answer your questions."

HOMECOMING

It would have been nice if Serro told us he was going to expose the existence of Specter along with all of our identities. It's impossible for us to catch a break. It's a shame Fesio and Auldin's names weren't mentioned when it came to who helped free Xenem. That being said, there are currently more pressing reasons for us to be infuriated. A mixture of anger, confusion and fear fill all of us as we look at each other in panic. It's nearly impossible to hear anything with all the shouting and questions coming from every direction. I know it wouldn't do me or any of us any good if we were to stay seated. A medic walks up to me and helps me up. As he helps me walk to the podium, our path is being blocked by people swarming me. I don't even hear what they are saying or asking me, but the medic has them move out the way with the help of other soldiers. I see a bright white light shining from across the room surrounded by people, I can only assume that is Somma. It takes a while to make it through everyone. Once I reach the podium, I see Rachel and Martin are the first ones to make it up. They look at me with worry in their eyes, I wish I could help them, but I'm just as worried as them. The rest of the squad slowly stumbles their way to the podium. I see a bright light move closer to us, I limp my way to the crowd and despite the pain, I reach my hand inside the crowd and once I feel Somma grab onto my hand, I pull her to us. We are all finally on the stage, but the trouble is far from over.

    The flashing of the cameras and the multiple people asking questions is enough to almost make me freeze in panic. I turn to Serro with fury in my eyes, which not many people can do and live to tell the tale. He looks down in shame, Blaine walks up to me,

"You hold him, I punch, got it?"

Though I would love that, now is not the best time. I ignore Blaine and turn to everyone,

"You all have to get out of here, I'll stay and take care of this."

Everyone looks at each other and stays where they are. Somma is still shining bright, I need her to relax because she is only getting brighter. Granted, her shine could give us the opportunity to slip away, but that doesn't seem like the best option. I pull Somma closer to me which causes me to squint,

"You need to get away from here. We'll be okay." I say while rubbing her arm.

Somma holds my other hand and takes a deep breath in, then breathes out. Her light dies down back to normal,

"I am not going anywhere without you."

"I'm going to get us out of here. Just try to relax." I respond while squeezing her hand tight.

Somma smiles and nods. She moves back in line with the rest of the squad. I slowly turn and limp to the podium. I close my eyes and block out the sound of everyone. After a moment, I slowly open my eyes and lean towards the microphone. The crowd finally quiets down.

"My name is CPL. Clark Parson. I will be speaking on behalf of all of Specter. I will try to answer your questions one at a time. *Quietly*."

I can tell the crowd wants to erupt, but they can see I am in no mood to deal with that. Multiple people raise their hands, I point at someone who looks like they are from Foli,

"How long has Specter been a squad?"

"A little less than a year. Next question." I respond before pointing to someone from Earth,

"Did it take you and the others from Earth some getting used to being in a squad with others from different planets? Do you think they respect you as a superior?"

"They had to get used to us more than we had to get used to them. As for if they respect me, I don't know. I hope they do. I know I respect them. I will answer a couple more questions."

The room is still filled with people with their hands up. I point to a man from Vespis in the back.

"I see you have sustained injuries, may I ask what happened?"

"I died twice. You all have one last question."

I point at someone in the front row from Tilo,

"Who is your next target? Many planets in the Chelorian Confederacy are still holding power and are becoming bigger threats than ever before."

"At the moment, we do not know our next target. I'm feeling more generous than I should, so I will answer one more."

Another man from Earth raises his hand, I point to him,

"No offense to your squad, but do you think if you had more higher ranking soldiers with more experience in your squad, SSG. Miner would still be alive and you would not have sustained your injuries? Perhaps freed and gotten out of Xenem faster?"

I exhale and grip the podium in anger, I grind my teeth.

"No." I say as calmly as I can, "The failures and injuries we faced are on all of us as a team. We regret the moments we failed together, but share in the glory of our victories together. No amount of experience could have stopped what happened, do not think otherwise. We are done here. Thank you all."

I begin limping away, Somma puts my arm around her and helps me walk off, the rest of Specter follows behind. The crowd erupts again and tries to swarm us, but Blaine moves in front of them, blocking them from getting closer. We see Fesio by the door opening it for us. We quickly leave the room, ignoring everyone. Fesio follows us and closes the door on the crowd. We make our way to an empty conference room. Fesio stays out of the room, realizing this is a Specter issue. We all sit down at the table and say nothing. I slowly place my head on the table and sigh. Somma holds my hand tight, but remains silent. We have absolutely no idea why Serro would do this to us. He was the one who was so dead-set on keeping us a secret. If the media knows about us, it's not long before the rest of the Chelorian Confederacy learns about us and begins to anticipate anything we do, Serro knew that and still went through with it. The one part of this that eliminates him doing this out of malice or hate is the fact he looked visibly upset by what he did and he genuinely respected Sarge and his leadership. We are all left completely baffled and enraged.

Serro slowly walks in, Blaine grunts and stands up out of his chair, seemingly prepared to tackle Serro. He begins to walk towards him,

"Blaine, sit down!" I demand.

Blaine looks at me then back at Serro. He swats his hand at him and drops back into his seat. Serro slowly pulls out a chair and sits. He looks down at the table.

"I imagine you all have questions?"

All of Specter erupts in anger. Serro tries to defend himself to everyone, but to me, it's all noise and chaos. All of the noise begins to get to me, I close my eyes trying to block it out, but the anger gets to me. In the midst of all the chaos in the room, I growl and slam my fist on the table causing the table to shake, it scares everyone, including Somma. Everyone is silent, I lean in towards Serro,

"What have you done?" I ask with my teeth clenched.

Serro shakes his head,

"You all would not understand."

"There is a lot we do not understand at the moment, what's one more thing, *sir*?" Mitchell asks sarcastically.

Serro sighs,

"Once the USC found out about Miner's death, Parson's injuries and everything else that happened on Xenem, they were furious. Most of the USC had no idea your squad existed. At the moment, Specter is still a squad that will still be used, but the USC is considering whether it is necessary. They appreciate what you have done, but they do not want to risk your lives running what they called 'suicide missions'. I will try to convince them to keep Specter, but it would be under their terms, you would have to answer to them. You would be a typical squad with a new leader. I know you all can do your jobs as intended, hopefully they will let your squad do what it was created for but under more supervision. It is the best we would be able to do. It is still up for discussion, I am fighting for them to let you work as intended. Please do not direct your fury at me. No part of me wanted this, I promise. They had me expose you publicly so all of the USC everywhere knows about you to support their case. I am truly sorry."

I understand why he did what he did. I do feel the USC is overreacting, but nothing we say would help. We are all shocked, we figured we had more time to take down other planets before being caught. Sero brings out key cards with random addresses on them and passes them to each of us.

"If it means anything, I have convinced the USC to provide safe houses for all of you around Vespis. Of course you do not have to stay on Vespis, you can go where you want for the time being, but the spaces are yours if you want them. We have generously provided furniture, work-out equipment and other amenities to show our appreciation. I know it will take more than that for forgiveness, but just feel lucky you are all still part of the USC. As for Miner's funeral and memorial, we will let you all know when it is, for now, enjoy your freedom and again, I am sorry."

Despite Somma and I deciding to live together, we still take a key card. Everyone grabs their card and storms out, without saying a word to Serro. A medic walks in holding a syringe and walks to Serro, he whispers something in his ear. Serro nods and walks to me with the medic.

"CPL. Parson, as one last sign of appreciation, the USC has allowed me to inject you with a healing serum, do not worry, I am not trying to poison you. We have spent a while working on this. You would be the first soldier who gets to use it, it would completely heal you within seconds. It has been tested, we are happy to report it is a success. We are rather proud of it."

I look at the syringe cautiously. Somma looks at me and looks back at the medic, she stands up out of her seat,

"May I give it to him?"

The medic looks at Serro and he nods. The medic slowly hands the syringe to Somma,

"Carefully inject it into his bicep." he says.

Somma grabs the syringe and sits back down next to me. Serro and the medic leave the room. Somma sees the worry and fear in my eyes, she knows I have had my fill of sharp objects going inside of me. She rubs my arm,

"Can you take your coat off, my love?"

I nod my head and slowly unbutton my coat, taking my right arm out of the coat sleeve. Somma kisses my cheek,

"I do not want to hurt you, ever. It will be okay, though. I trust it. Do you trust me?"

I nod my head again and move my arm towards her. Somma smiles at me and carefully injects the syringe into my bicep. She clicks a button on the syringe which injects the serum into my arm. It hurts like hell, I groan in pain and put my head on the table trying to suppress the pain. It sure feels like poison, but if Somma trusts it then I can only assume the pain will pass in a moment. Somma holds my hand tight trying to help me through the pain. I squeeze her hand and do my best to not hurt her. After a few moments that feel like an eternity, the pain finally goes away. I lift my head off the table and slowly let go of Somma's hand. She moves her hand away and shakes it in pain. I slowly grab her hand and look at it, luckily I don't see any visible damage or feel anything broken or out of place.

"I'm sorry, I didn't mean to hurt you."

"I know, I am okay, my love." she says before kissing my hand, "How do you feel?"

I press down on my thigh and side and feel no pain. As

far as I can tell, the serum worked. I don't know if I trust it yet, but so far all seems normal.

"It feels better. Thank you."

Somma lifts my shirt and the wound is gone, leaving only a scar. It's safe to assume my thigh's wound looks the same.

"It worked!" she exclaims.

I'm glad it worked, but at the end of the day, it's just another scar. I stand up on my own, which feels odd, but it's nice I no longer need to be carried around. Somma stands up after me and holds my hand,

"Do you want to leave?" she asks

I kiss her cheek,

"Thank you for carrying me around."

Somma blushes and looks down shyly. I try to walk, but Somma pulls me back closer to her,

"I want more, my love." she says playfully.

I smile while pulling her closer to me by her waist and kissing her on the lips passionately. Somma giggles and kisses me on the lips again,

"Now we can go." she says while grabbing my hand.

I put on my old coat over my uniform as we grab our bags and walk out, doing our best to avoid people, but it seems impossible as we enter the first floor of the USC Headquarters. We walk with our heads down, but we hear people whispering to each other. They can whisper about us all they want, it beats having people swarm us and shout questions. As we are about to leave, we hear a woman gasp,

"There he is!"

I sigh, thinking it's the media about to surround us, but I look up and it's my mother and father running to me. They wrap me in a tight hug, I can hear my mother sniffling and my father sighing in relief. I haven't seen them since the Xenem prison cell. I am beyond happy that they are safe.

"We heard about all your injuries, and how you also died? Here you stand, a true hero! We're so glad you're okay."

my mother says.

My father laughs,

"Man of Steel! We're so proud of you."

It's been so long since my father has called me that. It may seem odd, but I saw it as a badge I had to earn. Maybe, that's why I put myself through so much hell, to prove I am like the Man of Steel. I really could have used his powers in Xenem. I turn back to Somma who is standing there smiling. I felt I had to introduce her to my parents. I didn't need to, but I guess I'm old-fashioned. I put my hand on Somma's back and walk her to my parents, I can tell she is nervous, but she smiles at them,

"Mom, Dad, this is my girlfriend Somma Juna-"

My mother pulls me towards her quickly, interrupting me,

"Clark, what are you doing with her? She was there on Xenem with that other Vespin man. She may look like a kind, beautiful Vespin but she is evil, both of them are. You can't be with her, please tell me you're joking!" she says while slowly backing away from Somma.

Somma lowers her head in shame, I pull myself out of my mother's grasp and stand in between them,

"You don't understand, she was there by force. Her father is the other Vespin you saw, GEN. Pyren Juna, he forced her to work for Xenem after he betrayed USC. He is going to be put on trial, but Somma had nothing to do with that, she helped you and everyone else escape. She's not evil at all, we have been together for a while now. Please trust me."

"We saw it. She stood by and watched as others were beaten and killed. She probably has blood on her hands as well. You may be a big hero of the USC, but I am still your mother, you cannot be with her, she can't be trusted."

I look at my father, hoping he would talk some sense into her, but he remains silent. I just reunited with my parents, fighting like this is the last thing I wanted to do, but she won't listen. I understand what they all went through was horrible, but I'm their son, I hoped my words would hold some power.

I look back at Somma, tears roll down her face as she looks down. I know Somma hasn't gotten over what she did. Attacking me, standing by as others suffered, everything. She will probably never get over it. She is already trying to regain the trust and forgiveness of the rest of the squad, my parents are just more people for her to remind her of her mistakes.

"Mom, please just listen to me. I-"

Somma steps in front of me, which causes me to go silent.

"Mr. and Mrs. Parson, words cannot tell you how deeply I regret what I did. I am truly sorry for the pain I may have caused you both and everyone else. My father became someone I did not recognize, he wanted me to become someone I was not, someone evil and heartless. I never killed anyone innocent, I did watch as they were killed which will haunt me for the rest of my days, but even when my life was threatened, I refused to do what I was told. I was beaten because of it, but I would never do such things. When I opened all the cells in the prison, I knew it would not be enough to gain forgiveness, but I truly am sorry for what you both went through."

My mother remains silent, my father steps forward,

"Caroline, I don't think she's 'evil'. Clark trusts her. That's enough for me."

"When she breaks our son's heart, I hope you remember this moment." my mother responds.

"Mrs. Parson, never in my life would I ever break your son's heart." Somma interjects. She holds my hands and looks me in the eyes, "Clark has been a true hero, not just for the USC, but for our squad and myself. I have never met a more kind, caring, loyal and strong man in my life. I love him with all my heart. When he died, I never cried so much in my life. I knew I did not just lose a squad member, but I lost what you would call my 'boyfriend', my *Relani*. I lost my best friend, I lost the only person I could trust, I felt like I lost everything. I cannot imagine my life without him. You both raised him to be the most incredible man I have ever met, for that, I thank you both. Please do not ever think I would hurt him like that. I will do anything to keep him safe, just like he does with me. Clark means everything to me, every day I am with him, I am grateful and cannot stop smiling. Before I met him, I was always nervous, scared, confused and felt weak. My father made it worse, but Clark treated me with respect and kindness from the moment we met. He has taught me so many things that have saved my life many times. He taught us all how to be true warriors with no fear. I am a stronger person because of him. You do not have to like me or trust me, but I know your son loves and trusts me and I love and trust him. I will never hurt him or any of you. I call him many things, but one thing he will always be is my hero. My perfect hero."

Somma kisses my cheek and hugs me. My parents and myself are stunned silent. My father walks up to Somma and extends his hand,

"Somma, please just call me Thomas. I am still a bit skeptical, but I knew one day, my boy would find his Wonder Woman. Just keep him out of trouble." he jokes.

Somma smiles and shakes my fathers hand. My mother slowly steps forward,

"I really don't know what to think right now, but I see the way you look at Clark. I've waited so long for a beautiful girl to see what we saw. We raised him to be everything you said, kind, caring, loyal and strong, but Clark was always the type of person who looked out for others before himself, so you need to look out for him. You lucky girl, I know my son, he looks at everyone the same, but I see him look at you and there is a light in there that I have not seen in ages. He's in love with you, I can't stop that, but I'll have to be okay with that. Unfortunately, he has had his heart broken many times in his life. Please do not be another heartbreak for him. He will always treat you right, I know it, so never take him for granted. So, Ms. Juna, I am trusting you. You may call me Caroline. It's nice to officially meet you."

My mother extends her hand to Somma, she shakes her

hand,

"Thomas, Caroline, thank you both. I will take care of him and love him every day. I promise." Somma says.

My parents smile at her before they turn to me. Both of them hug me, I hear my father whisper something,

"Make sure to call her beautiful every day, women love that!"

"It's true." my mother added, "Take care of her Clark. Just be careful. We love you. If you really do love her, when you're ready, give her this."

I feel my mother slip something in my coat pocket. They let go and wave goodbye to Somma and I. Somma bows her head to them as they leave. I grab Somma's and and my bag, she gently grabs my face with her hands and passionately kisses me on the lips,

"No one has ever defended me like that before, thank you."

"They didn't listen to me, you changed their minds. I appreciate what you said about me. I will always try to be your hero."

"I know you will, my love. Where do you want to go?" she asks while looking out the window.

I smile and pull out the key card Serro gave us. Somma smiles and looks at the address, she gasps and grabs my hand. We run out of the building to what I assume is the address. Judging by her reaction, Somma knows exactly where the address is. If I never took that serum, all this running would absolutely devastate me. Leaving the USC Headquarters, we see Fesio leaning on a wall, he nods at us. I don't know if Serro or anyone gave him a place to go or any reward. Seeing as I don't need my own safehouse, Fesio should use it. We walk over to Fesio and I hand him my keycard. He grabs it and smiles,

"Good, a place for me to hide, thank you." Fesio pulls out a communicator, "My call code is 826. LT. Serro gave me one to stay in contact with you and Specter. You both may call me if you need me. Hopefully, I can call you if I need it."

"Of course, I'm sure we'll need help soon. Be safe and thank you for everything." I respond.

I shake Fesio's hand and Somma does the same. She immediately grabs my hand and starts running again, dragging me with her. We're running so fast, I barely have time to see and appreciate the beauty of Vespis. I've only been here a few times, usually to go to the Headquarters, I never got a chance to sight-see. All the running does lessen the chance of us being stopped by people wanting to ask us questions, that's really the only benefit of all this running. We finally stop at an outdoor area where people can board Ranna's to take them to certain locations.

"You're fast." I say to Somma while trying to catch my breath.

"We're not done yet!"

We run onto a Ranna that's heading west. The Ranna is full of people. Some of which I can tell recognise us, but luckily leave us alone. I spot one seat available, I walk Somma to it and sit her down.

"Are you sure you do not want to sit?" she asks while pulling me closer to her.

I look around, but there is nowhere else to sit. I decide to sit on the ground next to her. Everyone is staring at me, but Somma quietly giggles and kisses my head. I don't mind where I'm sitting too much. Like everything on Vespis, the floor looks pristine. I take off my coat and put it in my bag as a little girl walks up to Somma and I, she looks at me in confusion,

"You are not from here." she says while poking my arm.

I smile at her,

"No, I am not. Is that okay?"

She smiles and nods at me, but her attention is quickly drawn to our uniforms.

"Are you soldiers?"

"Yes, we are!" Somma says while leaning over,

The little girl gasps and rubs the USC patch on both of our coats,

"Thank you for your service. Please stay safe!" she says before hugging Somma and I.

The little girl runs back to where she came from. Out of all the interactions we have had ever since we got back, especially concerning who we are, this has been my favorite. After about ten minutes, the Ranna stops. Somma pulls me up to begin running again. We reach a building and run inside. It's looks like an apartment complex. By the looks of it, not many people live here. I'm not sure if anyone else is here in general. We enter an elevator that takes us up to the floor where our safe-house is.

"I used to come to this building all the time as a child with my brother and sisters. We thought it was so beautiful, we dreamed of living here one day. As soon as I saw the address, I could not believe it. A shame no one lives here anymore. I'm not sure why." Somma says.

The elevator doors open and we reach an empty hall. We walk down the hall and reach the third door on the left. Somma looks at the key card's address. She smiles and points at the door. She hands me the card and I unlock the door. We slowly walk in and see a beautiful looking space. Wooden floors, exposed white brick walls, comfortable looking furniture, a bookcase, a sound system for music and as mentioned by Serro, workout equipment. The piece of equipment that catches my eye is the punching bag, I'll probably use that and the sound system the most. Somma and I remain silent for a moment, in shock that this is where we will be living together. I can see why Somma and her siblings idolized this place. Somma steps in front of me and takes her shimmering hair out of the braid. She takes both my hands and backs up slowly, pulling me with her to the center of the living room.

"We made it." she says softly with a smile on her face.

I imagine the others have places as nice as this, they deserve it. I don't know where Fesio ended up, but I hope he is somewhere comfortable and safe. Xenem's don't exactly fit in here. Fesio can survive a lot, but an angry mob I am not too sure of. I hope that the USC will take care of him. There are so many things I want to do, but something I know I need to do first pops into my head. I kiss her hands and walk to the sound system. I select the song that the band in Tanli was playing during our celebration, Flower in Rain. I walk back to Somma who is waiting for me with the same smile. I grab her hands,

"Will you dance with me?"

Somma laughs and tears up. She moves closer to me.

"I will gladly dance with you. Always."

I still don't know much about dancing, besides what she taught me in Tanli. I place my right hand on her waist, she places her right hand on my arm and with her left hand, she grabs my right hand. We start moving slowly to the music. I feel much better about dancing this time, mainly because I don't think a surprise ambush is coming our way. I'm doing a lot better than I was the last time we danced. It's easier for me to keep up with her. Just like the first time, Somma tries to trick me again by taking a quick step back, expecting me to fall, but I follow her movements and stay up. Somma laughs,

"My, my, someone has been practicing!"

I kiss her cheek,

"If you knew how long I have waited to dance with you again." I whisper while we continue to dance.

I twirl her around, her shimmering hair follows her in what seems like slow motion. After a few minutes, the song ends. Somma looks around,

"Sad, the music ended."

"The music never ends." I respond while twirling her again.

Somma smiles,

"How do we dance without music?"

I begin humming the song from memory. Somma smiles again as she places her head against my chest. We continue to dance with me humming. After another couple of minutes, I stop humming. I softly chuckle,

"I'm sorry, I forgot how the rest goes."
"Now how do we dance?"
"We just move."

We continue dancing all around the room in blissful silence. We move in front of the window, the dimming lights of Vespis pierce through the windows and shine between us. If someone had asked me years ago if I would dance for longer than ten seconds, I would think they were crazy. If they had also told me it would be with a beautiful and incredible girl like Somma, I would know for sure they were crazy. At this moment, I realize that everything I went through, all the pain, torment and suffering led me to this moment, making it all worth it. I thought it would never end, but if this is the universe's reward, I will gladly go through it all again.

"Look who is teaching *me* about dancing now." Somma says before kissing my cheek.

Despite still not knowing too much, I decide to lead. I grab Somma by her waist with both hands and lift her off the ground. She laughs as her legs wrap around me. I twirl around with her in my arms as we continue to laugh, realizing this is the happiest we have ever been. I lose my balance and drop her on the coach while I fall on the floor. Even dizzy, I know to protect her. She can take the couch, I'll gladly take the floor. Somma crawls off the coach and goes to me, giggling as I am laying on the floor also laughing.

"Maybe I should lead, my love." she says as she goes on top of me.

"I did my best." I respond, putting my hands on her waist.

"You were amazing. I think I found my perfect dance partner."

Somma passionately kisses me on the lips while on top of me. She moves away with a flirtatious and mischievous grin. She moves off of me and grabs my hands. She lifts me off the ground,

"Come with me, my love." she says while pulling me into

a bedroom.

We haven't seen any other room here, but that won't stop me from enjoying what's to come. Somma takes me next to the bed and takes off my coat and shirt, which normally I'd hate, but right now I don't mind it at all. She playfully pushes me on the bed, she takes off her coat and goes on top of me. She kisses me passionately again while running her hands along my body. I take off her shirt, gently caressing her whole perfect, smooth, sparkling body with my hands. Before I know it, we're taking all of each other's clothes off. We continue on into an evening of pure love, joy and ever flowing passion, ending what has become the first of what I am sure are many magical nights with Somma.

DAY ONE

I keep thinking something bad is about to happen. Everything seems too good to be true, being in bed with Somma, an actual bed, is something I never thought would happen. I have every right to be nervous considering everything I went through. I don't know if Somma is nervous too, but she is enjoying every second of her time right now. After everything we did tonight, Somma is exhausted. She lays next to me and has her arm around my body, trying to stay awake. Weirdly, I'm not too tired. I'm more than fine laying here holding Somma, it's one of the things I've wanted to do for a while, but I was hoping to explore more of the safehouse, maybe see the books on the shelf. I feel Somma slowly falling asleep, I gently lift my arm away from her to let her sleep, I was going to let her take the bed anyways, I want her to be as comfortable as possible and an empty bed is a dream scenario for someone exhausted. I try to get up, but with a random burst of energy, Somma wakes up and grabs my arm,

"No, wait, where are you going?" she asks in a worried tone.

"Don't worry, I'm just going in the other room. I was going to let you sleep."

Somma gently tugs at my arm,

"Come here."

I lay back down next to her and she kisses my cheek, she lays her head on my chest and holds me tight,

"I want to sleep in your arms."

I kiss her head and close my eyes. I'm still not that tired, but I figure if I close my eyes, sooner or later I'll fall asleep.

With my eyes closed, I feel a blanket get thrown over me. Somma kisses my cheek multiple times before laying down again, I chuckle.

"I love you." I whisper.

"I love you, too, sleep well. Goodnight, my love."

Somma falls asleep within minutes. It always took me a while to fall asleep, even before I joined the war. After everything I've been through, falling asleep got harder for me. Many nights, I found myself having the urge to shoot up out of bed because I thought someone was about to attack me in my sleep. Spending nights in the wilds of Xenem only made that fear worse. I can't shoot up anymore, though. Not with Somma holding onto me, I don't want to wake her up. I'm hoping that her holding onto me will be a reminder that I'm not in the middle of nowhere surrounded by dangerous people, I'm safe.

An hour later, I finally fall asleep. Sometimes in the middle of the night, I start seeing random, painful images and moments in my head from past experiences. Tonight, I keep seeing flashes of that soldier in Vonra choking me and stabbing Somma, Sarge getting shot in the head, Teni kneeling over me with a knife about to kill me, Juna stabbing me, and Tyro slashing me across both cheeks. All of those moments keep replaying in my head, no matter what I do, they won't stop. I feel myself breathing harder and harder, my head shaking left to right, but the scenes keep replaying with sounds of high-pitch, deafening ringing and the chilling cackle of Tyro. It gets too much for me, I quickly wake myself up and sit up in bed as slowly as I can, gently moving Somma off of me.

Luckily, Somma seems to be in a deep enough sleep to not notice or feel her being moved. My heart is racing, my hands are shaking, I'm drenched in sweat, my anxiety and panic through the roof, this is a typical night for me. I sit up at the edge of the bed with my feet on the floor and lean over. Sweat covered pieces of my hair fall on my face, I still feel myself breathing heavily. I cover my face with both hands and shake my head, I really thought I was past this. I still hear the ringing in my ears, but I feel something behind me gently touch my back. I hear Somma say something, but her voice is muffled by the ringing. I don't respond to what she is saying, she speaks again, but it's still muffled. Somma quickly jumps out of the bed and goes on the floor in front of me, trying to calm me down. It's as if my eyes don't register that she's in front of me, her voice remains muffled as she puts her hands on my knees trying to get me to focus on her. Her attempts were unsuccessful, inside I wanted to collapse and hold her, but my body was frozen.

Somma looks around the room for something to help with a panicked expression on her face, her skin starts shining brighter. She looks into the living room and smiles, she moves the hair out of my face and wraps her arms around my neck. Through the ringing, I hear her humming something while holding me. At first, I don't recognize it due to the ringing blocking it out, but as seconds pass, the ringing gets quieter and I can hear her. She is humming the song we danced to earlier in the living room. Somma gently places her forehead against mine with the shine on her skin dying down, her eyes closed while smiling and continuing to hum to song. The ringing goes away completely, my breathing starts slowing down and my anxiety and panic wash away, but a tear does roll down my cheek.

All I hear is her humming and it's beautiful. I slowly wrap my arms around her body, hugging her tight. I softly kiss her cheek as I move away.

"Thank you. I tried to be quiet, I didn't want to wake you." I say softly, lacking eye contact.

"I do not want you to go through that alone. Ever." she responds, wiping the tear off my cheek.

I look down and slowly stand up,

"I'm sorry I woke you up. I'll lay down on the couch and let you sleep." I say while fidgeting with my fingers.

I start walking out, but Somma gently grabs my arms and turns me around.

"I get nightmares too." she continued, "In Tyro's tower, I would have nightmares every night about losing you and everyone else I loved and had left, but I had no one there to cry to or hold me. All I wanted was you to be there so I could hold you and know I was safe just like I did with you. I have waited so long to sleep in your arms. Please come back to bed and just hold onto me, it will be okay."

She walks me back to the bed and sits me down. She lifts my face to her and smiles,

"It is going to be okay, my love, I am here." she says before she kisses me on the lips.

Somma gently lays me back, she gets in the bed and lays next to me and holds me again. Despite not wanting to wake her up again, I decide to stay. I put my arm around her,

"Thank you." I say quietly while rubbing her back,

"Try to sleep, I will be right here. Nothing will happen."

For some reason, I'm able to fall asleep a lot faster. It could be the fact I have a bit more peace of mind, it could be multiple reasons, but I'm just glad I am able to sleep. In time, I'm sure I will have to comfort Somma when she gets a nightmare, I know I will be ready. The night flies by, I open my eyes and from what I tell outside, it's the morning. Enjoying the morning air on Earth was something I always loved doing, I imagine the morning air on Vespis is even better. Somma is still asleep, I slowly move out of the bed to get dressed. I open my bag to see loads of black clothing that undoubtedly belongs to me. I grab a long sleeve shirt, ripped jeans and my black boots and change into them.

It has been way too long since I've worn my own personal clothes. I guess when we were all getting cleaned up, Serro had our personal clothes put in our bags. I've never seen anyone in Specter in regular clothes, besides the celebration in Tanli. Even then, it was still formal. I leave the building and step outside, the air is incredibly clean. I don't know what time it is exactly, but it was the perfect moment to step outside. I take a walk around our building and see a beautiful patch of flowers across the street. I walk up to them and it's like looking at a rainbow up close. Every color imaginable in one flower, I've never seen anything like it before. I suppose these are normal on Vespis, but it blows my mind. I don't know if I'm allowed, but I pick a few to bring back to Somma. It's the least I could do for waking her up last night. I spend a few more minutes walking around before heading back inside.

I quietly open our door and walk into the bedroom where Somma is still sleeping peacefully. Beams of light shine through the window, making Somma look like royalty while she sleeps. I sit down on her side of the bed next to her and watch her sleep. I don't understand how someone so stunning loves me like she does. I don't know what I did to deserve her, but it was worth it. I gently move her hair away from her face and kiss her on the cheek, I couldn't resist. The kiss wakes her up a little, she smiles and opens her eyes a little. She looks at the spot next to her where I was laying then looks around and sees me sitting next to her.

"Good morning, handsome." she says with her eyes barely open.

I don't respond to her, but I smile watching her wake up. Somma giggles,

"I finally get to wake up and see you."

I grab the flowers and show them to her,

"These are for you. I hope you like them."

Somma's face lights up and giggles. She grabs them and looks at all the colors.

"Laviell flowers! I love them, thank you!"

She puts the flowers down on her nightstand next to her and grabs my face before kissing me on the lips. I put a blanket over her as she lays back down, she still looks tired and probably wants to sleep some more.

"I'll let you go back to sleep, I'll be in the other room working out, if you need anything, let me know."

"One more kiss, my love." she responds with her eyes closed.

I chuckle and lean over, giving her a kiss on the lips. She smiles as I get up and go into the living room. I change into a black tank top and sweatpants, I grab a towel before working out. I recall being excited about the punching bag, but I want to see what else was brought here. By the looks of it, it's mainly weights, a few pieces for cardio, but that's about it. I spend 15 minutes on each item, it's been a while since I was able to work out, especially alone and peacefully, but luckily it feels like I never stopped. After using the weights and doing cardio, I move onto the punching bag which helps me get out my frustrations especially when it comes to what happened last night. I end with core and floor exercises which I've always hated, but I know I need to do it. I spend another 15 minutes on each exercise, push-ups, sit-ups, planks and other exercises that felt like hell. I end with sit-ups again, after I finish, I let myself fall flat on the floor while out of breath and covered in sweat. I'd say I worked out for a little over an hour, it felt good.

I remain on the floor breathing heavily and wiping the sweat off my face. I grab my towel and drop it on my face, hoping it will do the work out getting sweat off my face. My arms are too tired to do it myself. While still laying down on the floor with the towel on my face, I hear soft footsteps approaching me, I lift the towel and see Somma sit on top of me, placing her hands on my chest,

"Are you all done, my love?" she asks.

Based on her outfit, I can see she wants to workout too. She's wearing a gray tank top and leggings with a towel over her shoulder.

"I just finished. I'll get out of the way for you." I respond while trying to get up, but Somma won't get off me.

"I would much rather workout with you."

I don't know what exactly she wants to do, but I'm exhausted. If she really wants to workout with me, I guess I'll have to power through.

"What did you want to do?" I ask, putting my hands on her waist.

"Do you remember how when we all met, you had us spar with each other? I never had a chance to spar with you."

Last time Somma and I did something close to sparring, it ended with me jumping out of a tower, so I'm not sure if it's the best idea. Somma sees the concern in my eyes, she laughs and kisses my cheek,

"Do not worry. We will not hit eachother, it will be who can get who on the ground first!"

I shrug my shoulders, reluctantly agreeing. Getting someone on the ground without hitting them is a tough challenge, I don't know how we're going to do it. Somma giggles as she gets off me. I get up and mentally prepare for what's to come. I can't underestimate Somma, she's strong, but her best bet is to use her speed, size and agility against me. Personally, I was fine with letting her win, but now my curiosity is peaked on who can really get who down first.

"Are you ready?" I playfully ask.

Somma smiles and nods as she puts her hair in a ponytail. I put my hair behind my ears and wait for Somma to make the first move. That's what Sarge taught me. Somma smirks and runs towards me, she goes down to her knee and slides on the wooden floor, trying to swipe my leg to trip me. She nearly gets me, but I move my leg out of the way. Somma looks back at me with a surprised expression. I walk to her and extend my hand to help her up, Somma grabs it and quickly pulls me down to the ground. I didn't expect her to do that, she caught me off guard and off-balance, causing me to hit the floor first. It didn't hurt, but it really caught me by surprise. Somma giggles and gets on top of me,

"Do not feel too bad, my love, you did great-"

I grab her waist and quickly roll to the left, interrupting her and causing her to lose balance. She falls over on her back with me now on top of her,

"You didn't do too bad yourself." I say while moving her hair out of her face.

Somma smiles and grabs my face, she pulls me in and

kisses me on the lips passionately. I get off of her as she begins her workout. I sit on the couch to relax and watch her. From what I can tell, she works mainly on core, cardio and some weightlifting. She focuses a lot on the lower half of her body, a lot of leg and glute exercises. I do the same workouts sometimes, but not as intense as her. Somma stops working out for a moment, she gets off the floor and moves the hanging pieces of hair by her face behind her ears. She runs to me lying on the couch and quickly kisses me on the lips. After giggling, she resumes her workout as if she used kissing me as a breather. It's hard to believe she's real. Somma's body, top to bottom, is like a sculpture. I always thought it came naturally with being a Vespin, but I am clearly wrong. Somma really works hard to stay fit, not just for looks, but because she knows she needs to for the USC.

After Somma finishes her workout, she lays on the floor and crawls to me by the couch. She sits up and lays back against the couch. I playfully hang my head off the couch next to her. She looks at me with a smile, I grab her towel and dab her head with it, Somma giggles and kisses me on the cheek.

"It makes me happy that you are here with me. I feel safer when you are near." she says while rubbing my cheek with her thumb.

"You will always be safe with me."

Somma kisses my cheek multiple times, but we're interrupted by a ringing on a table. Somma and I look around confused. I quickly stand up and help Somma off the ground. We approach a nearby table with a flashing blue puck shaped device. I slowly press on the device and a hologram of Serro comes out of it. He has a confused expression on his face while looking at Somma and I,

"CPL. Parson, why are you with PVT. Juna? You have your own safehouse."

"Well, sir, I died for a third time and she is helping me come back to life." I respond, knowing damn well that my answer is going to piss him off.

"Hopefully she can find you a brain, too." he continued, "SSG. Miner's funeral has been arranged, it will be held at USC Headquarters tomorrow morning. As for Pyren Juna's trial. It will be held at the Vespis Palace of Truth and Justice. It will begin within a couple months. I need everyone's testimonies. The memorial will be at 0800 tomorrow, do not be late. Now, some good news. The USC will be awarding Specter with the Medal of Torious. Despite all the trouble, the USC does appreciate what you all have done. The ceremony will take place after Miner's memorial. I will se you both tommorow."

The hologram disappears. I'm personally not exactly thrilled about the Medal of Torious. It's awarded to those who accomplished something incredible under dire circumstances or adversity, which we did, but it's just a piece of tin. I still appreciate it, though. Somma slowly walks away and sits down on the couch without saying a word, unaffected by the news of her receiving a medal with all of us. It was almost as if Somma forgot about her father's trial. Spending time with each other felt like a dream, but this brought us back to reality. I sit next to her and place my hand on her thigh, she holds my hand and lowers her head.

"I will soon be the last of the Juna bloodline."

"If it's to end with you, there is no one better it should end with." I respond.

Somma looks down and doesn't respond. I really am unsure if I said the right thing, but what else could I say. The USC doesn't take too kindly to traitors. I'm put in a tough position that has been lingering in the back of my mind for a while now. As someone who was personally affected by GEN. Juna's actions, resulting in my death, I feel no sadness with the idea of his execution. I wish I could do it myself. The problem is and has been that Somma still has some love for him. I understand he is her father, but she saw what he has done. I doubt she will speak against her father, but I know everyone else will and expect me to do the same. I want to speak, but I don't know what that will do to my relationship with Somma.

I feel like for the first time, she and I can actually be in a regular relationship, all that is in jeopardy with the decisions I make from here on out when it comes to the trial. Somma lays down on the couch on her side with her head laying on my lap. I place my hand on her arm trying to comfort her, she reaches and holds my hand,

"Can you call everyone, please? Fesio too. We need to speak with them about the trial. Hopefully, speaking with them early can help them change their minds if they are thinking of speaking against him. They can say whatever they want at the trial, but I cannot have it end with my father's execution."

I sigh and pull out my communicator. I connect with everyone in Specter and Fesio,

"I'm sure those of you in Specter got Serro's message by now. We all need to talk about it. Meet us at USC Headquarters as fast as possible. That's an order."

The lines remain silent, until we hear a scoff,

"*Look who's the leader now.*" Blaine responds mockingly.

I don't respond, putting the communicator away. No one responded to me, but I know they heard me. I sense they know what needs to be spoken about. Somma sits up and kisses my cheek before she hugs me tight,

"Thank you, my love. I need you now more than ever. Please stay by my side." she says while squeezing me tighter.

I kiss her cheek and help her off the couch. I hold her hand as I take her back to our room where she gets changed in her casual clothes. Other than the celebration in Tanli, I've never seen her or anyone in Specter wearing casual clothing. As expected, Somma's casual clothes look like they belong to someone of royal blood. I guess that's just basic fashion on Vespis. I never really paid attention to what people wore any time I came here. She puts on a white long sleeve shirt, with slit sleeves that flows with the breeze and light gray pants that are also slit at their bottoms. Surprisingly, for shoes, she goes with what looks like basic white slip-on shoes, perhaps the most normal looking item of clothing she owns. She puts her hair in a side braid and puts on her Noli and arrow and feather necklaces to complete her already incredible outfit. I shouldn't be surprised with how great she looks. Somma is lucky enough to look good in just about anything, even a Xenem uniform. I feel underdressed compared to her. The clothes I wore during my walk earlier in the morning are what I decide to put on again, but I put on my old coat and my necklaces too. Somma waits by the door for me to finish getting my boots on. I see her leaning against the wall with her head down. I can tell she has a lot on her mind, but I want to get her mind off of what's going on, as much as I can.

"You look beautiful." I say softly.

Somma looks up and smiles at me. She kisses my cheek and holds my hand while opening the door. She opens it slightly before stopping and looking back at me. She closes the door again and grabs my other hand.

"May we dance when we get back?" she asks.

"We have some time. We can dance right now if you want."

Somma kisses my right hand and walks me to the center of the room. She stands in front of me and smiles as she looks up at me. I try to walk to the sound system to play a song, but she pulls me back.

"I think you should hum it again. I like it better that way." she says while running her hands along my arms.

I give a shy smile while looking down. Somma moves closer to me as we get in position to begin dancing. I put my hands on her waist and she wraps her arms around my neck. Somehow, I remember a lot of the song and begin humming it. We move to the sound of my hums, within less than a minute, Somma begins humming the song with me as we dance. Something always felt off when I would hum the song. I was never able to do the harmony's on my own, but Somma joining in filled the missing pieces. Her shirt shows her stomach, with my hands still on her waist, I move my left hand up and feel the scar on her side. It makes me think back to that disaster on Vonra. It's seen by most as a day of celebration and a success and while that is true, it's also a day filled with pain and torment. Though she and I never get tired of dancing with each other, Somma slows down once she notices where my hand is. She looks up and sees me looking down, she can tell I'm thinking about the day she got that wound and how it happened. Somma gently touches my cheeks with her hand to get my attention,

"I can change shirts if you want. If the scar bothers you, I can wear less revealing clothes."

"You don't need to do that. I'm sorry." I respond, slowly moving my hand away from her scar.

It's clear she's more okay with her scars being shown than I am. My guess, her beauty distracts others from it or she doesn't mind showing them in general, either way, I don't have that luxury. Somma puts my hand back on her scar, then lifts up my shirt revealing my scar in the same location oddly enough. She places her hand on my scar and tilts her head,

"Interesting." she whispers to herself.

I've never noticed that our scars were practically the same. Same location and received the same way, stabbed. I hate to compare, but the way she got it was a bit more heroic than the way I got mine. My eyes narrow as I observe both scars, Somma chuckles softly,

"It seems we are more connected than we thought."

"And just as reckless." I jokingly respond.

Somma playfully hits my arm and kisses my lips, she moves closer to me as we continue to dance. We have both stopped humming, but it doesn't stop us from dancing. After a few minutes, I slow down,

"Are you ready to go?"

Somma slowly nods at me. I kiss her cheek and walk her to the door. I open it for her,

"You really do look beautiful." I say.

Somma shyly looks down with a smile, she looks up and

smirks,

"Thank you. I would say you look handsome, but- " she quickly pulls my hair out of its ponytail and giggles, "You need to fix your hair!"

I shake my hair like a wet dog in her face, which messes up her hair a little.

"Okay, I am sorry! You look very handsome, my love." she responds while laughing.

Somma fixes her hair then moves the hair out of my face. I decide to keep my hair down, I prefer it that way. She kisses me a few times on the lips before we walk out of the room and head to the elevator. Somma's overall mood seems to have gotten a bit better, she swings my arm back and forth as she holds onto my hand in the elevator as we go down. I was expecting to run like we did before, but I'm pleasantly surprised to see we're walking. I was starting to think Somma ran everywhere. As we pass more and more people, they look at us holding hands. They have a mixture of confused, off-put, and concerned looks on their faces. From what I understand, Vespins and Humans don't typically have relationships with anyone outside of their planet. I think we might be the first interracial relationship on Vespis.

Somma was never like other Vespins. While Vespins are generally friendly and welcoming, it's rare that they approach you and try to strike up conversations. Somma did both of those with ease. How she was raised by GEN. Juna baffles me. Her mother must have been where she gets her kindness from. As kind as most Vespins are, there are still some, like Somma's father, who are cold and rude. As Somma and I walk to the station where we first got on a Ranna, a man walks past us and lets out a disgusted groan. He smacks our hands off of each other.

"You should be ashamed, child." he says.

Somma skins flashes a bright white light, she growls and tries to approach him, but I hold her back and shake my head. What he did pissed me off too, but it's not something I would see as a reason to fight or get violent. There's too much useless violence going on around the galaxies as it is.

"He cannot do that to us. If I was with someone like me or him, he would have never done that. It is not okay." Somma says while holding my hand again, but she holds it tighter in anger.

"I hate it, I know," I respond, "but people like that are everyone. I don't let it bother me. The only Vespin opinion that matters to me is yours. People can say what they want, as long as we're happy, then none of what they say matters."

Somma's scowl steadily turns into a relaxed expression. She kisses my hand and starts walking. The man is lucky I calmed Somma down, she would have broken bones he never knew he had, like a spine. Somma stops walking again and pulls me to the side, in an alleyway. She kisses me on the lips,

"There is a lot I have done in the past that I am ashamed of, but I want you to know that what I have with you, this love, is not one of them. I am not ashamed at all. I knew how others would react to us. I know I should not have tried to react poorly, but I do not want anyone to insult you, making you feel bad or embarrassed. I love you always and I will never be ashamed of that."

"You'll see that I embarrass myself all on my own." I joke before kissing her on the cheek, "I love you."

Somma smiles and hugs me tight, we hear the Ranna land at its station. Somma gasps and grabs my hand, we begin running to the Ranna. I should have known walking was just a short lived luxury. We run onto the Ranna and sit down. I put my arm around Somma and she moves closer to me. Naturally, we get some of the same looks others have been giving us, but it's easy to ignore. We can't go five minutes without another issue arising, but this time, it isn't about Somma and I.

We hear arguing near us, we both lean forward and see a man harassing a woman sitting down. I don't hear what he's saying, but the lady looks scared and uncomfortable. Even though I don't know what he's saying, I would feel bad if I let him go on. I look at Somma who is also watching the man. She looks up at me and nods her head. I close my eyes and sigh. I slowly let go of Somma and stand up. I make my way to the man who looks drunk,

"Sir, please leave her alone. You can have my seat, just move away and stay quiet."

I spoke as calmly and softly as I could. I truly just wanted to grab him and throw him off the moving Ranna, but there are women and children watching. Besides, most of the people here aren't that crazy about me. Whether it's because they saw Somma and I together or know about Specter, maybe both. The man laughs in my face and shoves my head, causing my hair to fly in my face. I keep my head turned away with my hair still in my face. I take a second to breathe, but the man shoves me again. I don't move, my feet stay planted. I see Somma stand up, about to help me, but I hold my hand up to her. I turn back to him,

"Are we done?"

The unnerving smile the man had turns to anger, he throws a punch at me, but I move out the way and grab his arm, twisting it behind him, immobilizing him. He cries out in pain.

"*Paolin seel! Poalin seel nol tine!*"

He obviously said something in Vespin which I don't understand, but it sounds like he's yielding judging by his cries and the pained expression on his face. With his arm still behind him in my grasp, I walk him away from the lady who bows her head to me with a smile. He doesn't deserve it, but I am still willing to give him my seat. I bring him to where I was sitting, Somma stands up and moves out of the way. I sit him down, motioning to the others on the Ranna to move away from him. After everyone moves away, I grab Somma's hand and walk away with her to find another empty space. People move down their seats to give us a place to sit, but there's only one spot available. Without thinking about it, I sit Somma down on a seat while I go on the floor.

I close my eyes and lean back against Somma's legs. I feel

her hands slowly run through my hair as it blows in the wind. I hear others talking about what I assume just happened, I try not to think about it.

"Vespis is not as magical and as perfect as people think. People here can be so rude and indecent." Somma says.

I shrug my shoulders with my eyes closed, it's not news to me what Somma said. I don't think anywhere has people who are all kind and loving, living in harmony. I was bound to deal with stuff like what has happened so far today anyways. Somma sighs,

"Despite the imperfections, it's home. There is a tall, beautiful tree at a park near the Headquarters. I would always go there when I was too stressed or upset about certain things and it would help me calm down and give me a peaceful space to think. I have been meaning to go back, I would love to show it to you!"

I smile as I look up at her. I would love to see the tree. After a few minutes, our Ranna reaches our stop. Once we finally reach the Headquarters and see Specter and Fesio waiting outside. It's midday, I realize we are a bit late, but Somma and I are still eager to get the meeting started. It won't be fun, but if Somma needs it, I support it. It may cause a divide within Specter, but at least we will all know where we stand in the case of former GEN. Pyren Juna. Seeing Somma in normal clothes was already strange, but seeing everyone else in their normal clothes is even stranger. It's not too often you get to tee the styles of different civilizations all in one place.

I've probably seen Blaine in casual clothing once when we first met and he looks the same. A beat up, red and gray T-Shirt with holes in it, dirty blue jeans and a pair of worn out combat boots. It seems at no point he thought of getting himself new clothes. As if telling the Lane twins apart wasn't hard enough, they wear similar outfits. Both wear white button up shirts with Mitchell's shirt being a slightly different tone of white. Both also wear Khakis and Oxfords. I feel like they are intentionally making it hard to tell them apart. Rachel is dressed closer to Blaine, just without the dirty clothes. She wears leggings, running shoes, a gray long sleeve shirt and a zip-up jacket. I don't know what exactly I was expecting with Carden and Kierra, but after seeing what they wear, it makes sense. I've never been to Foli or Matu, so I am unsure if this is the normal, everyday wear for them. Carden wears an all black cloak that covers his entire body. His legs have seemingly disappeared within the cloak. Kierra wears a beautiful, long buttoned-up coat with the colors of Matu, white pants and open-toe sandals. Bradley's outfit is incredibly predictable. A gray blazer with a white pocket square, white button-up shirt, gray dress pants and leather shoes. In no way is that outfit casual, but if he's comfortable, then it doesn't matter. Admittedly, it looks good. Fesio is wearing what the USC gave him when we washed up, a gray long sleeve shirt with the USC logo on it and gray pants and his boots. Other than Bradley, those of us from Earth are underdressed. It's nice to see that everyone in Specter is still wearing their necklaces.

Blaine sees Somma and can't hide his shocked expression. I don't know how I didn't expect this, but as we walk past everyone, Blaine stares at Somma's cleavage not so subtly. Somma snaps her fingers in his face as she passes him, breaking his trance.

"Try keeping your eyes up." I say to him.

The one time Blaine looks at Somma in a positive way, of course that's what he does. We enter the building and walk towards an empty conference room. Everyone stares at us, I'll admit, we do look like an unusual bunch, especially out of uniform. I open the door for everyone, they all walks past me. Somma is the last one to enter as she was holding my hand the whole time. She slowly lets go and begins to walk in. She stops and turns to me, with a look on her face that she wants to say something, but is unsure of what to say before going in. I kiss her cheek and rub her back with my hand,

"It'll be okay."

Somma smiles and rubs my cheek with her thumb. She

closes her eyes and sighs before finally walking in. I close the door behind me and stand at the head of the table where everyone is silent.

"GEN. Juna is going to be put on trial soon. I called you all here to see what you're all thinking. We're not ordered to go and testify against him, but Serro really wants us to. He is also going to testify. Juna's betrayal is known throughout the USC, so either way, he will be imprisoned. I know Somma won't testify, what about the rest of you?"

Everyone looks at each other, but no one says anything. I knock on the table to get everyone's attention, hoping someone will answer me. Kierra looks up at me,

"I will not speak either. I believe in prison he can reflect on what he did. Perhaps a fate worse than death."

Somma and I smile. We thought the same thing, but a divide is slowly being created as Bradley scoffs,

"Who cares if he reflects on anything? He betrayed everyone, forced Somma to turn on the USC, helped Tyro imprison us and basically killed Parson. He would kill us if he had the chance, I say we offer him the same mercy. I'm speaking at the trial."

Bradley makes a good point, I just wish it was in favor of the outcome Somma wanted. Kierra and Bradley represent the divide to come from this trial. I never thought we would all be on the same page, but convincing everyone to stay out of it is going to be harder than I thought. Blaine nods his head,

"I'm with the rich kid, Juna has been a pain in the ass even before he turned. I don't care who's father he is, I want a punishment he won't come back from."

"His death serves no purpose." Fesio interjects, "You all have work to do as Specter, while you can anyways, going to this trial would be a waste of time. Juna will face punishment, why wish for more death? Have you all not seen enough already?"

"You haven't known CPL. Parson long." Rachel responds to Fesio, "Try working and getting to know someone for months and building respect for them just to watch them get essentially killed. Not by just anyone, but a General we may not have liked, but trusted. It's too much, I say let him die. I'm sorry, Somma."

Somma lowers her head, in her mind, I think she sees both sides of the arguments as valid. The arguing goes on for a while. Carden and Martin have aligned themselves with Somma, Mitchell has taken the side of Juna's death. It's five, including Serro, for testifying, basically ensuring his execution, versus five for not going and letting him get thrown in prison if possible. I'm the only one who hasn't voted on the matter because the truth is, I have no idea what I want. I hate it, but I do want to be avenged in some sort of way. I barely made it out of my fight with Juna alive, plus he's a terrible father to Somma, I don't want him around anymore. Prison isn't enough. On the other hand, I love Somma and I know she doesn't want her father to die. He's all she has left of her family. I want to be on her side in all matters if possible, but I am completely torn. It's been a little over an hour of heated arguments between everyone, I've never heard us all speak so much.

"You all have to understand he is all I have left." Somma continued, "I do not have any other family. I know what he did was wrong, my father will pay in prison for his crimes, but he does not need to die. He is a General to you all, but he is my father first."

Bradley, whose blazer is off and his sleeves rolled up, smacks his hand on the table,

"Somma, I'm sorry, but your father is a traitor, a killer and a coward. As we speak, I am sure he is thinking of ways to get revenge on us if he gets out and I really don't think he will spare you. You have to testify, I know it's hard, but do it for the USC." Bradley stops and rubs his eyes, "I don't know how relationships work on Vespis, but your boyfriend was beaten and killed by your father, CPL. Parson barely made it out alive by some miracle. Yet you want to save Juna. Don't you care?

Don't you care that your boyfriend basically died in your arms? It hurt us to watch, but did it not hurt you? Did you not care? Your father did that and you don't care? I guess when he inevitably escapes from prison and finishes your boyfriend, you won't care then too? He can only come back to life so many times. You want Juna to live despite all of that, you just don't care, right? I really don't understand."

Somma tears up,

"No, I do care- Of course I- I just-" Somma tries to speak, but is taken back by Bradley's barrage of questions.

After stumbling over her words a few more times and looking back at me with tears rolling down her face, she stops speaking. She stands up out of her chair and walks out of the room in defeat. The room goes silent. I don't know where that fire from Bradley came from, but even outside of Specter, I can't have him speak like that to anyone. I quickly stand up, about to leave to catch up with Somma, I stop and turn to Bradley,

"What were you thinking?"

"I seem to be one of the few people who are thinking in this room. When I first joined this war, everyone asked me why I did it, it's because I was sick of bad people getting away with everything. Sure, my family was wealthy, but that just made us targets for contestant robberies and death threats if we didn't give up any money. No one did a thing to help us, so people took what they could from us. They got away. I am sick of bad people getting a break, prison is no break, but it beats death which is what Juna deserves. You need to think with your mind rather than your heart. With all due respect, sir."

For so long I was one of the people who asked why he joined, I never would have figured that was why. I understand where he is coming from and why this issue is so important to him. I guess I am partially on his side, but I'm still undecided. Still, he can't speak like that to Somma or anyone in Specter. I don't respond to Bradley, but I sigh and rub my eyes in contemplation of what he said while leaning on a wall. The

398

room erupts into more arguments and debates, after hearing a lot more of people's thoughts, I've finally had enough and at this point, I just want to be alone with Somma, away from the chaos. I quickly walk out of the room which is still filled with the sounds of everyone yelling. I'm sure we'll see where everyone landed soon enough.

    I look around the first floor of the building trying to find Somma. I can't find her. After a while of searching, I get worried, but I remember what she told me on the Ranna about a tree she loved nearby. It's a safe bet she went there after Bradley's outburst. I run out of the building and see a massive tree nearby, I don't know how I have missed it all this time, that has to be the tree. I run to the park where the tree is. I am blown away by the sheer size of it. It looks like a regular Oak tree, but a thousand times its regular size which I guess is normal here. I stop and look up in amazement. I begin to slowly walk around the tree, inspecting it. During my walk, I feel someone grab my hand from below me and pull me back. My hand being grabbed breaks my trance as I nearly trip while being pulled back. After catching myself, I see it's Somma who's holding onto my hand, sitting on the ground against a wall. It's no secret that she has been crying. Her skin is shining brighter, but the park is empty which is probably for the best. I go down to my knees and wipe the tears from her face,

    "Is everything okay? I was looking-"

    Somma interrupts me by wrapping her arms around my neck, hugging me tight while crying,

    "I do care. I promise I care. I promise, I am so sorry, I do care, I do. I am sorry. I care, Clark, please believe me." she says while weeping and holding onto me.

    "It's okay, I believe you. Everything is okay, I'm right here."

    Somma continues to cry while her arms are around me. Bradley did a number on her, but I think it was more than just him that caused Somma to break down like this, now that I think about it. It was probably everything. The different sides, all the yelling and debating and their situation itself isn't ideal. It was getting too much for me too. It's been five minutes of Somma and I on our knees at the park hugging each other. Somma has not stopped crying, despite my best efforts.

"Don't listen to Bradley. He was just heated and went over the line. Nothing he said was okay, but don't worry about him. I'm here now, just breathe for me." I say while rubbing her back with my hand.

Somma begins to slowly stop crying as much, she starts breathing steadily. The right side of my shirt is soaked from her tears, but I don't mind. For all I know, shirts soaked in Vespin tears are probably lucky.

"I cannot do this." she says with her voice breaking.

"Don't say that. This isn't easy, but you can get through it, I'll be by your side no matter what. We have to be strong."

Somma moves away and looks into my eyes,

"It'll be okay, I promise." I say while caressing her cheek with my hand.

Somma smiles and kisses me on the lips as she places her soft and cold hands on my face,

"I do not want you to ever think I do not care about you or what happened. The image of you on the ground bleeding out in my arms replays in my head every day and I hate it. I care. I am sorry if it ever seems like I do not."

"I know. It's okay. Let's just sit here okay?"

Somma smiles as I sit next to her. She lays down next to me, placing her head on my shoulder. I wrap my arm around her as I look at the tree again.

"It gets bigger every time I see it." she says softly.

I laugh in amazement, I never thought I would ever see something like this. Another thing that amazes me is that none of Somma's clothes have gotten dirty at all from sitting and laying on the ground. Either the ground everywhere in Vespis is perfectly clean or it's impossible to get clothes dirty here, maybe using some sort of fabric. I quickly decide it's just her fabric since I see my jeans have gotten dirty. I don't really mind it, but I try to swipe off the dirt from my knees and legs. Somma gasps and goes to her knees.

"We can get up if you want." she says while rubbing my thigh.

I smile and pull her back in close, staying on the ground. Somma giggles and moves in closer with my arm around her. I've never cared if my clothes got dirty. If I had to crawl through mud, I'd do it with little to no hesitation, dust on my coat, no issue, wet shirt, I don't care. It never really bothered me, so having some dirt on my clothes from sitting down isn't a big deal to me. Wiping it away was just a way to try to make it not look as dirty. Somma looks at the tree is wonderment, as if it's her first time seeing it,

"This tree has been here long before I was born. My mother was the first one to bring me here with my brother and sisters. We all loved it here. My father does not care much for it, not since the war started, but according to my mother, they would always go here together. I would always see people walking around the tree with a loved one, a *Relani* and *Telani* together. It is believed that circling the tree with someone will provide eternal love and protection to them both, blessing their relationship. That is what my mother taught us. I made a promise to myself that if I ever had someone so special in my life, I would walk with them around the tree. It probably sounds odd to you, but I have always believed it."

I look at the tree again, I smile and stand up. I extend my hand to Somma on the ground. She looks up at me and smiles, tearing up while grabbing my hand. I pull her up and we begin walking around the tree while holding hands. During the walk I hear Somma giggle,

"Is everything okay?" I ask.

"I was just thinking about how my mother told us how magical it will be once we find someone to walk around the tree with. She was right. I never thought I would find someone to walk with. I am beyond happy that I am walking with you. Thank you, my love."

Somma kisses my hand and holds onto my arm as we continue to make our way around the tree. I respond by kissing her head. The walk is longer than I thought, obviously this tree isn't normal, but I didn't think it would take this long. I am not complaining, but I feel like I need to say something so Somma doesn't get bored. Speaking was never my strongest ability. Somma is aware that I am quiet, I just hope she doesn't get bored. We finish going around the tree, Somma goes off to the side with me towards the tree, we both lean on it with our shoulders. I look up at the branches, but Somma gently touches my face, drawing my attention to her.

"You look very handsome, my love." she says softly.

I smile and shake my head in playful disagreement. Somma moves closer and kisses my cheek,

"We have been together for a while, but you still do not speak much. Is something wrong?"

"No, I'm sorry. I'm just a quiet person. I'm really happy to be here with you. Thank you for showing me the tree."

"I like hearing your voice. It always makes me smile. It is strange, I know what you are saying even when all you do is smile at me or look down because you are shy, but I will always want to hear your voice."

"You are not real." I say quietly while rubbing her cheek with my thumb.

Somma places her hand on mine and kisses me on the lips.

"I am very real, I love you."

At that moment, after everything she just said and that last kiss, I decide something that I have been thinking about for a while. I never found a right time or place to do it, with Sarge's funeral, Juna's trial and the all around mess Serro caused, it was hard to find a right time for what I am about to do. We live lives where tomorrows are not guaranteed, so I want us to take the next step, not because of fear of dying soon, but fear of dying without us being more than just boyfriend and girlfriend, *Relani* and *Telani*. It may seem soon, but I truly want this and I think she does too. I love her, she's everything to me. This is going to truly force me out of my comfort zone and I am terrified, but if I can survive the wilds of Xenem, survive death and live to tell the tale, then I should be okay. I close my eyes and take a deep breath in, I open them to see her leaning against the tree smiling and staring into my eyes while my hand is still on her cheek. Her beauty is what is making this hard, but is also making me want to do it more. I reach in my coat pocket and grab what my mother put in there. She didn't tell me what it was, but I knew. It's a diamond ring and a box. I didn't have anything to say planned out, but I knew if I spoke from within, I would say the right thing.

"It was a rough day for you and I'm sorry, but hopefully this helps." I say.

I kiss her cheek and slowly go down on one knee. Somma watches me go down with surprise in her eyes. I slowly pull the box out in front of Somma, she covers her mouth with her hands. I slowly open the box, I smile as I look at the beautiful diamond ring, then look back at Somma who's still in disbelief, her eyes sparkle like never before. I gently grab her left hand, pulling it closer to me,

"Somma, I'm not great with words as you know, but I love you with all my heart. My mother already told you, she sees the way I look at you, it is unlike the way I look at anyone else. Every time I look at you, every time I kiss you, every time you hold me, every time we dance, every time you do anything, I fall in love with you all over again. You are the most beautiful girl I have ever seen and I don't know what I did to make you even look at me in any other way besides a soldier, but I am glad I did it. My life has only gotten better since we got together. I feel safer, loved and cared for. I never thought anyone would treat me like you have and I will never be able to repay you for everything you have done for me. There isn't a single second where I am tired of being with you, I always want to be by your side. With this ring, I promise to always love and cherish you, protect you and our lives, treat you with love, kindness and respect every second of every day and never make you feel alone and hurt. You are all I'll ever want in this life and the next. You are beautiful, funny, strong, passionate, smart and so much more. I feel safe and protected from everything when I am by your side, you are truly the girl of my dreams. Someone I think I have spent my whole life waiting for. You wouldn't believe how much I need you in my life and I swear I will always be there for you whenever you call, no matter what I am doing or how I am feeling, I'm all yours and I love you with every inch of my being and I always will. You are all that I want and need. I could go on forever about how much I love and cherish you and how amazing you are, but I have one question. I may be doing this too soon, but my beautiful diamond queen, my everything, Somma Terra Juna, the girl of my dreams, will you do me the extreme honor of making me the happiest and luckiest man in all the galaxies and be my wife?"

Somma laughs while crying, she goes down to her knees in front of me and nods her head while touching my cheeks with both hands,

"Yes, my love. Of course I will marry you!"

BITTERSWEET DAYS

The ring fits Somma's finger perfectly. She cries tears of joy as she looks at the ring on her hand. She laughs and launches at me, wrapping me in a tight hug. I didn't expect to propose to her right then and there. To be honest, I had no idea when or where I wanted to do it. I guess hearing the stories about her mother teaching Somma and her siblings about the tree and what it represents, especially for people who love each other, gave me the idea to do it. The tree obviously means a lot to Somma, I don't think there could have been anywhere better. I sometimes thought of proposing at the Heleia Fields on Vonra, but doing it here felt right.

Somma has not let go of me and is still crying. I even start to tear up. I will always be baffled when it comes to how I got with Somma in the first place. I often think about how I originally wanted nothing to do with this squad, but who knows where I'd be today or if I would even be with someone if not for this squad and everything we have been through? I hear Somma chuckle while holding me,

"'Somma Parson', I love the way that sounds!" she says before kissing me on the cheek.

This tree really is magical. It'll always have a special place in my heart. Somma has never held onto me for so long, she is holding me just as tight as she when she first wrapped her arms around me.

"My mother would have loved you. I wish she could see us right now." she says with her voice breaking.

"She's been with us this whole time."

Somma sniffles and holds me even tighter. I'm sure I

would have loved her mother. Somma's kind nature can only be the result of being raised with her teachings. GEN. Juna made her a good soldier, but her mom made her a great person. Somma eventually lets go and moves away. She wipes her tears and laughs,

"I was not expecting that, but I would have gladly said yes no matter when you asked. You are the only man I have ever wanted since the moment I met you. You have made me so happy, my love."

I kiss her cheek and look at the ring again with her. It's the ring my father used to propose to my mother, she kept it with her all the time. Growing up, I've only seen this ring a few times, but I never noticed how beautiful it is. The ring isn't anything too fancy, the diamond is a decent size on a golden ring. The diamond blends in with Somma's skin though. I look down and chuckle while wiping a tear away. Somma lifts my face up and smiles at me,

"What is it?" she asks.

"I was just imagining you in your wedding dress. So beautiful, I can't help but smile and-"

Somma smiles as she launches herself at my face, kissing me on the lips passionately which interrupts me. She runs her hands through my hair while kissing me as we lay down, it's lucky no one is around. People would make it awkward, especially with how much she is on top of me. Somma moves away and giggles,

"I am sorry, but I had to kiss you." she says while shyly moving pieces of her hair out of her face.

"You can kiss me all you want."

Somma smiles and grabs my hand, she stands up and pulls me up with her. We are about to walk away, but Somma goes back to the three and looks up at it one more time. She kisses her hand and places it on the trunk of the tree, I hear her whisper "Thank you." before slowly walking away. I feel it would be rude if I didn't do the same thing, so I go to the tree and do the same thing. I slowly back away from the tree taking the view in one more time before we go, Somma pulls on my arm,

"Are you ready to go?"

I smile and nod. I haven't gotten to enjoy the sights of Vespis yet, so Somma takes me around the city to show me her favorite places. As for the rest of Specter, I don't know if they are still in that conference room or not, but we'll just see them at the memorial tomorrow, hopefully in a more peaceful manner. Somma takes me to an old library she used to always go to, then to beautiful water fountains and parks. We get the occasional weird and disapproving looks, but we don't mind. We sit down on a fountain together, Somma gasps and pulls out a camera from her bag. It's a floating camera, I've never seen one in person, but I've heard of it. It's a ball where you toss it in the air and it floats, taking photos from any angle. She tosses it in the air and moves the hair out of my face. The camera points at us, she kisses my cheek while I smile at the camera. The camera takes the photo and while I don't look that great, Somma looks amazing. All in all, I love the photo. Somma is usually happy, but I've never seen her this happy. What happened at the meeting really crushed her, I'm not sure if she is even thinking about it. I didn't propose to her just to make her feel better, but I'm glad it helped. It's been an emotional few days and it's going to continue tomorrow with Sarge's funeral, so I want her to be as happy as can be today because tomorrow we are all going to feel his loss more than ever.

We stay at the fountain for a few more minutes before getting up and walking around a nearby street market. Everyone is selling an assortment of items, food, clothes, rugs, just about anything. It takes us a while to walk through since Somma keeps stopping to say hello to everyone and see what they're selling while also doing her best to show off her ring without being too obvious. I try to be just as friendly so people don't look at me too differently, but I just end up drawing more attention to myself and inviting those looks we've been getting all day. For the most part, people don't say anything about us, even though I can tell they want to. One older lady that runs a shop that sells pottery saw Somma's ring and scoffed while pointing her bony finger at us,

"Young lady, do not tell me you are to be married to this man."

"I am." Somma responds while pulling me closer.

"He is from Earth! They are weak and cannot be trusted. He will hurt you. Run while you can."

I step forward, about to say something, but Somma pulls me away. I try to calm myself down, but my breathing gets heavier in anger. Somma takes me to a secluded area away from the market surrounded by trees. It's a quaint spot to help me calm down and get away from the crowds which she knew I didn't like. She leans me against a tree and hugs me, the hug does help me calm down, but I'm still pissed off about what that lady said.

"She's wrong. I'm not going to hurt you, ever." I say while hugging her.

"I know, my love. Nothing she said was true. Do not listen to her. Do you want to go back?"

I take a deep breath in and sigh. I nod my head, Somma smiles and kisses my cheek while holding my hand, walking us back to the market. To be honest, I didn't really want to go back. I never liked being out in public and I was getting tired of the weird looks. We didn't get too many at the market, but it was still frustrating. I go back with her though, she was having so much fun speaking with everyone and I knew she wanted to be with me, which still surprises me. As we walk back into the market, we hear a familiar voice speaking with a shop owner, we turn and see Sarsey from Tanli Village. I haven't seen him since he gave me the arrow and feather necklaces for stopping his store from being robbed. It hurt like hell stopping the thieves, but it's nothing compared to what I've been through now. It's good to see him, but I didn't feel like saying hello, I'm not as open to conversations as Somma. It's not that I want to be rude, it's just not who I am.

"We should say hi to him!" Somma exclaims while pulling me towards him

I wasn't going to try to stop her, besides it might take my mind off what happened. Somma taps Sarsey's shoulder, he turns and sees us. He looks confused, but he looks closer at us and smiles,

"Look who it is! The Heroes of Tanli! I hope you do not mind, Geb or I suppose I should say Ben, has told me all of your names. It is so good to see you both. I hope the rest of your squad is doing well!"

"It is good to see you!" Somma exclaims, "Unfortunately, our leader who was with us Tanli died."

"Yes, we all heard about that. SSG. Richard Miner, I remember him. My sincerest apologies to you all. At least you are all okay. Clark, thank you again for what you did for my store, no one has ever done something like that for me, I truly appreciate it. I see you are both wearing the arrow and feather necklaces I gave you and beautiful pieces of Noli, very nice, I hope it protects you both!"

"Thank you, sir. I'm glad you are doing well. What are you doing here?" I ask

"I am a trader! I try to come out to Vespis when I can to sell my goods. I have not been here in a while. The Confederacy made traveling between systems nearly impossible, but ever since your squad took care of them in our system, traveling has become much easier and-"

Sarsey stops himself after seeing the ring on Somma's finger,

"Oh my, Somma, what lovely ring! Who is the lucky man?"

Somma giggles and holds my hand. Sarsey smiles,

"Of course! I should have figured! What a beautiful and strong pairing you two make. I have to get back to my rather cheap friend over here, but it was truly good to see you both again. Stop by Tanli when you get a chance, we are still cleaning up Vonra, so we have to stay in Tanli a little longer, but at least we are safe. Nonetheless, stay safe and congratulations!"

He bows his head to us and turns back to the shop owner. Somma kisses my hand and we continue walking. There was a time where we would get pissed off if anyone exposed our names to anyone, we used to be extremely cautious of people knowing the existence of Specter and our identities. Ever since Serro exposed the existence of it all, it doesn't really bother us anymore, but it'd be better if we can keep Specter as much a secret as possible while we can.

Time flew by in my time with Somma. Within what seems like a couple hours, we spent the entire day together, Vespis gets darker and I could tell Somma is tired, as am I. Today I will never forget, but we do have to wake up early tomorrow for Sarge's funeral. We are walking back to the station for a Ranna to take us home, I pick Somma up off her feet and carry her. Somma smiles and wraps her arms around my neck,

"What a gentleman, thank you." she says before kissing my cheek.

She lays her head on my sounder as I carry her to the station. We are not too far from it, but Somma does fall asleep in my arms. I make it onto a Ranna and sit down while holding Somma. It's hard for me not to fall asleep while sitting down, but I force myself to stay up long enough for the Ranna to reach our stop. Doing my best to not wake Somma up, I slowly get up and walk off the Ranna. The elevator ride up to our room is quiet with the only sound being the elevator mechanisms and Somma's soft breathing as she sleeps. As the elevator goes up, I watch Somma as she sleeps peacefully. Admiring her beauty, I internally congratulate myself for proposing to someone so incredible. As much of a struggle as it is while holding her, I open our door and close it shut with my leg. I take Somma to our bed and gently lay her down, I cover he with a blanket and try to take off the ring so I could put it on her nightstand, but she wakes up a little and stops me,

"I want to keep it on." she says while pushing the ring back on her finger.

I chuckle and rub her cheek with my thumb,

"Yes, ma'am. I'll sleep soon, I just have to take care of some things, okay?"

She smiles and nods with her eyes closed. I kiss her cheek and walk away, but she calls my name. I turn around and walk back to the bed. Somma moves the covers off of her and goes on her knees while in bed. She wraps her arms around my neck and smiles,

"You have made me the happiest girl in all the galaxies. I love you more than you could ever know. Thank you." she says before passionately kissing me on the lips.

"I love you, too. Get some sleep, a bed has to be cozier than my arms."

"Not true at all." she responds.

Somma lays back down and I cover her again. She closes her eyes and quickly falls asleep. I chuckle as I quietly walk out the room and close the door. I sit on the couch, with Sarge's funeral tomorrow, I take the time to reflect on my time with him. I think about all the lessons he taught me from life advice to how to be a good soldier to which alcohol is best. I didn't always understand him or his methods, but he truly cared about me and everyone in Specter. I hope he's happy wherever he is. I sit on the couch in reflective silence for half an hour, leaning forward on my knees staring blankly. I hear a door open, Somma walks out wearing her nightgown, an all gray short silk skirt with her hair down. She sits down on my lap and puts her arm around me,

"Are you okay?" she asks while gently running her hand through my hair.

"You look so beautiful," I continued, while rubbing her thigh, "What are you doing up?"

"Thank you, my love. I woke up and saw you still were not in bed, I was worried."

"I was just thinking about Sarge. I guess I miss him."

"I miss him too. I remember my first day as a part of Specter, he came up to me and said 'We are going to do great things.' Sarge saw how nervous I was though, he put his hand on my shoulder and said "No need to worry, if I am nowhere around, just listen to Parson, he will keep you all safe. He is quiet, but do not be afraid to approach him or ask him for help. He is always there for everyone. It baffles me how he is like that.' I trusted him and he was right. He was right about us doing great things and he was right about you. Sarge saw the best in all of us. I will always be grateful for him."

"I didn't know he said that about me. Thank you." I respond while wrapping my arms around her waist.

Somma and I hold each other for a few minutes in silence, both of us thinking about Sarge. After a few moments, I kiss Somma's hand,

"We can go to bed now if you want."

"Yes, my love, but I think I prefer you carrying me now." she jokes while putting her arms around my neck and her legs over my thighs playfully.

I chuckle and lift her up. I carry her back to the bed and gently place her down, pulling the covers over her. I go to the bathroom and get ready, putting on my sleeping clothes. It's nothing like Somma's outfit, it's just a black tank top and sweatpants. Similar to what I wear to workout. I find that no matter the scenario, I always look underdressed compared to her. I go back into the bedroom where Somma is waiting for me. I set an alarm for 0600 hours, I lay down next to her, she moves the covers over me before moving next to me. She lays her head on my chest and has her arm around me. I put my arm around her and kiss her head, hoping for a peaceful night with no nightmares or panic attacks.

"Goodnight, Mrs. Parson. I love you." I joke

Somma giggles,

"I cannot wait to be called that. Goodnight, Mr. Parson. I love you."

She kisses my cheek a few times before laying her head back down on my chest. She falls asleep quickly, as I don't really need the covers, I put them back on her so she doesn't get cold. A part of me is scared to fall asleep. I'm going into tonight trying to be positive, after all I just proposed to a beautiful girl who actually said yes and meant it. All things considered, I'm doing very well. I fall asleep, but it felt like my eyes were closed for mere seconds before the alarm goes off at 0600. Maybe that's just how it feels to sleep peacefully. Somma and I wake up at the same time, I sit up in the bed, she sees that she has all the blankets on her,

"You need to keep yourself warm." she says while tossing the blankets over me.

"You're too sweet, but I'm okay, we need to get up."

Somma groans playfully and pulls me back in bed next to her,

"Lay with me just for a few more minutes."

I lay on my side and watch her with a smile on my face for a couple minutes as she slowly wakes up. I move her hair away from her face and kiss her cheek.

"Alright, beautiful, we have to get up now." I say while moving the covers off of her.

She slowly sits up and rubs her eyes, causing them to sparkle more. I grab our uniforms off the hangers and lay them down on the bed. Somma gets out of bed and we get ready and wash up in the bathroom, afterwards she takes off her gown and I take off my clothes. We both put our uniforms on for Sarge's funeral. She and I both put our hair in ponytails, luckily for Somma, she doesn't need to wear makeup to look beautiful and presentable, but she puts some on anyways. Her white ribbon from Tanli keeps her hair up, she has kept it with her this whole time. We leave at 0730 and head to the USC Headquarters. Somma and I were both pretty quiet while getting ready, we mainly communicated by smiling at each other, with Sarge's funeral today it's hard to be happy or talkative. That doesn't stop us from holding hands though, I grab her hand as we walk down the hall. She squeezes my hand tight as we enter the elevator to head down. While the elevator is going down, Somma looks at my uniform,

"You look very handsome." she says.

"Thank you, you look beautiful."

Somma giggles and kisses my hand, the elevator door opens and we walk to the Ranna station. It's pretty busy with everyone trying to head to their jobs or wherever else they need to go. People see our uniforms and try to politely let us get on a Ranna before them, but we let them pass, both Somma and I don't want special treatment. We make it onto a Ranna and sit next to each other.

"You slept peacefully last night. I am glad." Somma says while leaning her head on my shoulder.

"Thank you. How did you sleep?"

"Do not worry about that, my love."

"What happened?"

"I kept trying to wake myself up just in case you had another nightmare or panic attack. I was asleep last time you had one, I woke up too late and I did not know what to do. I was lucky I was able to help in some way. I want to be there for you if you ever start panicking again. I know I could help if I could be there as soon as it starts."

This is what I wanted to avoid. I never wanted to bother her or anyone with my problems. Somma is losing sleep because I can't keep my mind together even in sleep, I'm sure in time I would have been able to get past that panic attack alone and let Somma sleep if I was only quieter.

"I'm sorry. I really do appreciate you, but you don't need to keep yourself up. When it comes to nightmares of panic attacks, I can handle them alone. I don't want you to lose sleep over it. I'm fine with moving to another room if it happens again. I've handled them on my own for years. Don't worry about me, but thank you."

Somma sighs and shows me the ring on her hand,

"This means you are not on your own anymore. You

have not been on your own in a long time, I was always there. Even without a ring, you knew how much I loved and cared about you. I would do anything to keep you safe. I will always worry about you. I do not care how much sleep I lose, I want you to be happy and safe, just like how you make me feel. I know some nights I will also have nightmares and panic attacks, I am sure you will want to be there for me too. No matter how much sleep we lose or no matter what happens in our lives, we handle everything together, okay?"

I smile and kiss her head. Even though I proposed to her, I still saw myself as someone who's all alone, but Somma is right, I have her by my side. Seeing how emotional today is going to be for everyone, I don't want anyone to feel alone. Last time we saw everyone, things left on an awkward note, I hope we can put that aside for now. Looking around the Ranna, we see other soldiers in uniform. It's safe to say they are also on their way to Sarge's funeral. I tend to forget how much impact Sarge has had on the USC that goes beyond Specter. I catch some soldiers eyeing our Specter patches, but I don't think they are looking at them with admiration. I sense some resentment or jealousy towards it, like they think they should have been a part of Specter. Maybe they're right, but if they have any respect for Sarge, they'll keep quiet about it. The effects of the USC forcing Serro to expose us seem to be long lasting. I often worry what will happen if they decide to disband Specter. I don't know if they'll send us to different squads or to different parts of the galaxies, but deeming us unnecessary would be a huge mistake. To an extent, I understand why they don't want Specter. We've had our fair share of injuries in pursuit of completing a job, there's a reason why regular squads and soldiers don't do what we do. It's too dangerous. That being said, when is the last time any squad took down a power like the hold Xenem had? I don't know how to convince them to see reason, but I just hope we can all stay together.

The Ranna stops and we get off to head to the

USC Headquarters. Floods of people including high and low ranking soldiers to people from all over the galaxies are making their way inside. In typical Specter fashion, the squad is off to the side away from everyone. They're all wearing their uniforms. Blaine is sitting on the grass with his back against a tree while Bradley leans on the same tree and the others are standing around waiting, remaining silent. I don't know how long they've been here waiting, but I'm just glad everyone showed up. Somma and I approach them, we all give each other hugs as we mourn the death of someone we looked up to and brought us together. I hear Bradley say something to Somma as he hugs her, I didn't hear everything, but I was able to make out,

"I'm sorry for what I said yesterday. I went too far."

I see Somma smile at him and respond, but I don't know what she said either, but as long as they're both okay now, I don't need to know. To my surprise, Fesio shows up and shakes everyone's hand. He only knew Sarge as a corpse I carried around, he didn't need to come to this, but I still appreciate it. Fesio can sense mine and everyone else's confusion as to why he is here,

"It is good to see you all again. I am sure you are thinking the same thing. Yes, I did not know SSG. Miner, but I watched someone carry around his body for miles without complaining or stopping. It made me think what a great man he must have been. He also brought you all together, Specter freed my home and I suppose I have him to thank for assembling the team that did it. If you do not want me to go, I understand."

"You're more than welcome to join us, Sarge would have liked you." I respond.

No one is Specter has any objections, I think they are all starting to look past the fact he is from Xenem. Before we enter I pull Somma to the side,

"Should we tell them?" I ask while pointing at the ring.

Somma smiles and nods, I hold her hand and we walk back to everyone,

"Excuse me, everyone? We have an announcement." I say.

Everyone turns to us, I lift Somma's hand up showing her ring. Everyone erupts in joy. They all give us another hug, except Blaine who remains seated and claps.

"A bit soon, but congrats." he says while clapping.

I didn't expect a big reaction from him, but clapping and a backhanded compliment works fine for me, it's the best we're going to get from him. We all head in and walk towards the cemetery behind the Headquarters where all soldiers are buried. We join everyone at Sarge's grave. We see his closed casket covered with the flag of the USC, at that moment, the emotions hit us all. Serro approaches us,

"It is good to see you all. I know SSG. Miner would be happy knowing you all showed up. I realize this is an emotional time, but we must remain strong. That is what he would have wanted. We will be starting shortly, we have reserved spots for you all up front. Take your seats."

Fesio, knowing he is not a part of Specter, finds a seat somewhere else while we head to the front row. Ben walks up to us to say hello, we all give him a hug. Sarge's death is even harder on Ben, it clearly hit him hard and seeing his casket didn't help. He did not say much to us, which is understandable, but he tried his best to keep his classic smile. I walk him to an open seat and sit him down before shaking his hand. I wanted to tell Ben about my proposal to Somma, but I could tell he wasn't in a celebratory mood, we'll tell him at another time. I know he will be happy to hear it. After I walk back to my seat, my parents walk up to me and give me a hug. They only met Sarge once in the prison cell on Xenem, but they knew how much he meant to me. They go to the others and shake their hands and give their condolences. When they shake Somma's hand, they see the ring. I fully expected both of them to freak out and storm off, but my mother and father both smile and congratulate us before giving Somma a hug. I figured Somma was worried about their reaction, but it's like my mother said, there was no stopping how I felt so she knew what to expect. I suspect they do have some concerns, but they are probably waiting till a better time to talk about it.

Just like Ben, I walk them to open seats and give them both a hug. There aren't enough seats for everyone, I was lucky enough to find some for Ben and my parents. The remaining crowd has to stand, but they don't seem to mind. Serro walks up to the podium next to Sarge's coffin. He looks at it for a few moments, holding back tears. He looks down and shakes his head in disbelief. We all sit down in our reserved seats, Somma and I sit next to each other, holding hands. I carried Sarge all around the wilds of Xenem just so he could get a proper burial. I must admit, I'm proud I was able to accomplish that. That being said, it truly hurts seeing his coffin, but it's what he deserves. He was a true hero, one who must be remembered. Always.

LIVES OF HEROES

The crowd quiets down. The only sounds being heard is the wind and people sniffling. It takes a while for Serro to speak, his relationship with Sarge seems to be closer than any of us thought. It makes sense, they've fought together for years. I remember Sarge was the only one who stuck around when Serro proposed his idea for the squad. Fesio gave credit to Sarge for creating Specter, but Serro had just as much to do with it. I recall at the time wishing I had never snuck into that meeting, Serro was about to kill me, it was a nightmare. Plus, I didn't like the idea or the thought of who would be in the squad to begin with. I had a lot of issues with the whole situation, but now, I would do anything to keep Specter together and safe. Serro straightens his uniform after composing himself, he leans towards the microphone,

"Hello, everyone. Thank you all for coming. We are here to mourn the tragic passing of SSG. Richard Jameson Miner. I worked closely with him for years and I never took the time to appreciate it, but he was truly a one of a kind soldier and a better person. In my time with him, he never once showed fear or cowardice whether he was facing an enemy or a peer. I recall asking him how was able to never show fear, he simply told me, 'The key to living forever is acting like you *can* live forever. Why show fear when you cannot die, right? Whether I am shot or stabbed or tortured, I know damn well I will be remembered for my actions so therefore, I know I will live forever and cannot truly die.' I did not quite understand what he meant at the time, but standing here, remember this great man proves he was right. As many of you know now, SSG. Miner was involved with a formerly hidden operation, a squad under the name 'Specter". He fearlessly led them for months before his unfortunate death while in pursuit of freeing Chancellor's Valkis Tyro's reign over Xenem. Specter is present here today and are welcomed to come up and say a few words if they wish."

  Everyone in Specter looks at each other, for the most part, everyone in the squad is quiet and does not say much. I know they all loved Sarge, but don't want to say anything. I know they don't mean to be rude, I'm the same way, I hate speaking, especially publicly. After a few moments, they all turn to me and smile. Somma rubs my arm and nods at me while smiling. I take that as code for they think I should be the one to speak. I was unsure if I was going to speak, but I guess it's decided. I look down and take a deep breath, I open my eyes to see my hands and fingers are covered in blood. From what? It could be anything. Everything I have been through puts blood on my hands. This is not an ideal time for something like this, I'm not sure if it's real or my mind is playing tricks on me, but my hands begin to tremble and I sit frozen. Somma places her hand on my hand, I close my eyes and open them again. The blood is gone, all I feel is Somma's hand. Finally relaxed, I kiss Somma's cheek and stand up. Serro smiles as I approach the podium. He shakes my hand as he steps away to the side.

  Standing at the podium, I look out into the crowd and I'm shocked by the amount of people who showed up. It didn't help my anxiety seeing all those people. Everyone in Specter, besides Somma, probably had no idea about my anxiety and the thousands of other issues I have, but now they can see what a mess I am. I look back at them while breathing heavily, they look confused and concerned, but I look at Somma who smiles and blows a kiss at me. That instantly calms me down. I look down and take a deep breath in then breathe out. I clench my necklaces, I look back up and finally gain the courage to speak.

  "Thank you, LT. Serro and thank you all for coming. My

name is CPL. Clark Parson. I speak on behalf of everyone in Specter when I say this is truly a devastating and painful loss. All of us in Specter and many others in the USC affectionately referred to SSG. Miner as 'Sarge', he didn't mind it. In fact, I think he loved it. We all saw Sarge as a father figure. We didn't have our families with us, so having someone like Sarge with us to teach us about life, how to fight and be a good person impacted our lives more than he could ever know. I didn't always see eye to eye with Sarge or agree with his methods, but he always knew what to do, I just never saw it. He was truly an incredible leader and soldier who saved our lives more times than we can count. I was lucky enough to be raised by my amazing parents who shaped me into the man I am today, but Sarge shaped me into the soldier I was born to be. I knew no matter what happened, he would always be there to make sense of things and would always be there to fight by our side. I don't like talking about this, but in our time in Xenem, we all witnessed Sarge die. His body was thrown away to the wilds of Xenem. After dealing with unfortunate circumstances of my own that separated me from my squad for days, I found his body in the middle of nowhere in the wilds of Xenem. I knew he did not deserve to rot in the middle of nowhere, least of all on Xenem. I decided to carry his body all the way back for a proper burial. I was lost and confused, I was in pain and exhausted from my time there. As some of you may know, I was declared dead while trying to get out of Xenem with my squad. In death, I saw Sarge. He was right there with me and I remember what he told me, 'I think I made the right choice picking you for Specter, you've become everything I knew you could be, son.' I didn't believe him. I felt like a failure. Doomed to spend eternity in the afterlife ashamed of what I didn't do, but he made me see it's all about what I *did* rather than what I didn't do. It was advice I appreciated, but it wouldn't do much good since I died. I was given a second chance though, he told me it's not my time yet, from there I woke up." I begin crying mid sentence, "He wanted me to tell everyone in Specter that he's proud of them and to always fight for what is right. Fight forever. Before I was sent back, the last thing he said to me was 'Till I see you again, kid.' There will never be another Sarge, but he was right. Someone like him who will always be remembered will never die. So, Sarge, I promise to make you proud every day and to always fight for what's right. We all love you. Thank you for everything. Till I see you again, sir."

I grab his arrow and feather and Noli necklaces from my pocket that I grabbed while getting ready and place them inside of his casket to get buried with him. I stand by his casket and salute with tears falling down my face. Serro walks up to me and shake my hand again,

"That was wonderful, thank you. You may take your seat."

I walk to everyone in Specter who are all crying. They all get up and we share an emotional group hug. We all sit down again, Somma kisses my cheek,

"That was beautiful. I know he is proud of you and all of us." she says while wiping my tears.

The funeral continues for another hour with his friends and remaining family coming up to speak, including PVT. Kemper. Ben also spoke, giving an incredible and powerful goodbye to Sarge. He spoke of his time with him and Auldin when they were younger. All the races they had to see who was the fastest, all the nights they spent exploring other worlds and meeting new people, all the games and conversations they had about random things. It sounds like they all had an amazing life and a one of a kind friendship. It's truly a shame how they were all estranged for so long. I know that Sarge wouldn't want all of us to sit around crying over him, but it's hard not to when someone has impacted so many people's lives. The funeral concludes with an old military tradition from Earth, mainly the United States, the Twenty-One Gun Salute. It's customary for soldiers in the USC to be buried according to how their home planet buries their soldiers. Keeping in tradition with customary burial for soldiers on

Earth, we all salute as the guns fire off. Afterwards, people walk up to the casket and drop flowers and various other gifts for Sarge. He is lowered into his grave slowly, we watch in tears and we slowly lose sight of it as it goes lower. We're all invited to toss dirt on his coffin before he is finally buried. A group of people, including Specter, walk up and toss dirt as one final goodbye.

We knew today would be emotional, but I've never seen any of us cry so hard or so much in my time with them. We all head back inside to a room for a small celebration honoring Sarge's memory. The room has food and drinks for guests. On the wall, there is a photo of Sarge wearing his service uniform, next to that are multiple screens displaying news articles all in various languages talking about him through his life. Sarge was a private person who didn't speak much of his past, so these stories and articles are new to us. We look through the old articles and they're all amazing, one headline reads *"Young USC Soldier Prevents Catastrophe, Saves Hundreds in Crash Landing."* Another reads, *"USC Frees Desha of Coalition Control, Under Leadership of Lieutenant Richard Miner."* There are hundreds of articles from the past being displayed all around us. I don't know how long we stood there watching and reading, but every article and headline was more interesting than the last.

"What are the chances people write about us one day?" Rachel asks while looking around.

"They already have." Serro says from behind.

We all turn and see Serro approach us holding a pad, he turns it to us showing a news article talking about Specter. There's a photo someone took of all of us standing at the podium the day Serro exposed Specter. We really do look shocked and confused in the picture. The headline reads *"Ten Unsung Heroes. Unknown Squadron Frees Xenem."* We all look at the article with mixed emotions. For the most part, we're all happy that the result of our sacrifices is now immortalized. That being said, we never wanted our identities to be revealed and an article about us. What we do could put those in the Confederacy on high alert. No one has revealed to anyone in the USC that Somma was forced to betray us, but a part of me is worried someone did find out and wrote about it. I'm sure I am worried about nothing, but it was all a nightmare that I still think about.

"I know none of you wanted Specter to be known about, but I must say, I would feel proud to have this written about me, anyone would. Now, come with me, there are some people who would like to meet you all." Serro says.

He leads us to a group of people, high ranking soldiers and officials. I stay back while everyone else shakes their hands and speaks with them. They all ask about where we came from and what inspired us to join the war. To be honest, I didn't pay much attention to what they said. I was already feeling uneasy from being around so many people, plus I still feel the loss of Sarge. It stopped me from engaging with the people we were talking to, but they didn't notice me staying silent. I look around and see an exit, everyone is busy talking, so I sneak out away from everyone. No one notices I left and they probably won't notice I'm gone. It's been that way since high school. I go back to the cemetery and approach Sarge's grave which has already been covered with dirt. His gravestone has a Christian cross on top and reads *"Here lies Staff Sergeant Richard Jameson Miner. A fierce soldier and inspiring leader. John 15:13."*

John 15:13, "Greater love has no one than this, that someone lay down his life for his friends." It's hard to imagine Sarge believing in any god or being religious, none of us even knew he was Christian. I think I spotted a cross necklace hidden away on him before, but I thought I was just seeing things. I stand at his grave in silence with my hands in my pockets. I know Sarge is out there watching and listening, I have so much I wish I could say to him, but speaking to his grave is the next best thing.

"Hello, sir. I hope you're doing well. I'm sure you'd kick our teeth in for crying over you, so I apologize for that. I guess you know about Serro exposing Specter and the USC considering disbanding us, I imagine you were just as pissed off as we were, if not more. I guess things only get more complicated now. It's not all bad, Somma and I moved in together and I proposed to her. For some reason she said yes. I should thank you, sir. You brought us all together. I met the girl of my dreams because of this crazy squad. I wish you were still here. You'd fight the USC to keep Specter and you know we would fight by your side. We all miss you, life isn't the same without the smell of your cigars all around us. I know you're watching over us. We'll continue to try to make you proud every day. We know if we don't, you'll just haunt us. I'm glad you caught me eavesdropping on the Specter meeting, it led me to becoming who I am today. Sure, I died a few times, but I'm happy and safe, not to mention a better soldier. I know Auldin is up there with you laughing at me, tell him we say hi. Strangely, I miss him. I miss you both. Keep us safe, sir. Thank you for everything."

I close my eyes and sigh. I hear someone walk up to me,
"I knew I would find you here." Somma says.

When I first met her and worked with her, it was nearly impossible to hear her footsteps or hear her walk up and behind me, but I think I've gotten better at hearing her footsteps. They're still quiet, but I guess I'm trained to hear it now. Somma holds onto my arm and rests her head on it while looking at Sarge's grave. We stay silent while looking at his tombstone. I hear Somma sniffle and feel her grab my arm tighter. I take my hand out of my pocket and wipe my tears, Somma turns to me and goes on her toes to kisses my cheek. She moves closer to Sarge's grave,

"Hello, sir. I am sorry, there is a lot I want to say, but I do not know where to start. I suppose I should start with I miss you. You always knew how to make me feel confident and strong, I never felt like I belonged anywhere, but Specter changed that. You have given me kind, strong and supportive friends and best of all, an amazing man I will spend my life with. I do not have much else to say besides thank you and I will never forget you. I also want to thank you for sending back Clark, we almost lost him, but you knew he was meant to stay with us. Help me protect him, please. You know how reckless he is. We will come back to visit soon."

Somma walks back and gives me a tight hug. We move to a nearby bench where we sit and hold each other in silence. We do not need to say anything, I'm just glad she's with me. Somma looks an empty grave near us and sighs,

"May I ask you a question, my love?"

I nod my head.

"I know you do not like thinking about it and if you do not want to answer I understand. How does it feel when you die?"

I remain silent as I think about my answer. I've never thought about it before. Even in the moment of death, I was filled with multiple emotions. She's right, I don't like thinking about it, but if she really wants to know, I guess I could try to come up with an honest answer. I sigh while taking a seat on a bench. I look down,

"I imagine it's different for everyone. Depending how they die or what happens, I'd think it's all different." I get up and walk to the empty grave, staring at it, "For me, I was angry. I was angry at how it happened, I was angry about who did it. I was also heartbroken, the last thing I saw was you and everyone else crying. I wanted to get up and hold you, telling you everything was okay. I wanted to use all my strength to get up and leave with everyone, but I couldn't. I tried so hard to make it out alive. It didn't feel real. It was painful and cold, it was a mixture of emotions. Anger, sadness, regret, pain. It was awful. I could've ended up in one of these graves or-"

Somma pulls me away from the empty grave, interrupting me and wrapping me in a tight hug. I hear her sniffling while holding onto me tight. I kiss her head, trying to make her feel better,

"I will not let anything like that happen to you

everagain. I promise." she says.

"I'm not going anywhere."

Somma kisses my cheek and continues to hold me. There's something oddly romantic about holding her at a cemetery. She holds my hand as we walk back into the building, I hear her giggling as she wipes her tears. She steps in front of me and grabs my other hand,

"You remind me of something I learned about your planet." she says while swinging my arms around, "Earth has these small animals named Cats and people believed they had nine lives. That sounds like you!"

"I guess I have seven lives left, I'll make it count." I respond while twirling her.

It makes sense. I should have died twice. Blaine referred to me as a walking corpse, maybe that's just what I am. That won't stop me from enjoying the time I have left, who knows when I'll die next? Somma giggles as I twirl her around,

"How lucky I am to marry the man with nine lives!" she says.

"It looks like I'm going to be here for a while, you're stuck with me."

"I am more than okay with that, my love."

Somma kisses my lips and pulls me inside the building,

"I know you do not like crowds or speaking to people, but LT. Serro really wants you to meet the people we were speaking with. They want to meet the legendary CPL. Clark 'Nine Lives' Parson!"

I shyly smile and look down, I don't care if they think I'm a legend. Personally, I don't think I am a legend, not even close. There's not much for me to tell. Somma knows more than anyone how I feel meeting new people. She lifts my head up, rubbing my cheek with her thumb.

"Do it for me?" she asks while smiling.

She knows it's essentially impossible for me to say no to her. I sigh and nod my head. She kisses my cheek and grabs my hand. She leads me back to the room. I suppose it was rude what I did, if they did notice I was gone, then it's a surprise to me. We reach the entrance to the room, we see the rest of Specter still speaking with everyone. I sigh and walk in the room with Somma right behind me going back to speak with other people, I don't know how she is so social. Serro marches up to me,

"Where have you been?" he asks while leading me to the group of people Specter was speaking with. "Everyone, this is CPL. Clark Parson, second-in-command behind SSG. Miner."

A General from Desha, named Orvin Cromwen, extends his hand to me,

"Good to meet you. How are you doing with all of this? I imagine you were rather close with SSG. Miner, especially after your wonderful speech." he says while shaking my hand.

"I am doing okay, sir, thank you."

"Those scars on your face, how did you get them?"

I break eye contact and look down,

"Two knife slashes, sir."

"I see. You do not speak much, do you, my boy?"

I shake my head. GEN. Cromwen nods his head, understanding my silent nature. Cromwen was an odd looking man, compared to what most people from Desha look like. He's a rounder gentleman, wrinkles cover his face and an old military uniform. I shake everyone else's hands, they don't try to speak much with me. They were right next to me when I barely spoke to GEN. Cromwen, they knew I wouldn't speak much to any of them. After introducing myself to everyone, I look at Serro who understands that I wish to leave. Without saying a word, he nods his head once. I nod back and turn back to everyone,

"It was nice meeting you all." I say while fidgeting with my fingers.

They all nod their heads and smile. I walk away, ashamed. I feel terrible for how I acted. I didn't want to offend anyone or make it seem like I wasn't interested in them. I guess I still have a long way to go as far as being social goes. I find an empty table away from most of the people and sit down. I unbutton my coat and lay my head down on the table in frustration and shame. It's not the best look, but I've already made a fool out of myself. I hear someone sit next me,

"I was never one for crowds, either." Fesio says.

I lift my head up and see him sitting next to me, I rub my eyes in frustration,

"I don't want this. I never wanted fame or glory or to meet all these people. We were just doing our job. I guess I'm weird. Everyone else seems to like meeting all these new people and having stories written about us. Even Kierra is speaking more than she ever has."

"I see. Well, you are to be married to someone who is very social, she is going to want you to be social with her, what happens then?" he asks, throwing me off.

"I've thought about that a lot. I would never question my decision to propose to Somma, but I don't know how to be the man she deserves. She grew up going to gatherings and dances surrounded by people, my life was the opposite. She knows that too, but still said yes to my proposal. I don't want her to regret her decision later on. I've been scared of losing her physically, but I know I can also lose her emotionally. I guess I just have to work on being more social."

I slam my head back on the table, Fesio remains silent letting me work through whatever is wrong with me. It's silent for a few minutes before I hear another person sit down to my left.

"Fesio, may I have a moment alone with him, please?" Somma says.

Her voice is always soothing, enough to calm me down, but the shame remains. Fesio gets up and walks away. She moves her chair closer to me and I feel her gently rub my arm.

"LT. Serro told me what happened."

"I'm sorry. I tried. I just can't talk to people." I respond with my head still on the table.

"I know. It is okay. Can you talk to me at least?"

I slowly move my head up and nod my head trying to make eye contact with her. It's an incredible mystery how I'm able to talk to her. Talking to people in general is hard for me, but talking to someone as beautiful as Somma is usually a much bigger challenge. I'm still quiet around her, but I feel more comfortable speaking to her than anyone else. Somma kisses my cheek and smiles,

"You can speak with me just fine, how is that?" she asks.

"I wish I knew."

She frowns and rests her head on my shoulder. If I had to guess, the reason why it's a little easier speaking to Somma is because it is easier speaking with people you love and you know loves you back. It feels safer to speak my mind. Despite our differences socially, I wouldn't want marry anyone else. I just hope she will always feel the same way. Somma moves hef head away from arm and rubs my arm slowly,

"I heard what you said to Fesio."

I look down, completely avoiding eye contact with her. She places her hand on mine, I look up at her.

"There has not been a single moment where I regret agreeing to marry you, she continued, "there will never be a day where I regret it. Yes, we are a bit different, socially, but that will never change how I feel about you. I will marry you and it will be the happiest day of my life no matter what. Spending my life with you is a gift I will forever cherish."

I kiss Somma's hand and sigh in relief. We sit together, watching people conversing with each other and reading the news articles. After a few minutes, Ben walks up to us and sits down,

"Well, I doubt Richard would recall meeting any of these people who claim to have known him. Though, he would have loved all the alcohol here." he jokes.

We still haven't told Ben about the proposal. We saw him somewhere in the room speaking with people earlier, but didn't have the chance to talk to him, none of us have. While we have him alone, now is as good of a time as any.

"How are you doing?" I ask Ben,

"It is a sad day, truly. There is solace in fact that Richard is in a better place, Auldin too. That was a lovely speech you gave, Clark. He was a great man. You remind me of him when he was younger, always helping people no matter the cost. Richard was a wild and reckless person, but he always wanted to do good, like you. You are a lot quieter, though."

"Thank you. We do have some good news we think will cheer you up."

Ben smiles. Somma lifts her hand up showing her ring. Ben gasps and laughs,

"Amazing! Congratulations, my friends! I had a feeling you would marry each other, a perfect pairing only the gods could have created. The people of Tanli would be thrilled to hear about this, they do ask about you all a lot. Would it be too much to ask for you all to visit for a little and perhaps tell them about your proposal. I understand Specter will be busy after this with your award ceremony, but if you could find the time, we would appreciate it!"

We knew Ben would be happy for us. As far as Specter being busy, we haven't been told any news or updates about anything concerning us. I'm more than happy to return to Vonra and Tanli. Despite everything terrible that happened to me there, it's still the place where Somma and I kissed for the first time. It'll always have a special place in my heart. On our last days there, I told Somma we'd return to Tanli someday, now's the perfect time.

"What do you think? We can spend some time in Tanli?" I ask Somma.

"I was hoping you would ask!"

Ben smiles,

"Wonderful! I will speak with others and ask them to join us."

Somma helps Ben out of his seat and walks him to the rest of Specter. I'm hoping we can all leave right now. I've embarrassed myself enough I'd say. Somma walks back and sits next to me,

"He is talking to everyone about it. All of us going back to Kana makes me think back. Do you remember where I first kissed you?" she asks while buttoning up my coat.

"You first kissed me on the cheek in front of Ben's outpost while I was keeping watch. You kissed me on the lips soon after that. It was also at the outpost after those thieves nearly beat me to death. I was resting on a cot while you were taking care of me, you kissed me and everything seemed so calm, peaceful and safe. Every kiss since then has felt the same."

Somma shyly looks down and smiles. She holds my hand and kisses it. I always think about that day, it's amazing what it all led to. Not many people from Earth, if anyone, can say they are engaged to a Vespin. One as perfect as Somma. She looks back up and giggles,

"I remember after I kissed your cheek, I immediately wanted to do it again. It was difficult for me to fall asleep afterwards, I kept thinking about you throughout the night. Then, when I closed my eyes as I kissed your lips, I saw a future with you in it and I knew it was all I wanted. In my time on Xenem, it was rare I had dreams that did not terrify me, but made me smile. One dream I had was you proposing to me. I did not know if it would ever happen, but I hoped every day it would. When you did propose at the tree, I was ready to say yes as soon as you went down on your knee, but I wanted to let you finish your amazing speech, it was so beautiful. It seems dreams can come true."

I smile and kiss her lips, I don't think I will ever deserve someone like her. Ben walks back to us with Specter, Ben looks so small next to everyone, especially Blaine.

"They have agreed to go, but I believe the USC will be awarding you all soon. Congratulations, my friends!" Ben exclaims.

The ceremony will be taking place in another room, one usually held for press conferences. We see people start leaving to go to the other room. Serro signals us to follow him. I quickly fix my hair and walk out with everyone. Walking into the room, we take a seat on the stage, I look into the crowd and see my parents. My mother is waving at me while my father gives me two thumbs up. I wave back at them, but I start to notice, I don't think I've met anyone's parents or families in Specter, besides Blaine's family and Somma's amazing father.

"Are any of your families coming?" I ask everyone,

Rachel scoffs and shakes her head. Along with Somma, Rachel is another person who I figured didn't have any family coming to see them. Just as well, if I met Rachel's father, I'd probably end up punching him in the face. Everyone else has their family coming to the ceremony. If my introduction to them is anything like what happened with people Serro introduced me to, they will not like me. To the left of us are high ranking members of the USC, some of which we have already met. Serro walks on the stage and takes a seat on the left side, GEN. Cromwen goes to the podium and smiles at the crowd,

"Please take your seats." he continued as people in the audience sits down, "Thank you all for coming. It is most unfortunate that we live in a time of great uncertainty, young men and women from all over the vast galaxies risk their lives every day to secure peace and hope for our homes. It is important that we honor and celebrate the brave warriors who fight for us, but there are soldiers who face great adversity to succeed in the field. Today, we are here to award the special group of men and women of the squad known as Specter. Through incredible odds, Specter survived the harsh and devastating environment of Xenem. Not only did they survive, but with the help of the rest of the USC, were able to effectively end the cruel reign of Chancellor Valkis Tyro. Leader of Specter, the late SSG. Richard Miner, died in the line of duty during his time in Xenem and unfortunately could not see his squad accomplish what others thought impossible or deemed too dangerous. Little is known of what happened in Xenem during their campaign, but we are thrilled that the rest of Specter made it out alive, but not unscathed. What they accomplished will be documented and celebrated for years to come, so it is my great honor to award CPL. Clark Parson, SPC. Blaine Carlston, PVT. Carden Reddina, Kierra Shuua, Rachel Denza, Somma Juna, Bradley Dillon, Martin and Mitchell Lane with the Medal of Torious. Their sacrifices in the face of danger shall inspire us all for years to come, we thank them all for their service. Congratulations, Specter!"

We all stand as the crowd cheers. Cromwen approaches us with another soldier standing by him holding a box containing nine medals. As he puts a medal on each of us, he thanks us and shakes our hands. After all the medals are put on us, we stand at attention as photos are taken of us. Cromwen signals me to the podium to make a speech. After my last interaction with him, I don't want to disappoint him further, so I reluctantly step forward. I lift the microphone up closer to my face, the audience quiets down. Two speeches in front of a crowd in one day is rough, but I don't have much of a choice.

"Thank you, GEN. Cromwen, thank you to everyone in the USC and those who came to support us today. As many of you can imagine, this is a difficult day for us, but on behalf of Specter and myself, we truly appreciate this honor. The thing is, there is one problem with all of this." I stop and lift the medal around my neck, "This award goes to those who sacrificed their lives through pain and tragedy and while I agree, Specter deserves this award, we aren't the only ones who should be getting praise. GEN. Cromwen mentioned how we had help from the USC to free Xenem and while that is true, I would like to mention a few people in particular who helped us. LT. Jovell Serro, PVT. Charlie Kemper and a couple people who aren't a part of the USC, but without them, we would not have made it out alive. Fesio Telkit, one of the bravest warriors I have ever met and can always rely on us to repay him for all he has done. Ben Tawin, a man who took us in during our journey to Xenem and offered us food and shelter as well as his friendship. He flew us out of Xenem safely and we are glad to have met him. I would also like to mention a man who we once hated. He was our enemy, but sacrificed his life to destroy Tyro's tower. Former Xenem soldier, CPT. Auldin Leezol. He wanted to kill me and my squad and we wanted to kill him too, but after Xenem betrayed him, we had a common enemy and in time, his desire to kill us went away, he was another casualty of Xenem's fall. He wasn't always the greatest person, but he proved what a good man he can be, giving me and Specter the chance to escape while destroying what was left of Tyro's reign. I want to thank them all for their help and sacrifice. They all deserve this medal. We are happy to be here and thank the USC for this incredible award."

The crowd cheers as I go back to my seat. Everyone is Specter is also clapping, Somma rubs my arm and kisses my cheek as I sit down. After the ceremony ends, we walk off the stage to greet our families before leaving for Tanli. I think I have spoken enough today, but I have to meet with their families. It's what Sarge would have done.

REST AND RELAXATION

I'm a bit nervous to meet everyone's families. Before I meet anyone's parents, I know my parents want to see me again. I walk up to them and they give me a hug together, I think they are happier that I got the medal than I am. After hugging me, my father asks where Somma is. I look around and see her sitting down on the stairs leading to the stage with Rachel. It makes sense, both of them unfortunately don't have family here, so I'd imagine sitting there waiting is the only thing they thought they could do. As I walk to Somma, I notice she's looking down at the ground, like she is thinking back to memories of her family wishing they were here. I approach her and kneel in front of her, she looks up at me and her face lights up with joy, giving me her classic beautiful smile. I reach for her hand and she grabs it, squeezing it tight,

"I thought you were the social one." I joke.
"How are your parents?"
"They want to see you."

Somma looks surprised, she quickly fixes her hair and stands up. She turns to Rachel and hugs her,

"We must not be sad. We have family right here, Rachel."

After letting go, Rachel smiles at Somma and grabs her hand in appreciation. Somma's hair didn't even need fixing, it somehow never looks bad. I pat Rachel's shoulder,

"Are you going to be okay?" I ask her.
"Yes, sir."

I lean and whisper,
"You can just call me Clark."

Rachel smiles and nods, playfully saluting me,

"Yes, sir." she responds mockingly.

I salute back at her. I'm starting to want just having everyone call each other by their names, I've never cared for addressing others by their ranks. Too formal for me. Whatever fate is ahead of Specter, I want us all to be seen as equals. No ranks or titles. Somma was the first person I let call me by my first name. I figured with Rachel being alone on a day like this, letting her be another person to call me by my first name would cheer her up a little. Somma holds my hand as we approach my parents. I think Somma is still concerned over how my mother feels about her, as am I. My mother is one of the kindest people I know, but I still don't know if she trusts Somma. We last saw them at Sarge's funeral a few hours ago, my parents didn't say much, but we didn't think much of it given the circumstances. They did seem happy about the proposal, my mom especially. She's hard to read sometimes. We approach my parents, Somma waves at them with a shy smile. My father, who was quick to accept Somma as a part of my life, opens his arms for a hug. Somma laughs and hugs him, he congratulates her, I was never worried about how he would greet her. Somma turns to my mother and gives her a hug, my mother also congratulates her.

Somma decides to stay and talk to my parents while I met everyone else's families. I've already met Blaine's family, they are clones of him, but I still feel it's right to say hello. Blaine has two younger brothers who constantly try to wrestle each other, but his parents, Johnny and Lisa, seem to have them on a tight leash. Trying to be on their best behavior, when I approach them, they all politely shake my hand when I greet them. I didn't spend much time with them, I only had time to say hello before going to everyone else's families. Carden, an only child, had very quiet parents, but were friendly enough. The Lane twins had a big family, 3 sisters and another brother, all of them loud and expressive, quite the opposite of the twins. They opted to hug me instead of shaking hands. Kierra is also an only child, her mother showed up, but Kierra didn't seem thrilled to be in her company. As I approach them, I hear her mother,

"I hear there is a way to turn your hair and eyes into that of a normal Matuan! You can be like the rest of us."

Before Kierra can respond, I walk up to them.

"I think she's perfect just the way she is. Hello, CPL. Clark Parson, wonderful to finally meet you, ma'am."

I extend my hand to her mother, Danila, she scowls at me before reluctantly shaking my hand. I risked a lot with my comment, but seeing where Kierra gets her insecurity from made what I thought inside slip out. Before leaving the already awkward situation, I shake Kierra's hand,

"Thank you, sir." she says with a smile.

"Call me Clark."

I try to find Bradley's family, but it seems they have left before I could meet them. I've finally met everyone, now is the best time to head out and go to Tanli. Everything was a bit of a blur to me. What I do remember is letting everyone know they may call me by my first name. They all looked happy to hear the news. Blaine didn't seem to care, he calls me by my last name most of the time anyways. I'd assume everyone is fine with me calling them by their first names and having others in Specter do the same. Somma and I gather everyone while saying goodbye to our families and other people. Somma and I say goodbye to my parents and LT. Serro, who thanks me for mentioning him in my speech, when I shake his hand he looks at me in a way that seems like he is saying "Work on your social skills."

After saying goodbye to a few other people, we say our goodbyes to Fesio, who also thanks me. We ask him if he wants to join us in going to Tanli, but he politely declines as he feels tired and is about to leave too. Martin asks Serro permission to take a ship to Kana as he was saying goodbye. Surprisingly, Serro agrees. We leave the conference room, heading to the landing strip where the USC keeps their ships. It's a mostly silent walk to the ship we'll be taking. It's not that we're not happy to return to Kana, but it's been an already emotional day, we expect people in Tanli to also feel a bit emotional. Sarge seemed to really like the people there and they seemed to really like him.

We board the ship, Kierra and Ben go to the pilot seats up front while we all stay in the back. Ben teaches her how to fly the ship. He was familiar with the model from when he used to fly with Richard and Auldin. Seeing the playful smile on her face, I feel like Kierra knows how to fly this ship. I don't doubt she knows how to fly anything, especially with all the reading she does. I thought I read a lot, but Kierra has us all beat. She still lets Ben teach her out of kindness. Kierra takes off the ship easily without any hesitation or confusion like she has been flying this ship for years. Ben laughs,

"Clever Matuan, I should have figured!" he jokes.

We leave Vespis and head for Vonra, it shouldn't take too long especially with this ship. I hold Somma's hand and Rachel looks at the ring,

"It's beautiful. Do you know where you're going to get married?" she asks.

Somma looks at me, waiting for me to answer. There are a few places I have thought of, but I haven't run them by Somma yet.

"Nothing has been decided, yet. The tree in Felv near the Headquarters would be nice, it's where I proposed to Somma. There's also the Heleia Fields on Vonra. We spent a lot of time there before going to Xenem. We're still thinking about it."

Somma smiles at me and kisses my hand before looking back at everyone,

"You are all invited, of course!"

Everyone smiles at her, on such an emotional day, it's nice to see everyone smile. The meeting about Juna's trail divided Specter, but it seems with the funeral and the news of the proposal, everyone has put it aside for now. As predicted, it was a short trip to Vonra. As we enter its atmosphere, we see Vonra. It looks completely different, still a work in progress, but it looks cleaner and less bleak. Ben looks at Vonra with a prideful smile on his face. We're all shocked to see the progress being made. Last we saw, it was a crumbling, filthy city covered with bodies and blood. It looks completely different. Freeing Vonra came at a cost for all of us, but I don't think any of us regret what we did. After Vonra, we pass by the fields of colored sand, it's just as amazing as the first time we saw it. When we first landed here, we weren't able to appreciate the beauty. I guess leaving a broken down ship after crashing takes your mind off such things. I have a feeling leaving Kana is going to be hard, it was hard enough leaving the first time.

    We land in Tanli Village near the markets, a part of me is anxious to get out. I know the people want to see us, but I still get nervous. We leave our bags on the ship and head for the door. We straighten our coats and fix our hair, we still want to look presentable. Last they saw us, we wore old, raggy clothes that were given to us by Ben. Seeing us in clean USC uniforms will shock them again, but I don't want them to look at us any differently. We first arrived in Tanli wearing our dirtied gear and uniforms, but I think they got to know us all once we got out of the uniforms and started acting like regular people. I consider taking my coat off at least, but no one else is. I think everyone else wants a bit more adulation than they will already get.

    I help Somma straighten her coat and fix her collar. I kiss her on the lips and take her hand, walking her to the door to wait for everyone. Somma and I take our hair out of our ponytails and after Bradley fixes his hair trying to make himself look like a celebrity, he smacks the button to open the door. As soon as it opens, we are surrounded by people who, at first, look confused, but once they recognize us all, they cheer and wave at us. We feel so much love and support from these amazing people, most of them I personally recognize from when I bought that ridiculous outfit for the celebration after freeing Vonra. It was great seeing everyone, even Ben was thrilled for us, cheering along with the others. It's not often we get this sort of praise, for so long I felt like the bad guy fighting in this seemingly pointless war, but after some time, especially here, I feel like a hero of sorts. We're all heroes here, at least to the people of Tanli and Vonra. We truly appreciate this reaction from everyone. We couldn't have imagined a warmer welcome.

The people here look great. In much better condition than the last time we saw them. It seems there is a governing body here that formed an alliance with the USC, I'd say that's how the progress in Vonra is moving so quickly. We all walk off the ship into the small crowd that formed around us. We shake the hands of as many people as we can. Most of them still can't understand us, but we're all still wearing the translator device Carden gave us, letting us understand everyone. It hasn't failed us yet. Everyone is shouting incredible kind greetings and compliments as we pass through. It's a bit overwhelming, but it beats a crowd yelling obscenities at us like they typically do.

Ben leads us through the crowd to the heart of the marketplace where the celebration took place. He walks up with us to a structure that's still a work in progress, but it looks like a sculpture. It is made out of different pieces of Noli and from what we can tell with what has been built so far, we see an arrow.

"All of us began working on this after we heard the news of Richard's death. When it is finished, it will serve as a memorial to Richard and a sign of appreciation to all of you. It is still a work in progress, but we are creating the Specter's logo. You all have done more than you realize, this is the least we could do." Ben says standing next to the structure.

We're all speechless. Never has anyone done such a kind gesture for any of us. So far, it looks amazing. After we thank Ben and everyone else, Ben subtly points at Somma's ring,

"I believe there is something else you wanted to tell everyone?" he asks playfully.

We haven't even mentioned to Ben how we found out he told everyone our names, but with everything going on, good and bad, it hardly seems important anymore, especially with the news Somma and I have. We hold hands and walk in front of everyone, Ben walks with us to translate,

"You have shown us all incredible kindness." I continued, "Helping you has been something that we will never regret and you can always count on us to be here if you ever need us. It is a sad day as many of you know. SSG. Miner loved it here and though you did not understand him often, he felt connected to you all, he would have loved the statue you're all making. Thank you. We do have some more news that we're very excited and happy about and we hope you all feel the same way."

Somma lifts her hand in front of everyone, they look closer and their faces light up. They all cheer, some people even tear up. People come up to Somma and I, shaking our hands again and giving us hugs. Someone walks up to Ben holding something round, covered with a cloth. Ben knows what it is, he laughs once he sees it. He grabs it and hands it to me, I slowly grab it and take the cloth off, revealing the wig I got for the celebration after free Vonra. I recall the wig being left somewhere away from Tanli when Somma and I danced for the first time before Xenem attacked. The crowd and even Specter erupts in laughter once they see the wig, I chuckle at the sight of it. It was an ugly, uncomfortable accessory to an already ridiculous outfit, but I knew I had to go all out. Despite my better judgment, I put the wig on again, causing even more laughter.

As far as the wig goes, not much has changed. It's just as ugly and uncomfortable. After a few minutes, I take the wig off and hand it back to Ben, Somma and I stay together as the rest of Specter goes off to their own things. After telling Carden and Kierra of new books they recently got at their library, courtesy of the USC, both of them decide to go to the library. Blaine and Bradley stay in the marketplace, Rachel and the Martin twins decide to help out where they can around the area. No one asked them to, but it's just who they are. Somma continues to speak with people with the help of Ben, I stand back and watch her. The way she smiles and her shimmering hair blowing in the wind, really, everything, it just makes me smile like a fool. I overhear a lady speaking to Somma,

"The way he makes you smile is something you can never take for granted. The way he looks at you is incredible. So much love and care in his eyes. You both are very lucky. Love like yours, love that goes beyond galaxies, is so rare. I know you will make him happy and feel loved and I am sure he will make you just as happy and feel loved always. We are very happy for you both."

Somma tears up and smiles, she gives the lady a hug and thanks her. Looking down, I tear up too. I don't think I was meant to hear that, but I'm glad I did. After Somma moves away, she grabs the lady's hands,

"You are too kind. Yes, we are very lucky. I have never met someone like him, I have never felt more loved in my entire life and I have never loved someone as much as I love him. I truly cannot wait to marry him. I hope it will be soon."

Ben translates, the lady squeezes Somma's hands and bows her head before pulling her closer. The lady whispers something to her, Somma smiles and nods at her,

"I completely agree."

After Ben translates, the lady laughs. Somma walks back to me and kisses my cheek, I forget how she has to stand on her toes to kiss me, the height difference never mattered to us though. I personally find it adorable. The crowd lets us walk away and enjoy ourselves, not that being with them was not enjoyable, but I guess they know we want some time to ourselves. Somma puts her arm around my arm as we walk around, but curiosity seems to be getting the better of me about what the lady whispered to Somma. I walk us to an empty alleyway where there are no people. I love the people here, but I just needed a break away from it all. I close my eyes, take a deep breath in and out as the wind blows my hair in my face. With my eyes still closed, I feel Somma move the hair out of my face and gently kiss me on the lips. I open my eyes to see her smiling at me, the wind also blowing her hair. I rub her cheek with my thumb,

"You look beautiful."

"Marry me, then." she jokes.

"I wish I could. I'd do it today." I continued, "What did that lady whisper to you?"

Somma giggles and looks down,

"She said you were very handsome, naturally, I agreed with her."

I smile and playfully shake my head. Somma pulls me closer to her and hugs me with her arms around my neck,

"Do you take me to be your wife?" she whispers.

"I do. Do you take me to be your husband?"

"I do." she moves away with her arms still around my neck, "As far as I am concerned, we are now what you would call husband and wife. Now, kiss me."

I lean in and kiss her lips passionately. I know this isn't official, but I truly wish it was. It's like Somma said though, as far as we're concerned, we're married. Somma leans on the wall behind her while kissing me, she pulls me closer to her. I unbutton her coat, but Somma moves away and grabs my hands. She giggles,

"I wish we could do more, but we are still in public, my love."

"I understand." I respond while backing away and sitting on a nearby crate.

Somma smiles and sits on my lap. She turns to me and puts her arm around me,

"When we have more privacy and I have you all to myself, we will have fun."

"Promise?" I ask while rubbing her thigh.

Somma smiles and takes my hand,

"I promise, I cannot wait." she responds while putting my hand under her shirt and leading it higher up.

Before she leads my hand any higher, she stops and kisses my cheek, pulling my hand out from her shirt. A devastating tease.

"You're pretty mean, Ms. Juna."

"Maybe, but you already proposed to me. I am all yours, you are stuck with me."

"Lucky me." I say before kissing her cheek.

I wrap my arms around her waist and hold her while she sits on my lap, leaning her head on me, watching the people pass by in Tanli. There are very few moments where I feel at peace, every one of those moments includes Somma and this is no different. No one is crowding us or yelling, Somma on my lap and holding me tight with the wind passing through our hair, it's hard not to feel at peace. I hope the rest of Specter is having a good time too, we try to take advantage of any free time we have.

It's been a rough and emotional day, days like these always make me exhausted. I can't help myself, I close my eyes and lean on Somma. I hear Somma giggle and pull me closer to her, she kisses my head and holds me tight. If we were in bed, I probably would have completely fallen asleep.

"I love you." she whispers.

I chuckle and hold her tighter, but my rest is interrupted by a ringing from my communicator. I sigh and lean up, taking the communicator from my belt and answering the call.

"Parson, this LT. Serro. I understand you and your squad are enjoying your time on Kana, but I have just received news of surviving members of Xenem's army going to different planets and building support to rebuild its army. We need Specter to find them and take care of them, deal with them however you wish. For the time being, you are the leader of Specter, at least while the USC still allows you all to operate. Get moving as soon as possible. I will contact the rest of your squad, I assume PVT. Juna is with you, like always, so I know she heard this. Be safe and do not do anything too dangerous. Good luck."

Serro hangs up, I shake my head and toss my communicator to the side. I'm glad the USC is still allowing

Specter to operate for now, but I wish we had more time to ourselves. Somma grabs my communicator and hands it to me. I grab it and put it back on my belt before leaning my head on her again.

"Ready to go?" I ask in a disapointed tone.

"Not quite yet." she says while getting off of my lap.

She extends her hand to me, I grab it and with a smile, she leads us out of the alley. I have no idea where she is taking me. I know I should have us go back to the ship and wait for the others, but I don't care at this point. As bad as it sounds, those soldiers from Xenem can wait. We reach the marketplace, Somma stops and looks around. She turns to me,

"Close your eyes, my love."

"Are you going to rob me?" I joke.

"Of course! I will do that later on, but not at this moment."

I smile and close my eyes. I feel Somma kiss my cheek and take my hand again. She continues leading me somewhere. I can't say I am a fan of being led somewhere with my eyes closed. I feel myself stumbling over a few times, not knowing where I am going while also trying to keep up with Somma. After a few minutes, we finally stop.

"You may open your eyes, my love." I hear Somma say.

I open my eyes and see the beautiful Heleia Fields in front of me. It's like I am seeing it for the first time again. Somma steps in front of me, she has taken her coat off, sporting the white tank top she wears under her uniform. I approach her and kiss her cheek,

"My beautiful girl. Thank you for bringing me back here." I say while moving her hair out of her face.

Somma smiles and presses my hand against her cheek. She points to the ground, I oddly understand what she is saying, I go to my knees,

"Do you want me to propose again?" I joke.

Somma giggles, she takes a moment to respond as she unbuttons my coat and takes it off, placing it on the ground next to hers. She places her hands on my face,

"You can propose to me again if you want, but having you on your knees makes this easier."

Somma pulls me in and kisses me passionately. She runs her hands through my hair while kissing me, I caress her body with my hands, eventually I take her tank top off and lay her down on our coats. I kiss my way down her body, but I stop for a moment and lift my head,

"Do we have enough privacy now?" I ask playfully.

"I do not care at this point, keep going. Do not stop, my love."

Somma gently pushes my head down towards her lower body where I continue kissing her while taking the rest of her clothes off and she takes off mine. With everything we just did, it would be an absolutely perfect moment, if only the sand didn't get in our hair. After what seems like hours of fun, Somma and I put our clothes back on, leaving only our coats on the ground to lay on. Somma lays down next to me and rests her head on my chest. With my black tank top, hers being white and us being so close together, I imagine we look like the Yin-Yang symbol. Not that Somma would know what that is.

Somma and I lay together in silence, enjoying each other's company while holding each other. Something Serro said keeps replaying in my head. He told me for the time being, I will lead Specter. I've been through a lot these past months, but I don't know if I can lead. I've always thought a good leader is someone who has no issue being loud and heard, like Sarge. In that aspect, Blaine would be a good leader, if he wasn't so quick to anger and making irrational decisions. I suppose his willingness to be loud convinced Sarge to have him co-lead Specter with me while he was away. Leading was easier when I knew Sarge would be there to fix anything that went wrong under our leadership. I know that doesn't sound great, but it helped. I'm not proud of it. I don't have a problem with Blaine still being second-in-command to me, but I don't know how he or anyone in Specter will feel about this new role of mine as leader. I hear Somma giggle,

"I am going to be married to the leader of Specter, how exciting!" she exclaims.

"I'm just the leader for now. I'm still just a Corporal, I doubt I'll be any good."

"You will be amazing, my love. I know it. You have earned it." she responds before kissing my cheek.

I sigh, my breath shakes as I exhale. Despite Somma's kind words, I doubt I will ever feel ready. Somma leans up and places her hand on my cheek,

"Do not be nervous. We have all seen you as our leader for a while. We listened to everything you said and we are all still here. I know trying to lead after Sarge will be difficult, but he trusted you. I know you will do a great job. If it means anything, I am extremely proud of you. I am always proud of you."

I lean up and kiss Somma on the lips. She has always had a way to make me feel better when it comes to just about anything. Somma begins to tear up after I kiss her, I wipe here tear and rub her cheek, waiting for her to tell me what's wrong,

"Do you remember when I told you about my brother, Tomlen?" she asks while holding my hand.

I nod my head,

"I know that if he had you as a leader, someone he knew he could speak with and to help him, he would have had an easier time. He might still be here today."

"I wish I could have been there. I would have done anything to help him."

Somma sniffles and hugs me. Who knows if Tomlen would have even come to me seeking help? It's not easy seeing signs in people who want to end their life. I am ashamed to admit I have gotten good at hiding how I feel. I was telling the truth, though. If I was there leading a squad with Tomlen and had he talked to me about what he was feeling, I would have done anything to stop him from doing what he did.

"My family would have loved you. I wish they were still

with me, by my side." Somma says.

"They never left your side. You have another family, though. We'll always keep you safe."

Somma giggles as she lays her head back down on my chest while I hold her tight. I wish I could bring her family back, it's a shame the only one she was left with was GEN. Juna. I don't want Somma to focus on her family right now, I want her back to a happier state. I feel terrible about what happened to her and her family to this day, but dwelling on the past again won't do her any favors. I have an idea that I am sure will help, I stand up and wipe the sand off of me. Somma lifts her hands towards me, I help her up and wipe the sand off her too. She giggles and messes with my hair, getting some sand out of it. I return the favor by messing with her hair, also getting sand out of it. Somma laughs and fixes her hair while I walk towards the cliff facing the fields. The setting sun looks beautiful on top of the glowing sands. I extend my hand to Somma, she wipes her tears and takes my hand, I twirl her around and pull her towards me. The plan is simple, dance the night away.

"As I recall, we're married now. I need to dance with my beautiful bride." I say while putting my hands on her waist.

Somma smiles and places her hands on my shoulders. I begin to hum our song and we start to move. Never have we danced in such a scenic setting. Last time we danced here, it was cut short by Xenem's attack. Somma stands on her toes and kisses me on the cheek, I lift her up and swing her around. Somma infectious laugh is music to my ears. I put her back down and continue to dance with her, she rests her head on my chest looking at the Heleia Fields. She looks up at me, placing her hands on my face. The constant winds keeps blowing my hair in my face, she moves the hair out of my face and smiles,

"We should get married here." she says while rubbing my cheek with her thumb.

"I agree, but we can get married anywhere, as long as it ends with you being my wife."

"That will happen no matter what, my love."

We continue to dance into the night. I don't know where Somma gets the energy to keep going, but I personally have had a long day. Somma, realizing how tired I am, lays me down on the coats, she leans over me looking into my eyes. I have no idea what beauty she sees or finds so mesmerizing, but I absolutely love the way she looks at me.

"I keep finding new things about you, my love." she says quietly while placing her hand on my cheek. "When you look at other people, people you do not know, your eyes narrow. They narrow like you do not trust them, you are waiting for them to attack you, staying focused and drawn to their every move. You look at LT. Serro the same way. When there are people you trust or know, your eyes relax a little, but it is something completely different when you look at me. When you look at me, your eyes relax, but I see the love and care you have for me. The lady I was speaking with earlier saw the same thing in you. It may sound foolish, but I look in your eyes and see love that will surround me my whole life. I see our future. I believe that is why I can never keep my eyes off of you. Your eyes are filled with love and kindness, they are beautiful."

I'm shocked. I do agree with everything she said about the way my eyes are with people, but I'm shocked at what she sees. It's true. I look at her with love, I have for a long time. Unsure of what to say, I lean up and kiss her on the lips. She giggles and lays down next to me, placing her hand on my heart. I quickly drift off while looking into the magical night sky. I sleep peacefully with Somma in my arms. I usually expect night terrors, but so far, my nights have been calm and peaceful.

The sound of a ship landing wakes me up. I slowly open my eyes, Somma is gone. I look behind me to see the ship we arrived in. The hatch is open with Blaine and Carden standing outside checking the ship for any repairs it may need before starting the task given to us. The sun is still rising as I fully wake myself up. I stand up, picking up my coat from the ground and wiping off the sand. I approach the cliff overlooking the Heleia Fields. I take a seat at the edge of thr cliff, taking in the view while I can before we leave. I know we will return, Somma and I are getting married here. It wasn't a hard decision. Being here with her made it simple. A few minutes into watching the sun rise, I hear footsteps walk up next to me,

"We finally had a magical night, but you still owe me a few more, my love."

I look up and see Somma, in uniform, standing next to me, also watching the sunrise.

"What do you mean?" I continued as I stand up, putting on my coat, "Is destroying an evil dictatorship and getting one step closer to saving all of the galaxies not considered a magical night?"

"Not to me." she playfully responds while holding my hand.

"Well, that will have to wait then," I continued as we walk to the ship, "We still have some work to do."

Somma and I look back at the sunrise one last time, enjoying the view before we go back to what we usually do as members of the formally hidden Specter, Sarge's master plan; Save the vast cosmos, help others and most importantly, be the Galaxy's Finest. The question is, are we ready to face this new chapter? More danger lies ahead, things are different now. Will we be able to handle it? I think so, but we will just have to see. It's time for us to move forward together.

Made in the USA
Las Vegas, NV
22 April 2025